Praise for *Bright of the Sky*
Book One of The Entire and the Rose

"At the start of this riveting launch of a new far-future SF series from Kenyon (*Tropic of Creation*), a disastrous mishap during interstellar space travel catapults pilot Titus Quinn with his wife, Johanna Arlis, and nine-year-old daughter, Sydney, into a parallel universe called the Entire. Titus makes it back to this dimension, his hair turned white, his memory gone, his family presumed dead, and his reputation ruined with the corporation that employed him. The corporation (in search of radical space travel methods) sends Titus (in search of Johanna and Sydney) back through the space-time warp. There, he gradually, painfully regains knowledge of its rulers, the cruel, alien Tarig; its subordinate, Chinese-inspired humanoid population, the Chalin; and his daughter's enslavement. Titus's transformative odyssey to reclaim Sydney reveals a Tarig plan whose ramifications will be felt far beyond his immediate family. Kenyon's deft prose, high-stakes suspense, and skilled, thorough world building will have readers anxious for the next installment."
Publishers Weekly Starred Review

". . . a splendid fantasy quest as compelling as anything by Stephen R. Donaldson, Philip José Farmer, or yes, J. R. R. Tolkien."
Washington Post

". . . a bravura concept bolstered by fine writing; lots of plausible, thrilling action; old-fashioned heroism; and strong emotional hooks . . . the mark of a fine writer. Grade: A."
Sci Fi Weekly

"Kay Kenyon's *Bright of the Sky* is her richest and most ambitious novel yet—fascinating, and best of all, there promises to be more to come."
Greg Bear
Hugo and Nebula Award–winning author of *Quantico* and *Darwin's Radio*

"[A] star-maker, a magnificent book that should establish its author's reputation as among the very best in the field today. Deservedly so, because it's that good . . . a classic piece of world making. . . . [H]ere is another of those grand worlds whose mere idea invites us in to share in the wonder. *Bright of the Sky* enchants on the scale of your first encounter with the world inside of *Rama*, or the immense history behind the deserts of *Dune*, or the unbridled audacity of Riverworld. It's an enormous stage demanding a grand story and, so far, Kenyon is telling it with style and substance. The characters are as solid as the world they live in, and Kenyon's prose sweeps you up and never lets go. On its own, [it] could very well be the book of the year. If the rest of the series measures up, it will be one for the ages."

SF Site

"The author of *The Seeds of Time* imagines a dystopic version of our own world. Reminiscent of the groundbreaking novels of Philip K. Dick, Philip José Farmer, and Dan Simmons, her latest volume belongs in most libraries."

Library Journal

"In a fascinating and gratifying feat of world building, Kenyon unfolds the wonders and the dangers of the Entire and an almost-Chinese culture that should remain engaging throughout what promises to be a grand epic, indeed."

Booklist

"With a rich and vivid setting, peopled with believable and sympathetic characters and fascinating aliens, Kay Kenyon has launched an impressive saga with *Bright of the Sky*."

SFFWorld.com

"Kay Kenyon has created a dark, colorful, richly imagined world that works as both science fiction and fantasy, a classic space opera that recalls the novels of Dan Simmons. Titus Quinn bestrides *Bright of the Sky* in the great tradition of larger-than-life heroes, an engaging, romantic, unforgettable character. The stakes are high in this book, the characters memorable, the world complex and fascinating. A terrific story!"

Louise Marley, author of *Singer in the Snow*

"Kenyon writes beautifully, her characters are multilayered and complex, and her extrasolar worlds are real and nuanced while at the same time truly alien."

Robert J. Sawyer

Hugo and Nebula Award–winning author of *Rollback* and *Mindscan*

"Kay Kenyon takes the nuts and bolts of SF and weaves pure magic around them. The brilliance of her imagination is matched only by the beauty of her prose. You should buy *Bright of the Sky* immediately. It's astounding!"

Sean Williams, author of *The Crooked Letter* and *Saturn Returns*

Praise for *A World Too Near*
Book Two of The Entire and the Rose

"One of the most imaginative creations in recent science fiction history."
SF Site

"Kenyon's latest has it all—plot, character, action, science, and the sense of wonder that all the cynics say can't be done anymore. A remarkable achievement."
Mike Resnick, Hugo-winning author of *Starship: Mercenary* and *Santiago*

"The fate of two universes hangs in the balance in this intricately plotted sequel to *Bright of the Sky*. . . . Tangled motivations, complex characters, and intriguing world building will keep readers on the edges of their seats."
Publishers Weekly Starred Review

"Kay Kenyon continues to offer some neat adventures for her protagonists in this really alluring offbeat universe she's created. . . . All the characters continue to be fascinatingly complex. . . . Every minor character is endowed with exceptional depth and reality. . . . The artificial universe known as the Entire remains a great conception and playground for adventure."
Sci Fi Weekly

". . . continues the promise shown in book one. . . . The Entire is a marvelous parallel universe . . . [and] the details of [the main character's] quest make for stunning adventure fiction, while the mysteries revealed about the Entire are completely mind-blowing. . . . It is epic fantasy and world building on a grand scale. It would be criminal if this novel didn't make year's best lists at the end of 2008."
Realms of Fantasy

Also by Kay Kenyon

BRIGHT OF THE SKY
Book One of The Entire and the Rose

A WORLD TOO NEAR
Book Two of The Entire and the Rose

PRINCE OF STORMS
Book Four of The Entire and the Rose

CITY
WITHOUT END

CITY WITHOUT END

KAY KENYON

BOOK THREE *of* THE ENTIRE AND THE ROSE

an imprint of **Prometheus Books**
Amherst, NY

Published 2010 by Pyr®, an imprint of Prometheus Books

Inquiries should be addressed to
Pyr
59 John Glenn Drive
Amherst, New York 14228–2119
VOICE: 716–691–0133
FAX: 716–691–0137
WWW.PYRSF.COM

14 13 12 11 10   5 4 3 2 1

Library of Congress Cataloging-in-Publication Data

Kenyon, Kay.
    City without end / Kay Kenyon.
        p. cm. — (The entire and the rose ; bk. 3)
    ISBN 978–1–59102–698–3 (hardcover: alk. paper)
    ISBN 978–1–59102–790–4 (paperback: alk. paper)
    I. Title.

PS3561.E5544C58 2009
813'.54—dc22

                                                                2008049650

Printed in the United States on acid-free paper

For my husband, with love

ACKNOWLEDGMENTS

IN THIS SERIES, I continue to owe thanks to those who good-heartedly agree to read drafts and advise me on science and technology. Deep gratitude to my husband and first reader, Thomas Overcast; science fiction writer Karen Fishler; writer of hard physics science fiction Robert Metzger; theoretical physicist Todd Brun; and, for advice on traumatic injuries, my EMT son, Matt Balser—all of whom were kind enough to read and comment on various parts of this book. Departures from the strictly possible and fictionally plausible are on my own shoulders. To my agent, Donald Maass, my sincere thanks for setting me on the path to this story. I am indebted to my editor, Lou Anders, for his suggestions and contagious passion for this series as well as for conceiving the perfect matchup of my story with the artwork of the superb Stephan Martiniere.

PART I

THE LITTLE GOD

PROLOGUE: THE ENTIRE

Beside the storm wall, Ahnenhoon,
Across the war plains, Ahnenhoon,
Over the armies, Ahnenhoon,
Around the Repel, Ahnenhoon,
Under the grave flags, Ahnenhoon.
—a marching song

H E STILL HAD DIRT UNDER HIS FINGERNAILS FROM HIS GRAVE. His massive hands with their knobby joints sported thick fingers, now grimed with soil. He had hoped for burial in a cloth sack. When he came to consciousness in a box with the sounds of shovels and light welling through the slats, he knew he'd have to work quickly. As dirt started hitting the lid, he blessed Wei who had given him a knife for ripping the planks.

And rip them he did, enough to get a shoulder free, covering his mouth to protect a pocket of air. With the burial detail eager for their warm beds in the barracks of Ahnenhoon, they'd dug the grave hastily and mercifully shallow.

Next to the looming outer walls of the fortress, Mo Ti quickly refilled his grave. In the distance he heard the sounds of the army's defensive guns. The Paion must be hitting hard, their zeppelins budding out of the sky to rain ichors on the army of the Entire. Good. Death was a fine distraction on a night like this; it might be just the advantage that would save him.

Though it was Deep Ebb, the darkest phase of all, the slumbering sky still burned lavender, throwing a bruised light on him. He must seek the hiding places of the hills. With his massive girth and height, he had never been one easily overlooked, nor, with his face like a tree bole, easily forgotten. Even weak from blood loss, Mo Ti could dispatch a soldier or two, but he had little chance against the terrible lords, thin and vicious, or the Paion, lurching through the grass inside their foul machines. Do not look upon me, Miserable God, he silently prayed. King of Woe, I am beneath your notice, a beetle in dung.

Before loping away, he spared a moment to read his grave flag. *Monster of the Repel.* Mo Ti smiled. Yes, I am a monster to you, high Tarig lords. He bowed his misshapen body in mock obeisance to the Repel, the lords' inner keep, where it bulked above the concentric defenses of the fortress. You will see me again, *gracious lords.*

He held much against them, but not burying him alive. That he had arranged himself. Once in the lords' custody, Mo Ti needed, above all, to escape Tarig questioning. In his cell he had removed the bindings on his wounds from the sword fight. Blood welled up, spilling onto the floor. Then he mixed waters and dyes to create a scene of death. Finding him an obvious suicide in their dungeon, the Chalin servants had given him a proper burial, it not being a custom of the *gracious lords* to appear unnecessarily cruel.

He drank deep from the water bladder that had been taped to his leg. Wei had done what she could to help him. But she was a stupid girl not to give him food, too.

Moving swiftly away from the fortress, he took what cover he could in the long grasses. In the distance, the storm walls swayed, sending their dark shadows across the field of contest. Three Paion dirigibles hovered over the killing grounds, their sides pulsing with the weird light of their alien homeland. Before disappearing into sphincters in the sky, they would throw down their poisonous gouts on the ranks of soldiers. Mo Ti hoped the sentries would be inattentive to the Repel's close vicinity. Soldiers often watched the wrong things.

As did the Tarig. For one thing, they were insensible to the dreams. Even if they could not dream, they were insensible to other sentients' dreams— dreams that might be spoken of if the Tarig cared whose sleep was troubled. The Inyx mounts spoke heart to heart and now turned the Entire's dreams to excellent propaganda. How delicious that the young girl the Tarig blinded—

his beloved Sydney, for whom he would give his life—had been the first one to see their fatal weakness. How fitting she would be the one to sweep the mantis lords from their sky city.

But now that carefully wrought future was in doubt. Because of the newcomer. The spider. A small, fierce human without a shred of pity for the worlds she would set to the torch. Titus Quinn must stop her, though he didn't know it yet.

The Rose spider, Hel Ese, came to ally with Sydney. To Mo Ti's alarm, she had succeeded, displacing him with powers and persuasion. Sewn into her clothes and brought from her world was a small god that Mo Ti did not understand and therefore feared. But the spider had made a strategic mistake. She had allowed Mo Ti to overhear her plans. Impressively cruel plans for a woman. For any sentient being.

He bent over in pain from the wound in his side. It was still two days' walk to the River Nigh where he would seek passage from the navitar. Rising, he looked into the waxing silver sky, the fiery river that warmed the Entire and his bones. The bright give me strength, Mo Ti thought. The bright bring me home.

He drove his body through the crumpled hills edging the plains of Ahnenhoon. He must find this man, Titus Quinn, the man for whom he had sacrificed himself yesterday during the fight. There had been no time then to tell him of the Rose spider who stalked them all. During that brief skirmish Mo Ti and Titus Quinn had fought off the guards who came in the first wave of defenders. When Mo Ti saw that he could fight three at once, he urged Titus Quinn to flee. He granted the man his life for one reason: instead of destroying the Repel and the land around it, Titus Quinn had repudiated his terrible weapon, sparing the land. And therefore Mo Ti spared *him*. Then the lords arrived, striking Mo Ti senseless. It was his good fortune the high lord's human captive, Johanna, was suffering a beating from the Tarig, an undertaking that distracted them from his immediate interrogation.

Thus had Titus Quinn escaped. Wei informed Mo Ti of this fact as he lay in his cell deep in the fortress. Wei was a common servant sent by Johanna to help Mo Ti. It was a fine gesture from a dying woman—a woman who, it was rumored, loved her Tarig lord.

He spit in the dust, thinking of it. Far better dead, Mo Ti thought, than in such an embrace.

A shadow fell over him. From nowhere, a zeppelin scudded above the hill, moving breathtakingly close to Mo Ti's position. He fell into a deep crouch, nearly blacking out from the pain in his gut. The fat-bellied conveyance motored over the next ridge.

Mo Ti stayed low, listening. Silence. The sounds of the airship motor had bled away. From the plains came distant reports of guns. He was just rising to an upright position when he saw it: silhouetted against the sky, a figure on the near ridge. Standing on two short legs, a Paion mechanical, its two multi-weaponed arms cocked at the elbow and ready. The machine almost looked like a man, but it was headless, giving it the nightmare look all children feared. In the hump on its back rode the passenger that drove it. A Paion.

He froze in place. But it was too late. The Paion turned to face him. Mo Ti had no cover; he was exposed to the alien's view.

Mo Ti ran down the length of the gully. Had the airship disgorged its battalions in the next basin behind the hill? If so, he was a dead man. Reaching the near slope, he forced himself to climb, putting distance between himself and the Paion ranks. Looking back, he saw that the Paion was following. It raised a carapaced arm.

Mo Ti flattened himself against the hill, and the beam went high but near. He admired such accuracy from a running soldier.

Another singular fact stood out. The creature was alone. The Paion always fought in masses, their glowing white shells forming tight knots of offense. But so far, this one was alone. It stalked forward, aiming again. Mo Ti twisted away, rolling sideways on the hillside, escaping the blasts even as he groaned from the exertion.

Forcing himself to his feet, he switched directions, loping toward the war plains. There, in the confusion of the larger conflict, he might divert this lone Paion to other targets. He topped the ridge, his inhalations coming hard and fast, each breath a slice of pain. On the grasslands in front of him, cannon smoke drifted, forming a curtain over hot spots from flaming equipment and bodies. Behind him, the foul creature lurched after him.

Mo Ti ran toward the mayhem, toward the flash of war engines spouting

fire, toward the rallies and sorties of battle. He had no weapon to meet the
Paion in arms, no chance against the streaming fire of its hand armament. Mo
Ti cursed the Paion and cursed Titus Quinn, too, for whose sake he was
fleeing for his life. It was good to curse, to keep one's strength up, to fend off
the pain each footfall brought him.

Looking behind him, he saw the Paion closing on him.

There was no time to run. Mo Ti turned to fight.

Staggering closer, the Paion raised its arm again. By the creature's gait,
Mo Ti thought it was damaged. He saw the weapon corkscrew out of the
carapace, bypassing the robotic hand. Fire spurted. Mo Ti lunged to the side,
falling heavily and driving the breath from his lungs. The pain nearly
knocked him senseless. He lost precious intervals forcing himself to his
knees. He was untouched. Trying to stand, Mo Ti saw that the Paion's hand
armament was smoking, hanging useless. It had backfired along the creature's arm, which now slapped at its side as the Paion advanced.

Encouraged, Mo Ti rose to his feet.

In its milky white casing, the Paion advanced, wobbling on its jointed
legs. In height it came to Mo Ti's chest. It raised its other arm.

No ichors streamed out. The creature's hand was a blade. So, it would be
a knife fight. That was good news for Mo Ti. He advanced, drawing his blade,
a short but infinitely sharp knife. He blessed Wei for the supplies of his
coffin.

They fell at each other, striking. Mo Ti parried the Paion's first jab, but
the second slashed his belt, scoring the braided leather instead of Mo Ti's gut.
Having overreached, the Paion staggered forward, giving Mo Ti time to
come at the creature from the back. Raising his arm in a last-ditch blow, he
struck at the hump, sending the Paion staggering. Moving in, Mo Ti knew
his knife would have little effect against armor. Instead of striking, Mo Ti
used his one undoubted advantage: his size. He fell on the Paion. In the force
of his sheer weight, he split the mechanical's carapace in a grinding tear. He
brought his fist up and hammered at the bulge again and again as the creature lay face down.

When he could raise his arm no more, Mo Ti collapsed, still lying on top
of the mechanical. Fumes of the body inside came to his nostrils. The Paion

could not endure exposure to Entire air. The biological entity within was disintegrating, leaking out of the rents in the armor.

Mo Ti rolled off the Paion. He lay panting on his back, fighting to remain conscious. At last he dragged himself to a sitting position. One hand of the mechanical was spinning round the wrist as though trying to sort out which weapon to bring up next.

"It is over," Mo Ti whispered. "Go to your gods." He had seen dead Paion mechanicals before, in his soldiering days. Even dead, they were ugly and unnatural. It was said the headless things took their vision from senses spread over the full carapace. And that no one could win against them one on one.

The hand produced another blade, this one long and thin. Then, satisfied it had done its best, the machine let its forearm clink to the ground.

Mo Ti rose to his feet and looked down at his adversary. Yellow blood seeped out of the hump where the Paion had ridden. Mo Ti looked to the ridge to check for further pursuit. The hills were quiet, feeding halfhearted echoes from the battlefield.

He stepped on the Paion's wrist and hacked his blade at the offered weapon. You never knew when an extra would be needed. He was, he reminded himself, still a long way from the Nigh. The blade separated from the wrist, and Mo Ti slid it into his belt.

He began his painful march once again. Rest was impossible. Once he lay down, he would sleep for days. Somehow, as the hours passed, he managed to keep his purpose before him: The River Nigh. Titus Quinn. Must tell him, and soon. Hel Ese, the spider, coming in for the kill.

Although Titus Quinn was a lifetime journey away from Ahnenhoon, Mo Ti did not despair. By the River Nigh, all places were near.

PROLOGUE: THE ROSE

I N THE MIRROR, LAMAR GELDE LOOKED AT HIMSELF in swimming trunks. At seventy-seven, a wreck of a man. His white skin hung on a six-foot frame, muscles trim but stringy, chest thin and leathery despite daily work-outs. His belly button sagged a good two inches from where it should be, and his toenails looked like ancient ivory. Grabbing his pool robe, he pulled it over his body, lashing it at the waist.

The face, at least the face, bore a semblance of dignity. The latest max-illofacial outcomes took thirty years off him, beginning with the nasolobial folds (receded) and the platysma bands wattling his neck (gone.) He peered closer: a few hairline cracks around his eyes argued for the next procedure, corrigator muscle update. He reminded himself that there was nothing ghoulish about being good-looking at his age. Everyone did it. Well, maybe seventy-seven was pushing it, but if he was going to live a long time, now was no time to start slipping.

Caitlin Quinn hailed him with a raise of her poolside drink. He made his way to her, noting that her thirty-five-year-old body still looked fit, though she had the bad taste to complain of it.

"What'll you have?" she asked, pointing her data ring at the house.

"Seltzer and lime."

She stranded the order at the smart wall, her smile wobbling. She'd called him here to talk about something. Anything she needed, he was the man.

As Caitlin made her way to the wet bar to retrieve their drinks, Lamar watched Rob and his son horsing around in the pool. He sighed. A nice little family scene on the surface. Underneath, nothing of the sort. Caitlin and Rob were on the outs. No doubt Caitlin was half in love with Titus Quinn, her brother-in-law, and Rob was clueless. Since they were living off Titus's millions, Rob no longer had to worry about being fired for being forty and hopelessly out of date with savant AIs. Nope. He'd had the money to quit outright before they fired him, and now he and Caitlin had their own little middie start-up company. They should take their happiness while there was still time.

Thirteen-year-old Mateo stood on the diving board, waving at Lamar. "Back dive, uncle Lamar, watch!" He danced on the board, then launched his body, folding in a way only a cat or youngster could manage, smoothing out in time to make a decent plunge.

Lamar clapped, impressed. Mateo waved like crazy and swam the length of the pool. Despite no little envy, Lamar was proud of the kid. Handsome, motivated, respectful. Liked his "uncle." Well, Lamar had promised to take good care of the family. Rob and Caitlin were Quinn's only family now—they and their children, Mateo and Emily. Lamar had grown closer to them in the interval of Quinn's absence. Nice kid, Mateo. It made Lamar wish he'd had a few of his own. But Caitlin, seated again next to him, looked unhappy. She had no idea how unhappy she had a right to be. It made him feel like shit.

She wouldn't be in on it. How could she be? She was a middie, smart enough to tend lower-level AI's, the savants. Same as Rob. But she'd never be a savvy, testing over 160. It wasn't her fault, but she wasn't up to dealing with the new world.

Mateo did a flying back somersault, landing on his butt. Rob roared with laughter, and Mateo hauled himself out of the pool, breathless but laughing anyway.

"Good kid," Lamar said.

"I know." Caitlin cut him a glance. "Not good enough, maybe."

He frowned, and the conversation sagged into the waiting silence.

"We got the results. He didn't ace the test."

Lamar gaped at her. Didn't ace the test? The Standard Test. Christ, the kid was the grandson of Donnel Quinn and the nephew of Titus Quinn, and he didn't slam the Standard? He hung his head, not looking at her. Genetics.

It was genetics. Mateo got his brains from Caitlin and Rob—no shame in that—but he was no savvy. Not like Lamar, or Titus. Christ almighty. A blow.

Caitlin pushed on, falsely cheerful. "He's bright. IQ 139. He'll be fine."

Fine. Yes, depending on your definition. Didn't Mateo have some big ambitions, though? Something about being a virtual enviro designer . . . well, not likely. Stanford wouldn't take him, or Cornell. Lamar could pull some strings. But the boy didn't have the right stuff to make it far; couldn't do calculus in his head or understand advanced quantum theory. Time was when even the average-smart could do real science, but that time was gone. The easy stuff had all been done, and now, talking to a middie—much less a dred—was like explaining sunrise to a pigmy.

"I'm sorry, Caitlin."

"Of course you are." Her voice didn't cloak her bitterness. Lamar was a savvy.

He shifted uneasily in the pool chair. He should have been prepared for this. Mateo was thirteen, the age they gave the Standard. What was he supposed to say: Brains aren't everything? Oh, but they were.

Mateo grabbed his towel and made his way to the adults while Rob did his pool laps.

"He doesn't know yet," Caitlin whispered.

"Ho, unc," Mateo chirped.

"Ho, young man." Lamar pasted on a smile, more rigid these days after his rhinoplasty.

Mateo took a sip of a half-finished soda, and Lamar watched him with dismay. The boy squinted against the July sun, making him look confused and wary. The spark in his eyes, that look of broad perspective, was missing. Lamar should have seen it before. The boy was a middie, poor son of a bitch.

"Want to see a double twist?" Mateo asked, jumping up. Assured that every adult within two blocks would want to see Mateo Quinn perform dive platform feats, he raced off, heedless of Caitlin's call not to run on the cement.

His departure left a vacuum in Lamar's heart. What a miserable mess. Mateo wasn't in the club. Bad enough to leave Caitlin and Rob behind, but now Mateo? Quinn would be unhappy. Quinn would carve Lamar a new asshole.

Lamar sank into a dark place, thinking of how his little revolutionary cabal was screwing over his adopted family. Thinking of how he'd have to face Quinn for leaving Mateo behind when the world change came about.

The fact was, even Lamar didn't want to leave him behind. He *liked* the boy, liked Caitlin and little Emily. For God's sake, how could he abandon them?

The topic didn't bear close scrutiny. It was a monstrous scheme. But if the world had to be abandoned, Lamar and his people couldn't be blamed. That responsibility fell upon the Tarig. They were intent on using the Rose universe as fuel and had been beta testing the concept for fully two years, if not longer. Lately the tally of vanished stars included Alpha Carinae, a rare yellow-white super giant, which people who bothered to learn their stars knew as Canopus. Few bothered. The astronomers were in a lather, of course. Particularly since over the last three months Alpha Carinae had been pre-ceded in death by Procyon, the lovely marquee star of Canis Minor, and 40 Eridani-B, a DA-class white dwarf. People paying attention, like Lamar and his friends, saw these vanishings as yet another hint the end was near. The stars had simply winked out. Impossible, of course. But not for the Tarig.

Nothing, really, could stop them, not for long. Lamar and company's little plan—with the very apt name of *renaissance*—would hasten that act of cannibalism, after first saving a few gifted people who the Tarig might tol-erate in their closed kingdom. We'll help you burn it. Let a few of us emi-grate, and we'll show you how.

Grotesque, yes. But who else could fight the monstrous Tarig, if not equally ferocious humans? These were Lamar's usual ruminations, fore-stalling the guilt that threatened to inundate his days.

But a new thought was forming. Perhaps—just perhaps—he didn't have to leave the boy behind. Lamar Gelde might, for example, bend the rules a bit. Given his exemplary service to the new renaissance, hadn't he earned some privileges?

Of course he'd have to face Helice, and she was fierce on the topic. But the hell with Helice, the little rat-bitch. He'd never liked her, and she wasn't in charge from across the universe. Furthermore, Quinn would appreciate the out-of-the-box thinking. Quinn would goddamn well owe him big time.

Lamar watched Caitlin as he sipped his drink. *By damn, I'm poised to do something good and decent. By damn.*

Mateo was going to get his numbers changed. Caitlin was going to re-test, too. Her numbers would come up strong, as well. Rob—well, no one would miss him. He was out of the equation. Lamar would have to pull off a bit of backroom manipulation, and normally such a switch could never escape the scrutiny of the mSap . . . but the thing was, he didn't need to fool the machine sapient that ran the Standard Test. He only needed to confuse the bureaucrats for a few days. By then, it would be too late.

Lamar murmured into his drink, hardly believing what he was saying to Caitlin: "I can get you in on something. You and your family." Now that he had said it, it filled him with a vast relief. In the midst of the coming storm, amid the colossal suffering to come, someone would have a reprieve.

Caitlin looked at him, waiting.

"I can't tell you what it is. Something's coming. Not a word to Rob or anybody, not even Mateo." He noted Caitlin's growing confusion. "It won't matter about the test. Very soon, it won't matter at all."

"What are you talking about? Are they coming up with a new test?"

"No, no tests. That's behind us now."

She scrunched her lips in thought. "It might be behind *you*, Lamar, but it's not behind *us*."

He fixed her with a pointed look as Rob, draped in a towel, ambled over from his swim. "I can't say more. Don't push right now. We'll talk, but privately."

She started to protest, but he shook his head as Rob joined them.

Poor Rob. He was a dead man. It made him feel like hell to know so much, while simple people enjoyed their barbeques and swims. But he couldn't let himself worry about Rob. *He's holding the race back. Propagating, watering down the neurons.* Rob wouldn't have a place in the future. Not like Lamar. Not like Titus Quinn. Men with the requisite IQ.

It was all based on merit.

And in the case of Mateo and Caitlin, on who you knew.

CHAPTER ONE

The most exalted of habitations is the Ascendancy. But the longest is Rim City.

—from *The Radiant Way*

IN THE NEVER-ENDING CITY, Ji Anzi and Titus Quinn finally found a magistrate willing to marry them. In this city of one hundred billion people, they had few friends. One, to be exact: Zhiya. And she was a despised godder, though appearances could be misleading. Anzi knew that Zhiya's network of contacts sent tendrils throughout Rim City, throughout the Entire.

One of Zhiya's contacts was this resin-addicted magistrate who lay before them. He was barely conscious, an impoverished legate who lived on the never-ending wharf in a hovel almost too small to hold the three-person wedding party. It wouldn't do to engage a fully conscious magistrate to officiate. The whole city was looking for Titus and Anzi, backed up by legions of Tarig, and perhaps Titus's enemies in the Rose as well. He was a man well hated, but beloved of Ji Anzi.

She held his hand now, ready to join their lives. It must be done quickly. With so many searching for them, they might be discovered at any moment. Titus said that marriage was a thing that would bind them now and forever, no matter what happened next. He was, Anzi knew from profound experience, a man who wanted a family. He'd had one. Now he had her, and it seemed he meant to keep her.

The legate had agreed to marry them, but Changjun stunk of resin-laden smoke and was so weak he couldn't sit up.

Titus turned to the godwoman Zhiya. "He's half dead."

Zhiya shrugged. "The less he remembers, the better."

Anzi looked askance at the magistrate, wondering how she had come to this moment, to marry Titus Quinn in a shack that smelled of drugs and vomit.

The legate reached in the direction of the voices, rasping something unintelligible.

"Certainly," Zhiya answered him. "Your fee to be paid in resin." She brought out a small chunk from her pocket, opening her palm to display it. "Yours very soon, honorable Changjun." Zhiya might serve the God of the Entire, but she was not above drug dealing and treason. Titus trusted the dwarf godwoman with whom he'd forged a friendship on his way to Ahnenhoon. Anzi took his word for it that Zhiya opposed the lords and supported Titus—a startling betrayal for a high-ranking Venerable.

A spike of laughter from outside reminded Anzi that amid Rim crowds were many who would gladly hand them over to the Tarig. After Ahnenhoon, she and Titus were notorious. But what, Anzi wondered, did people think had happened at Ahnenhoon to make both her and the famous outlaw fugitives? She doubted the realm's sentients knew the All needed the Rose for burning. She doubted they knew Ahnenhoon was the sight of more than the Long War. Its fortress was the repository for the great engine that was already burning stars, allowing the Tarig to test their plans for further burning.

Looking around the filthy hovel, Anzi wondered if the legate could be roused to conduct the civil ceremony. He was saturated with the drug and had pissed himself. This was not the marriage she had dreamed of. Was it a good idea? They hadn't had time to think it through. Titus loved her and was taking her for his second wife. Second, if Joanna was still alive. This was doubtful. But for Titus's sake, she hoped Johanna lived. The burden of her death was something Anzi hoped he would be spared by the God of Misery.

Zhiya checked again at the door—as though she could stop a Tarig from entering. Zhiya was hardly a soldier: barely four feet in height, with a sideways gamboling walk and a persistent disregard for her service to her religious order.

Zhiya smiled at the reeking legate. "Hurry, Excellency," she crooned, "Marry them and celebrate with the heavenly smoke."

The legate roused himself onto one elbow, but it was only to reach for the nugget. Zhiya surged forward and shook him by the shoulders. "By the mucking bright . . ." she began. But the man fell back, eyes rolling up. He had passed out.

From just beyond the walls came the sound of the sea splatting against the breakwater. Changjun's room had a glorious location next to the largest sea in either universe. But then everyone in Rim City had more or less the same location, the city being many thousand of miles long and a stone's throw wide.

Titus glanced at Zhiya. "Check the street. We're leaving."

Zhiya didn't budge. "I could perform the ceremony."

Anzi stifled a gasp of dismay. "No. You're a godwoman. The Miserable God would curse us." Anzi cast around for another solution. "Find us a priest of the Red Throne."

Zhiya kicked at the slumbering legate, muttering. "My dear, it's a charming thought to be helped by a Red priest. Unfortunately, it would get us all killed. But if you get another idea, be sure to keep it to yourself."

"But," Anzi continued, unfazed, "the Society of the Red Throne—"

"Believes in the lords, commerce, and the three vows. No, Anzi, I'm afraid you're stuck with me. Only three can do the job: a legate, a ship keeper, or a godder." Motioning toward the comatose legate, Zhiya said, "You're down to two choices. See any ship keepers?"

Titus looked at Anzi, saying softly, "Let her do it, my love. What more can the Miserable God bring on us?"

Anzi raised an eyebrow. What more could He do? What, besides threaten the Rose universe with extinction? What, besides give Titus a weapon to save the Rose, and then, diabolically, make it a weapon he couldn't bring himself to use? The cirque he'd brought into the Entire, the small silver chain around his ankle, had proven to be a molecular weapon that would erase not just the Tarig threat but the whole of the Entire. At Ahnenhoon, as Titus was at the very moment of depositing the weapon at the base of the engine, Titus's first wife told him to make peace with his God. In this way she let slip that Titus was about to die. That everyone in the Entire was about to die, since the weapon would destroy the Entire. He'd asked her what she knew of the cirque and how she *could* know. He learned that he'd been tricked by Lord Oventroe to bring a doomsday weapon to Ahnenhoon. Oventroe, who had inspected the cirque and promised it would take down only the engine.

They had fled Ahnenhoon, he and Anzi, with the job undone, the engine still churning. But they were forced to leave Johanna behind. She had no doubt been caught at the foot of the engine, the place she was forbidden to be. No doubt it all came out, eventually, what she was there for.

A saving grace was that Johanna would be forced to reveal that Titus had the overwhelming weapon. That he left with it. It could still destroy the Tarig land. Therefore the lords did not dare to simply cross over to the Rose and kill the Earth to forestall future aggression. The lords would most certainly do so if not restrained by this most useful deterrent: the cirque in Titus's possession.

But the problem was he had thrown the cirque away.

Titus said again, "Let her do the ceremony, Anzi."

He looked at her with such longing it nearly stopped her breath. Anzi slid a glance at the godwoman, considering whether she could bear to be married by a godder.

Zhiya blurted, "You think I *want* to do it? If you ask me, Titus should marry *me*. I've lusted after him from the first day I saw him." She shrugged apologetically at Titus's bride-to-be.

Titus was still focused on Anzi. "Marry me, Ji Anzi, and let the Miserable God do his worst."

At the blasphemy, she raised two fingers to her left eye. "Beloved, never say it."

"Someone has to stand up to him."

Anzi turned to Zhiya. "Yes, then," she whispered. "You're not so despised a godder as most."

Zhiya sighed. "By God's balls, a fine compliment. But shall we get on with this?"

"Yes, Venerable," Anzi said, almost inaudible. "Bless us." She closed her eyes, unable to meet Zhiya's gaze.

Without preamble, the godwoman muttered the blessing. Anzi heard it

in a blur of resin smoke and adrenaline . . . *counter of sins, creator of misery . . .*
do not look on this paltry couple, do not bring thine eye to their small, mean, and plod-
ding lives . . .

"Anzi," Titus said at last, nudging her from a sickening reverie. He drew
her into his arms, whispering, "My great love. My wife."

"Is it over?" she asked.

"Yes," Zhiya snapped. "Many days of bliss to you both." She peeked out
the door. "We'll raise a toast at the whorehouse." She ducked an apology to
Anzi. "My side business, but they do know how to have a party."

"Titus," Anzi said. He paused, waiting for her to go on. "Have you
thought what will happen if they catch us?"

He nodded. "Yes. They won't catch us."

"But, if they do?"

Zhiya sighed. "The longer we stay here the more chance there is that they
will catch you. Go now. Talk later."

Anzi fixed Zhiya with her gaze. "No. There is no later."

Titus grew wary. "What is it?"

"It's the chain. It's gone. Lying at the bottom of the Nigh." The chain as
a deterrent was the only chance left for the Rose, and Titus knew that as well
as she did. He just didn't want to admit what it meant. "If we separate, and
one of us is caught, we can claim the device is with the other person." She
saw him resisting this idea. "The chain still has power—if they believe we
have it. They'll be afraid to move against the Earth if they think I'll open the
links and let out the plague. Or you will."

"No, Anzi."

"Pardon, but I think yes."

Zhiya rolled her eyes. "What a fine beginning to marital harmony."

Ignoring her, Titus said, "No. If we're caught we'll just say we gave it to
someone for safekeeping."

"But who would that be? Among all the sentients of the Entire, who
loves the Rose? Only you and I. The lords would suspect us."

"Anzi," he pleaded. "No, I don't like it."

"I might choose to go without your agreement."

They looked at each other for a long moment. Titus was processing this.

He had already heard the wisdom of what she said. She thought he'd already decided, but was postponing saying so.

She went to his arms. "My love," she whispered. They held each other.

Anzi pushed away finally. "Wait for me, Titus."

He held her at arms' length. "I hate this. Go, if you think best. But don't pretend to have the cirque. I can't ask it of you. I won't."

"No. Don't ask." He was always wanting to do the right thing. He had done so many awful things that he weighed small things too hard because they were easier to grasp. This was a small thing.

When he saw her resolve, he said, "Come home to me."

"Yes."

Zhiya regarded the leave taking with growing impatience. "Where will you go, girl?"

"To a far primacy. Somewhere you can't guess."

Zhiya flicked her gaze at Titus. "I'll put her on a vessel, then."

He nodded. After a pause he said, "Give us one hour alone."

The godwoman smirked. "What? Here?" She noted the unconscious legate sprawled on the only bed. "You don't have the luxury of an hour."

"Give us some goddamn time, Zhiya."

Anzi put a hand on his arm, getting his attention. "We'll have our time." It was something she was not quite ready to believe, but she said it anyway, her heart cooling. She lifted her hood and yanked it forward, moving to the door.

Titus intercepted her at the door, pulling the hood back. Cupping her face, he kissed her in a way that instantly heated her.

She pressed him away at last. "The Chalin never say farewell. I won't say it now."

"No," he agreed. "Protect yourself first. Promise me."

"First before what?"

"Before me."

"I promise."

Zhiya took Anzi's arm. "Pull that hood over your head, and let's get out of here." She cut a reassuring look at Titus, but Anzi could not look at him again.

She and Zhiya slipped through the door.

Once out in the street, the godwoman hurried alongside Anzi toward the wharf, where a navitar vessel might be found. "You have no more intention of putting yourself first than I do of going celibate. You are an impressive liar, Ji Anzi."

Anzi nodded under her hood. "Thank you, Venerable."

CHAPTER TWO

Lies seek the light like Inyx do the steppes.
—a saying

YDNEY RAN INTO SLEEP, INTO HER DREAMS, eager to share in the carnage. Dreams were the battlefield, the only arena where the mantis lords were vulnerable. Each night she lay her head down to sleep, to fight. She was no Inyx, could not join the raids of her Deep Ebb army, but her thoughts urged them on. At the head of the Inyx forays was her beloved mount Riod, slicing into the minds of those who slept, sending poison. The worst kind of poison for despots: truth.

The gracious lords have deceived us all. They are not flesh and blood, but way-farers in bodies of their creation, fearing to live, tethered to their ancestral home, far outside of the Entire. The lords are simulacra, fearing carbon-based life. They do not die or have children. To them, birth is stepping into a form for a time. Until they scurry back to the Heart, where they exist as unholy burning things. Denizens of the Entire, should we venerate such creatures? Should we trust the radiant lords, who can retreat at any time to their true home—the Heart? It is a hellishly burning place where their minds swarm in chaos. Only here in the Entire can a Tarig have a body, a life, and worshippers. Would you be subject to such as that?

The dream took Sydney, as Inyx dreams could, filling her drifting mind with urgent sendings. Then it cast her up, like a wave tosses a shell on a beach. She lay sweating in fear and excitement, sticking to her bedclothes, as the storm moved on. She knew that the same kinds of dreams were harrowing the sleep of sentients throughout the Entire. Each one interpreted the send-

35

ings in their own dream-logic. Lacking perfect coherence, the dreams still suggested truths, sowed anxieties. All part of her plan, of Mo Ti's plan: to bring the Inyx herds together in one common force, then use their united dream-sendings in an insurgency of the mind.

Mo Ti's plan, when he'd brought it to her so long ago, had been simple, breathtaking: *Discredit the Tarig. Undermine them. Crush them.* And though Mo Ti was at present far away, Sydney executed that plan, joined by Riod, greatest of the hoofed and horned magnificent Inyx. She didn't know how she would crush the mantis lords. That part was yet to unfold. But it began with a dreamtime rebellion that could penetrate Entirean distances. Each night, a new dream swooped into the minds of sleepers, like a bird landing lightly on a branch, waiting to peck at vital parts.

She sat up, too stimulated to sleep. It was Between Ebb, nearly morning, and Riod would return soon. She rose quickly and dressed, thinking of him, but not too strongly. He shouldn't be distracted from his work in the fields nearby. There, the herds grazed and dozed, looking harmless, while forging their heart-sight into a sword.

Sydney moved quietly, not wanting to disturb Helice, asleep on the other bed. They shared a tent and compatible ambitions; most ebb-times, they spent hours talking. For the first time in the Entire, Sydney had a woman friend.

As she washed and dressed, she glanced at Helice, thankful for her but also blaming her. Helice had brought word of the cirque. In response, Sydney had no choice but to send Mo Ti to stop her father from using it. To kill him. The decision sickened her. It was an ugly thing, even if her father *had* abandoned her and steeped himself in privileges and princedom. How he could have done so, she would never understand. It didn't matter anymore.

When she drew back the tent flap, she was surprised to find the herd surging from the pastures into camp. Their sendings began to filter to her. *Look up. It comes.* Her eyes cut to the sky. Nigh-ward, a shadow cut a crease into the curdling lavender folds of the bright. At great speed, the speck grew. It could only be one thing.

A brightship.

The camp was in chaos. Tarig strode across the field—by now empty of the dreaming herd—cutting a swath through the encampment. Only three Tarig debarked from the ship. As they approached they looked cumulatively like a tripart fighting machine, tall, taloned, and glinting in the morning bright. Sydney rushed back into the tent where Helice was hurriedly dressing.

"Leave!" Sydney hissed. If the lords found a Rose woman among them. . . . "Hide!" Sydney could hear footsteps approaching. But there was no time for Helice to leave. The tent flap flew wide. The lords were here.

Helice bowed deeply, like a servant.

The one in front had the slightly leaner physique of a female, and affected half-gloves that would not impede her in her fight. This one glanced at Helice, then turned to Sydney.

While the two other Tarig stood somewhat back, the gloved Tarig said, "The Rose child, ah?"

She didn't like this Tarig. "I'm not of the Rose. I'm of Riod's sway."

The lord looked down from a height of seven feet. In Sydney's ten years of captivity she had seen the Tarig so infrequently that their physical aspect could still intimidate.

The lead Tarig said, "You will use proper address, small girl, lest my cousins take offense." The other Tarig watched Sydney with black eyes.

"Yes, Bright One."

"You may call us Lady Anuve."

"Yes, Lady Anuve," Sydney made herself say. Her mouth gone dry, Sydney forced herself to breathe. Had they discovered the dreamcasts? Her thoughts raced. Was their rebellion over already? *Riod*, she thought, presuming he would be reaching out to her mind, *Stay far from the tent. You will hear all that transpires. We can't change what comes now. Be brave, my heart.*

"I will dismiss my servant," Sydney said, waving Helice out of the tent. The Tarig ignored her as she passed—small, scarred, and bald—hardly a personage.

Lady Anuve flicked out a talon. Snagging a length of Sydney's hair, she murmured, "Hair the color of soil." The talon whispered down the side of Sydney's face. "And eyes to match." The claw stopped at Sydney's left eyelid. Once, long ago, a talon like that had blinded her, as this Tarig lady surely knew.

Sydney, despite her defiant stance, started to shake.

Retracting her talon, Anuve shoved Sydney in the shoulder, pushing her through the tent door into the morning air. There the herd had begun to gather in front of Sydney's pavilion, among them Adikar the healer, Takko the Laroo, Akay-Wat her Captain of Roamlands, and all their mounts.

Riod stood at the forefront, looming as tall as the Tarig. *Tell her this is my sway, and she must speak with me*, Riod sent.

"Riod is master here," Sydney told the Tarig lady. "You should speak with him. I'll tell you what he says."

"One hears that riders in this place have bonds with Inyx mounts. Is this so?"

"Yes."

"You will use proper address, or we will kill you."

"Yes, Bright One."

Anuve looked at her, calculating. "Do you love this beast, then? So one hears, that the bond is close to love."

"I have such a bond with Riod, Lady Anuve."

"Ah." For the first time Anuve looked at Riod, and then at the mounts behind him. "Send them away, and all their riders."

"But Riod . . ."

"Riod may stay."

Riod, beloved, Sydney thought. But he had heard Anuve's command. He told the gathered Inyx and their riders to move off, out of hearing, out of harm's way. Akay-Wat, riding Gevka, was among them, looking dismayed. It reminded Sydney that it had been a long while since she'd spoken with her old Hirrin friend. Sydney concentrated on a reassuring thought, trusting that the mounts would hear her and relay it to the riders.

Helice was on foot, refusing as always to ride her designated mount. She turned to leave, first locking glances with Sydney as though to say, don't betray me.

When Riod and Sydney were alone among the Tarig, Anuve fixed Sydney with a cold, accusatory stare. "Your eyes have been tampered with."

Relief flooded over her. They'd come because of her sight, only her sight. Sydney released the breath she had been holding. She must take exquisite care. Some lies were needful. Others were useless.

"Yes, Bright One," she finally said. The Tarig were the first who tampered with her sight, and she had tampered back. The mantis lords wanted to spy on the Inyx through her eyes, so they could watch for Titus Quinn. But then Helice had removed the tampering.

"Now we wish to know how this was done. You will tell me now, small girl, how you took back your sight and also how you *knew* to take back your sight. Hnn? We are curious to learn these things."

When Sydney didn't answer, Anuve said, "It was your father, one assumes. Yes?"

"No. My father never came here, Bright One."

"You will tell me who it was, and how it was, that your sight came to be restored." Anuve nodded at one of the other Tarig. He took out a tiny flechette and flung it at Riod, where it stuck into his hide at the shoulder.

Riod shied as Sydney rushed to his side. Grabbing at the barb stuck in Riod's hide, she tried to pull it out, but the protruding end was too sharp. Riod staggered, then collapsed into a sitting position, his legs folded under him. He didn't respond when she touched him or frantically called to him in her mind.

Anuve nodded. "Now you shall tell, yes?"

Sydney barely controlled her fury. "I knew you had my eyes by the way I felt when you looked out of them, my lady. My body rejected your surgeries."

Anuve regarded her quietly. "Think of another answer, girl of the Rose." She flicked a gaze at her two Tarig companions, and they moved away, beginning a search of the camp. She went on. "There have been events at Ahnenhoon. You will not have heard, we suppose you will say, that your father brought a weapon to our great Repel. Lord Inweer stopped him from using it. The darkling fled. Here, ah?"

Fled. Titus fled. Still alive, then. "No, lady, he isn't here. Search as you like." Titus wasn't dead. Somehow, Mo Ti hadn't killed him.

The Tarig lady put a finger under Sydney's chin, tilting it up to lock their gazes. "Your eyes did not repair themselves. You will have some time to think over what you are saying. The Tarig are gracious. We understand sentients have bonds with those called father. But if he is not here now, then you have no reason to deny he was once here. Tell us, and we will spare Riod's life."

Riod's life? Sydney was instantly stricken.

Anuve nodded at Riod. "As he is now, so he remains until I release him from the inhibitor. So he remains until my cousins draw their claws across his neck. By the first hour of Prime of Day. Go to the tent and think carefully."

Sydney looked at Riod, her emotions in turmoil. Nothing, nothing from Riod. His mind was locked in, his body helpless.

Anuve pushed her toward the tent, and Sydney staggered at the casual strength of the Tarig's arm. She ducked through the tent flap, standing alone, wild with fear. The bright lit up the cloth pavilion roof as though it were a normal day, as though the day had in store a ride with her mount and the usual pleasure of his company. She sat on her cot a long while before she could even begin to think. The questing, fearful thoughts of the mounts reached out to her, and she formed a thought for them to take: *Let me think what to do. Wait, my friends.*

As the bright waxed overhead, Sydney sat on her cot.

The Tarig didn't know about the herd sendings. All they knew is that Sydney had foiled their attempt to confiscate her sight. All she had to do was give up Helice, to say: *Helice came to me for help, having sneaked into the realm. I gave her sanctuary. She fixed my eyes. She has a little machine* . . . But Helice had value, almost infinite value. She had the renaissance plan. Of the herd and its riders only Riod and Akay-Wat knew about this, so Sydney diverted her thoughts from the subject quickly.

Sydney walked to her clothing chest and opened it. She took out her best jacket and riding pants. They were white, or nearly white. She changed into them, taking the one item she needed most. She stepped outside.

One of the Tarig stood there, keeping guard. Anuve was nowhere in sight. "I want to be sure Riod is all right," she said to the lord. "Let me approach him."

A nod granted her permission. Coming up to Riod, she knelt and whispered to him: "I've never been afraid to die, Riod. I love you." She took out a knife and pressed it to her own throat. She spoke so the Tarig could hear her clearly: "Come near me or my mount, and I will kill myself."

The Tarig lunged forward. But Lady Anuve shouted out, "Stop. Let her be."

Anuve came into view, her metal skirt slit to allow her long stride. She approached within ten feet of Sydney and Riod and looked down at them. After a minute she said, "You will tire of holding up the knife."

"I'll do the job before then."

Anuve stood as still as Riod and watched. Apparently, as Sydney had gambled, they didn't want her dead.

Thoughts from the herd fell on her like rain. *Come back, mistress. If Riod's time has come, he goes bravely. Sydney. Come back. Mistress.* And, amid the cacophony of anonymous thoughts, Akay-Wat's impassioned plea: *Give them the Rose woman, Akay-Wat begs you. Stay with us, oh stay . . .*

Sydney found she wasn't afraid. Once she had decided to die, the rest was—if not easy—at least peaceful. She let her mind go blank, beyond emotion or logic.

She waited.

Sometime during this profound calm, the camp stirred around her. Sydney hardly registered the movements. The heart-sendings grew stronger, more difficult to ignore. At last, reluctantly, she came back to full presence.

Insistent thoughts came pulsing to her from the herd: *A brightship comes. Another ship.*

Sydney moved slightly. Turning toward Riod, she saw him still immobile. Where the flechette was stuck into him, a trickle of blood had dried, forming a red crack down his side.

After a time, a new Tarig strode into view. The lord stood next to Anuve, taller, more commanding.

The newcomer and Anuve were speaking, but they kept their voices out of hearing range. The other two Tarig were also joining in, as though there were no difference in standing among them. The conference ended.

The new Tarig approached Sydney. He crouched next to her in that way Tarig had of appearing all knees and elbows, inspiring her expression, *mantis lords.*

"Do you know this Tarig lord, young girl?" he asked.

She shook her head, unable to summon the spit to speak.

"Lord Inweer. One has come from Ahnenhoon. You know Ahnenhoon?" She nodded.

"At Ahnenhoon, Johanna was our companion. You have before you that lord. Do you understand?"

Again, she nodded. "Stay back," she croaked. Though, in truth he was close enough now that he could easily grab the knife. He was also close enough that she could stab him in the eye, the best way to kill a Tarig.

"Your father was here, and he must have had means to return your normal sight. One can forgive you this small treason. Do not lie to us, and this lord will help you."

"Riod . . ." Sydney whispered. "Remove Riod's barb, and we can talk, Bright Lord." She looked into his implacable face and found herself saying, though she hated to say it, "Please."

Lord Inweer stood up and yanked the barb from Riod's side. Flecks of blood spun off it as he flung it away.

Riod's chest expanded, grabbing air.

Sydney whispered, summoning the required lie: "My father fixed my eyes. Then he left, Bright Lord."

"Ah. That is a good answer. Where did he go?"

"He would not tell me."

Inweer watched her. Then he did something Tarig never did. He blinked. It made his face look almost human. "We will tell you of your mother, now. Johanna is dead. One could not save her. She helped her husband when he came against the great engine. My cousin killed her for this crime. We buried her at Ahnenhoon."

Dead. Sydney felt a pang at the news. Her mother had been dead to her for a long while—but now she was dead in truth. The news hit her with some force. How strange that recently she had sent Sydney a scroll with a moving image of herself. There were times, deep in the ebb, when Sydney looked at that image and wondered about her mother. Now, she would never know more.

Inweer went on, "This lord held her in regard."

This was the lord she had so despised, the one her mother had been living with as mistress of his household and of his bed. She had hated them both. Now he was going to help her. She felt numb with all that was happening. *Riod*, she thought passionately. *Johanna is dead.*

Riod's awakening mind sent: *I am here. Always here, best rider.*

Inweer had no part of their private heart-sendings. He watched them as though he knew they were talking, though. "One has the power to raise you up, small girl. This lord will do so for the sake of Johanna. You will ask no questions, but accept all conditions."

"And Riod will be safe, my lord?"

"You may keep your beast. One has no interest in his fate."

She lowered her hand. She couldn't drop the knife because her fingers were frozen in their grip. Inweer pried her fingers open and took the weapon.

He said, his voice very deep and soft, "She asked for you, pleaded for your safety. This we granted, giving you leave to rise up among the Inyx. Now you will need further protection from cousins who find you distasteful. You will have a position. It will mean you must leave this sway. Do you agree?"

At her side, Riod trembled, coming to full alert. She touched him. *My heart.*

Shall I kill him? Riod sent.

"No, Riod," she said aloud. "Lord Inweer can help us." The lord was waiting for her reply. "Where will I go, Bright Lord?"

"We have considered the idea that the Chalin Sway should be yours. The master of that sway can be dismissed. You may do well there. In return, you will entrap your father the next time he appears before you. That is the condition. He cannot be loose in the Entire. We do not discuss this or compromise. Ah?"

Well, that was easy to agree to. "Yes, my lord."

Satisfied, Inweer rose from his crouch and conferred with the other Tarig.

Riod pulled his front legs under him, lumbering up, front first, then back. He dipped his head down to allow Sydney to hold on to his fore horns. Then he lifted his head, and Sydney rose up using his strength.

Someone approached them from the ranks of the riders who had been gathering at a distance. Takko the Laroo brought Riod a pan of water and

Sydney a cup. He nodded at her, his face conveying relief. Sydney felt her skin crack at the effort of smiling.

The Tarig group turned to Sydney and Riod at last. Anuve spoke, "We like not the idea of the Chalin sway. It is too much to give, and it has its master, Zai Gan." Anuve and Inweer exchanged glances like cuts. Surely she could not overrule Lord Inweer, who was, after all, one of the ruling Five. "We have in mind, however, that small girl might go to Rim City. She can be magister of that city."

Sydney was not dead. No, and she was being given a great prize, instead. Numb, she could only listen.

Anuve regarded her. "It may suit our purposes. She may prove herself a loyal sentient."

Rim City. At the foot of the Ascendancy. "Wherever you send me, Bright Ones, I have to bring Riod." Sydney blurted it out, then saw how the Tarig regarded this interruption. They stared at her with expressions that silenced her.

Inweer said, "Take two or three companions, then." He turned to Anuve. "She will need loyalty around her."

Anuve said nothing; Inweer outranked her. Sydney's thoughts were giddy. Rim City was said to encircle the Sea of Arising, so it was within spitting distance of the Ascendancy. Oh, Riod. Oh, Mo Ti, she thought.

Inweer went on, "We would have her be mistress of a sway. Thus we will invest Rim City as a sway. It shows the Bright Realm that she has earned our respect. It shows that she is pardoned for her Rose birthing. It is well to pardon from time to time." He nodded. "One concurs with you, Lady Anuve. She will go to Rim Sway. It is a place no one else could want and no master of a sway need be cast down."

Anuve fixed Sydney with a black look. "And you will bring Titus Quinn to us?"

Sydney nodded. "Yes. He'll come, Bright One."

Anuve growled, "He tends to slip away."

"I'll help you, my lady."

"The daughter helps to snare the father? Even a father who helped her realign her sight?"

"Yes, my lady." They had no clue what her relationship with Titus was. That when he was a prince of the city, he had left her to her enslavement among the Inyx before she had found Riod to champion her. He had let the lords blind her. And he had lived like a king.

Lord Inweer was eager to be on his way and took his leave. Sydney and Anuve watched him stride back to his ship. He must feel satisfaction, Sydney thought, that he'd done a favor for Johanna. Now she was left with the after-taste of *accepting* a favor from him. As the brightship slipped silently into its ascent path, Anuve murmured, "We must wonder how the lord gives credence to you."

"The bright lady must know I do not love my father."

"Do not all children love their parents?"

"Not all, Lady Anuve."

"This will favor our purpose, Rose child."

The phrase grated. "I am not a Rose child, my lady."

The gloved hand came back and across Sydney's face, sending her staggering backward. "You are what we say you are, ah?"

Sydney regained her footing and nodded, shrugging the pain of the blow away.

Anuve persisted, "We say you are a decoy."

I am your death. Sydney smiled. The Tarig had learned that humans smiled. They just hadn't learned all the reasons why.

Already, Sydney's mind was on Rim City. Oh Mo Ti, she thought. In that far city she would finally take on her new name that Mo Ti had devised for her: Sen Ni, to give her darkling name a Chalin style.

One step closer to raising the kingdom, one without Tarig lords and ladies.

The camp was in a state of watchful brooding. The news spread quickly that Sydney was going to Rim City and that Riod would go with her. The shock of these revelations hit hard. Knots of riders stood talking in low tones, fearful of drawing the attention of the Tarig still in camp.

Helice stood in one of these groups, listening hard, trying to grasp what had happened, though her language skills were still imperfect. The riders didn't despise her as much as before, since many had accepted her surgery to restore their vision. Blind riders might have been the fashion once; no longer. Helice had ingratiated herself with the riders, but her refusal to bond with a mount kept her an outsider.

That wouldn't matter anymore. She was going to Rim City. She'd be among that select group Sydney brought with her, no doubt about that. The girl needed her. For renaissance. One couldn't think about that subject among the horse-beasts, though. She turned the thought aside.

She looked around her, trying to guess which of the nearby Inyx might be probing her mind. She disciplined herself to not dwell on certain matters. The beasts could pick up thoughts, but only with effort and only if the thoughts were strong and well formed. Helice kept her mind skittering over her plans, touching on them and darting away. But even if the Inyx glimpsed her intentions, what could they do? She had been more or less honest with Sydney. Their goals were compatible, at least for a while.

As plodding as the Inyx were, even they could grasp the significance of Sydney moving to Rim City. There, Riod would be close enough to the Tarig home base to fine-tune their dream probes to greater effect. There were still pieces of intelligence Sydney and Helice needed. Rim City was a perfect base camp for the final assault. The riders said that the city was under the very shadow of the Ascendancy. Perfect.

Though the day was hot, Helice pulled her scarf up around her neck. She was self-conscious about the infection that had taken hold in her burns. The injuries she'd sustained from the rough passage into the Entire hadn't healed well. Just when she thought she might be getting better, the burns on her neck and chin began to fester. The mSap's medical knowledge was equal to any possessed by Earth's finest physicians, but the tissue sample she'd analyzed yielded a culprit bacterium unknown to Rose medicine. To find a pharmaceutical treatment, she needed a laboratory, test subjects . . . it would mean weeks, even months of painstaking work.

Certainly the camp healer with her local remedies was of no help. Maybe Rim City would have better doctors, although she couldn't afford close scrutiny. She didn't know what medical technologies the Entire had, but it was a disturbing possibility that a physician might notice she was a little . . . different. Chalin were human, or seemed to be. Who knew, though, if their physiologies were exactly the same?

No time to worry. Helice was buoyed by the prospect of being at the center of things. She had always savored being at the locus of events, decisions, and power. Not because she wanted power for herself—that was a side benefit—but because it meant working at the top of her game, using all the neurons the gene lottery bestowed. There was no better thing.

She wasn't without sympathy for those who couldn't think on her level. She was well aware that most people would view such sympathy as condescension. In a culturally correct world, everyone was equal in some cosmic sense. The problem with cosmic sense was its fuzziness. It led to illogical conclusions such as that people deserved to be kept warm, fed, and entertained by virtue of being human. And if such humans had been able to take a suitable role in contributing to society, she would have been in favor of tithes for the mentally disadvantaged. However, these days there were so few suitable occupations. Nan bots built and maintained physical structures; AI-powered services of all kinds performed humble tasks. The unfortunate majority, with their average intelligence—hovering within fifteen to twenty points of one hundred and wickedly called dreds by some—led lives stuffed with virtual entertainments. Truly a circus maximus of the latter-day Roman Empire.

Well, they could live as they wished, of course. But the problem was— and here is where it affected Helice and her circle—they were yoking the intellectually gifted to their little cart.

That state of affairs was coming to an end.

Well, there was a bit more coming to an end, but it would be best not to dwell on it in front of the Inyx.

CHAPTER THREE

How can the Adda float so high?
—They have no memories to weigh them down.

—a child's riddle

FROM THE OPEN DOOR OF HIS QUARTERS, Quinn could watch the great sea. Time was when he had spent years looking down on this sea. Now he saw it from a new angle, like most of the things in his life.

He saw Anzi anew. They had begun badly, as she drew his escape pod into the Entire; a girl playing at magic like the sorcerer's apprentice. Although that act had possibly saved his life and the lives of his family, it had also damned them. That seemed long ago. Since then, they had shared terror and deliverance so many times it was hard to imagine life without her. He saw the Entire through her eyes, he supposed. He saw himself through her eyes.

What would she think of him now, with his new face, courtesy of one of Zhiya's back-alley healers? He'd changed features once before, in what had become a continuing distortion of the man Titus Quinn, played out on his face and elsewhere.

He walked to the small porch jutting out from his upper-story sitting room.

Where are you, Anzi? I'm not supposed to know. Still, where are you right now?

Johanna had released him from his marriage. She had moved on, and so, she claimed, should he. Their marriage had not survived the Entire. How could it? How could anything of the Rose survive this place?

Now, two weeks after Anzi had left, Quinn was well lodged in a small but luxurious suite of rooms in a node of the city where a reclusive resident might have privacy. Zhiya had arranged it at her own expense. A godwoman—even of venerable rank—must have a side income, and Zhiya did: her cadre of exclusive consorts who hired her to procure. His hideaway wasn't far from her own quarters—although *far* was a troublesome concept here. By navitar vessel, every place was close in Rim City, a city girdling the Sea of Arising.

From this sea five rivers spread out like arms on a starfish. This was a radial universe, a cosmos with a geography; a place that couldn't be, except as a profound construct of a stage-four civilization. Contained by storm walls, lidded by the bright, and pierced by the rivers Nigh—all this had become sensible to him, even inevitable. They called this place the Entire, as though there *was* nothing else. Sometimes that, too, made sense to him. A convenient mind-set, since he was stuck here. And since he probably wasn't welcome in the Rose.

Did you deliver the weapon to Ahnenhoon, Quinn?

—I got it to the place.

And did you destroy the engine there?

—There was a problem.

What problem could matter enough? They're going to burn us for fuel.

Quinn tried to conjure an answer. Minerva misjudged the nan. It would have destroyed this universe. Helice had warned him, but he hadn't believed her. His thoughts stuck on this point. Why had Helice tried to protect the Entire? She must have seen some profit in the place, but what profit could matter if the Earth was threatened? Somehow the trade-off had seemed worth it to her. He'd very much like to know why.

Standing on the porch, he gazed at the distant pillars that seemed to bear up the Tarig capital city. Inside those conduits of exotic matter, lifts rose and fell, conveying functionaries and petitioners intent upon the chores of the colossal meritocracy. Commanding the summit, the Ascendancy, a stationary, misshapen moon. The floating city was the most formidable sight in the Entire *or* the Rose—and Quinn had seen many sights. He had captained star vessels. He had seen the Repel of Ahnenhoon. But this was a sight to stop one's breath. Exactly as the Tarig intended.

Below the city in the sky, navitar vessels on the sea sparked in and out of existence. As Quinn watched he saw, out toward one of the five primacies, a congregation of Adda cruising slowly, far from their usual cross-primacy routes. A trick of perspective, to see so far. Today was especially good for mirages. Quinn gazed at the closest storm wall where it stopped short at the shore in a view that appeared to be twenty miles away. He squinted, trying to see the storm walls of Sydney's primacy too, but as most things relating to his daughter, they were obscured by time and distance. Yet by navitar vessel, she was close. That was the overwhelming reality of the Entire. Immensity and immediacy were two sides of the same coin.

Could anyone choose to destroy this? The Entire endured. Earth was under threat. He could have traded these two circumstances. He hadn't.

At a noise downstairs, Quinn found his knife—a beat too slowly, but fast enough.

Zhiya appeared in the doorway, key in hand. Nodding her overlarge head at the sea, she said, "Anzi's not out there."

Quinn slipped the knife back into the folds of his shirt. "No. Out in the void."

"Don't try to guess."

"Was I?"

Zhiya gamboled in, joining him on the balcony. "Even I don't know where she went. No use trying to ply me with sex, I won't tell you." She threw a lock of her white hair over her shoulder. "On second thought, you could try."

Quinn smiled, saying nothing. In the nearby public square he could glimpse from his balcony, a God's Needle jutted up from the city, where sentients left offerings for the god whom they hoped would not notice them. The needle looked neglected. This was a city favoring a different religion, the faith of the Red Throne. He didn't know which he preferred: the Red, with its fatalistic and pious acceptance of all futures, or the Misery, acknowledging that the more you attracted notice, the worse God dealt with you. Having experienced the foretelling powers of the navitar Ghoris, he was inclined to believe that if any being was close to a creator, it might be the red-robed pilots. The navitars didn't encourage such devotion. They were oblivious to it. An excellent clergy, and immune to corruption.

Zhiya led him back to the sitting room. "Let me look at your face." She hauled a chair closer. "Sit."

He got to her level, and she examined his bruised face, where the needles had instructed his face to move and his face had responded with slow, painful morphing.

"My drunken physician did well. But you look tired. Did you sleep?"

"Badly."

"Dreams?"

"Of Tarig."

Zhiya shrugged "A plague of nightmares. We all have them."

"I dream of fighting them."

"Good idea."

Ever since she'd given him a ride in her airship, she'd had in mind that he'd lead a revolution. In Zhiya's peregrinations, she'd always looked for someone who'd take the role. Unfortunately, she had settled on him.

He rose. "So, you approve the new face?"

"Lovely. But I fancy a soldier, dear one. Strap on a sword and you can have me on the balcony."

"I'm no soldier. You've mistaken me for a hero." He went back to his post at the doorway. "I'm Ji Anzi's husband."

Zhiya blinked. "Hm. Well, for my part, I liked you better when you were important."

Quinn turned from her. He gazed at the pillars of the Ascendancy. Once he'd thought of slicing the legs off that hovering beast. Now his chance was gone. The cirque lay at the bottom of the Nigh. The cirque, that flawed device he'd brought from the Rose. Flawed, full of changeover nan. Escaping, it would have rushed out and enveloped the world, along with the bright sky, the dark walls. All. It was not a limited device, as the Rose engineers had promised. It would have taken it all.

So the engine at Ahnenhoon remained, churning into the Rose. Whether he'd chosen rightly or wrongly, the moment was past. No one man could destroy so much. *He* could not. The cirque was gone.

"I suspected you would turn me down."

He turned back to Zhiya, cocking an eyebrow.

"About taking a little comfort in my arms." She swept her hand toward the door. On cue, a stunning woman in deep purple and gold entered, bowing. A courtesan. She drew the eye, locked it on.

Zhiya avoided Quinn's look. "One of my girls. Your lovely wife won't mind. It isn't our way to put too much meaning into physical delight."

"It isn't my way to pay for sex."

"My treat," Zhiya said.

He left the porch and approached the woman. "Your name?"

"Ban, Excellency." She glanced at the quarters, noting that she'd be entertaining a man of means.

"You may leave, Ban. Thank you."

Zhiya signaled Ban to stay. "It will do you good, Ni Jian," she said, using Quinn's new name. When Quinn didn't answer, she drew closer. "She'd want you to live naturally—while she's gone."

"I *am* living naturally."

"Staring at the sea? Thinking too much about what's gone, what's done and not done?"

"I'm recuperating."

"Some things still work, I'm sure," she muttered. After a long moment, she gestured Ban out of the room. "You're no use to anyone if you let yourself go dark."

"No use to *you*."

Zhiya put on a hurt expression. "As though I've ever asked anything of you."

It was true. She'd helped him in the bad times, never calling for a favor in return. But she hated the Tarig, and counted on Quinn to share that hate. Maybe do something about it, if the day ever came.

Softening his tone, he said, "Don't ask me to go back to what I was. There's no going back."

"There's going forward."

"I do go forward."

She smiled, shaking her head. "Stuck in place, dear one. Someone has to tell you."

He saw how it was with her. She remembered him striving, half mad with despair over Sydney and guilt over his wife's suffering. Zhiya had seen him engulfed in pain and thoughts of revenge. Maybe she liked him better that way.

"I'm not dark." He had the words, finally. He knew the feeling that had lurked there these last days. "I'm at peace." Amid all of this, it was the simple truth. The world was at war, but he was relieved of duty. "I've become a plain man. I'm glad of it." He knew how it sounded. Like he was settling for less. There was a big difference between peace and surrender, though. "At peace. Do you know how good that feels?"

Her response dripped with sarcasm. "I can just imagine." She went to the chair where Ban had left her shawl and picked it up. "Recuperate, then. I can see you need more rest before you pillow a beautiful woman who is the best of my whores and who, besides, is your own height."

He smiled at her. "If I was going to pillow with anyone—which I'm not, because I'm done betraying the women in my life—it would be you."

She threw the shawl over her white hair that was the hallmark of Chalin women. "Recuperate, Ni Jian. Let me know when you're worth talking to again." Before closing the door, she gave him a sideways glance. "Anzi might be gone a long time, you know."

"I know."

The longer she was gone, the safer it was for the Rose. Standing at the door again, and looking at the God's Needle nearby, he almost threw out a prayer. It wouldn't do, though, to have the wrong god hear it.

Days passed. Quinn counted them. Ten, twenty. Zhiya came and went, reporting on Tarig presence in Rim City, listening for news, spying out new sources. But to what purpose? She wanted him to bring them down, and Quinn only wanted peace.

At times, he was able to sleep. Sometimes he dreamed lucidly. Tonight was such a night.

He pivoted to avoid the slashing blow. The Tarig lord missed, but more Tarig swarmed around him. He was dreaming, he knew, but he still fought for his life. Each Tarig he felled was replaced by another, jumping up from the ground, created from soil.

They replicated wildly; not born, but sprouting unnaturally. They were made of dirt, but no less strong for that. Within seconds of springing up, their skin hardened off, congealing under a thousand years of fire curing. The foremost creature came for him out of nowhere, her talon aimed for his eye. Before the claw went in, he had time to see it was the Lady Chiron. She was supposed to be dead. No longer.

To escape blinding, he woke.

It was Deep Ebb, what passed for night in the Entire. Through the haze of broken sleep, Quinn noted the lavender sky with clefts of purple, shedding a dour twilight. Though every day Zhiya begged him to secure his doors, he left them thrown wide to his deck for the view of the sea, where Anzi had set sail.

A creature poised on the balcony. Small, misshapen, ominous.

Quinn rolled to his feet, his hand clamping on to his knife. He circled around the creature, trying to see how many there were. The room in shadow. The creature, a monkey.

A Ysli. Simian creature, but sentient. He wore a belt with tools hanging from it. It sprang at him. Before Quinn's knife had completed its upward swing, the Ysli jumped high to crash into Quinn's chest. Quinn sprawled onto his back; the Ysli rode him down.

A knife was at Quinn's eye. "Calm," the Ysli said in a hissing voice. "No movement."

Quinn felt the blade press at the corner of one eye. He remained still.

"No knife," the creature said, still whispering.

Quinn released his grip on his own knife, and the Ysli kicked it away, still sitting on his chest like a nightmare.

"I'll pay you more than the Tarig can," Quinn whispered.

"Under sentient," the creature hissed. "I serve the mistress, don't I? Ghoris. You remember?" He grinned at Quinn's reaction. "You know her, so no cause to draw knives. You drew yours first, or I wouldn't have jumped. Can you be calm? I'll let you up."

"Yes."

The Ysli climbed down, placing the knife in his tool belt. The back of his arms and thighs bristled with hair, as did its chest and groin. Golden eyes peered out at Quinn from a bald and wizened face. Quinn knew this ship keeper. "Ghoris says you must come."

"To her ship?"

"Does a navitar leave her ship?"

"Why does she want me?"

"She doesn't. The visitor does."

"Visitor?"

The Ysli frowned, massive eyebrows meeting in the crease of his forehead. "Coming or not?"

Quinn grabbed a cloak, leading the way down the stairs to the street.

Anzi, he thought. She's here, somehow on Ghoris's ship. Ghoris had taken pity on him and would give them a cabin to indulge their longing and bodily hunger. But remembering the navitar, he thought not. Ghoris was barely aware that she *had* a body.

Nighttime made a splendor of Rim City. The isthmus of lights extended out on either side in a hot strip of molten colors, a neon foam on the endless shore. The tracks of the longest city in the universe, in any universe.

Quinn and the ship keeper walked quickly through the lanes of the nearest residential quarter, offering glimpses of the sea peeking between courtyards and back passageways. They stayed off the great Way, the circular road that meandered more or less parallel with the shore. Keeping to back ways, they passed into a more humble sector with a chaotic assortment of shops and apartments above. The only rule in this city was never to block the Way. In theory, a citizen of the Entire could walk the full circumference of the sea, the better to see the lords' glory. One step at a time, it would take thousands of years.

When the back ways came to a dead end, the ship keeper reluctantly led him into the Way. Fortunately, few sentients were abroad at the late hour.

On the sea side of the Way, habitations and wharves huddled, blocking off a view of the mercurial waters. His instinctive caution made him wary of this ship keeper. But if the Tarig knew him to be at Zhiya's hiding place, they didn't need a ruse to bring him out.

Ghoris was an ally, if a slightly mad one. She had brought him out of

Ahnenhoon. She had predicted Johanna would be the key to Earth's future. And Ghoris had been right.

He hoped the navitar had good reason to bring him out into the streets. As long as he stayed hidden, the lords would think he had a doomsday device. That piece of deterrence would argue for leaving the Earth alone, and the Rose. As long as he remained hidden. He cast a quick look at the Ysli, taciturn, working hard to match strides with Quinn.

They came to a pier hidden in a shed and entered through a locked door which the Ysli resealed behind him. Quinn heard the slosh of exotic water against the boardwalk. Here in the deep shadow, no light shone from the wharf or from the ship. The navitar's ship hunkered there, a mere outline.

Quinn let the Ysli take his arm, guiding him to the ship ramp.

On the upper deck, a brief flash of light and a glimpse of red cloth: Ghoris moving in her quarters, maybe keeping watch, or maybe just careening from porthole to porthole, staring madly.

The Ysli led him to the main cabin, leaving him at the threshold.

Then Quinn turned and found he was not alone. He faced a massive presence in the room. Neither of them moved. "I've come in good faith," Quinn said at last. "And you?" When the presence didn't answer, Quinn said, "Turn on a light."

"No lights," came the gentle voice.

River matter sloshed gently against the ship's hull. The two of them faced off, shadow against shadow.

"I know you," Quinn ventured, remembering.

"You do. I am Mo Ti."

The man who'd covered his retreat from Ahnenhoon. "The one who fought off two soldiers so I could escape."

"Three."

"I'm glad you got away. I'd hear your story if you'll tell it." He heard Mo Ti move a little, and the floorboards creaked.

"Someday. Mo Ti is here now, with news."

"Who are you, Mo Ti?"

"First, a story."

Quinn sat on the bench under the porthole. Mo Ti took the bench opposite. His leathers stank of sweat in the small cabin, as though the man had run ten miles under the full bright.

"I come from a far sway, Titus Quinn. Your daughter's sway." Quinn waited.

"I was her protector, but she sent me away, taking on a vile advisor in my place. I wish to save her from ruin. No matter how I betray her today, Mo Ti serves her forever. You understand?"

"Yes," Quinn breathed.

"I do not know you, nor care one gobbet for you, darkling. But I saw the thing you did at Ahnenhoon. You had the chain and did not use it against us. All would have died. You spared us. Mo Ti remembers."

"I made my choice. For my own reasons."

"And Mo Ti, too, has his own reasons. Listen." The giant—for he was a massive man, larger than any Quinn had seen—leaned forward in the dark. "Before I left the primacy of the Long Gaze of Fire, someone came to us whom you know. Someone from the dark universe. It was she who told us about the chain and what it held."

Helice. Quinn knew that when she slipped away from their former mission, she went to Sydney.

"The woman is a spider, Titus Quinn."

"Call me Quinn."

"You brought the spider here."

He accepted the rebuke in silence. Helice had followed him, and he hadn't thought fast enough to prevent it. From upstairs came a rattling sound. Ghoris at the door, trying to come down. The ship keeper had locked her in, then. The door rattled again, louder.

Mo Ti stopped, listening. Unperturbed, he went on: "The spider has a machine she built up from parts sown into her garments. Like a mechanical thing with a mind, it has magical properties. Your Hel Ese used it to take a blight from Sydney's eyes. My mistress carried the sight of the Tarig, and to forestall them watching us, wore a blindfold. The spider healed her. For that she won Sydney's high regard and prevailed on Sydney to send me away.

"Further, she told Sydney you had a device that would loose a plague on our land. That you would put it at the foot of the engine at Ahnenhoon, but that the plague would kill all the world. My mistress believed her." Quinn could imagine what a monster his daughter must think him. Mo Ti continued, "But you did not use the chain." He paused. "Was it because you love the Entire, darkling?"

"Yes."

Mo Ti was quiet for a moment, perhaps mulling over whether to trust a man who would betray his own world. "Strange."

"Is this the news you came to tell me, Mo Ti? That Helice has turned my daughter against me?"

"No." They were interrupted by the ship keeper, who came inside and, without speaking to them or lighting his way, ascended the companionway to the upper deck. They listened as the Ysli unlocked the door and entered the navitar's cabin. Ghoris barked a laugh, and the ship keeper slammed the door behind him, murmuring to the navitar.

Mo Ti went on. "Here is the news I came to tell: The spider told us in private counsels she would come to the Entire with a large force of darklings, but not too large. They would take refuge here, and she would let the Tarig burn the Rose. She has a great machine in the Rose that matches the forces of the Ahnenhoon engine. Working together, the two machines will ignite a great fire in your realm. Thus she removes all threat of the Rose sending another plague into the Entire. She purges her fellow darklings whom she hates. She begins a new sway, and breeds humans to long life here. That is the spider's plan."

For a moment Quinn couldn't quite grasp the size of it. He sat, waiting for Mo Ti's words to stick. Instead, they swirled: matching engine; a great fire; breeding humans . . .

"She has a darkling word for this plan. *Rena Sance.* To renew darkling life. To begin your culture over again. This pleases her. Also long life in the Entire. That is Mo Ti's belief, that she comes here to live one hundred thousand days."

Quinn was shaking his head. It wasn't possible, even for Helice. "The Tarig can already burn the Rose for fuel. Why have another engine?"

"She says using a matching engine can hasten the Rose collapse. What would take many thousands of days can be done in one."

Still pushing away, Quinn shot back: "Why? Why should the Tarig rush? They have time to burn us one star at a time."

"No. She would get it over with. As it is now, there are armed forays forthcoming from the Rose. You were one. If there are others, best light the Rose fire now, rather than wait. So the spider told us."

A moan from upstairs. Perhaps Ghoris heard this, despaired of it.

Quinn sat in the dark, thoughts circling. It stunned him—not just the plan, but that Helice had even thought of it. How could a universe collapse in an instant? But it could. A quantum transition, occurring everywhere at once; the universe and all its atoms moving simultaneously to a lower energy state, falling inward, heating to incandescence.

"I don't believe you, Mo Ti. Why the hell should I?" In the heavy dark, the giant's silence reigned. "Why doesn't she go directly to the Tarig?" It would be like her to go to the top.

"The spider says she needs assurances that the Tarig won't take her engine without first letting her people come. She seeks the Tarig weak point. So do we all. But she might find it first. She has her little machine. It is the only part of her I fear. The machine is a little god."

Worse and worse. A machine sapient, of course. She had brought an mSap with her.

They sat facing each other while Mo Ti waited and Quinn churned. One part fit: Helice had warned him the nan device was out of control. She tried to save the Entire. She wanted it for herself, then. Herself and *a force of darklings.*

"And you, Mo Ti. Why help the Rose—against your own mistress?"

The giant didn't answer. Quinn let the moment stretch out. Why would the devoted Mo Ti go against Sydney, against the Entire?

Even in the dark, the two men faced off with hostile eyes.

Mo Ti shifted his weight. "Mo Ti has reasons."

Oh yes, reasons. Mo Ti had them aplenty. Hel Ese wished to bring darklings to the All. A human sway, a settlement of thousands. The lords would crush her for the mere suggestion. When caught, Hel Ese's downfall would take Sydney as well. But if he and his mistress were to die for treason, let it be their own treason, and their own goals: to raise the kingdom. First envisioned by High Prefect Cixi, then transmitted to Mo Ti, the dream was for a kingdom of diverse sentients under the daughter of the Rose. It was Cixi's perfect plan, and Mo Ti and Sydney were bringing it to fruition.

As for fuel needed, that was a problem for another day.

He was not ready to divulge to Titus Quinn Sydney's plan. Quinn need only assist them by removing the spider. It suited the man's interests to do so, and it suited Mo Ti to set him upon it.

"The Entire is for the Entire," Mo Ti said, finally. "I want no hoards of darklings here. Especially not ruled by the spider. Go away once you rid us of her. You to the Rose, we for the Entire. It is the way it has always been."

They heard the ship keeper coming down the stairs in a great hurry. Entering the main cabin, the Ysli bore a small lantern. By its light, Quinn looked at Mo Ti in his leather tunic, torn leggings. His face, bulging at chin and cheekbones and his hair drawn up into a top knot, in the warrior style. Just as he remembered him.

"We must depart," the Ysli rasped. "Ghoris says our presence is suspect. Ready yourselves for the binds."

Quinn glanced out the port hole, but the enclosed pier remained empty by what light was cast from the cabin. He addressed Mo Ti. "My daughter wouldn't help kill the Earth. She wouldn't help Helice."

Mo Ti snorted. "What ties does my mistress have to the Rose? Whatever ties there were, they are gone. Sydney is a power in the land, and her loyalties are here."

While the two faced off in silence, the Ysli spat out, "We leave now. Be ready!"

Mo Ti said, "Run with us. You are the only one that can stop the spider."

"There's you."

"Mo Ti is easy to see, and all will seek me. You are like other men. Go abroad in the bright realm and remove her."

So much for being at peace. The war would never be done with him. He was enlisted for the duration. Already he felt something uncoiling within him. A striking force, gathering rage from the words of this hulking messenger.

From upstairs they heard Ghoris cry out, "Ship keeper! Cast off, cast off!"

As Quinn hesitated, Mo Ti sneered, "Tarig, no doubt. Did they follow you? Do you want to live?"

"If you're lying, wherever you go, I'll find you. We'll have the fight we should have had."

Mo Ti grinned. In the cerulean light, he looked like the Miserable God himself, gloating from the side of a godman's cart. "I am waiting, darkling."

If it was Tarig who approached, his best chance was with the ship. Quinn glanced at the ship keeper. "Cast off," he said. The ship keeper nodded. Upstairs, the navitar seemed to know. The vessel lurched, then began a slow pull out of its berth.

The ship gained speed, spearing out of the pier. Within the next moment, the funnel came down with a splash, sucking in the fuel of the exotic water. Leaving Rim City behind, the vessel sped out to sea.

CHAPTER FOUR

The light of your ambition leads you, burning its promises for fuel.

—Hoptat the Seer

"THE BINDS," THE SHIP KEEPER WARNED FROM THE GALLEY DOOR. "She goes steeply in. Be ready." Then he disappeared into his galley and his hammock.

Quinn found a seat on a bench. Outside, a bluish light stained the deck and fizzed along the edges of the portholes. On the bridge, Ghoris shouted something incoherent. The ship yawed, dipping the starboard deck. A gout of the Nigh swilled off the porthole. They were headed down, lopsided, into the knots of time. Mo Ti, less accustomed to ships than Quinn, staggered and grabbed a wall for support.

The ship sank deeper, bleeding off the lights. Quinn heard Mo Ti seek his own berth, settling heavily. The vessel, calmer now that it had made its dimensional transition, fell slowly into the depths, thickening the air inside the cabin, bringing a familiar nausea. Quinn stared at the porthole near him. Inside the Nigh was an intermittent, querulous light. Some said the light source was the ship itself, and others, the mind of the observer. They were travelers in space-time, traversing the galactic distances of the Entire the only way common people could, by leave of the navitars—unlikely pilots though they were. No wonder simple people revered them, made of them red-clad prophets, though few ever spoke to a navitar, and none sensibly.

Outside, light ran in slicks on the back of long waves. Sleep beckoned. Quinn pushed it away as thoughts fell like sediment through his mind.

Drifting down, drifting deep. Across from him, Mo Ti lay on his bench barely awake, eyes rolling up, his body splayed on its too-small bed.

Quinn tried to focus on the warrior's face. Devoted to her. Betraying her. Jealous of the new advisor. Spared Quinn's life. Big enough to kill with a blow of his fist. The body muscular but longing to go to fat. Mo Ti was a eunuch.

"Who gelded you?" Quinn asked, barely able to form words.

A long time later Mo Ti whispered, "The mantis lords cut me."

Quinn closed his eyes. Here was a sentient who hated the Tarig. It moved him to trust Mo Ti a bit more, that they shared an enemy. He had hoped to find a great flaw in the man; some reason to dismiss the things he'd said. But on this edge of consciousness, Quinn abandoned himself to instinct. Mo Ti had told the truth. Quinn let himself fall into the hole that was waiting for him: Helice's almost inconceivable plan. She was a demon. Some people had rotted hearts; no saving them. From his first encounter, he'd thought her shriveled and feral. *Must learn to trust first insights. It wasn't racial purity she was after, but intellectual. The new monstrous. Guise: small young woman with sporty smile.* He slept.

The dreams, when they came, were all of the Tarig. They were bodiless, waves riding in light, pulses crying out in a shrieking brightness. He followed their essence, tracing pathways of pure thought that converged and separated. Here was Lord Hadenth, half mad, his pathway stuttering, dimpling into a momentary dark fold. Over there, Chiron, her presence swelling and beating like a heart. They had no true form. They chose bodies to suit.

He drifted, just beneath consciousness. On the deck above, Ghoris roared, still strong in her command of the binds: "They ride, ride. See the horned beasts, coming through the air! See who rides the beasts? It is the girl of your loins, Titus. She. She brings the dreams."

At first all he could see was eddies of fire. But there, a shadow flying above, throwing a silhouette of an Inyx over the deck.

Quinn was burning up. His mouth filled with molten consciousness. The porthole view showed a flying beast, horns curving backward, leading a wingless armada. The shadows passed overhead, sparks shedding from their hooves, hitting the submerged deck like hail.

The ship was moving up, river matter slipping past the portholes. Quinn struggled to sit up. Shaking off his stupor, he crawled over to Mo Ti, who was still unconscious.

He shook the big man. "The dreams," he croaked, trying to find his voice. "They're Inyx dreams. Inyx, aren't they?"

Mo Ti stirred, pawing at the air around him. Quinn moved off, waiting for the big man to come round. From the galley, Quinn heard rattling, signifying that the ship had surfaced and the ship keeper was preparing food. Ghoris would be starving.

Quinn settled himself cross-legged on the floor, waiting for Mo Ti to wake. Ghoris was quiet in her pilot's chair above. But she'd already told him: *Sydney rides the beasts. She brings the dreams.* Could the Inyx send their minds so far? Could Sydney ride with them?

Mo Ti roused slowly. He sat on the bunk now, hands on his massive thighs, breathing like a bellows.

"Tell me about the dreams, Mo Ti."

The giant stared at him from underneath heavy brows. "To each man his own dreams."

"Except if they're all the same."

"Mo Ti's dreams are different from other men."

"I don't think so." Quinn paused while the ship keeper passed through the cabin, carrying a fragrant tray of food up the companionway. "Did you dream?"

"No."

"I think you did. About fire." When Mo Ti wouldn't meet his gaze, he ventured, "Everyone's dreaming of the Tarig. Anzi dreams of them, and I do. Not a coincidence, is it."

Mo Ti stood, rubbing his great arms. "Mo Ti takes a piss." He went out to the deck.

Quinn heard the ship keeper talking to Ghoris, urging her to eat. He thought about the visions in the binds; had he really seen the Inyx flying overhead, or was it the navitar's words that made him imagine it?

Out on the deck, Quinn found the ship riding a sliver of the endless Nigh, a good mile or more off the storm wall. The dark palisade rose hugely into the sky, a storm-clad wall that bordered the river on one side to the limit of sight. Far above, the bright met the wall in a curdle of gravity and shadow. Nothing else rode the river, nor was there any sign of life on the shore.

It was into this river—some version of it—that Quinn had thrown the cirque, letting the river take it, transform it. The *threat* of the cirque, however, was still as powerful as ever.

He approached Mo Ti, who stared across the river into the colossal stretch of the primacy, whichever primacy this was. They stood side by side for a few minutes.

"You've told me part of it. Now tell me the rest, about my daughter."

The giant regarded him.

Quinn pressed on: "I'm a worried man, Mo Ti. You shouldn't worry a man with a big weapon."

Mo Ti noted the change of tactic. "The weapon? But Titus Quinn loves the Entire. So he said."

"That was before. Before I knew Helice was here with a bigger weapon." He wondered whether, if he actually had the cirque, this time he would use it. "It'll distress me to bring down the Entire. But I will."

Quinn pissed into the river. His stream pierced the river surface and fell deep without seeming to mix. I *would* use it, he thought. And the conviction made him like himself better.

Moving around the prow for a view of the storm wall, Mo Ti gazed up at the silent, hovering turbulence. "Mo Ti did wonder when you would get your warrior's balls."

Quinn joined him at the rail. "I want to know about the dreams. The Inyx aren't just sharing thoughts among themselves and their riders. It's spreading beyond."

Mo Ti cut him a sideways glance. "Show me the chain. I would see this killing bracelet."

"It's not with me. Near enough, though."

Mo Ti gave him a flat stare. "Are you a man who desires power?"

"I'll do what I have to for the Rose. Then I don't care."

A cynical smile exposed the giant's yellow teeth, big as knuckles. "What man does not wish for power?" Quinn didn't answer. "Would you take the Ascendancy from the Tarig?"

"If I could." A new thought broke in. Sydney wanted the power. This was what Mo Ti was asking: was he a rival to Sydney? It almost made him laugh. His daughter wanted to destroy the Tarig. Perhaps, in the aftermath, she wanted to take the Ascendancy. This is what Mo Ti meant when he said she was a power in the land. Ghoris said his daughter rode the Inyx. All of them. If so, and if they accessed dreams or minds, she might well be a power in the land. Would he stand in her way? Not a chance.

Would you take the Ascendancy from the Tarig? "If she wants it, she's welcome to it." It was almost impossible for him to think of an eleven-year-old girl who loved to climb trees and use electronic paints planning to bring down an autocracy. But it wasn't the disbelief that gave him the sickening stab in his gut. It was the sudden clear view of how little he knew his daughter anymore.

"Now tell me about the dreams."

They were alone on the deck. Through the porthole Quinn glimpsed the ship keeper setting down a tray of food. Mo Ti stalked the deck, moving around to the port side, looking out again on the land. Quinn followed.

Mo Ti spoke quietly, in that way he had of making you lean a little closer to him to hear. "A story," he began. While he talked, Mo Ti continued to scan the horizon, watching for pursuit. The man was alert, distrustful of appearances. Perhaps he didn't understand that they were on board the ultimate stealth vessel.

"A thousand days ago, in one Inyx encampment, Sydney rebelled, saying she would have a free bond with her mount, who was Riod, an Inyx given to mischief and raiding other herds. He was fast and strong, and these qualities Sydney loved. Together they were all for speed and wildness, and each came to love the other, and their bond was free indeed. Soon I joined them on Distanir, and we were four, free-bonded, and calling others to join us. Riod fought Priov for chieftainship of the herd and won. After that, Sydney sent the Hirrin Akay-Wat to the outlying herds urging them to end enslavement of the riders. A great stream of riders and their mounts came into Riod's encampment. They pledged fealty to Sydney and Riod. The separate Inyx herds joined together, although the lords can never understand it, how voiceless beasts can form a great sway. Or if they do understand, they do not object. The Inyx make excellent war mounts."

Quinn had known that the Inyx mind powers were highly valued on the battle grounds of Ahnenhoon—even if the species showed no deference to the Tarig.

Mo Ti continued, "Then you attacked the Tarig in their own city, and they knew you were back, looking for the daughter. They thought to keep watch for you through her eyes. They offered to cure the blindness she suffered, and she agreed. You have heard how those seeds bore fruit, how it won my mistress's heart to the spider. She used her small god to undo what the lords had done, and Sydney was fully sighted, honestly sighted.

"So the sway was filled with the Inyx of many camps, their riders, their hopes for new sight such as Sydney had found. Already Hel Ese is assigned to restoring the power in their eyes, and the mounts do not object, being won over to free bond. The line is long in front of the spider's tent.

"But each night in the great field, the Inyx were questing. Their powers are small when they act alone. But together, they can cast their thoughts far. Very far. Each night they joined forces to probe the Ascendancy itself, looking for a way to bring it down. They discovered that the Tarig return to a home far away to restore themselves. They do not live as ordinary sentients, but cowardly, shrink back to their home place. At Sydney's bidding, the Inyx send the image out in dreams, so that all sentients may loathe the false lords." Mo Ti snorted. "And the Tarig remain ignorant. They do not feel us in their minds, nor do they dream. We may spy as we like and thus Riod does, with the herd's power. For Sydney's sake."

Quinn listened in silent amazement to Mo Ti's claim of all that his daughter had dared to begin.

The big man went on: "Our aim is to drive the Tarig from their nest. And we may yet claim a victory." He noted the doubt on Quinn's face. "There is much you still do not yet know."

Quinn didn't move or breathe.

"The Tarig love to say how they descended into form from the Heart and now choose to live in the All. This much they admit. But it is not so noble as they say. They require their land of fire and do not stray far from it. Their visits into body are for a short time or a long time, as the will moves them. No Tarig dies, but returns to his homeland. There, each mixes into the greater like water in a pitcher. Find their entrances to the Heart, their means of returning, and you can control them. If we succeed, your goal also succeeds."

They mix like water in a pitcher. A stunning discovery, if true. "You know how they return?"

"Not yet." Mo Ti squinted into the flatness of the primacy, a view so flat that, using a telescope, one could see the opposite storm wall, there being no curvature of this world.

Quinn felt a stirring, a revelation. "The lords don't die?"

"No, nor are they born."

"I've seen their children."

"You have not. They are small adults, made dull of mind."

Small girl floated in the water. She who had wanted a toy boat. This was an imbecile? She had been more subtle than that, hadn't she? Yet Mo Ti said she was only a Tarig made small and dull. He stared into the midlands of the primacy, letting the thought shed its liberation on him. *I never killed a child.* Small girl was no child. It mattered, and it didn't matter. At the time he'd thought she was a child, and he held her face beneath the water. Perhaps there was no reprieve. Still, "Thank you," he whispered.

The disclosure kept rippling out: *The lords don't die nor are they born.* He thought of Lady Chiron. Well and truly dead, he hoped. He said as much to Mo Ti, describing how Chiron had died, with nothing left of her body.

"Riod says the Heart remembers them. Can spit them out, good as before." Mo Ti's face showed what he made of such a thing.

Quinn pieced it together. "Then Chiron's consciousness could come back. Some earlier version of her, kept safe as a . . . memory? . . . in the Heart."

Mo Ti shrugged. "So Riod thinks. Who knows what the fiends do?"

The ship keeper came out of the cabin. "Food. The pilot's leavings, if you care for them."

He nodded thanks to the ship keeper, but they couldn't eat yet. The Tarig wanted or needed to go home. But where was that home? Was it a physical entity in the Rose? Or might it be a universe unto itself? "Will you find these doorways, Mo Ti? Will Riod?"

"We live in this hope."

"Maybe I can help. I have a thing that might be useful." The correlates.

In the secrets of how, where, and when the Entire corresponded to the Rose—and perhaps to other universes as well. He turned to the cabin. "Mo Ti, share a meal with me. The ship keeper brought us food."

"First tell me your scheme."

"Over a meal." Thoughts came in a storm of hope. He had not killed a child. He had not. Amid the larger menace, an unguessed-at reprieve.

Mo Ti quirked his mouth into what might pass for a smile. "You think a man can eat after telling his captain's secrets?"

Quinn smiled back. "Sure."

They went for the food. And while they ate, Quinn disclosed a few revelations of his own. Mo Ti chewed his dumplings slowly, considering with profound interest Quinn's claim that if the Heart was another universe, Quinn might just know how to get there.

Jaq the ship keeper plunged his hands in the soapy water, muttering as he cleaned the pilot's meal plates. A ship keeper's duty was to see that the ship kept its customs. And having guests in the navitar's cabin was not customary. He slammed the cleaned utensils in their drawers. Like all ship keepers he deplored departures from ship custom. But there the two of them were, pressing their mundane concerns on her, and she barely able to sit up, keep her caftan on, and remember not to pass gas in company. Not only that, but the fat eunuch and his companion had eaten all the dumplings, and now Jaq had no luncheon except some pickled momo, a gift from three Gond who had a good journey.

He could stand the situation no longer. Drying his hands, he went to the foot of the companionway to see if he could overhear the conversation. The big man stood at the head of the stairs.

"In," the monster said, cocking his head toward the cabin.

Jaq hastened up the companionway, fearing that Ghoris had taken on one of her fits. But she was sitting up, smock pulled modestly up, with good color back in her face after the meal. He hurried over to the basin to bring a damp towel for her mouth and chin, but she waved him away. Nearby the two passengers stood, none the worse for the passage through the binds, and now waiting expectantly as though he should do more for them than he already had.

The navitar gripped his arm so fiercely he winced. "She will wait."

"Who will wait?" Her hair hung in slimy ropes around her face. She needed her cleaning up and here they were having conversations.

Ghoris only smirked, but the smaller man took pity on Jaq's confusion. "You'll leave the ship for a time, under the navitar's orders. A short absence, desperately needed."

"Leave?" Incredulous, Jaq turned to the navitar.

The passenger continued, "We would go. But we're hunted." At the monster's side he looked like a mere upstart. But between the two he was clearly in charge. Jaq paid him closer attention now. The passenger needed him to run an errand. But what had Jaq and his pilot to do with a venture of the worldly world? Ghoris needed him, *had* needed him for these five thousand days? That could not change.

"You tire of the river, ship keeper," the navitar said, crisp as you please.

"No, not . . ."

Still holding on to his arm, Ghoris drew him down to look into her rheumy eyes. "That's the *story* you'll tell on your long journey. Everyone likes a good story, even lying ones, so long as it's true *somewhere*."

Jaq would have marveled at this long speech from his navitar except that he could not get past the words *long journey*.

"I'm going on a journey?" The ship rocked at anchor, a motion he barely felt, so long had he been on the river. He could not imagine the life of the un-Nigh and had no intention of ever leaving the pilot's side, especially not for these mere passengers.

"Here is a nice story," Ghoris said, smirking again. "This man is the one everyone wants. Looking here. Looking there. But Titus Quinn is right here. Husband of Johanna, she at the center of it all. She misses him, except she can't remember him." She shrugged. "All stories are true somewhere."

Jaq gaped. Titus Quinn?

"Was it necessary to tell him so much?" the one designated as Titus Quinn asked.

But the question was too much for Ghoris, and she began picking at her shift, finally deciding to haul it closer to her face to clean her chin.

The monster said, "Give him his task." He pressed his hand to his side as though he were in pain, and sat heavily on a bench.

Jaq could only stare at Titus Quinn. He didn't look like a man who could kill a grown Tarig and straddle the brightships. He looked like a passable soldier of Ahnenhoon: fit and lean, but no general. But if his navitar had said so, it was true.

Titus Quinn nodded at him. "You'll go to Na Jing in the Shulen Wielding, Jaq. From there up the minoral to the reach, where you'll meet a scholar and give him a message. As I said, we'd go ourselves, but we're hunted. With luck and good winds, you could be home to the Nigh in a couple of arcs."

Twenty days to cross the primacy and travel up the minoral and back again? Nay, more like forty days, or one hundred days, what with intransigent bekus and the haphazard migrations of the floating grain-eaters. It made him sick to even think of traveling by Adda, by the huge Celestials. And what would the pilot do without him? He asked that.

"Mo Ti will be her keeper," the monster said.

Jaq stood, hands at his sides, shaking his head. Titus Quinn. A great journey. He looked to his navitar, but she had already forgotten him, staring out the window at the Sheltering Path primacy, the God-blighted primacy where no one ever went. The pilot had dismissed him, sending him as a messenger.

"The big man is unwell," he noted, hoping he was too ailing to be ship keeper.

The monster snorted. "The wound needs only rest and *less talk*."

Jaq stood before them, resigned and stunned. "What is the message?"

"To use the correlates to find the doors to the Heart."

"I don't understand."

"No," Titus Quinn said. "But the message is for a scholar. His name is Su Bei. He'll understand. Tell him: The lords travel to and from the Heart. We need to control those doors. And Su Bei must identify the locations."

The lords travel back to the Heart from whence they came? Jaq tried to grasp this. He could not, and clearly they weren't going to explain things to him, explain treason. He beseeched the navitar with a look.

Ghoris stared out the window, insensible. His navitar had commanded him to undertake a journey for Titus Quinn. How was this any business of his navitar and himself? Still, Ghoris refused to look at him. He saw how it would be; he must go. They had told him secrets. He was part of it now.

"Who is Su Bei?"

Titus Quinn, the great fugitive, appeared to relax somewhat. Jaq had not noticed until now how tense he had been. "A friend of mine from the old days. A scholar who taught me the Lucent tongue. I gave the correlates into his keeping. Can you remember the message?"

Reluctantly, Jaq repeated it. And then again, until he got it right.

"Tell him to find me in Rim City in the company of the godwoman Zhiya."

Now Jaq knew it all: Quinn's location, his plans, his knowledge of something called the correlates. Jaq could go to the Tarig and tell where the fugitive was. But then the lords would throw his pilot in the great river, and she would sink like a boulder. That he could not bear.

As he left the bridge with Titus Quinn, he reflected on the fact that Ghoris didn't even know his name, had never known it. *Ship keeper* she had always called him. He looked back at her, hoping to at least hear that fond term.

An unaccustomed and labored smile drifted across her face. She lifted a hand in farewell.

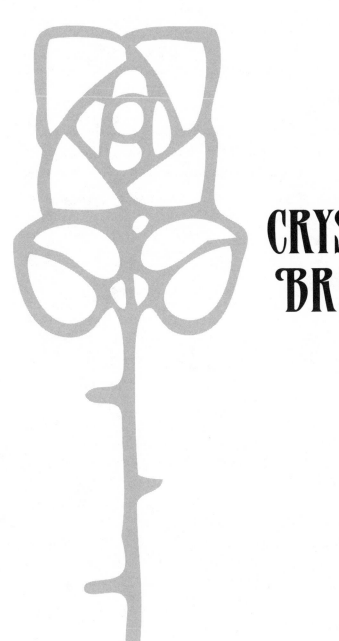

PART II
THE CRYSTAL BRIDGE

CHAPTER FIVE

Rose. 1. *A dimension said to exist outside the All.* 2. *A flower found on a remote planetesimal.* 3. *(informal) A fleeting state of being.*

— from *Hol Fan's Glossary of Needful Terms*

THE PORTHOLE IN LI YUN TAI'S SLEEPING CHAMBER shimmered with a silvery light. Tai and his lover paid dearly for a burrow with a window unto the depths of the sea. But today the porthole seemed wan and cold. Wei Bo was gone.

The moment Tai entered his burrow, he knew. The bed was unmade, Bo's pillow gone. Heart in a clench, he threw open the doors of the clothing chest. Bo's silks, gone. His dance slippers, gone. Tai clicked the doors shut, stunned and lost. Mementos were missing. The painting of Gu Lou the navitar, the one they had bought together. Gone. Bo was gone. Tai sat on the bed next to the sea wall, staring into its phantomy depths. The anti-bright. The light he and his fellow morts preferred to the glaring sky. He sighed. You drive away the thing you love. By wanting too much of it.

Not that it had been love. Neither Tai nor Bo ever said love. That was a hag word; it dragged you down, taught you to cling and skim. Their life in their burrow had been flash and deep. Now it was nothing.

Returning to the wardrobe, Tai stripped off his work clothes from the dumpling kitchen, stuffing them in a corner of the wardrobe and rummaging for his blue chemise. No, too nice. He reached for the short orange tunic, the cling work boots, and the crinkle belt for added spark. He threw them on, regarding himself in the wardrobe mirror. He was tall, trim, young, and pale. He was flash. What more did he need?

He set out, plunging into the main street of the undercity, no aim in mind. Marquis lights gilded the streets; vhat drum rhythms pulsed from wine dens. Here and there, portholes showed the dim eye of the water. It was a better light than above. The undercity was very like the Rose, with something almost like night. The Rose: the place of short lives, deeply felt. By the Navitar's Mind, that was the only way to live.

Morts, who usually stayed in the underground city, avoided the life-lengthening rays of the lords' glaring sky. The Reds considered this practice heresy, coming to the undercity solely for worship. Both Reds and morts revered the navitars. But the Reds were the conforming side of things; morts, the flash side.

A few Reds hurried down the street, casting sideways glances at him, disapproving of how he was dressed. They disapproved of most things. The undercity used to be theirs alone, a place to honor the navitars by peering into the foaming waters. Morts weren't welcome, but the Society couldn't keep them out. The Entire had no forbidden places, much as Reds might wish it otherwise.

His mood lifted. If he could shock a Red, then he must look blossom.

Pedi cabs swept by, stuffed with revelers, oglers, and wish-I-weres, daring a taste of the undercity but by day keeping to the ways of the All. But why be Entire when you could be Rose? Li Yun Tai had answered that for himself halfway through school, leaving his family seaside domicile and the life of the bright, the only life his parents could imagine. They'd sacrificed everything to come to Rim City to start their textile business and sew silks for the middling merchants and their haggish children. They had swathed Tai in silk from the time he was a baby. He grew up with the iridescence of silk and its eye-shattering colors. It had made him want an iridescent life. When he started to sleep days and wake in the ebb, his mother said, eyes full of tears, "You are tired of us." But when he left the silk shop it was for love of silk, not despising of it. He hadn't seen her or his father in five thousand days. They wouldn't like what he'd become. A mort. Soon to die. Kept out of the bright. Live a modest span, then walk into the sea. Like the river pilots. When you're done you're so done.

The Dark Flower was crammed full, but the door keeper let him in, liking the orange with the work boots, nodding to Tai, saying something Tai couldn't hear in the thrumming drum beat. Through the dancing bodies, some wearing feather masks—so overdone—he caught sight of the drummer hammering the giant vhat pans, attacking the drums with staccato hands, his body muscled, beautiful—so flash in a world already flash. It struck Tai with bitter clarity: here was a world evaporating even as the dancers tried to claim it with reaching arms, jutting pelvises. *Grasp, cling. Lose it all.*

That's what Wei Bo had said. Why he left.

A woman with a red outcrop in her hair asked Tai to dance, and why not? He wasn't too proud to dance with her, and it shocked his brethren. He held her close, grinding hips, but laughing.

"Like the flower?" She bobbed her head. It was a blossom made of silk. Very mort. By the end of the second dance she'd given it to him, and Tai wore it behind his ear.

Feeling good now, Tai accepted another cup of wine and drank it like nectar; it didn't faze him. A woman in a green feather mask stood before him.

"Nigh fizz?"

Feather girl held up a foaming drink served in a spilling-over cup, forcing him to lick the overrun. They danced, but he found tears pushing at his eyes. The Nigh fizz let him feel his heart. Oh, Wei Bo. Not love, of course. But they'd shared a burrow for six hundred days, and they'd been fond of each other. And others. And then just others.

She led him to a stairway. People were doing it on the landing, and on the stairs, every which way, girl to girl, boy to everything that would stay still. But though he was throbbing, he didn't want to just pluck the flower of the moment. He didn't want the moment at all. He just wanted to die. The Nigh beckoned him through the wall, portals discharging gargled light. Come down, down to me. You've lived your flash. Come down.

Too much drink. He wanted to ditch the girl.

"Sorry," he said. But she was already gone. In her place was an apparition: an indigo blue feather mask hid the eyes and cheekbones, but he was beautiful. He wore plain gray silks, his skin so white, he might have been birthed from the Nigh itself. "You look sad."

"No time to be sad."

"Sure there is. It just is what it is. And then we swim."

Tai looked out the porthole. Swim like a Navitar. Float like a river spider.

Blue feathers had him by the hand, gently leading him up the stairs, past the copulating bodies, past all the dismal ecstasy. They walked down a corridor, dark, heavy with incense. Despite his mood, Tai was stunned by the masked boy. The night turned the corner of possibilities. They entered a room of light. Tai shielded his eyes. The light came from a full wall porthole. The opening shimmered in time waves, waves buttered with light.

"Over here," blue boy said, his voice deep and direct, saying what he wanted. Over here. Against the porthole. Turn around, lean into the glass. Yes, like that, press your face against the wall, let the sea light kiss you. The pane was cold against Tai's cheek. Roused, Tai pressed his passion against the cold surface, feeling it like heat. Hands around his waist, pulling his buttocks out. No play time then, just straight to the point. Don't cling. Want, but don't want too much. Tai bent, compliant, tears wetting the glass, the side of his face slipping. His silks pulled up in back. Yes, if it will make you happy, blue feathers. Just be flash. With me. With me. Tai pushed back, receiving him.

He could see their reflections in the glass. Gray on orange, bird on boy, flash on flash. Blue boy's face so exotic in the waters, his perfect mouth filled with the foaming Nigh. Tai turned around, and blue boy finished him off, blue feathers quaking with an exotic urgency.

Breathless, Tai leaned against the sea window, then sank to the floor beside his partner. Tai turned toward him and pulled the mask down. Transfixed, he drank in blue boy's face, a perfect sculpture. Not only that, blue boy was smiling. And staying.

Mustn't cling, Tai reminded himself. To break the spell, he forced his eyes away from his face, but blue boy put his hand on Tai's chin, turning him back.

"Fajan," blue boy said, giving his name.

"Tai."

"Talk to me. Let's watch the sea."

The two of them moved back to a place where they could view the full wall porthole. Fajan wanted to talk, and the night and the party downstairs stretched on.

Fajan turned to him when they'd had enough river-watching. "Come back tomorrow."

Oh, yes.

CHAPTER SIX

If you do not know your own mind, ask an Inyx.

—a saying

DURING QUINN'S AND MO TI'S TRANSIT OF THE BINDS, the bright had fallen to Shadow Ebb, yielding a violet sky that made the river a spill of wine.

Bearing a full pail, Mo Ti lumbered down the companionway and went through to the outer deck. He pitched the contents over the side of the ship. When he returned, he set the stinking bucket down and turned to Quinn.

"There is food in the galley."

"No thanks," Quinn said. "But noted."

Ghoris lay moaning on her upper deck, having had a bad time of it, attempting the transit in one swoop from the Arm of Heaven primacy, where Jaq had departed, to the Long Gaze of Fire. The evening was calm except for the distant storm wall, that towering companion to the river. Quinn had been on the River Nigh many times, but this time was startlingly different, given their destination. The Inyx Sway was the place that had eluded him for so long, his daughter's home. Oddly, though, he'd come here not for Sydney, but for Helice.

Mo Ti moved more easily at his tasks, now that Quinn had properly dressed his wounds—wounds that Mo Ti had taken for Quinn at Ahnenhoon. The man was built like a boulder, and injuries that might kill a smaller man had already begun healing. Now Mo Ti had light duty as ship keeper, doing the navitar's bidding and her personal care. As bad a duty as this might be at the moment, the ship was the best hiding place for both of them. Mo Ti could never hide his distinctive physical aspect, that was certain. For this reason, until Jaq returned from his assignment, this ship would pick up no passengers.

Mo Ti paused by Quinn's side at the railing, looking out on the river. He had just given Quinn a detailed description of his last hours in the fortress at Ahnenhoon. That report had included an account of Johanna Quinn's death. The big man said, "It gave me no pleasure to tell you about your wife."

"I know that. Thank you."

"She was no soldier, but she died like the best of them."

Quinn nodded. Died. He'd guessed she had, but now it was confirmed. After all the bad news Mo Ti had delivered to Quinn, this was the final, awful piece.

Though Mo Ti hadn't seen Johanna die, he said no one could survive the beating Lord Inweer gave her in the great keep of Ahnenhoon. Of course, Lord Inweer could have healed her if he had wished, but why would he? Johanna had betrayed him.

Mo Ti's news left Quinn feeling strangely cold and remote. A few weeks ago he had seen Johanna after years of separation. Then, within that same hour, she was dead. He couldn't put it together. How to feel. Except that he should have died with her. But that wasn't it, either. Hadn't he learned by now that he wasn't going to be excused from the fight? The war still enlisted him, preempted his life.

Except that he had remarried. Despite Anzi's conviction that she was the second wife, she was no such thing. Johanna had freed him of their vows. There was only one woman in Quinn's life, Ji Anzi. He missed her terribly, and despite all the good reasons for not knowing where she was, he would gladly, at this moment, picture her as safe. When his thoughts drifted to her, he tried not to guess where she had gone; but he did guess, anyway: perhaps back to her nominal uncle and aunt, Yulin and Suzong?

Mo Ti nodded toward the door. "We are coming in to shore. Ghoris says it is the roamlands."

They went to the starboard rail, looking out. The shore was straight, the plains behind it shadowed and endless. If Sydney wanted to hide here, he could never find her.

This land had for so long been the object of his yearning. Sydney dwelled in the Inyx Sway; said to be a slave; then rumored to have risen to a high position. Speaking through the telepathic mounts, she had told him clearly not to come. Riod, her mount, would kill him. He steeled himself for her hostility, but in his own mind, he'd never abandoned her. Though he'd slept with a Tarig lady, it had given him no power to refute Tarig edicts. Still, he knew how it looked to the outside world. Some days it looked like that to *him* as well.

He had practiced what to say. Forgive me, was a start.

Now he had arrived at her shore, but not with any hope to take her home. The purpose of freeing his daughter was long out of date, superceded by what the war required of him and by her own preferences. Well, she was about to see him again, whether she wanted to or not.

From the bridge came a garbled shout. Ghoris. After a moment Quinn heard his name and began to ascend the companionway. He looked to Mo Ti for permission. He was ship keeper now. Mo Ti nodded and followed him up.

Ghoris slumped in exhaustion on her navitar's dais, watching the door. She beckoned to Quinn, and he approached. The portals were open, letting in a breeze off the primacy, clove-ridden and welcome in the stinking pilot house.

Ghoris pointed to a stool, and Quinn brought it close, sitting next to her.

The navitar's hair hung disheveled around her shoulders. Directly over her head was a membrane that gave way when she stood up to command the forces of the exotic river. He had seen her do so once, but could hardly remember what he had seen, and much of that was hallucination, he was sure.

She looked at him with beady eyes tucked into folds of fat. "She's not here."

Quinn waited. You could never be quite sure who Ghoris was speaking of. He'd been wrong before.

"She went away. The girl—both girls—passed us in the binds."

"Sydney? My daughter? And Helice with her?" He took the navitar's silence for a yes.

Quinn heard Mo Ti utter an oath. The big man wanted Helice disposed of almost as much as Quinn did.

Ghoris tried to shift her considerable bulk in the chair, but gave up on the effort. "Still being the father," she murmured. "Leave it. Leave it."

"She's my daughter. I don't walk away."

Her face swelled with anger or pain, he couldn't tell which. "The good father. You . . . can't . . . have both." Her voice became eerily normal. "I told you before."

It was true, she'd said he had to choose, but he had thought she'd meant choose between the Entire and the Rose. That was when he'd come to the Ascendancy to rescue his daughter and Ghoris had said he had a bigger problem than that. Bigger, it was always going to be bigger than his life, these demands of duty. He waited for her to go on.

"Out there." Ghoris pointed out the porthole toward the primacy of the Long Gaze of Fire. "Things you need to see. Take a trip. Not by our vessel. See the Paion, yes?"

She didn't go on. Every word was an effort. She needed to sleep, and for a moment Quinn thought she *was* asleep, as her head slumped forward. Then she jerked awake. "Go and find something useful." He tried to ask a question, but she waved him off. "Here's the place where . . . they used to . . ." She frowned in confusion. "They were here, don't you see? Have you never thought of *them*? You can't see, can you? I talk to deaf men! Jaq, where is Jaq?"

Mo Ti came forward. "You sent him on a mission to Su Bei's reach. I'm your ship keeper now."

Ghoris looked at him as though he'd just eaten Jaq. She pointed at him and growled, "We come to shore. Prepare, ship keeper." Then she snatched Quinn's hands in hers, in a grip like a wrestler's. "The Scar, Titus. It's here. You can go."

"Ghoris," he said, knowing she was trying to tell him things, but fearing he would never understand. "I've got to find Helice, or she'll ruin my world. Where is she?"

The navitar murmured, "Where *is* she or where *will* she be?"

He frowned, trying to step through the land mines of her conversation. "Where is the place where I'll find her?"

"Under the sea."

"I don't understand."

"Try harder, Titus Quinn." When he remained silent, she said: "Paion live nearby. Go to them, under-sentient." She added, rather unhelpfully, "If you must have daughters, have them. Have more daughters if the one does not suit."

"Paion live here? Are there Paion among the Inyx, is that what you're saying?"

Ghoris groaned, but whether in discomfort or frustration he didn't know. "Paion were here, and *will be*. Attend, can't you? *Try*, Titus."

Mo Ti came forward, putting his hand on Quinn's shoulder. "She must rest. Ask more later."

Quinn stood, and saw the navitar shake her head wearily. "You were supposed to be so *smart*." She closed her eyes.

The two men left her, descending to the lower cabin.

Their mission now seemed pointless, but with the navitar vessel heading in to shore, they went out on deck to watch. Along the strand, shadows bulked—perhaps storage buildings. It hardly mattered, if what Ghoris said was true, the two *girls* were gone. Quinn watched the shore approach. Passed them in the binds? So they had been here just hours ago.

They came steadily to land. Now he could see the dark shapes resolve themselves into a welcoming party. Inyx. Some fifteen riders sat their mounts in a stolid line. The riders: various sentients including Ysli, Hirrin, and Chalin. The mounts: massive beasts with a double row of horns down their prodigious necks.

Prow funnel tilted up, the ship slid onto the muddy strand, spreading struts to stabilize it, though its draft was not deep. The ship came up a few feet onto the beach and settled.

Quinn asked Mo Ti, "You know them?"

"Mo Ti does." He nodded at a Hirrin who was dismounting from an Inyx who folded his front legs to help her accomplish the maneuver. "Akay-Wat."

Mo Ti let down a ramp secured with ropes. He motioned for Quinn to descend.

"You'll come?" Quinn asked.

"I'll attend Ghoris first. Guard your thoughts here. They need not know I have confided so much to you. Do not dwell on the dream forays."

Quinn nodded his agreement and descended the ramp to the flats, avoiding the meandering slicks of Nigh water. When he stood before the

Hirrin, she looked at him directly, but not in the way of a blind person. He knew then that she was sighted. No doubt she had been given the same *gift* as Sydney had. So here would be another friend of Helice.

"I am not a friend," the Hirrin said by way of greeting.

Quinn was taken aback by the comment that seemed to read his thoughts.

The Hirrin was soft gray, with a long neck and wide nostrils. Her brown eyes gave her a doe-look. He noted her prosthetic leg, one that skewed her stance.

"I'm Titus Quinn," he said, putting aside all pretense in this gathering of Inyx.

"Oh, we all know. I am Akay-Wat. We rode hard to get here when we heard you approaching."

"Thank you," he said, putting the best face on his reception party.

Akay-Wat nodded at her mount. "This is Gevka."

He bowed at them both. "I've come to talk to my daughter. If she's here."

Akay-Wat shook her head on its long neck. "Come at last, oh yes? Come for the daughter, have you?"

He could see where the conversation would go. "I'd see her if I could." He allowed himself a moment to survey the other riders and their mounts. One was a catlike creature who rode upright. He had rarely seen a Laroo up close. Voices pressed on him. No, not voices, thoughts. The mounts snorted and swayed, giving the impression of being mentally active, while remaining in position. Those farther away might not hear all the conversation, but they heard it by relay from Gevka. So he'd been told. Many things about the Inyx were guesses on the part of sentients who'd never seen one.

Akay-Wat said, "She is not here."

"My daughter . . ."

The Hirrin interrupted him. "Call her Sydney, that is best among us. We are her family, I think."

When he hesitated to go on, she added, "I am no friend to the Hel Ese woman. Speak freely."

He looked back at Mo Ti for some support, but he was still with Ghoris. Turning back to the Hirrin, he said, "And her companion too? Helice is gone also?"

"Yes, and Riod too. Oh dear, gone to the longest city."

City? The Inyx had no cities . . . And then the thoughts in the minds of the mounts and their riders came flooding into him: she was in Rim City. The Tarig had freed her from banishment. They'd given her a sway. The news brought a spike of hope. Sydney might have her freedom. But Akay-Wat was guarded if not hostile, and he needed backup. "May I ask Mo Ti to join us?"

Akay-Wat nodded. "He is a friend."

At a gesture from Quinn, Mo Ti descended the ship's ramp, his duties to Ghoris apparently fulfilled for now. As he came closer, Akay-Wat's expression changed to one of open relief. She went to Mo Ti, and her long neck stretched forward, allowing her to rest her head on his arm for a moment in a gesture of obvious affection. They spoke in low tones for some time.

When Mo Ti finally approached Quinn, he said, "We will share a campfire."

The cook fire burned down to embers. They'd prepared a meal for him, and he'd accepted, though it was nothing more than small baked bricks of food. They were nomads, comfortable under the bare sky, living and sleeping. Many of them slept now, the riders flung upon the ground with only a travel pouch for a pillow.

Mo Ti stood, signaling his impatience to be gone. "Ghoris waits," he said.

Akay-Wat sat on her haunches, apparently sobered by Quinn's long story of all that had happened to him since first suffering capture in the Entire. Quinn wasn't sure whether she believed everything, but he hadn't withheld any of the terrible things he'd done. She listened carefully when he told of going to Lady Chiron's sleeping chambers, of killing Small Girl, of almost— but fatefully, not quite—rescuing Sydney when he had received permission to travel to the Inyx, back when he was still incognito in the Entire. All that was long ago now—just how long ago could never quite be parsed. A year and a half had passed here. At home, it was longer, if it was not shorter.

He had hesitated to tell Akay-Wat of Helice's plan to destroy his home. She might be in favor of that. But he told her anyway, subterfuge among the Inyx being pointless. Given Akay-Wat's hostility to Helice Maki, he thought they were safe.

"Mo Ti," Quinn said, "stay a moment."

The big man watched him stonily. Mo Ti's suggestion was to beat Sydney and Helice to the Rim City and take Helice down on the quay. Quinn was susceptible to Mo Ti's urgings. But he couldn't leave yet.

Seeing that Quinn would not soon leave, Mo Ti turned away to thread among the cook fires. He had many friends here, and they accepted him as a rider. Quinn wondered if the big man might choose to stay among the Inyx, waiting for Sydney's return. But Sydney wasn't coming back. Even Akay-Wat seemed resigned to that.

Left alone with the Hirrin at the fire pit, Quinn asked, "Have I any hope for her?"

Akay-Wat hooved a stray ember back into the pit. Gevka moved to her side, looming over both of them. The Hirrin nudged Gevka with her nose. Perhaps they conferred privately on what to say.

"Hope is not a bad thing, Akay-Wat thinks." The Hirrin cut a glance at him. "But Sydney will measure you, as she does everyone. In your case the measure falls short."

That said it clearly enough.

"Here is a thing to know," Akay-Wat went on. "When we lived in the barracks, before we had free bond with our mounts, she had a book, yes? I heard her in the ebb, pricking the pages, making her account of the day. All the things the day brought. Or did not bring."

"Pricking the pages?"

"We were blind."

That he had momentarily forgotten chagrined him. "Go on, please."

"She keeps the book with her always. It is the list of her days. You are in the list, Akay-Wat thinks. Oh yes. As—this you must remember—when we had word you stole all the brightships. As when Sydney asked Riod to watch the bright, waiting for one of those ships to come into our skies to bear her home."

Quinn's eyes felt hot as he stared at the coals.

"'The bright,' she would say to her mount. 'Do you see anything, Riod? Look again.'"

The words cut him, somewhere deep enough that he could bear it.

"Through our mounts, we all saw her lift her face to the bright, waiting, waiting. Mo Ti told her, 'He is not coming,' and she nearly killed him for it. Not for saying you would not come, but for saying out loud that she cared."

The embers fell, darkening. "You wonder what else is in the book? Akay-Wat wonders too; wonders what Sydney said about this Hirrin. Once she called me a good captain. That I will always remember." After a long pause she said, "She took the book with her. Still using pin pricks, so no one else can read it. Still saying who did what and why."

If she meant to give him hope, she did so begrudgingly. But it was true there was more to come, and Sydney, along with many others, would be taking his measure. He didn't know if that was comforting, or not.

Mo Ti loomed over them. He never spoke much, and didn't need to now, either. He wanted to be under way.

Quinn rose, thanking Akay-Wat and Gevka for the meal. Standing so close to an Inyx made a strong impression. He could not imagine how it would be to ride one. His shoulders did not reach even to the animal's back.

He turned to the Hirrin. "The navitar said there are—or were—Paion here. Do Paion ride with you, Akay-Wat?"

She looked at him, her eyes large in surprise. "No one has ever seen a Paion."

"So I thought."

"Once they fought near here. Did the navitar mean the great battle?"

Quinn was puzzled. He'd been told the Paion always attacked at Ahnenhoon, never elsewhere.

"Once," Akay-Wat said, "the Paion fell upon the Entire nearby in great numbers and the Tarig themselves came to repel them. Their entrance point is marked by the Scar." She turned down-primacy, nodding her head. "Many Paion were slaughtered, and even the Tarig died, or they laid down their minds in dead corpses and picked them up again, later." She swiped a quick glance at him to see if he'd dreamed such things. "So it is said."

"The lords do not die," Quinn murmured. "I've heard that, too."

Akay-Wat gave out a puff of air through her lips that passed for a sigh. "Oh, but they do not *live*, and that is more shameful."

"And the Paion?"

The Hirrin gazed down-primacy again. "There is only a great scar on the storm wall. It has been there since ancient times, many archons. But no Paion anymore. Akay-Wat has been to and fro across the primacy."

Blind, though, Quinn inadvertently thought.

Instantly a thought came into his mind: *The riders see through Inyx eyes. Even a Gond is not so ignorant.*

Apologies, Quinn thought, as hard as he could, but whether Akay-Wat's mount heard him, he didn't know.

"Akay-Wat, have the Inyx ever read a Paion's mind? Inyx often are recruited to the Long War."

She turned to her mount to let him answer.

The thought came eerily clear: *Yes. Their thoughts are all on conquest.*

The Hirrin went to her pack, drawing something out with her prehensile lips. She cocked her head, and Quinn understood he was to take the object.

It was a small hoop with a handle, like a miniature sports racket with the strings missing. Quinn studied the worn metal of the thing. Along the perimeter were intricate but faint designs, almost invisible.

"Akay-Wat was Sydney's captain, her messenger to the herds across the steppe. In the journeys I once found the Scar, yes? Too close, you are in danger of the storm wall. But at a distance, my mount kicked up this object." She added, "It is no Inyx thing, nor Jout, nor any thing the riders have ever seen."

Paion thing, Gevka sent.

"Perhaps," Akay-Wat mused out loud.

Quinn thought again about Ghoris urging him to go to the Scar, but from Gevka's mind came the image of many days' travel, and he knew he didn't have that long.

"Does it have any use that you've discovered?"

"No. The middle of it is empty, lost." She still hadn't taken the hoop.

Mo Ti was waiting.

Akay-Wat kept Quinn in her steady brown gaze. "Navitars know things, yes? Perhaps you are meant to keep it. So you have not come to the Inyx Sway for nothing."

He looked into those enormous eyes, eyes that, these days at least, seemed to see more than most. "Thank you, Akay-Wat. But it's already been for something." He tried to give the artifact back, but she made no move to accept it.

"Give my greeting to Sydney, Titus Quinn. You will?"

He promised, knowing that the day would not be far off when he saw his daughter again. He was certain now. Amendments were needed to the book of pin pricks. He clutched the gift of the small metal hoop and then he and Mo Ti made their way back to the vessel, a black hump against the darkened river.

CHAPTER SEVEN

The station of navitar is neither sought after by petitioners nor bestowed by the Magisterium. Far otherwise! The pilot is chosen by the Nigh.

—from *The Radiant Way*

ON BOARD THE NAVITAR VESSEL, Sydney's hair whipped around her face. She was sailing toward the Ascendancy, toward civilization, and toward her confrontation with the Tarig. She could not have said at that moment which of these she found more exhilarating. *Oh, Mo Ti, they handed it to me. Rim City.* Since the day Mo Ti had suggested a scheme to supplant the Tarig, she'd known she would return to the Ascendancy. Now she'd be a stone's throw away. *Mo Ti, look at me now.*

She welcomed the wind in her face like the breath of the steppe as she rode her mount, like the future hitting her fresh and hard. Having emerged from the binds, the ship skimmed over the Sea of Arising, bearing only her, Helice, and Riod. And her watchful escort, Lady Anuve.

Before her lay a smudged curve of land that was the closest shore of Rim City; behind and much further away, the glowing pillars of the Ascendancy. She wondered why they sailed at all, when the pilot could have aimed closer to their destination. Happily, the navitar provided this slow approach, perhaps for her to savor. If she craned her neck she could see the floating city, the home of all her enemies and her one friend.

Cixi, she thought, *I'm almost there. Cixi, I have a sway.*

The riders had told her all about Rim City, city of ten billion souls. Around the campfire, they had told her of the never-ending city pierced by the five rivers and linked by bridges. The great crystal bridges arched over not only the rivers, but leaned far away from the storm walls like horseshoes set at an angle in the sand. By this means, a sentient could set out at any point and, with enough time, travel the length of the city, back to the starting point. She was Mistress of this Sway. Although not much more than a decoy, she thrilled to her new prospects.

Riod, however, fared poorly. He lay on a bed of straw in the lean-to the ship keeper had constructed for him. When the vessel had plunged down to the binds, he'd fallen into a festering sleep. Inyx were known for their aversion to the Nigh; he would recover quickly once on solid ground, she trusted. By his side, she had stroked his neck, murmuring that the ship didn't really descend in the usual sense, and the river didn't really spill into the hut, as Riod thought. It was an illusion, the mind's construct to explain sensations. The river matter wasn't a physical substance, but exotic foam, a turbulence of time and quantum particles—so Helice had explained.

If Riod's mind was too sensitive to endure the Nigh, no logic would help. She turned from the view and made her way back to him, ducking behind the blanket that served as a privacy curtain.

Helice, standing at the rail, watched Sydney disappear into Riod's shed. She avoided looking up at the bridge. The Tarig bitch had begun to take notice of her, peering down now and then from her billet in the navitar's cabin. There was no help for it, though Helice tried to act like Sydney's minion, one whose voice was ruined by burns from a cook fire.

But not even Anuve could ruin her happiness. She was on her way. Incredibly, all was well on track. Quinn hadn't used the cirque yet. She wondered why he held off. Did he believe her that the device was too virulent? She'd tried to tell him that, but he was *so* mistrustful.

His daughter was more malleable. That was because she and Helice shared the same goals: They both wanted to kill Titus Quinn and have the Ascendancy. That made for solidarity, yes it did. Even the horsy creatures were partners, as queer as that was. Well, it was helpful to be able to read the minds of your opponents. Nice little role for the beasts. All working out nicely now.

Except that Quinn was still tromping about with the nan. Dangerous, nasty nan. Can't control the nan, but *can* control the man. That was her mantra, and she was sticking to it.

Her first concern, though, was to save the Entire. Some people might conclude it was the wrong universe, but that would be sloppy thinking. Despite being a native of the Rose, she had always felt like an outsider, even as a child. As she'd grown older she'd formed her viewpoint that the world's capable and energetic were blackmailed by the clueless and indigent. Support us, keep us on the dole, or we'll rise up.

One might wish to believe in equality. Helice wished to. Unfortunately, people were divided among the haves and have nots. Some have advanced intelligence, some do not. Even those at the level of the somewhat capable, the somewhat educated—the middies—depended on the savvies to grasp the world of the math-based sciences. What did the average citizen know of bio-molecular manipulation or quantum processing, to name but two essential fields? It was all very well to share—but sharing had become a system of enti-tlements: subsidized food, housing, virtual entertainments. All so gradual that the yoked no longer noticed the dent in their shoulders.

Fatally, it hadn't occurred to the average citizen that the beast of burden might refuse.

Not that she would have been a revolutionary under normal circum-stances. It was just that these weren't ordinary circumstances. The Tarig wanted to kill the Rose, and they were surely going to succeed. It wasn't her fault; it wasn't her *choice* that the Tarig planned to burn the Rose. But since it had to happen, she would make sure someone got out alive.

And now, who would that be? The folks with capabilities near the lower end of the scale, where nuanced thought just cannot occur, or the mathemati-cians, physicists, biologists, engineers, and what have you?

It didn't take more than a femtosecond to make *that* pick.

She was acutely aware of how it looked, however. Like she was killing the Rose. People who thought so would just have to remember that the Rose was doomed anyway, and therefore they had no right to destroy humanity's only refuge.

While the Earth's predicament was regrettable, someone really ought to consider the *up* side. Renaissance. The renaissance of humanity. Two thousand individuals, selected by an empirical test and, because of time constraints, a little favoritism. The few and the smart. These would cross over and begin things anew in a nice little sway a bit removed from Tarig paranoia. She was sure she could come to terms with the high lords.

Taking a deep breath of Entire air, she let the rays of the bright fall on her skin. The bright might have an effect on regenerative senescence, extending Entirean lives. But it might also have effects on cancer-suppressing proteins and a host of disease- and infection-suppressing genes. All these restorative effects might be the function of some other Tarig technology— but if so, why did the Tarig fret that human lives would be extended here, and therefore attract mass migrations? Whatever the source of the Entire's healing, she'd be sure to fold that into her list of requests.

The damn Tarig bitch. Still gazing out the window. Not yet, ugly thing. I'm not ready for you yet. Not until my mSap works out exactly where your transfer sites are. A little leverage is a wonderful thing. Pulling her attention away from the view, Helice decided to duck into Riod's lean-to and give some moral support. A nice thought, and one that Riod might even be reading out of her mind at this moment. She was always careful to think generous and civil thoughts. You never knew when horse-face might be listening.

In the shed, Sydney sponged Riod's head as he lay on a bed of dried grasses. Though his coat was slicked with sweat and his lovely green eyes were dull, he sent pulses of gratitude to her as she swabbed and curried him. *Beloved*, he sent. *My heart*, she formed in her mind, trusting he reached for her thoughts.

Helice sat by Sydney's side, rubbing ointment into Riod's hooves and polishing them. The woman of the Rose had once fascinated Sydney, but over her days with the herd, her reluctance to share thoughts or any bond with her mount kept her a stranger. Though the two women were allies now against the Tarig, Sydney was uneasy. Helice had a cold center. But she also had an mSap. Riod felt they needed no machines, but an mSap was no mere machine.

Sydney heard footsteps on the deck and looked up in time to see the curtain pulled aside.

A young man stood before her, dressed in a navitar's caftan and blinking in the deep shade of the lean-to. When he spoke, his voice was flat and high. "Shall I purge the Inyx? Sometimes that helps."

The idea startled Sydney. "I don't think you'd want to be purging an Inyx. Once on shore he'll be fine."

He bowed. "I am Geng De, ship's pilot."

Riod raised his head, taking an interest in the visitor.

"I saw a mount die on a ship once. That was a sad occurrence; but we are almost to our berth." The navitar turned a pale gaze on Helice. "You're the servant calling herself Hei Ling. As you see, I know all my passengers by name."

Helice made a proper little bow of her head.

Turning to Sydney, the navitar said, "You are a personage, indeed: Mistress of Rim City. The longest city is eager to have a view of you, Sen Ni."

Sydney exchanged glances with Helice. It made her wary that the navitar knew the name she planned to adopt.

Riod lowered his head once more, beginning a plunge into a nauseated sleep.

He went on, "We should talk quickly, before the Tarig lady comes snooping." The navitar folded his hands in front of his little paunch belly. "We should get to know each other, Sen Ni. Would you like that?"

It was hard to believe this youngster was a navitar. She'd heard they were half mad, and this one seemed almost normal. "What do you want?"

"Many things, like anyone. I've seen a great deal I *could* want. They aren't *things*, though, not like dwellings or jewels. A navitar cares nothing for that."

He sounded older now, as though he *had* seen many things.

"What I want today is to tell you about the foaming chain. Where it is." As the two women stared at him, he said, "Would you like to know?"

"Yes," Sydney murmured. If he was referring to the chain her father brought as a weapon, she would very much like to know. "Tell me, Geng De."

"Oh, it's locked away. In the river, where it can't hurt us. Aren't you glad? I hope you're glad, because I came all the way down from the bridge to tell you."

"In the river?" Sydney asked. "It fell in the river?"

"No. Your father *threw* it in the river. It sank right down, and the river sent its contents out of the binds, transferring its energy into a good form for transit. So it's still down there, but empty. Now, as for the molecular poisons themselves, it would be impossible to describe to you where those have gone. I don't suppose under-sentients care much for such explanations."

Sydney was still trying to comprehend their new circumstances. The nan, gone. The weapon, disarmed. "He *wanted* to throw it in the river?"

Geng De cocked his head, thinking. "I didn't see any coercion. I just saw the chain sink, and Titus Quinn's hand flinging it. You knew that navitars see things in the binds?" When Sydney nodded, he went on, "Other navitars saw it too. It's a reliable reality."

She exchanged glances with Helice, seeing her own doubt reflected. Helice was bursting to break into the conversation, but her language skills were too weak.

"Why would my father do that?"

Geng De shrugged. "Fear, perhaps."

Maybe he did the right thing for once, Sydney thought. Helice looked triumphant. Perhaps she took some credit for this.

The navitar moved to the doorway, where a gap in the curtain allowed him to watch the deck. "I'm glad you liked my news. I could tell you other things, too." Geng De nodded toward Helice. "We should talk alone."

Sydney let an awkward pause stretch out. Then: "Leave us, Hei Ling," she murmured. She didn't like how Helice's face darkened. But at last Helice left the shed.

Geng De stood in the murky light, shaking his head. "Not good, that one. Anything that you get she'll want for herself."

She was disturbed to think Geng De had seen a bad future; on the other hand, he could be making it up. It was too dangerous to discuss these things with him, and she remained silent. He was only a pudgy young man with too much sentience.

"You might need me, Sen Ni. You might need me very much."

She remained quiet.

"You think she'll bring fire to the Rose. But what if her plots merely escalate the war between here and there? If war comes, you'll never get what you want."

"You know what I want?"

He blinked, as though puzzled that she questioned him. "Most of it. But don't worry, I won't tell." Glancing out the doorway curtain again, he went on. "The more you threaten the Rose, the more they'll want to kill us. She brings powers into the All—powers that are bad for us."

"The Rose already wants to kill us."

"Not really. The people who created the chain never wanted it to kill *everything*. They just put it together wrong. So you see, you don't need to take on so many enemies. You've divided your efforts"

Sydney grew very quiet. What other enemies did Geng De think she had? How did he know so much?

He murmured. "I know you'll move against the lords."

Her heart shrank in her chest. It was unsettling to hear it said out loud, and with Lady Anuve so near.

"You need someone like me," Geng De said.

"I'm mistress of a sway. I'm not sure I do need you."

"You should listen to me. I'm not demented, like the others. If you help this woman and her schemes, you bring Titus Quinn against you. He won't stop even if it means crushing you."

Sydney had heard all she needed to. He was nothing but a pudgy youngster playing future-reading games. She went to the door, holding the blanket open for him to leave.

He held his ground. "You're bringing bad threads together. Titus Quinn is a strong thread, if you only knew."

"I'm not afraid of him."

"You should be."

"Maybe he should be afraid of *me*."

"He would be, if I stood at your side."

He glanced out toward the deck. "Do you know how strong the knot is, the one that ties Sen Ni with Geng De?" He locked the fingers of his hands together. "This strong. Strong as the brane that keeps the world. Mighty as the river of the sky."

"I choose my own counselors."

"I don't think you do. She drove Mo Ti away, didn't she?" Then he shoved past the curtain and headed for the bridge.

He knew her secrets. Did he see things in the binds, as he claimed? She watched as the navitar made his way down the outside deck and ducked into the central cabin. Letting the blanket fall, she sat next to Riod on the floor. She delayed waking him, though she wished for his comfort and advice.

She considered Geng De's claim that her father had thrown the chain away. Ill-advisedly, she'd sent Mo Ti to kill him, then. She had almost been responsible for her father's death. Though Helice could not have known it would turn out that way, she was the one who had urged the assassination, to keep the Entire safe. Sydney sat and thought about those who were for her, and those who were against. The sorting was a hard task.

Soon the ship keeper came to say they would dock. She went on deck, filling her lungs with cleansing air. There was no sign of Geng De or Helice. In the crowded waters near the port, ships plowed their courses, hulls streaming mercurial spray, shifting to neon greens and watery sapphire, if her eyes saw true.

As she rounded the prow of the ship, she saw a startling view of Rim City. The metropolis lay in a vast arc before her. With ebb-time lights just emerging, the coast bore a necklace of glittering stones, with the nearest node of the metropolis a central diadem.

Glancing up at the pilot house, she saw Geng De looking down at her. Anuve was nowhere in sight. Geng De bowed, and she nodded a little in return. She might not want him for an advisor. But she didn't need him as an enemy, either.

Then she turned back to the bejeweled city. She had never lived in a city, much less the largest city in the universe, but she wouldn't let it change her. She was a child of the roamlands. She knew how to ride an Inyx, command the loyalty of the herd, and fly into the mind of the Tarig. Whatever Rim City would bring, it couldn't be harder than what she'd already done.

Helice joined her at the railing. "What did he want?" she whispered in English.

Sydney realized with surprise that she was going to lie to Helice. "He wanted to sell us more information."

Helice was watching her with a considering gaze. "I didn't think navitars were so worldly."

"I didn't think so either. This one is different." It was easy to claim to foretell and to boast of having seen things happening far away. Perhaps he knew little, and only shared the navitar propensity for visions. She would have preferred him as a normal pilot. She would have preferred not hearing that a knot bound them together. She chose not to believe it.

But if she didn't want him for a friend, she was not so sure she wanted Helice, either.

CHAPTER EIGHT

*The student asks: If my redstone necklace had every view of every
veil that ever brightened, would I be wise?*

*The master answers: If I had a thousand pieces of a priceless
vase, would I be rich?*

—from *The Veil of the Thousand Worlds*

Su BEI WATCHED AS HIS LAST SERVANT LEFT HIM, riding a beku down the minoral. Zhou had been with him ten thousand days and had begged to stay with his master, but Bei had been firm. My work is coming to an end, he'd said. I'm too old for scholarship. He hoped old Zhou would believe it.

Their farewell had been perfunctory at the end, with Zhou crushed and Bei impatient to get back to his treatise. His treatise on the cosmography of the Rose would be his crowning achievement. Bei rubbed his hands together to fend off the chill of the storm walls. It was a black day, and no mistake. But here at the very tip of the minoral it was always black. The storm walls made it so: one on that side, one on this, converging at the crucial veil of worlds. No other place worth living, even if it meant isolation and talking to stone well machines instead of flesh and blood. Well, goodbye to Zhou. Never say farewell; in a life of one hundred thousand days, they were sure to meet again. Time enough to see one's friends more than enough and grow tired of them.

Bei raised a hand in blessing, but Zhou was by now well down the minoral, cape billowing in the storm wall turbulence.

He hurried to the lift and closed the doors for the descent into the cavity. There was no sense building the veil above ground. No stability. Furthermore, it was hard to keep stone wells functioning what with the dust and the electrical charges. No, deep underground was the place, and Bei now had its warrens to himself and his studies.

Unless you counted Ji Anzi. Well, the girl did not count. Stone well literate, but no scholarly training.

The lift door opened, and Bei hastened down the corridor to the veil of worlds room.

Ji Anzi had promised to stay out of his way while she hid here, though why she came to him, he could not have said. Certainly, his minoral was no haven from the Tarig. Time was when the fiends had watched him closely, coming in their brightships, checking on him, suspicious that since Bei had known Titus in the Ascendancy, he might have seen him again. And so he had; and sent him on his way again, to seek out the correlates.

He'd succeeded in finding them and now had sent them to his old friend. Yes, the dear boy had sent him the great secret of the Entire: the algorithms predicting the specific alignment of the shifting universes, the formulas identifying how and when one might safely travel from here to there and back again. And, if one were not in a traveling mode—as Bei most certainly was not—one could use them for scholarship, to add to his map of the Rose universe. It wasn't clear the correlates could be used for anything else. Nor that they should be.

Titus was growing in power, just as Bei had predicted; but whether he would ever use his power to make inroads against the Tarig—well, that dream was far beyond the man. Time was that Bei had thought Titus Quinn possessed a high destiny; but he'd yet to prove he had a whisker's weight of ambition.

He hastened through the great stone well room, empty now except for snaking, disconnected cables. He'd ordered the computational engines moved down the corridor to his sanctuary to concentrate all resources on his great task.

Bei fondled the redstones strung around his neck. The correlates were the very thing Titus Quinn had come seeking in the first place. Given into Titus's hands in the form of redstone memory nuggets by none other than a Tarig lord, Titus had sent them to Bei for safe keeping—either because he thought he wouldn't live long or because he feared losing them, Bei didn't know. So while Bei was curious what the man was up to, he wasn't going to waste the opportunity of having the stones in his possession.

It was only a few arcs ago that the messenger had arrived with the precious packet, suggesting that a high lord was involved, and the need for utmost secrecy. Of course, Bei well knew which lord was likely to be involved: Lord Oventroe, the very lord that Bei had known so long ago at the Ascendancy. So: Titus had managed to convince Oventroe to help him. Titus could be persuasive, Bei remembered. Obviously, he wasn't ready to take his daughter and use the correlates to go home. Instead, he'd made sure Bei had them. Should Titus be captured or killed, Bei was to find a way to send them to the Rose woman known as Caitlin, sister-in-law to Titus.

How Bei would be expected to *find* the woman, he had no idea. But Titus wasn't dead yet.

There was also the question of the ethics of giving up the correlates at all. Bei could well imagine an influx of Roselings into the Entire, a cultural upheaval devoutly to be avoided. No, he'd have to make Titus see the error of that. And meanwhile, the redstones were perfectly safe in this obscure minoral and scholarly reach.

He entered the veil-of-worlds room, noting the quick transitions on the gel surface, flicking past a thousand correlations every increment, casting a strobing light onto the racks of stone wells and discarded drinking cups. He seated himself at the table where his enlivened scrolls lay in piles. No sooner was he settled and organizing his thoughts, than Anzi appeared at his door.

"I thought you might like some company, Su Bei." She stood in that still and self-possessed way she had—as though she would wait all day for the answer she wanted. She wouldn't get it this time.

"Company is the last thing I want. Don't you have the midday meal to make?"

"It's waiting for you in your quarters."

As though he had time for meals, now when all of his scholars were gone and only himself for the work. He gave her a quick look. Maybe she could help . . . but no, there was no time to train her. He wanted no students. They couldn't be trusted with the correlates, couldn't be trusted to even *know* about the correlates—oh, it was a dangerous knowledge that Bei now had; Lord Oventroe's messenger had made that clear. No one must know. But Anzi already knew; knew about the lord himself and his fascination with the Rose. There was no good reason to send her away, so here she remained at this scholar's retreat, as useful as legs on an Adda.

Anzi watched the veil-of-worlds bring its sight to bear on the Rose. The scenes flicked rapidly. "Are these of Earth?"

"Earth? Do they look like Earth? It's the cosmos, girl, it's darkling space, have you no wits?" Earth was the least of his concerns. The *Rose* was his field of vision, the *universe*, not just a world. Each flick of the veil registered a place in the Rose cosmos, one rife with relation to every other place. It must all be coordinated into his grand scheme of cosmography. Where was Earth in such a perspective? It was less than a pimple on a flea on a beku's arse.

He waited for Anzi to leave, but she went on, "How long will it take you to make your map?"

"Longer than it would if I had peace to make it."

"An arc, a sequent, a phase of time? How long, Master Bei?"

He pulled on his beard, his mood darkening. "A thousand days. Two thousand days. Why should I know or care? I work until I finish. Then it is done."

"By then we will be at war. No one will finish the map."

"Not finish? That would be a catastrophe of the highest order. Of course I will finish it. I've already written the introduction. Leave me in peace so I can write the rest."

She began her protests again, but Bei pointed a finger at the girl, silencing her. "Lord Oventroe won't let them burn the Rose. He is a powerful lord and will arrange it."

"Easy to say, not so easy to do."

Bei strove for patience. "These are matters for the Ascendancy, girl. Best to leave politics for those with a stomach for it."

She continued as though she hadn't heard him. "But you have the correlates, Master Bei. You have the power to help."

"Ah, power. It's what we're fighting about, isn't it, young Anzi? And is it your *scholar's* opinion that the correlates can engender power—matter to burn, fuel to keep the bright bright?" He waited for her to dig herself a scholarly hole.

"You could forge ties between the worlds. You could find ways for us to have converse."

He stared at her. "You think conversations will prevent war?"

She shifted her feet, caught without a rebuttal.

He picked up a scroll and activated it, but she blurted out, "There must be a way for people to cross safely back and forth. Bring some people of the Rose here. And let some of us go there. How can we find peace if we know nothing of each other?"

Bei remained silent, staggered by her naiveté. Had this been her philosophy from the start? Get people talking and they'll love each other? Is this why she had fatefully snatched Titus Quinn from the Rose so long ago, bringing all this danger upon the world?

As though remembering the same thing, Anzi murmured, "It's worth some risk."

"It would be worth it indeed, if there was any likelihood of success. Unfortunately, people in the Rose are trying to shatter the storm walls. Do you suggest that I am supposed to bring more of them over?" His voice had risen a little too fast, too sharp. "Anzi," he said, trying a more reasonable tone, "you must understand, the more we know of each other, the less we'll like each other."

"Just the opposite, master. Remember, Titus once hated me. Now I am his wife."

Oh, *that*. She and Titus had been thrust together, shared dangers, and now they called their feelings of gratitude *love*.

He sighed. Why was he wasting his breath? He had work to do. "I do not have time to try to ferry people back and forth, even if I had a way to do it, which I do not."

It was true. He hadn't figured out how to refine his investigations in so narrow a fashion. He was just sketching out the grand structural elements of the Rose, with its clusters of galaxies, its curtains of globular clouds. Chasing after planetoids was outside of strict scholarship. He looked at her obdurate expression. Well, perhaps for Anzi and Titus he might arrange a chapter on

Earth correlations, with a few mathematical expressions of affinity. Titus would appreciate a nice chapter.

"He has the war chain, you know."

This new tactic brought him up short. "The chain, is it? Is he going to kill me with it, then?" He rose from his chair, agitated and aware of the day's work slipping away. "For not complying with your directives?"

She held her ground. "You should be grateful he didn't use it to destroy us."

Bei sighed. "I *am* grateful. My ancestors are grateful. My bekus are grateful. But gratitude can't shape scholarship, or we would only have scrolls celebrating our mothers." He fixed her with his most severe look. "No, Ji Anzi. Titus put the correlates into my keeping. He trusted me with them, not you. And it is I who will decide how to use them. Now leave me."

"I could help you."

He stared.

"I was a student of Vingde."

"Yes, a terrible one. He said you were a hopeless scholar, and a thief, besides."

She had the grace to lower her gaze. "A soldier has to make do."

"You never went for a soldier."

As she opened her mouth to argue, Bei shoved his palms in her direction. "I am done with talk."

"It is a wrong use of the knowledge the lord gave you. It must be *for* something. Not just a map, not a diagram in a book on a shelf no one will ever read."

He jumped up. "No one read! You think that's what all these scrolls are? Treatises no one will read?" He waved his hands at the tightly packed scrolls lining the walls. "I know every thesis, every scroll, every line of them! It is a lifetime of study, more precious than jewels."

"But they are of no use."

"Use? Use? What use is loyalty? What use is poetry? You talk of use!"

"The correlates should be used for passage, not study."

He sank into his chair, lowering his voice. "That is as it may be. Few will read my treatise. I accept obscurity. It is a triumphant obscurity."

She was silent, gazing at the floor. No doubt she finally saw how far she had overstepped herself.

Then her gaze flicked up. "But master, how can it truly matter, your map of the Rose universe? There are a hundred universes. Your map will never be significant among all the maps that could be drawn."

Bei narrowed his eyes. "A hundred universes?" He waved his hands at the library. "Where does it say there are a hundred universes?"

Anzi was silent a moment. She was getting confused, over her head . . . "The lord said so."

"You spoke of such things with Lord Oventroe?"

"He said it. On the Nigh, when he helped Titus approach Ahnenhoon."

"That there are a hundred?"

"He didn't say the exact number. There are many."

Bei's thoughts quickly sifted through this claim. All scholars knew it was unlikely there were only two universes, yet in other primacies in the realm the veils showed little. His own primacy pierced the Rose. Every minoral in this primacy was productive of Rose correlations. All scholarship, therefore, concentrated here, in these minorals. If there were other universes . . . Bei pulled on his chin, wondering if Anzi had stumbled upon something important. Perhaps it was a minor comment of the lord, taken out of context. . . .

"Titus bandied the subject about? And the lord allowed that it might be so?"

"The lord said the various realities are like bubbles in a foaming brew. That what we know of life is on the surface of these bubbles. The Entire is such a surface. And the Rose."

Bei stared at her. Out of her mouth had just poured a stream of either wisdom or foolishness of the highest order.

"Why would Lord Oventroe discuss such things with Titus Quinn?"

"Because Titus wanted to know why Oventroe could not just suggest to his cousins that they burn a different universe, and save him the trouble of going to Ahnenhoon to prevent the burning of the Rose."

Bei looked at her as though she were a talking beku. "And?"

"And the lord said that, yes, there are other universes, but none of them have much in them. And so, therefore, they are not productive of burning."

Feeling for his chair with the back of his legs, Bei lowered himself into his seat. "Bubbles, you say?"

"And they touch. Where it becomes possible to go from one to the other."

"We are a bubble too?"

"Differently shaped. So he said." Anzi made a gesture of probing. "We are multilobed, pushing into the other realities."

"Bubbles," Bei repeated.

"In foam."

"Surely the Rose is the greatest of them," he whispered, fingering his scrolls, his notebooks, his life's work.

Anzi's hand came down to gently cover his own. "Your work is still important, Master. It is a piece of the whole."

Bei contemplated the veil in front of him for a very long time. When he looked up again, he found that Anzi had fetched him a small plate of food and a glass of spirits, frothing with bubbles.

Ghoris's ship had fallen deep into the River Nigh, plunging quickly, making Mo Ti feel nauseated and impatient. He lay on his cot, blaming Quinn for the delay. They should have rushed to Rim City where they might have had the chance to kill Hel Ese when she debarked.

He glanced at Quinn as the man lay on the nearby bench staring out the porthole, his eyes filled with a blue fire reflection from the Nigh. In Quinn's hand, the Paion hoop, Akay-Wat's gift.

"We have waited too long," Mo Ti growled. Quinn didn't answer. They were on their way now, and they'd arrive when they arrived, all depending on Ghoris and if she truly understood the need for haste. Apparently she didn't understand, since she'd urged Quinn to chase after Paion back at the Inyx Sway. That was what came of taking counsel from madwomen.

"Too long," Mo Ti muttered again, when Quinn didn't answer. The stupor of the Nigh pulled on him, but his distress was too great for sleep.

Hel Ese had the small god, the thinking machine. Too much power for such a one as her. The small god could give the Entire to the spider. But the Entire must be for Sydney. Mo Ti believed this with all his heart. Who but a woman born to no home sway, a woman who was more than one sway, could ever supplant the Tarig? This was Cixi's logic. Cixi, the one part that he had not told Titus Quinn. The matriarch of the Great Within wished to topple the lords.

And wasn't the man of the Rose the one with the best chance to succeed?

A Tarig lord had given Quinn the secret of passage to and from. With this knowledge, Quinn might locate the place the lords went to renew themselves. A fine trap. Still, Sydney might not approve the alliance. It was a dangerous game, to trust Titus Quinn.

Now they depended upon Jaq to reach the man who held the correlates in safe keeping. Mo Ti hoped the witless ship keeper could even *remember* the message he was to deliver.

Barely conscious, Quinn muttered, "She has a book of pin pricks, Mo Ti. It measures me."

Mo Ti snorted in disgust. A man at the mercy of family frowns was forever weakened. Quinn had wasted two hours talking to Akay-Wat about things that could not be changed and would not matter if they could. Sydney's heart had been broken by the man when she was a child. She was now a woman grown, and it no longer mattered whether her father had run after her or not or eaten delicacies in the Ascendancy while Sydney ate bricks of straw. That time was past.

The portals were clotted with lightning. Still gazing at Quinn, Mo Ti saw how the light fell on the man's face, silvering it like a mask of a dead god. He was a great personage, no doubt; but always on the brink of failure. Perhaps the correlates would transform him. A little taste of power inspired most men.

As Ghoris sailed them onward, Mo Ti relinquished consciousness at last.

They dragged themselves up from the binds, Ghoris shouting for her ship keeper and the two passengers staggering into consciousness.

Mo Ti was the first to get to the rail. Just a few miles distant, under an Early Day sky, the lower precincts of Rim City lay thin and long on the shore of the Sea of Arising. But where in all this far-flung town was the ship that carried Sydney? Many navitar vessels streaked into local harbors from points away, some of them manifesting suddenly, rocking as they birthed from the river.

Quinn met him at the rail. "Now we find her."

Mo Ti murmured, "Hel Ese or Sydney?" It defined what the man was made of. He had to name his goal.

"Both of them," Quinn answered.

CHAPTER NINE

Caitlin Quinn stared at the letter. An actual paper letter, it bore the mast-head of the United States Bureau of the General Standard. She hadn't known until this moment that Lamar had been serious about altering her son's scores, and her own.

She and Mateo had been recategorized from "forward capability in key skill sets" to "advanced capability." From middie to savvy in one fell swoop, changing their status, not only to savvy, but to felon. Now the question was, what was she doing breaking the law? And just why did Lamar Gelde think they could get by with it?

She read the letter again, with its simple, bald statement of fact. Previously, the wrong records had been forwarded to the Quinn family. The present documents would confirm new standings for the Standard Test. Relief accompanied the guilt she felt. Now she wouldn't have to sit down with Mateo and explain his scores and his future. Now she and Rob wouldn't have to tell their son that being of forward capability instead of advanced was a fine and worthwhile status. The two of them would have pointed to themselves as evidence that it was possible to make a good life as a middie: the new software company, their close-knit family, their lovely home—all despite the fact that they lacked the designation of ultrasmart. They would have painted the brightest picture that they could. Lied.

They had meaningful work because Titus's millions were on loan to them, financing their software company, complete with a dedicated mSap. True, the family was together, and perhaps Rob loved his wife. The lie was that she still loved *him*. Because though it had been a year and a half since Caitlin had last seen Titus, it was unfortunately *that* brother she loved. Next

113

to Titus, Rob seemed ordinary, without fire. And because Rob wasn't his brother, she had shut her heart to him. If she could have changed her heart, she would have. Titus had said, *I'm not in line if you get a divorce. I can't be and still live with myself.* The problem was, didn't that imply that if he were not the brother-in-law, he *would* be in line?

She fingered the letter that might be Mateo's passport to the best future. Nearly every day Mateo asked if the test results had come in. *Not yet*, she'd said. Little Emily didn't help by declaring that *she* was going to be a savvy like Titus. At only eight years old, it would be awhile before Lamar would have to alter *her* scores.

Tucking the letter into her jacket pocket, she wondered how she was going to explain this to Rob. Not to worry. According to Lamar, the price for the switched scores was that Rob *not* know. But how long before the Bureau of Standard Tests figured out the mistake? How long before Mateo's improved access to the best schools came to Rob's attention? It couldn't be kept secret. And Lamar didn't care, said it wouldn't matter. Because something he called the transform was coming.

Now that she was well and truly into this mess, she was determined to get answers from Lamar. He was going to tell her the truth, and he was going to tell her today, or she'd tear up the letter and tell the Bureau of their mistake.

She grabbed her satchel and left her office, hoping not to see Rob. As she walked down the corridor of the plush central offices of Emergent Corporation, she stranded a command into the embedded data structures in the walls calling for her car. People nodded at her from their cubicles in the refurbished warehouse, site of their by now three-hundred-strong workforce in educational software development.

Rounding a corner, Rob saw her and waved. Deep in conversation with one of the team leaders, Rob was energized, busy and happy. She pointed at the door, mouthing *Have to go out*. He dashed down the hall to kiss her goodbye, a peck on the cheek.

"I'm running out to see Lamar."

It felt like a lie, and was, in any case, just a partial truth. Just as it had felt like a lie when she hadn't told Rob that she and Titus had almost made love on the floor of her office, before Titus pulled back and remembered that you didn't screw your brother's wife.

"Lunch with the old man?" Rob asked brightly. He had mostly forgiven Lamar for riding herd on Titus about his duties in the adjoining region. Rob forgave easily, and she hoped he'd do the same for her when it came her turn to be faithless. To be part of *the transform* when Rob couldn't. Whatever the hell the transform was. If Minerva was on the verge of a breakthrough in computer platforms—say to biological/DNA integration—if this was the mysterious transform, she could understand it being kept secret. But what did that have to do with the Standard Test?

"Have fun," Rob said, noting another section chief who was waiting to talk to him. And he was gone—happy, clueless. Hurrying outside before he changed his mind, Caitlin stepped into the glaringly bright day to wait for her car to drive itself up from the underground garage. It was her one true luxury, almost embarrassing in its perfection: a bright blue Mercedes sedan large enough to carry the four Quinns—on those few occasions when they were all together.

She wished Titus was here. For the millionth time in the last months she wished she knew more about where he was. *There are some things over there that can hurt us*, he'd told her before he left the last time. But insofar as she was privy to Minerva's secrets because she was family, she still knew only fragments: A parallel universe. Time passes differently than here. Titus engaged in great events that might kill him. In consideration thereof, Rob and Caitlin received all Titus's considerable monetary compensation.

And now there was the transform. By day's end she'd know what that was, but even in her determination, she had the feeling she would regret finding out.

The Columbia River lapped up against Lamar's house, a little slap, slap, from one of the world's great rivers. The Columbia slid by Portland in a whisper, barely noted by Portland's four million inhabitants whizzing over bridges in Meshed public transport and private autos. Lamar was more connected to the river; he lived on it. His houseboat was small, compact, and lovingly detailed. For all its tungsten countertops and mahogany trim, it was surprisingly modest. Caitlin supposed Lamar spent most of his money on his face, a gesture to vanity that was becoming increasingly foolish.

"Caitlin," Lamar said. "I got your message." He waved her on board, happy and nautical-looking in his silk shirt and captain's cap. She joined him on the deck, accepting a glass of wine and settling into a deck chair. He guessed why she'd come.

"You might say thank you," he murmured.

"I don't know what to say. We've now lied to the US government." She held the letter in her lap, marveling that even Lamar Gelde, formerly of the board of directors of the Minerva Corporation, could get the system to *think* it had erred—and then admit it, in writing.

He eyed the letter. "Just hold on to that. It's your ticket."

She watched as a few sailboarders skimmed by, riding the winds from the gorge. Some people were perfectly happy being middies, or even dreds. She had once been rather happy herself. Why now, all of a sudden, was she being made to feel that she needed to be something else?

She folded the letter lengthwise, making it easier to gesture with. "I'm not sure I want this."

"Oh, you want it."

"Convince me."

"I can't do that. Not today. Give me some time, for God's sake."

A little slick of oil creased the river, twisting the blue sky's perfect reflection in its rainbow waters. "I have—*we* have—all the money we need," Caitlin said. "Savvy or not, we're wealthy. I don't care if you're on the verge of some tech breakthrough. I'm not going to lie to be a part of it."

One of Lamar's improved eyebrows went up. "Speaking for Mateo, are you?"

"We can't keep up a pretence. Sooner or later Stanford or Harvard will figure it out. We can lower our sights. Maybe a state college."

Lamar put his drink down and went to the ship's rail, looking out at the industrial waterfront on the Washington State side of the river. "Well, that's fine. Not a bad idea. State college . . ." his voice tapered off. When he turned around, his face was pained.

"What the hell is this about?" she spat at him. His expression was locked down, and she meant to shake it loose. She stood up, leaned against another part of the railing, and held the letter over the water. "Tell me what's going on, or this goes in the river."

Lamar started, putting out a hand to restrain her. "That's your future."

"Convince me." Louder, she said, "Tell me what the hell is going on with my family and the Standard Test, or I won't have anything more to do with you ever again, much as I love you. So help me God, I won't." Her hand was shaking. Until this moment she hadn't realized how much tension she'd built up around this subject.

It was a standoff between them. The day was warm for late fall, but the deck took on a chill.

Lamar had only a few moments to marshal his strategy. He had to tell Caitlin something. But he judged her incapable of the cold, hard truth. She stood there in her expensive smartSuit, and her comfortable morality, demanding to be pure. All right then, if pure was what she needed, pure was what he'd give her.

"Titus is calling for a few people to go over. You're among them. You can bring Mateo and little Emily."

That piece was maybe the biggest she could absorb for now. He brought up her chair and pressed her into it.

He nodded at her consternation. "Let me lay this out. Titus has found a world called the Entire. It's not perfect, but it has a fundamental advantage: it's got the science of a million years from now. There's a civilization over there. They've been around much longer than we have, and they have the means to give us the keys to the universe."

Her voice was profoundly small. "A civilization?"

"The Entire. That's a word you're never going to use except when we're together. You understand?"

She nodded.

"Those who control this . . . Entire . . . are afraid of an inundation of our people into their lands. Understandable. So we're starting small. Two thousand people will cross over, to establish a base, a community. To begin bridging the cultural and technological differences. We need wives, husbands, families, children. The last thing we need is to look like a military operation."

He was proud of this spin so far. It was already beginning to settle Caitlin down.

"The reason the Standard Test matters is that Minerva is insisting only savvies go over for now. We need our sharpest mathematical and analytical minds, obviously." Even though Minerva wasn't involved, not as an entity at least, it was the most likely way to spin this thing.

"Minerva knows I'm not a savvy."

He shrugged. "They're not going to question three new names on the list, not if Titus asked for them."

"Why aren't we hearing about this publicly?"

"There are issues. We need to keep this under wraps for a bit."

She sat very quietly, then, seemingly looking at the river. Lamar gave her time. At last she said, "Why does Titus want us and not Rob?"

The next part was the cruelest lie; he needed a moment before he could utter it. "Quinn wants a few people he can trust—not just technological smart asses chosen by Minerva." He shook his head in mock frustration. "No, damn it, that's not it. The fact is, he wants you." He *did* hate himself.

But the lies would save her life. The Earth was in Tarig gun sights. No one would survive the coming storm, no one on this side of the brane interface. Rob wouldn't, nor all the other middies and dreds. He looked away, upriver, gathering his story. "Quinn confided some things to me. He knows you're unhappy with Rob." He turned halfway around, but couldn't face her. "He hopes you might find some happiness with him."

"With Titus."

He coughed. "Yes." He didn't want to see the look on her face. It would just about break his heart, so he didn't turn around. "Go across and be at his side for a few months, Caitlin. Give him the support he desperately needs right now. Johanna is dead. Sydney is likely dead as well. He doesn't have family anymore. He's a lonely man, with a lot on his shoulders. Go and help him. Then, if it doesn't add up for you, come back. Or wait for Rob to join you, in the next wave."

On that safer lie, he faced her. "Once the kinks are worked out, there'll be a modest influx of colonists. Rob can be in that number, if you want—if he wants." He spread his hands in a gesture of reasonableness: "It's the biggest opportunity in history. It's a chance to meet an alien civilization, and come to terms with it. Mateo and Emily would grow up with astounding resources at their fingertips."

"What is the Entire, Lamar?"

She's hooked, he thought. He drew his chair closer. He told her what little he knew. The picture built up from Minerva debriefings of Quinn when he returned last time. And he told it all—all except for the fact that the Entire was on its last lump of coal. That it needed a source of fuel as vast as a universe. And that there was nothing we could do about it. Lamar presumed that by now Helice had convinced Quinn not to use the nan device on the Tarig engine. Barring a total destruction of the Entire, there really *was* nothing to be done about the Tarig threat.

Satchel over her shoulder, sunglasses hiding her dazed expression, Caitlin was ready to go, eager to leave to be alone to think, no doubt.

"Be ready to go," he told her. "Be packed." He wouldn't say how the team of two thousand was preparing for the crossover, just that it was a few hours' drive away on the Hanford Reservation in Eastern Washington. He warned her not to go there; although she was now on their list, her savvy status was only a piece of paper. A few questions, such as "Where did you take your graduate degree?" would mark her as counterfeit.

She stopped at the ramp to the wharf. "Why do you call it a transform?"

Lamar got a kink in his chest. Damn. He improvised: "When the first wave comes home—those who decide to come home—there'll be an utter transformation in our society, at every level. You can't keep knowledge from changing the world. And believe me, it will."

He watched her make her way down the pier toward her car.

Brave girl. Took it like a champ. The things he did to keep Titus Quinn happy. This was a gift to him: your niece and nephew, saved from destruction. As for Caitlin, well, she wasn't an unattractive woman, middie though she was. Let Quinn do with her as the spirit dictated.

Dizzy with his performance, he slowly lowered himself into a deck chair. Meanwhile, Caitlin stood by the Mercedes. The sun glinted off the perfect blue three-coat gloss of the hood, and she stared at it until her eyes hurt.

She tried to imagine the Entire. Its fire-laden sky, its limitless extent, all folded inside a geography. Its alien peoples, some of whom were very much like us. Her thoughts circled around Lamar's descriptions like a plane looking for a place to land.

But most of all, she thought of Titus. Titus and her.

CHAPTER TEN

To stand next to the master is to see with the corner of his eye.
—Kan Shi, Red Throne Scholar

ILINARD THE JOUT STOOD BACK FROM THE ALLEY WALL of the under-city, admiring his handiwork, another likeness of the fugitive. Here, among the dregs of the Entire, a man like Titus Quinn might find anonymity. And more: among the morts, he might find accomplices.

The view spray would last for an arc, and then Milinard would return and squirt up another poster. Maybe across the way. Or down there. But not too many places, as the undercity was sacred to the adherents of the Red Throne, and the gracious lords would not have religions disrespected.

Now *that* was a subject he'd like to broach with the darkling Quinn himself: if the lords were so blameworthy, why was it they allowed all sentients to live as they liked, even worshipping foolish gods instead of venerating the Tarig as was proper? In the lords' generosity, they had even created the under-city, these burrows, so that the Society of the Red Throne could meditate in front of portals and ascribe to navitars the qualities of gods.

Do contemptible leaders tolerate such folly? Yes, let us ask *that* of the man who destroyed the brightships and killed the Lord Hadenth and now subverted the Entire with unhealthy crimes!

Of course, while the lords were supremely tolerant, the Magisterium was less so. The Great Within sent spies into the undercity, of whom Sublegate Milinard was one. Let the dregs do what they wished, but watch, watch them.

Milinard himself had a network of informants. Some of them were even

Reds. He was proud of those inroads into the undercity. Perhaps one of them would provide an important clue in the matter of the fugitive. Milinard imagined himself reporting personally to the High Prefect Cixi, the old dragon herself, perhaps receiving an advancement to full legate. The petals of the Jout's skin fluttered in satisfaction.

The Reds might be peculiar, but at least they were proper citizens, often rising to high positions—in Rim City especially. They thought of themselves as travelers on life's river, open to the best futures—futures they believed the navitars could see. The Society urged right actions to enable the most propitious futures to come forth. Time was when the cult had been more prominent, in a day when religions of striving were more popular. Nowadays sentients wanted religion that made no demands, which explained the resurgence of interest in the Miserable God. Milinard sighed. It was a sentient's choice.

As he packed up his squirter, he saw a young man gazing at the poster. By his outrageous attire, he was a mort, one of those flash boys so common here. Noting the sublegate, the young man turned away, striding as fast as he could in his skirt and boots.

"Hold, young fellow." Milinard beckoned him, and the youngster obeyed. The sublegate made it a point to occasionally, and at random, question a denizen of the undercity, especially morts. The morts claimed to venerate the navitars—so technically they were Reds—but Milinard had little doubt that all they desired was to carouse in the undercity out of sight of their families.

"Name?" he asked of the boy dressed like a girl.

"Li Yun Tai."

The young man called forth an insulting bow, hardly a nod. Well, that would merit a sterner tone. "You will say Excellency."

"Excellency."

Still, a tone of voice. "Come closer, Li Yun Tai." When the young man did so, Milinard gestured at the poster. "What opinion do you have of this man's aspect? Is he fair, do you think?"

"He is a darkling. That says enough, Excellency."

An evasive answer. Morts like this one might well give Titus Quinn refuge. They practically worshipped the Rose, hoping to copy those sad, short lives. Indeed, the man of the Rose was practically a hero among these odious boys.

Milinard persisted. "But would not Titus Quinn be fine to invite to your burrow for pleasures? It can't be easy for a boy in a girl's skirt to find company."

"Oh, but it is. A girl's skirt with something extra in it is what some people prefer, Excellency."

Milinard's temper edged upward, but he restrained himself. "Yun Tai, I have a pleasing duty you will perform."

Now the youngster looked worried. Did he think Milinard would demand sexual favors? But Milinard was still contemplating the happy pillowing with his wife last ebb and needed no adventures today.

He put a hand on Yun Tai's shoulder, drawing him closer. "I'll spare you the rigors of my physical prowess, mort." He released him, noting that the boy was shaking. "You might say, thank you, Excellency."

"Thank you, Excellency."

Milinard slapped him across the face. "That is an insult to me personally."

Yun Tai murmured, "Your pardon, Sublegate. I meant no offense."

"Very well, then. You can pleasure me some other time. Here, then, is your task: You will watch for the man whose image you see on these burrow walls. If you see anyone who, even in the least way, resembles this fugitive, you will rush to the Ascendancy and report to me. Your entry is assured when you mention the name Sublegate Milinard. You understand?"

Yun Tai did. He might be a mort, but he was no fool.

Milinard dismissed him to slink back into the murky streets. On that excellent note, the sublegate left the burrows, climbing the broad stairs to Rim City.

Night deepened in the undercity, bringing its accustomed throngs. Storefronts opened windows, exposing wares to the passersby, pedi cabs made early passes down the streets trolling for passengers, and vendors presided over piles of scarves, music redstones, and navitar trinkets. The first wave of sentients trickled in, dressed for the night.

Tai passed the dumpling stand, declining offers of a sample. Before meeting the disgusting Jout he was famished, but now his appetite waned.

But he wouldn't let thoughts of Milinard the Gross weigh him down; rather, he let thoughts of Titus Quinn lift him up. Titus Quinn, who came from the Rose, who defied the lords, who stole the brightships and sent them into the storm walls. They called him a *hsien*, an immortal hero. But he was, before anything, a darkling of the short, deep life—a life that had meaning because it was not long and tedious.

Truly, if he came across the personage Titus Quinn, Tai would never turn him in. He pictured himself befriending him, even helping him evade the lords. The idea excited him. Such actions would be full of risk, but they would be bold and meaningful, unlike his life at present—largely empty, he thought with sudden dismay. The idea of sex-right-now was only a pretence at intensity. For a truly vivid life, you had to find a worthy goal. Could it be that, posturing and needy, he had been wasting his days?

A matronly shopkeeper beckoned him to inspect her pile of navitar icons—framed portraits of bloated, misshapen pilots in their red caftans. He ignored the vendor. His insight was growing: Even the navitars were beside the point. They weren't to be venerated, but pitied. Morts and Reds thought that navitars were open to all experience. But they were closed to it. What can you know of life, cooped up on a vessel and seeing futures that would never come?

His appetite had returned. He entered a foodery and ordered a serving of deep-fried momo. Washing down his meal with mouthfuls of steaming oba, Tai reflected on the idea of a superior cause. It wasn't likely he would encounter Titus Quinn on the street. Why would the man of the Rose come to a place where he could be so easily cornered? Tai's goal would perhaps not be so grand. He didn't have a clue what that new goal might be. But at least he knew that he didn't know, and that was a start.

The street was surging with eager, spark-driven revelers. The influx would soon overflow into the dance pits, the fooderies, the wine dens. Just outside the window of the foodery, he saw the lit-up, skittery looks of faces seeking thrills. He could relate; he'd done that himself. No more, he vowed.

Still, tonight he had a date. He'd honor his rendezvous with blue feathers, as he secretly called the boy he'd met at the Dark Flower. He paid his bill and headed to the den where Fajan and his friends were gathered.

After their tryst at the Dark Flower, Fajan asked to see him again. Perhaps sex against the porthole wall didn't define Fajan any more than it defined Tai. And without his mask, Fajan had the face of someone who could be wise as well as fatally handsome.

The burrow, when he arrived, was jammed with morts and pulsing with music. He watched the crowd: the plasmic girls, the Rosy boys, and there, a Ysli in a gold cape . . . now *that* looked street major. Several very flash morts were wearing capes. He stopped, feeling out of place and wishing, suddenly and with fervor, for time alone.

"Tai!" Fajan hailed him from the corner next to the room-spanning porthole.

As Tai approached, Fajan waved him into the group settled on the floor away from the general din. Fajan slipped an arm around Tai's waist. His face was ethereal in the wan light of the exotic water. There were introductions, nicely received all around, and Tai felt easier.

He relaxed in the company of Fajan's friends, and together they gazed at the porthole, as though the silver waters might confer a special benediction. In this meditative frame of mind, Tai whispered to Fajan: "Do you ever hope for something more?" At Fajan's raised eyebrow, Tai added, "Something with a purpose?"

Fajan smiled a little, as though he *did* have a secret purpose.

Tai persisted. "What if we had to risk our lives for something worthwhile? Would you?"

Some of the morts glanced at him, annoyed by the distracting whispers.

"Just watch," Fajan murmured, giving Tai a hug. A bowl of smoking resin made the rounds, but Tai handed it on unsampled. Tinny music came from a stone well computational box in a far corner, music chosen for its weird scales and hypnotic base. The river was layered in gray and yellow light.

Fajan whispered, "You're tense. I'll help you relax later."

"Let's go now," Tai suggested.

Before Fajan could answer, a murmur went through the room. Someone cried out and was silenced. Something hung in the depths outside the porthole. There in the foaming waters hovered a form, wavering in the uncertain light. Fajan gripped Tai's hand. All of them were leaning forward, eyes alight.

"Rivitar," Fajan whispered.

Rivitar. A being that lived in the sea, in the Nigh. Tai had heard rumors of such things, but they were impossible. Nothing could live in such waters.

"I've seen them before," Fajan said. "Just watch."

If it was a creature, it was like none other: it was shaped like a box.

"Will it see us?" Tai asked.

"Hush."

The apparition approached. A sigh vented from the crowd; they would get a special vision this night. As the cube snugged up to the porthole, an image appeared on one of its surfaces. It was the face of a Hirrin. But on an adjoining surface, a Chalin face. Each visible side of the cube showed the face of a sentient.

Fajan gripped Tai's hand harder, barely containing his excitement.

A girl stood up and walked to the porthole as though in a trance. She put her hand against the glass. This brought the cube closer, and the room fell into disarray, with sentients—Chalin, Ysli, Jout—pushing forward, surging toward the girl and the bubble, the girl and the rivitar.

On the side of the cube closest to the porthole was a Chalin man's face, with a pleased, relaxed expression. No one else dared touch the glass lest they break the girl's reverie, or lest the rivitar flee. Her hand pressed on the glass. The rivitar's face pressed too, from the other side.

"Speak to him," someone said, and then others urged the girl to say something, as though anything could be heard through the thick, clear wall. The crowd stood transfixed and worshipful. Then, as quickly as it had appeared, the object winked out, flattening to a vertical slit, barely visible. The remnant broke up into segments and vanished.

The girl collapsed. People caught her, ministering to her. She stirred, murmuring, perhaps making more of her role than her smoke-infested gestures deserved.

Tai sat down, shunning the celebratory mood of the room as the music got louder and people shouted over it to compare stories.

Fajan's eyes were lit up. He knelt in front of Tai. "Like our rivitar?"

"Has it ever said anything?"

"It can't. It's in the river. But someday we'll speak to it. It will tell us mysteries."

This thing, whatever it might be, was fascinating, but Fajan's attitude was foolish. Fajan had—all of them here had—taken a reverence for the River Nigh to an extreme. Perhaps, once, Tai would have done the same.

Tai shook his head. "I think we've all had too much heavenly resin."

Fajan sat back on his heels. "You're not ready. You can't hear the rivitar if you're not ready. You're still living for sex-right-now. I used to do that, too."

This condescension was too much for Tai, after he had come to this burrow with a new vision of life, feeling above all the flash. He stood up, and Fajan did too, facing off with him. They were on the verge of saying things they couldn't take back.

Let the truth come, then, Tai thought. "That thing in the river is a machine. Anyone could paint faces on a box. Whatever it is, it isn't going to save you."

A patronizing shake of the head. "You're so Entire."

"And *you're* so Rose?" Fajan's calm silence drove Tai to say: "What if whatever is inside that box is attracted to other faces and has no more intelligence than an Adda? What if it's a prisoner? What if it's trapped inside the cube?"

Fajan smiled in his self-important way. "When you're ready, you'll see it differently."

Tai shook his head, murmuring, "I already see things differently." He turned and made his way through the crowd to the door, eager to be alone.

The air of the undercity was never fresh, but compared to the burrow it was sweet. People thronged: hurrying, loitering, posturing to be seen. Fajan did not come after him, Tai was thankful to note.

The rivitar had stunned him; but so had the reaction of Fajan and his friends. Whatever the apparition was, why idolize it? The rivitar might be trapped in the river. Its faces had looked happy, but that might be because it hoped the light-filled window offered escape. Tai knew what it was to be trapped in a land that wasn't his true home.

As to belonging, Tai thought he knew where he belonged. He'd been pushing it away too long. He wondered if he belonged in the Rose. Titus Quinn had shown it was possible to pass through the veil-of-worlds. Maybe Tai could too. Was it a far-fetched dream that someone like himself might go to a place so far away?

The thought solidified. Perhaps he really did belong in the Rose. Perhaps he had always been striving for it—through his pretensions as a mort, through his striving for intensity. A new vision came to him, that he would go to the Rose—somehow, he would go.

He walked home in a daze of startling clarity.

Zhiya huddled on Quinn's divan, her short legs curled under a blanket against the cold. She was glad to see Quinn. He'd been missing for the last four days, and her imagination had been running to Tarig torture and worse.

"You might have sent word," she murmured.

"You don't seem happy to see me, Zhiya."

"Oh, I'm happy. Last time I saw you, you were determined to be a common man. So disappointing." She pushed back her long hair that had fallen over her shoulders. "I rather fancy a driven man."

And she did like him more, now that he was back in the game. Not that it *was* a game: Hel Ese and her twisted idea of saving her people by killing them. Zhiya shook her head. That was taking zeal a little too far.

"Mo Ti might have made up this business of the matching engine, have you thought of that? To get you to kill the woman for him." She wondered who would destroy their own land, their own home. Traitors were common as bekus, but this betrayal was breathtaking.

"It's hard to credit," Zhiya went on.

"She doesn't like dreds." Quinn was gazing out his veranda doors at the sea of Arising, even though, in the heavy fog, he couldn't see it.

"Dreds?"

"An average person. She can't stand average."

The breeze was cold off the veranda and Zhiya snugged her blanket more firmly around her. "Close the door, my dear."

"Do you suppose my daughter is down in those streets somewhere? She could be."

"No, she's playing the part of the Mistress of the Sway. Up in her mansion."

Still looking out he murmured, "She has a sway. My child was a slave. And now . . ."

"You were a slave once, too. Quinns have a way of rising in the world." A gust rattled the porch doors. "Shut the doors," she muttered. For the last two days a heavy fog had hung over the city, stoving up her joints and making her hair frizz. It was not a good day even before Quinn dropped the news that he was going to track somebody down and kill them.

He moved away from the porch doors at last and began pacing the room.

Zhiya got up and shut the doors herself. She turned to Quinn. "I'll send one of my people to get rid of her. How convenient the little gondling is *in town*. That's to our advantage."

He shook his head. "I'd like a few words with Helice before we put her out of her misery."

Yes, Zhiya could well imagine. But was his disgust directed at Hel Ese or himself? She imagined that Quinn was kicking himself rather hard for not dealing with Ahnenhoon when he'd had the chance. She wasn't about to bring *that* subject up—the little matter of the chain that could have destroyed Ahnenhoon lying at the bottom of the Nigh where Quinn had thrown it in a fit of moral goodness.

Quinn went on, "I need to find out where her engine is. That's the important piece."

Zhiya sighed. "Haven't you figured out, my dear, that your daughter has set a trap for you? Why do you suppose the Tarig brought her here? To show their love of a scrawny Rose girl who's caused them so much trouble?"

Quinn managed a bitter smile. Hiding a lot of pain, that smile, Zhiya guessed.

"I know it's a trap."

Now *that* surprised her. Quinn usually clung more tightly to his family illusions. She raised an eyebrow.

"Helice is there. I may never get closer to her."

Somewhere in the distance, a short burst of fireworks shattered the silence; a little practice session for the big celebration. Purple and orange thudded into the sky, smearing the fog. Someone shouted, and horns blared. Then once again the fog cloaked the neighborhood with white and silence.

The denizens of Rim City had been told to express joy at their new status of sway, and in ten days time they would oblige. The massive celebration would include a grand procession, galas, fireworks, floats, public drunkenness, and food venders lining the Way. It was a fine excuse for a street party, and Rim City denizens knew how to throw one, having the longest street in the Entire, the Way that circumnavigated the sea.

It might be odd to have a woman of the *Rose* as mistress, but since the city wouldn't pay much attention to a leader anyway, she might as well be a darkling. At least she'd taken a proper name. *Sen Ni* had a Chalin sound, though it was just a transcription of her Rose name.

"Let me have my helpers bring Hel Ese out," Zhiya said.

Quinn picked up the Paion artifact he'd brought back from the Long Gaze of Fire. He turned it in his hand, as he often did, gazing as though into an empty mirror where lost things might be seen—such as a daughter whose childhood one had missed.

"No," Quinn answered. "They'll never get her out. The place is guarded by Tarig; it's up on that bridge."

Yes, the damnable bridge. Sydney had taken residence in the biggest house in the lower Rim. Occupying the central span of the arch over one of the Rivers Nigh, her mansion was inaccessible by boat and had only one street passing near: the Way. The Way crossed the five great crystal bridges spanning the Nighs, leaning away from the storm walls that came to an end at the sea. The crystal bridges. Lit from within, spectacular in the Deep Ebb, now one of them was essentially a fortress.

Zhiya challenged him. "How can *you* get her out?"

"I don't have to. I'll question her there. Then, to escape, it's just me."

"You think your daughter won't give you up to the Tarig. By the bright, you really think that."

He didn't answer.

Zhiya bit her tongue, but it had to be said. "You're going to convince her you've been a loving father."

"No. I'm going to ask her to forgive me."

Zhiya stared at him. "Forgive you? She sent the big eunuch to kill you. Not a forgiving sort, that girl."

When he didn't answer, an ugly thought struck her. "You *want* her to betray you. That way you can pay off your debt." She shook her head. "You're a man with too many corners."

"You wanted me to be a *hsien*." He smiled. "This is my big chance."

She'd rather meant for him to immortalize himself by bringing down the Tarig, not by winning this little skirmish between the Rose and the Entire. But changing his mind was hopeless.

"What will you have me do?"

"For starters," he said, "you could find me someone who isn't afraid of heights."

CHAPTER ELEVEN

Nascence: 1. A finger of land, often temporary, protruding from a minoral. 2. A state of impermanence. 3. (informal) Difficulties on all sides.

—from *Hol Fan's Glossary of Needful Words*

ANZI WOKE IN DARKNESS. An odd, insistent noise pounded at the walls of her bedchamber: a distant chugging punctuated by sharp, zinging cracks. This was no ordinary sound, even for the stormy minoral.

Rising from her bed, she threw on her long silk pants and padded jacket.

The door opened with a whack. Bei stood there, a candle in his hand. "Get dressed."

Stuffing her feet into her boots, she asked, "What is it?"

"The reach," he said. "We're leaving. Take what you must." He waited outside, giving her privacy to dress.

By the urgency in his voice, Anzi didn't question him, but hurriedly stuffed into her shirt the precious redstones on a thong. Earlier that evening she'd copied the correlates, and when Su Bei had burst into her room just now she thought he'd discovered this. The correlates were far too valuable to be in the scholar's keeping if he planned to hoard them for mapmaking. Sneaking into his library tonight, she'd feared discovery at every moment and worried as well that Bei might detect her use of the computational device to fashion a copy. Titus would need the correlates for a means of escape from the All. Or if not, perhaps to bring over a force of people to support him.

But Su Bei had larger matters in hand. "The veil has split apart," he said,

breathless. Back in the corridor, no globes lit their way. The candle Bei held
lit a ghostly path as he led them in a rush toward his library.

"The veil?"

"Yes! The veil of worlds, are you deaf? It split. It's gone, gone blank,
gone."

In the library, the shelves were in disarray where Bei had already been
stuffing their contents into packs. She went through to the veil-of-worlds
room, where the destruction of the veil was plain: it had burst, and from
behind it extruded a mass of viscous gel. Its push into the room had overturned stone well computational devices, no doubt ruining them.

"Help me," Bei cried from the library, and Anzi rushed back to him. An
unholy noise erupted from behind the wall, and it ballooned toward them,
shattering the shelves that lined it, sending scrolls clattering to the floor.

"Master, what's happening?"

"First the scrolls. In the packs. No, not that one, those!" He pointed
toward another shelf.

Anzi began shoving the live scrolls and loose-leaf manuscripts into the
nearest satchel. "A storm," he said. "It's raging up there. It began an hour
past and built to a frenzy."

"Wouldn't we be safer down here?"

"No, we're not safer! The minoral is cracking. Aren't you listening?" He
shoved an armload of material into another pack. "Go fetch the beku if you
can't pack. Bring them up from their stalls to the lift doors. No, bring them
down here and we'll load them. Now run, Anzi."

She dashed to the door and turned around. "But Master, how can the
minoral be cracking?" Nothing cracked in the Entire, much less a minoral, a
whole valley. How could it?

"We'll figure out *how* if we survive. I'll write a treatise! Now, by a beku's
balls, run!"

"If we're in a hurry, we should leave these scrolls."

"*Leave* them? My studies, my texts?" He was stacking scrolls in the
middle of the room, away from the debris of the bookcase wall. Already he
had a pile that would never fit on the two remaining bekus. "Off with you,
now." He thrust a lit candle at her.

Grabbing it, Anzi ran. The ground trembled, and a sift of pulverized stone fell in front of her. The tunnels were shifting. Underground was not the place to be, Bei was right. But what was it like *above*?

At the stalls, the two bekus were snorting and tossing their heads, eyes wild. Anzi managed to saddle the beasts, which settled them a little. Then she slipped on the bridles and led them from their stalls. Shying at the noises, the bekus yanked and fretted at the reins until they stopped at an unexpected turn to the inhabited section and refused to enter.

Anzi hauled on the reins, but the beasts got the better of her, pulling in opposite directions and making a freakish braying sound she had never heard before. She tied off their reins to a stanchion in the wall and pelted back down the corridor to the library.

Bei was hauling the great packs of scrolls, carrying more than he could possibly manage. "Where have you been? Where are the cursed bekus?"

"Master, the bekus won't come. Even if they did, they can't carry all this down the minoral."

"By the vows, I'll drag them here . . ." He peered down the corridor, and Anzi put her hand on Bei's arm. "Take the redstones with your treatise." She added, to hide her theft, "And the redstones with the correlates. We'll come back after the storm has passed."

"The correlates . . ." Bei said, looking stricken. He rushed to his table and took them out of a lacquered box. Anzi helped him thread them onto his scholar's necklace and he pulled it over his head. He eyed the stuffed satchels around him.

"We'll come back," she murmured. She gently tugged him down the passage.

When Anzi and Bei approached, the bekus reared up. "Shhh," Anzi crooned at them. "There, now, good bekus." She led them to their service lift, and they complied, with Bei following, silent and sober.

At the service lift, Anzi filled leather pouches with water from the stable spigots. The lift doors rattled as the conveyance came down to them and the doors opened. Bei moaned. "My studies . . ." She could offer no consolation. They had to leave while the lifts still worked. As they ascended the shaft, the ground through which they passed registered thundering and fractured harmonics, setting the bekus into a frenzy. At this rate, the beasts would never go into the storm.

The lift disgorged them into the small storage area. Here the turbulence of the reach surrounded them, barely muffled by the walls of the shed. Anzi knew immediately it wasn't a normal storm. The walls shuddered heavily and thunder barked from afar and then near. Although there were no windows, Anzi saw flickers from what she took for lightning firing up the deepest cracks in the adobe walls.

"Master, are we to travel in *this?*"

"No choice," he muttered.

The child's song came to her: *Storm wall, where none can pass/ Storm wall, always to last.* What lies we tell children, Anzi thought. You *can* pass through them. And they *don't* last. The lords were running out of fuel. The walls were powering down. The sickening thought hovered just out of reach: Maybe it wasn't just the minoral that was coming apart. Maybe it was everything.

Bei had himself under better command now, and he turned to her, hand on her shoulder. "Out, now, Anzi. We'll have to try." He took one beku's reins, and she the other.

Cautiously, she opened the door.

Ozone-laden wind blasted into their faces. The valley was in chaos. Around them, the storm walls, one on each side, roared and danced with lightning. Anzi's silks whipped against her and her hair danced with static. Converging in this narrow valley, the storm walls had always seemed ready to fight each other. For all that they were called *storm* walls, this was, at last, a storm worthy of them. It was a terrifying sight: as far as she could see down-minoral, the walls boomed and frayed with fire.

The pack beasts refused to budge. They brayed and squealed, digging in. Anzi gave a great kick to the rump of her beku, but it had not the slightest effect.

A splintering roar came from outside, flashing a spray of light onto the hut. Anzi spun around, squinting into the distance. There, a shape floated in the air. Something was approaching, or trying to. A sky bulb was coming in, but it wasn't going to make it.

"Su Bei! A sky bulb!" The dirigible was stopped, its mooring ropes whipping about. The airship floated crippled, perhaps struck by lightning.

"Yes, I see it. You want to ride closer to the bright than you need to, girl?" Bei was looking at the distant wedge of the sky, turned green and sickly, riven with lightning.

"Wait here!" she shouted and bolted out the door. Whoever was on that dirigible needed help to debark, or might be persuaded to leave again, with passengers. Sprinting across the intervening distance to the sky bulb, Anzi lunged for the nearest rope, grabbing it. She looked up to the hatchway, blown open and revealing darkness within. She'd have to climb the mooring rope. Wrapping her legs around the rope and pulling with her arms, she shinnied toward the hatch, her weight pulling the sky bulb over to one side. No help came from the gaping dark of the craft's doorway.

Reaching the hatchway, she crawled through. In lightning flashes she saw someone in the operator's chair, slumped forward. Making her way to the navigator, she found a dead Jout, a trickle of blood leaking from one eye. In the main cabin she stumbled over piles of baggage and supplies. "Anyone aboard?" she called.

No one answered, but she spied a passenger on the deck, lying in a heap. A Ysli.

The smell of charred flesh came to her nostrils. One of his boots had blown off, exposing a blackened and bloody foot. His eyes came half open, but he didn't register seeing her. She leaned in, "I'll help you."

Garbled words came from the Ysli's lips.

"Don't try to talk." She rummaged without success for a blanket, finally dragging a tarp over.

He swiped at her arm, grabbing on to her. "Su . . . Bei," he whispered.

"Yes. He's coming. You've arrived." She tucked the stiff tarp as best she could around him, trying to ignore the smell of cooked flesh lurking under his skin.

"Su Bei . . ." he said again.

She had no medical supplies with her and doubted even Bei would know how to treat the Ysli's burns. Rushing back to the navigator's post, she pulled the Jout's body away from the controls and tested the engine. It came to sputtering life. It might be dangerous to fly the thing, but if the storm worsened, speed might be an advantage.

At the hatchway, she waved wildly at Bei, who was still standing in the shed doorway. "Bring the water," she shouted, but her words were snapped away by the wind.

Back at the Ysli's side, she tucked the tarp more firmly around him, feeling helpless.

"Heart," he whispered. Anzi crouched lower to hear. "He bid me say . . . the Heart. Come all this way. For Su Bei."

"Yes, soon. First we have to get you to a safe place. What's your name?"

He waved at her in agitation. "Jaq. Ship keeper to Ghoris . . . the navitar. He'll block the way . . . to Heart . . ."

His eyes rolled back and he was silent a few moments. In growing excitement, Anzi considered that this ship keeper had come from a navitar whom she knew. Ghoris, who had once shown Titus a vision of the future.

He said, "Titus of the Rose needs Bei . . . to find doors."

Anzi bent closer to the injured sentient. "Titus?"

"Secret, all secret . . ."

"I'll keep your secrets. I'm his wife." Anzi put her hand on the Ysli's cheek so he could feel her presence. "I am Titus Quinn's wife. If you have a message, tell me now, for the sake of the bright."

In the faint gruel of light from the Deep Ebb sky, the Ysli's eyes glinted. He knew he was dying. She cupped his face with her hands. "I'm here with you, Jaq. You can tell me."

"Lords. They go home to Heart. Back and then forth."

He seemed unable to say more. Anzi hurried over to the hatchway, watching as Bei struggled to stay upright in the gusting wind, but finally making it to the flailing ropes of the sky bulb.

The nearest rope whipped out of Bei's grasp. She looked back at the wounded Ysli. To her consternation, he was babbling, and now she feared she had missed what he meant to say. She went to his side. "Tell me again, Jaq. And I will tell Su Bei, I promise."

His voice was weaker, but with great difficulty he enunciated, "Lords go home. To Heart. Titus Quinn will control doors."

She recognized that his words held great import, but she was having trouble concentrating. Ghoris—or Titus—had sent Jaq here to give Bei information. She scrambled back to the doorway, this time determined to help Bei climb up. She grabbed hold of the rope secured near the hatchway and swung out, holding on. Sliding down, she reached the ground and hollered for Bei to climb as she held it taut. The storm pelted them with fists of wind as Bei pulled uselessly on the rope, unable to haul himself up.

"I'll pull you up!" she shouted. Anzi yanked the rope around Bei's waist, tying it loosely. Then she climbed back up, managing to avoid kicking Bei in the face, and leaned over to pull him up. Useless. He was far too heavy. When he saw her struggling, Bei's face screwed into a determined scowl, and he began a feeble hand-over-hand climb, gaining inches. Anzi heard the Ysli moaning, but she couldn't leave Bei now. Gradually, Bei's old arms pulled him within reach, and Anzi leaned out, grabbing him by the armpits. They hung like this, with her arms loosing their strength, and Bei shouting for her to leave him. Then, with a supreme effort, she hauled one of Bei's shoulders over the lip of the entry. This brought the rope around his waist within reach. She seized it, and, with her last strength, pulled. Bei lay half in, half out of the sky bulb, and after a moment's rest, Anzi dragged him from the opening into the cabin.

They lay on the deck of the dirigible, panting and helpless. When she could move again, Anzi untied the rope from Bei's waist and hauled in the other mooring rope. She closed the hatch. A relative peace flowed over them, but now they were on a pitching and trembling deck. She noticed that Bei had thought to bring one of their water pouches, still anchored across his body with a strap. She uncorked it and gave him a sip.

He nodded at her. "Get us under way, can you?"

"Yes." A roar of thunder seemed to contradict her remark, but she staggered to the navigation station and turned the sky bulb around. Out the viewport, she judged her trajectory down the minoral and set the dirigible on its course. Daring to leave the steering, she tottered back to Bei and told him of the passenger and his message.

With her help, Bei managed to get to his feet and come to the Ysli's side. He was barely breathing.

"Jaq," Anzi said. "Su Bei is here."

Bei leaned closer to the Ysli. "Speak now, lad. I am Titus Quinn's oldest friend in the All. Tell me."

The Ysli's eyes fluttered. "Correlates. Su Bei a scholar. Find doors to Heart. Correlates find doors. Give them to Titus." He looked blindly up at Bei. "You see?"

"Yes, lad. I see."

Anzi hoped he did, because she didn't.

"Where is Titus Quinn?" Bei asked.

The fellow rallied his last strength to say: "He . . . is . . . Rim City."

Bei leaned closer. "Rim City is big, lad. Where might Titus Quinn be in the longest city?"

"Zhiya . . ." the Ysli said. He strained to say something, but his body, which up to now had been full of tension, fell slack. Anzi put her hand on his throat, feeling for life. But he was gone.

"What did he say?" Bei asked.

"He said, 'Zhiya.' She's a godder." At Bei's questioning look, she said, "I know Zhiya. She's a friend."

Worn out, Bei sat down heavily against the bulkhead, leaving Anzi in charge.

She pulled the tarp over the ship keeper's still form and made her way back to the navigator's bench. On her way, she picked up the water pouch and drank until she gagged. She was exhausted and dehydrated. But she and Su Bei were headed down the minoral.

An hour later they were still in progress. Bei and Anzi argued about ejecting the bodies to save weight and fuel. Anzi was horrified at the prospect, but eventually they agreed to let the Jout go. They opened the hatch and threw him out, the most sickening act Anzi had ever committed. Following the Jout went every piece of luggage and extra equipment that the dirigible contained.

But at Jaq's disposal, Anzi balked, and Bei could not prevail on her for a change of mind.

They motored on, with the storm walls booming insanely around them. As they passed a nascence, it erupted in a fountain of green fire. Hearing the explosion, Bei rushed to the viewport. "Gone," he whispered.

"They sometimes go," Anzi said, her voice quavering. The tiny lobes that jutted from the minorals were temporary places, but she'd never seen one evaporate. The storm wall moved in, closing off the juncture.

Bei eyed her. "Can you make this thing go faster?"

She shook her head. "Where are we? Which nascence was that?"

"Who bothers to name them?"

Anzi murmured, "If the minoral collapses, will it tear open the Entire?" Where the minoral joined the primacy, there was no barricade to staunch the leak into what undoubtedly was the black void.

"That is an answer," Bei said, "we are about to learn." He stared out the viewport for a long while, then sat on the bench next to her, watching their skittering progress down the valley.

"I should have brought my stone wells," he murmured.

"We'll buy them, or trade," Anzi said.

"Trade with what?"

"We have a dirigible."

"Which is not ours."

"It is now." She glanced at him. "What will you need computation devices for? To help Titus?"

He snorted. "Yes, to help Titus. No point in scholarship anymore. And it's a scholar's challenge, in any case. To find the doors. If there are doors."

The Tarig used doors for passage to their home. How Titus had learned this, Anzi didn't know. Didn't the lords live in the Entire? If they didn't, why would they choose to go back and forth to a home place? If they needed to do so for some reason, then of course Titus wanted to control those doors. If it was critical to the Tarig, then this was the way to force them to spare the Rose. But the Ysli's message was still coiling in her mind, not connecting.

"How will the correlates help?" she asked. It looked like Bei already knew the answer, and didn't like it.

"The Heart, girl. What universe is that? Not ours."

"The lords have said they came from the Heart."

"And just what did you *think* the Heart was?"

"Where the lords came from."

He smirked. "Yes. And where is that?"

"Well, if you know, Su Bei, kindly tell me."

"I didn't know, until now. But the only reason Titus needs the correlates to find the *doors*, is if the doors lead to another cosmos." Bei saw her questioning look. "The correlates can tell us how two places in different universes match up. And *when* they match up. But in the process, we also learn where each of the matching places *is*. You see?"

Bei stared out the viewport, the prospect of an adventure with Titus not yet galvanizing him. Anzi could understand. This minoral had been his home for tens of thousands of days.

"I could look for the doors," Bei said, "but not here. For that I must have access from other reaches, other primacies."

Lightning cracked the air nearby, sending the sky bulb careening. Anzi held her seat and grabbed Bei to steady him. The storm wasn't tiring; if anything, it was getting worse. "Master," she said. "I took something of yours."

Bei pursed his lips, watching her.

"I took the correlates to copy them so I could find Titus a way home." She had to look away. "I'm sorry."

Bei nodded. "I know you did." He gazed out the viewport, and his voice went soft. "Keep your copies, Anzi. It's always a good idea to have more than one set of valuable data. I presume you have them in a safe place?"

She patted her waistband.

"Well, then." They traveled in silence for a time, with the only sounds the thumping of wind against the sky bulb and the frequent thunder. Bei had already forgotten her theft, looking instead to what came next. "By the time I've looked for Titus's *doors* in each minoral in each primacy, I'll be too old for scholarship."

"I can come with you. I'll help you."

The minoral dragged by, sand and rock and storm walls squeezing in from each side. It seemed improbable they would ever get out of there, but they talked as though it would happen.

"I might need an assistant," Bei murmured.

"You'll need someone to secure a few stone wells."

"Yes. Someone good at *bargaining*." He looked around him. "This conveyance we might need to keep."

"I'm sure Jaq would have wanted us to have it."

"Are you, now?"

She shrugged. "Ownership is a fragile concept."

He pointed ahead. There, an unmistakable glow pierced the gloom.

"What is it?" Anzi breathed, leaning closer to the sight.

"Primacy."

They were coming to the end of the minoral.

It took another hour, but eventually the sky bulb motored into the flat basin of the colossal Arm of Heaven Primacy. There they were set free of the buffeting winds and Anzi brought the dirigible into one of a series of mooring masts staged at the entrance to the minoral. She shinnied down the rope and made the craft secure.

Once Bei clambered down, they used what means they had to make a shallow grave and laid the ship keeper into it, imploring the Miserable God to take no notice. They wrote a small paper grave flag: "His greatest voyage, up a minoral."

They slept for a time in the shadow of the sky bulb. When the minoral finally collapsed, the noise woke them. With the howling sound of wind through a pipe, the minoral seemed to stretch longer and thinner. As they watched, they couldn't know if the world was ending or preserving itself. Then the storm walls of the minoral fell away like evaporating foam. Anzi thought for a moment that she saw the void beyond the Entire. But in the next moment the primacy's great storm walls swept together like a curtain closing.

CHAPTER TWELVE

There are only three barriers to reconciliation: The past, the present, and pride.

—Si Rong the Wise

A S AN ENORMOUS HORN BRAYED, the longest parade in the history of the universe surged into the never-ending Way. Out into the fog-drenched streets came the citizens of Rim City, costumed in festive satins, masks, and headdresses. They were dressed for a mixture of veneration and revelry and for most there was no difference. With them came banners, kites, ropes of beads, jars of wine, cymbals, flutes, gongs, and bells, all pressing, banging, blowing, and ringing in general mayhem and the occasional impromptu riff. From more organized enclaves emerged painted floats, carts loaded with children, and caparisoned bekus ridden by as many revelers as could hold on. The massive fog banks that had nested over the lower Rim for so many days dampened few spirits; the bright gnawed at it, tattering it, throwing random scenes into spot-lit dioramas.

Everywhere around the shore, the dwellers of Rim City flooded into the Way. At the third hour of the third phase of day—a time all sentients knew by birthright, there being no clocks in the Entire—the Great Procession formed a complete circle around the sea. To anyone marching in the lower Rim today, it did seem that the line of revelers was never-ending, stretching to the limit of sight in both directions. At the bridges over the Rivers Nigh, the parade crossed over and streamed into the next primacy, with the marchers charged to walk and ride as long as the spirit moved them, with all homes open to those who might require rest before returning home.

One person was missing from the celebrants, but she had the best view of all. On a private balcony of the Ascendancy, the high prefect of the dragon court looked down on the Rim Sway. Cixi couldn't hear the braying of the processional horn, or even see the procession, except for the silent eruption of fireworks thirty thousand feet below.

It had been on a balcony like this one that, four thousand days ago, a young girl of the Rose had threatened to throw herself over the side. The girl didn't know what the Entire was; she couldn't conceive of what the Ascendancy was, much less the floating city or the great sea below. Sydney had looked at these sights, eyes wild. Cixi had coaxed her back, and the girl had come into her arms, clutching her with a ferocity that shocked the high prefect. No one had held Cixi for one hundred thousand days, and it loosened her, showing her that her heart was not dead. The girl and the high prefect began by sharing a secret hatred of the lords; soon they shared a bond very like a mother and daughter. And now Sydney was mistress of a sway. Incredibly, Rim City was celebrating the girl from the Rose grown to womanhood among the Inyx. As Cixi gazed at that portion of the city she could see from the under side of the Magisterium, she felt tears moving through her, though she was far too old to have any water left in her. Thank goodness they didn't spurt from her eyes. It was destructive of the makeup that took two hours to apply and would astound the functionaries of the Great Within, with its myriad clerks, factors, stewards, sublegates, legates, and preconsuls.

My dear girl, she mouthed through tiny, painted lips, and ordered the tears back down her throat.

In the Way itself, the processional chain was now formed, comprised of billions of inhabitants and their conveyances. No one would be indoors today. For one thing, the lords had decreed that the dwellers celebrate. For another, it was an event no wanted to miss, since becoming a sway was a great event in the history of the city. How anyone could hope to organize or govern such a place was a problem for another day. Rim Sway was an idea that caught on, gave sentients pride—so long as the girl of the Rose changed nothing, raised no new taxes, and got in no one's way, Rim City was happy to celebrate and drink to her health.

And the lords were watching to make sure they did.

Tarig were about, their tall forms glimpsed here or there, some of them wearing diamond nets on their skulls. Eddies of sentients gave way around them. Merchants and vendors here were used to Tarig presence, living as they did within sight of the Ascendancy, that brilliant mountain hanging above the sea. No event was too strange for Rim City, settled by people who had seen it all. Navitars did the city's bidding, giving passage to points on the great circumference. There was little that could impress a sentient who lived in this place at this time under the bright.

Nevertheless it was a hell of a party.

And Titus Quinn was in its midst, glad that the parade gave him an excuse to be where he was, glad for the obscuring fog. Joining the crowd of citizens going counterclockwise, as he thought of it, he made his way toward the mansion on the nearest bridge. In the press of revelers, it would take some time to get there. No one would remark that he carried a pack on his back, nor that his face was masked in paint. The Tarig were using the parade to flush him out, of course. And he was using the festivities for cover. So as to who was deceiving whom, it might be argued either way.

He cinched the pack straps more tightly around his shoulders and plunged into the crowd. Just off the square he was passing through stood the God's Needle he could see from his balcony. It looked like a lighthouse in a New England fogbank. At towers of worship like this sentients sometimes dared ask for the Miserable God's notice. No one ascended those holy stairs today. Far behind him the flotilla of Adda was mustering for a stately pass over the shoreline. The flock was led by an old behemoth so outsized she barely cleared the ground. Ahead of him, invisible in the fog, the crystal bridge.

The Sea of Arising, the center of the radial universe, was the mother sea of all the Nighs. Five rivers flowed out from the sea, down one side of each of the primacies. By its five arms the Nigh held the Entire into a coherent society. One could journey from the nesting forests of the Gond to the Reach at Ahnenhoon; the expanses of the impassible Empty Lands were no impediment; one need only a ship, a navitar, and an adventuresome spirit.

In his stall in the mansion on the bridge, this thought comforted Riod. By merely boarding a vessel he could be in the roamlands in but a few intervals. From his stall next to Sydney's quarters, he looked down at the disturbing sea. To be suspended over exotic waters made him uneasy and irritable. His hope to lead the great herd into the dream world of the Tarig was slipping from him. The herd circled near each night but could not find him. He had felt diminished from the moment he boarded the navitar's vessel and worse each day he spent next to the sea. Thus Riod had learned that an Inyx must never be separated from other Inyx. It was not enough to have his beloved rider nearby and his heart connection over distance with his herd mates. It was not nearly enough.

Deng, the Chalin servant assigned to Riod's care, came in, bearing fragrant grasses and making a new, fresh bed for the massive creature. Then he carefully emptied and refilled Riod's trough of water, doing everything as he had been instructed. Deng felt uneasy around this mind-snatching creature. He had learned a poem to say over and over that assured he would not leak secrets to Sen Ni's mount.

In the floors above Riod, the palace of the Mistress of the Sway was largely empty. Most of the staff of Sydney's residence and offices was gathered with her at the front terrace of the mansion, accepting acclamation from the Great Procession moving past. Sydney, on view by the masses, wore a red satin chemise over slim pants and embroidered slippers. Her hair was pulled back into a cinched band, making it appear as though she had long hair; Anuve had supervised her grooming with care. But Sydney knew her stature in the sway would change the moment her father was in custody. For this reason it was doubly worrisome that Riod was incapable of his nightly spying on the Tarig. He wasn't recovering from his bad trip by boat, and Sydney's goal of examining the Tarig weak points at close range was slipping away.

She hoped her father would not try to come to her today. The longer he delayed, the longer Riod would have to recover his strength. And the longer she would have to adjust to the idea that she would betray Quinn to the Tarig. She had told Anuve that she didn't care. Some days she wasn't so sure.

Feeling hot and confined by her clothes, Sydney kicked off her slippers to cool her feet. No one would notice that she stood barefoot, and if they did, let them complain.

Down the way came the next pulse of sentients: Here was a dragon, a silk-tented carapace with many feet carrying it along. The whiskered face jumped up at the sound of cymbals, and the bodies carrying the dragon skin danced and stomped. Sydney's household clapped and threw candies. For a moment, in the din of the parade, Sydney thought of Mo Ti. He should be here to see her in her role as Rim City mistress. In fact, she watched for him, thinking he might find her today. Had her father killed him or merely escaped him? And if the latter, then where was Mo Ti, and why hadn't he come to her?

A Jout in a puffy costume of yellow and red broke out of the crowd and approached the stairs separating the mansion from the Way. He rushed up the stairs, holding out a gift—a tasseled crown of good craftsmanship, if cheap materials.

Sydney picked up the golden tiara and smiled at the Jout, waving her thanks. But now she had a dilemma: should she presume to wear a crown, even this fake one? She turned to the window at the back, almost hidden from view. There the Lady Anuve watched without being seen. If Sydney declined the crown, then she'd insult the Jout and the merrymakers who surrounded him, half drunk though they were. She had a moment's pause as she considered whether putting on the crown might signal more of her plans than was terribly wise.

But she placed the tiara on her head. A burst of fireworks fountained into the sky, plowing a hole through the fog. In the dazzle of color streaming down, the crowd spilled up the stairs, trying for a better view. Amid the surge, Sydney noticed a strange person: a grinning and dancing dwarf with long white hair. Barging her way close, the dwarf thrust her stubby hand straight up at Sydney, saying quietly, "Read this in private if you want that crown for real." She pressed a note into Sydney's hand.

Then the dwarf laughed and pushed her way back to the procession, as Sydney's servants hurried to take control of the steps.

The many-legged dragon jumped and pranced, disappearing into the fog. The Jout in the puffy costume cart-wheeled behind it. The parade kept coming.

Tai stood at the base of the bony ladder leading to the belly of the Adda. He'd never ridden an Adda before, but neither had most of the people assembled on the wharf. He was one of thirty handpicked men who would ride the trailing ladders in the procession. It was the best-paying job he'd had in the three weeks since he'd resolved to better himself. Looking at the other riders, he knew why he was chosen: they were all beautiful and young, and like him, they were willing to exploit it. They were all dressed identically in fine green silk with square hats to match. He knew what Bo or Fajan would say: that he was corrupt to be part of a Tarig celebration. But the twelve primals he was paid for looking flash in a parade and riding the tail of an Adda was a fine start to his savings. A man doesn't go far without money in this world. And he certainly couldn't cross to the next world with nothing in his pockets.

His was the ninth in the line of Adda. Thirty celestial beasts were caparisoned with braided and jeweled rigging, tassels dangling close to their huge eyes, streamers tied to their cartilage ladders that formed the boarding steps. The great creatures floated in a firm line, tethered to the wharf, ready to set sail. Normally confined to riding the prevailing winds, today the Tarig provided a narrow stream of wind to take them along the coast in one direction, and then back along the same route to this staging ground.

Tai looked up at his Adda and found to his consternation that she was looking down at him. He bowed. She blinked, her pearlescent eyelids faintly green, her eyelashes long and coarse.

Shreds of fog obscured the forward line of the Adda where the lead behe-moth waited the signal to move. This was Beesha, an old favorite in Rim City, reduced these days to taking sightseers on sea outings, but beloved for her age and size. Tai would have loved to ride that one, but ninth in line was not haggish, either. He hoped to glimpse Sen Ni, she of the Rose, perhaps on her balcony. With luck, she might wave at him.

The Great Procession turned, and as it did, the fog began twisting away, evaporating under the bright.

In her quarters in the mansion, Helice felt dazed. She had only been in the world a few weeks; most of that time had been in the desolate tundra lands of the Inyx. Within a space of two weeks she had come to the center of the universe, almost under the shadow of the Ascendancy, and seen a fabulous city put on a display of grandeur. It was Mardi Gras, Chinese New Year, the Fourth of July—all magnified to Entirean standards.

As she looked out from her balcony, she saw in the distance a line of Adda approaching, the creatures of near mythical proportions that Quinn had described to her once and that had lived in her imagination ever since. She was here. She was standing amid all the glories that were the Entire. She loved it more than she could express. She was giddy with it. Happy, perhaps for the first time in her life. That stopped her. Hadn't she been happy? Testing savvy, rushing headlong through her doctorate degrees, climbing in the ranks of Minerva? No, never happy. Happiness was what she felt today: life's infinite possibility.

To make the day perfect, they would capture Titus Quinn. That would effectively remove Quinn from his position as the goddamned Christopher Columbus of the new universe. But even if he didn't come today, he was irrel-evant. He'd drowned the chain in the Nigh. That was the best thing he'd ever done. Maybe she didn't hate him quite as much as before. Any man who couldn't kill a whole world . . . but this was where she got into a bit of trouble. She planned to kill the Rose. So that made her a monster by most people's standards. Until you remembered that the Tarig were bloody well going to burn it with or without Helice Maki. They were, in fact, burning some of it right now, those little beta tests of the big engine, those little flash deaths of stars in a faltering Rose universe. Helping them hurry it up just a tad did not make her responsible for the fact that it was bound to happen.

She checked on the mSap. It was computing away, good little thing. She'd set it to detect electromagnetic spikes in the Ascendancy, thinking they might coincide with Tarig transfer points. But there were such profound turbulences here next to the storm wall that the mSap couldn't distinguish any pulses from the background fluctuations. Nor was Riod, the pathetic thing, doing any better with his side of it. Strange that a creature so massive should be the only one to sicken in the Nigh, though as to sickening, she had her own health worries. She put a hand to her face. The scabs still festered.

She patted the mSap. Keep going, she urged it. Once she had the transfer points identified, she'd have her security measures against the Tarig. They'd need to actually deal with her and not just dismiss her or kill her.

Replacing a wad of clothes on top of the mSap, she hid it again. The mSap would identify her as a foreigner. So far in the mansion she'd passed as Sydney's fellow rider Hei Ling; that fiction had to be sustained for a while longer.

The cap she wore to deflect undue notice of her baldness chafed today. She threw it onto her bed and ran a hand over her head, feeling a growth of fuzz. Going to the mirror in the commode, she used a razor to quickly skim herself smooth again. She allowed herself a closer look in the mirror, touching her face where the infection still lingered. It wasn't getting better. It was worse on her neck, but even her lower jaw now oozed in places. Helice had never been vain, but now she was worried. The burns from her crossing from the Rose had festered despite all the ointments and the ministrations of healers.

Pulling her scarf securely around her neck, she went to join Sydney. Mistress of the Sway against all odds, now the girl wanted to be queen. She hadn't a clue how unlikely that was. Perhaps Helice would let her keep Rim City, though. Remarkably, they seemed to want the same things. It had been a brilliant stroke to hook up with the girl. So long as she was malleable, Sydney might do well in Helice's regime.

Far below the mansion, on the river, a navitar vessel hung just outside the fogbank. From here the grand celebration looked ghostly, with fountains of skyrockets obscured and smeared by fog. Mo Ti looked up to the pilot house, seeing Ghoris staring out her viewports. Was she watching the Great Procession or some vision in her own head? Hard as she was to judge, he thought that lately she had been sad.

"Jaq," she had said one day when Mo Ti was bathing her. "Jaq"—and her eyes might have held tears. She missed the ship keeper. Jaq had been sent away by the mistress he loved and served. Mo Ti knew the pain of that. Sydney had sent him to kill her father, to prevent him from using the world-wreaking chain. Mo Ti had not done so, and worried that Sydney might see that as disloyal. Nor was this his only slip. Sydney had also found him withholding intelligence from her; she had unfortunately discovered that Cixi had been the one to send him to protect and advise her. But as high prefect of the Magisterium, Cixi worked in exquisite secrecy, especially among the mind-intruding Inyx. Add to all this, now Mo Ti had gone against Sydney in something she might never forgive. He had told Titus Quinn about the plan to raise the kingdom. He had told Titus Quinn about the Tarig doors home. It was a moment of trust, one that Sydney might never understand. It might do little good to tell her that Quinn had the means—the correlates—to find the doors to the Heart. If Quinn found them first, he said he would deliver the Tarig kingdom to Sydney. She might think Mo Ti a fool, or worse, to believe him.

He looked toward Rim City. The fog was parting, disappearing like soap bubbles left too long in the bowl. *Sydney*, he thought, as though his heart would burst.

On land the procession turned. The citizens were marching toward something, but the goal did not matter. What was important was to be on the Way at the moment all other city dwellers were. Most could not have said why it thrilled them to circumnavigate the sea; but few would have missed saying "I did the Great Procession on the first day Rim City was a sway."

A shower of candy hit Quinn as a float passed by. He waved at the acrobats performing their routines on a motorized float. It hummed by, wheelless, suspended a foot above the Way.

Suddenly at his side there appeared an outrageous-looking, very short woman. It took him a beat to realize it was Zhiya.

"By the bright, we are a sway!" she said, in the prearranged signal before disappearing into the oncoming procession. So, Zhiya had gotten the message to Sydney. It settled on him with a jolt that Sydney was nearby. She now held the note he had written in his own hand. He wanted to ask Zhiya: what does she look like? He would soon find out.

He was approaching the crystal bridge. He had been tracking the progress of the line of Adda that were sailing up the shoreline toward the mansion. Through the thinning fog he caught glimpses of the symbionts. Time to cut down to the Pearl Wharf. Everything now depended on timing, and Zhiya's man riding the Adda with the purple fringe, the man who was not afraid of heights. Quinn made his way down to the shore, his mind now on nothing but Sydney. *Show me that you still love the Earth. Child of the Entire you might be, but Earth is still your birthplace.*

And the Great Procession turned.

Firecrackers clapped out a long burst. Even deep in the mansion, Helice could still hear the cacophony of the parade crossing the bridge. She'd promised Sydney that she'd check on Riod, but now that she'd used the time to check on her mSap, she might just let that assignment go. A slight breeze hit her from a side corridor. Her scalp felt it. She'd forgotten her hat.

Turning back, she hurried down to the level of her quarters, just rounding a corner when she saw the Lady Anuve disappearing into the doorway of Helice's own apartment. She froze. Why would the Tarig bitch be in her room? She mustn't have time to search, to find the mSap. Helice rushed to the doorway.

It was too late. Anuve knelt beside the mSap, having pushed aside the heap of clothes covering it.

Helice swung back out of the doorway, pulse thudding, mind racing. How to explain the mSap? There was no way to explain it except for what it was. She would have to kill Anuve.

Not damn likely.

Helice found herself in a nearby room, pasted against the wall, panic banishing normal thought from her mind. She had to get the mSap from Anuve. The mSap was her only power in this universe.

She rushed to Sydney's quarters a few suites down. Empty. Everyone except Helice and Anuve was on the terrace. Helice stood in the doorway and screamed.

Ducking back into Sydney's room, she tore over to the windows over-looking the sea. She opened the casement and stepped through onto a small lanai, shutting the windows behind her and leaning against the wall. In a moment's assessment, she had her route planned out. First, she had to get from the lanai to the adjacent servant's quarters; a window ledge offered footing. She climbed onto it. Helice now stood hundreds of feet above the confluence of the Nigh and the sea with nothing to hang on to. Sidling along, praying Anuve would not look out the windows, she came to Riod's quarters. The windows were thrown open, blocking her passage. She flung them shut with her feet, crossing in front of Riod as he lay on his pile of straw observing her.

"Stupid, mind-sucking cripple," she thought murderously. "Die and get it over with."

Riod's voice smashed into her consciousness, though she willed him away from her. *Jump. That is the best way for you.*

Snarling her contempt, she passed on, scrambling finally onto her own lanai. She peered inside. Anuve was gone, having rushed off to investigate the scream. The mSap was still there.

Moving quickly, Helice jumped into the room and pulled her long scarf from around her neck. She cradled the mSap inside it. Grabbing her hat from the bed, Helice jammed back through the lanai doors, moving away from the window panes. She had the mSap. But no disguise, no money, nowhere to go. First things first. She had to get down from the bridge.

Deng rushed toward the sound of the scream. He was supposed to be waiting on the Inyx, but instead he'd been lolling next to a window to look at the procession. Clattering down the stairs to the residential quarters, he heard someone rounding the corner to come up. It was a Tarig. He crashed into her. She lifted him up by his shoulders.

"Did you scream, ah?"

Flabbergasted to be in the grip of a Tarig, he shook his head furiously. "I heard it, Lady."

She dropped him and, spinning around, strode back down the corridor, darting into rooms, one after the other. Deng was frozen in consternation. Who could have screamed? And why? The sight of a Tarig slinking and darting in the corridor filled him with a sickening fear. He trailed after Anuve, wanting to flee but understanding he must serve her.

The lady came out of one apartment and stood stock still. She drew a knife out of her waistband. Deng was going to die. She hurled the weapon at him. It landed at his feet, embedded in the floor.

"Find the woman Hei Ling. Search everywhere. Use any means to stop her from leaving."

"Yes, lady." He yanked the blade from the floor and went in the opposite direction from Anuve, piss running down his legs.

On the terrace, a team of acrobats passed by on a float. Sydney gripped the note in her fist, but she needed privacy to read it. The dwarf had referred to Sydney's ambitions. No one knew about those; no one should know.

The acrobats were wildly popular, bringing cries and applause from the onlookers. The servants on the terrace steps clapped gleefully. Anuve had been absent for several minutes from her post at the window. Now was the time. Sydney turned to the nearest attendant. "I will use the washstall."

She hurried into the foyer and into the nearest washstall. There she read the note; reread it. She leaned over the fountain, sick to her stomach. When the wave of nausea passed, she gripped the basin and looked into the mirror. He won't see me like this, she vowed. She splashed water on her face and straightened her hair. A woman in red stared back at her, eyes like dark wells.

Entering the great hall, she looked for Anuve. If the creature had been in view, she might have gone to her, shown her the note. Might have. But didn't.

She rushed down a back staircase to her apartment. She was going to do this. Stupid, stupid. But this wasn't just to see her father; he was, for the first time, offering her something. She wanted to consult with Riod, but there wasn't time.

Rushing into her quarters, she threw open the window to the largest porch on the Ascendancy side of the mansion. She turned to gauge the approach of the Adda. From out of a great bank of fog, a huge beast emerged. The lead Adda. She strained her eyes into the murk to see the one with the purple tassels. Still back in the line of beasts. She crumpled Titus's note and threw it over the railing.

The Adda bore down on the crystal bridge.

Tai's arm was weary from waving. He rode the pliable ladder, having hooked one leg around a cross bar. Holding on with one hand, he shamelessly waved at the citizens gathered along the quay, those who could pull themselves from the procession for a moment to see the great passing of the Adda.

The line of symbionts was riding low, perhaps lower than it ought if it was to pass properly before the mistress's review up on the bridge. The Adda just in front of his was particularly low, ruining the line of the procession. It was caparisoned in a purple headdress, dangling streamers and elaborate fringe. Now a man was rushing up to that Adda, trying to catch the ladder. To Tai's surprise, the green-clad rider in charge of the beast reached down a hand to him, helping him gain purchase on the lowest rung. For an instant, the two men clung to the Adda's trailing ladder, and then the beast climbed back to position, just as if it were all carefully planned. So, Tai thought: the rider in front thought to give his lover a ride in the fabulous Adda.

For a moment the two men on the purple Adda hung on, then one climbed into the orifice. The remaining rider turned for a moment, looking around him, and met Tai's gaze.

It felt like a punch in his midsection. Tai stared in a heart-stopping moment of incredulity. It was *he*. No. It was not. Looking more carefully, it was not. The face was not the same as the pictures . . . but in other ways it was. Tai had gazed so long at the likenesses of Titus Quinn that he knew him by face shape, by expression, by *essence*. By the Rose, Tai was sure. He found himself moving into a profound bow.

And on the other Adda, Titus Quinn bowed back.

With the mSap on her back, Helice had to face the building as she inched along the ledge on the outside of the mansion. Keeping her weight pressed forward, her forehead slid along the rough adobe of the mansion's facade, abrading her already sore face. By the time she got to the end of the building, she was frantic to find solid ground. Already, a Chalin servant had come looking out on one of the balconies; he hadn't seen her, but it wouldn't be long before someone did. Reaching the next balcony, she jumped down, sweating and frantic to hide.

She leaned over the railing to look at the bridge beneath her. A great superstructure held up the dwellings and the Way. If there was even as much as a thin girder to walk on, that was her way down. Pulling her cap more securely over her head, she sidled over the railing. Crouching on a plinth at the base of the lanai, she held on and took a closer look at the understructure.

Smooth and glassy. Well, she hadn't expected *stairs*.

Shadows approached through the fog. A giant Adda was lumbering down on her. Then she remembered: the parade of gas bags planned for that afternoon.

A noise from above. Someone had opened the door to the lanai. All they need do was look down and they would see her.

"Hnnn," came a sound from above.

Helice flattened herself on the ledge and craned her neck to look below. Just within reach, she saw a foothold and a handhold to pull herself under the mansion toward a fretwork of supports. She slid her foot in that direction. Bending her body double, she took hold of a strut with one hand, and then with all her remaining strength heaved herself to the new perch. To her profound relief, she heard a door closing above her. Anuve must have retreated inside.

Helice curled herself into a ball. Below her, navitar vessels bobbed on the sea. Someone pointed up at her, shouting. But it was the parade of Adda he noted, not her. A movement over her shoulder caught her attention. A few feet away Helice saw the hanging, cartilaginous ladders of the Adda sweep by.

Deng had found no one in his sweep through the mansion. Other Tarig were searching, the ones that had been hiding out of sight. Unsure what his next move should be, Deng returned to the residential quarter and was about to enter the mistress's suite when he heard the loud snorting of the Inyx. Diverted, he ran into Riod's stall and found the beast had hugely defecated in his nest.

Water, came the Inyx's thought. Deng would clean the straw later, but he took a moment to change the beast's water.

In the suite next to Riod, Sydney was waiting at the open doors, hoping that Riod could occupy the stable boy who might at any moment come looking in her suite.

The moment was almost upon her. Here came the Adda with the purple fringe, the ladder swinging low. It bore down on her. She lifted her hand, waiting. When it came over the balcony, the huge creature threw a cool shadow over her. A man with a painted face stood high on the ladder, crouching down, reaching out his hand.

Sydney grabbed the ladder as it swept along the balcony floor. She stepped onto it just as it began to rise again to clear the balustrade. She climbed, and the man above her climbed backward, still holding out his hand. He gained the entrance to the cavity, and then she took his hand, and leapt into the Adda's travel pouch.

The man with the painted face turned to the one other person inside, a man dressed in green silks, and said, "Climb into the sinuses, Yat Pang, I need privacy here." The man obeyed, but Sydney hardly noticed him leaving. The voice. It was her father's voice.

The line of Adda completed their pass of the Mistress of the Sway's mansion and went just a little further than they needed to along this route to find a place to make the huge swing around. Zhiya had bribed the leader of the Adda processional to take his time. Still, Quinn had only a few minutes to see his daughter.

"Sydney," he said, his voice deadened by the Adda's fleshy girth. "My face is altered. Do you know me?" Say that you do, he thought, not even knowing exactly what he meant.

She stared at him, wild-eyed.

And he stared at her. She was slender but athletic. She looked not at all like Johanna. Dressed in deep red silks, her face flushed, she looked both beautiful and fierce. Close-cropped dark hair, wide brown eyes. He knew better than to look for welcome in those eyes.

"Please sit," he said, kneeling on one side of the Adda's entrance orifice.

After a moment, she sat on her heels on the other side. Through the hole appeared the shoreline of the Sea of Arising, exotic waters foaming against the land. He wanted to reach out across the space between them, but he had no right to touch her.

"I've loved you all your life. I still do."

He saw a shadow of derision cross her face and hurried to say, before she could: "I was a prince of the city, but a hobbled one. I wore their clothes and ate their food, but they kept watch on me, never telling me where you were. But I lived under their roofs, and took my days from them. I failed to find you. I never forgave myself. It's the greatest regret of my life, Sydney. That I failed you."

Sydney's voice was grown up, a woman's voice: "I watched for you." Her face revealed nothing, not the slightest opening.

He knew she had waited for him. He didn't want to make an excuse, but he forced himself to say the truth: "I went home to tell the Earth that the Tarig will destroy them. I had one chance to go home to deliver that message. I took it. I had to."

She was still evaluating his face, tracing the changes. Whether she was disappointed that he looked like someone else, Quinn couldn't tell. "Heroic," she said.

He saw how this would be. Let her lash out at him, in anger, in sarcasm. It was what had to happen. But there was no time for the father, for the daughter. The Adda would soon be making the turn, and she had to get back to the balcony.

"You don't have much reason to care for the Earth."

"For the Rose? No. I don't remember it. There've been too many things . . . here."

"I've come to plead for it in any case."

A flicker went over her face. Maybe he should have said, I've come for you; come home with me. Just to offer it once. But he couldn't. He was here for the Rose. He saw how he must seem to her: the loyal soldier, the man without feelings. How far that was from the truth she might never understand. He wanted to say, I threw the chain into the Nigh. For you, Sydney. I gave up the Rose, and put it at the mercy of the Tarig.

He didn't say it; there wasn't any time.

Outside the orifice, Quinn could see that the Adda were swooping around to retrace their path.

"I know Helice's plan," he said. "I want her. She'll betray you in the end. I know her so well. . . . I don't expect you to believe me. But I'm going to stop her. Give her to me and I'll give you something in return. By God, I'll give you the Tarig."

An ironic smile. "They belong to you? I didn't notice that."

Her words were all measured and controlled. Oddly, amid this momentous discussion, he noticed that she spoke English with an accent. How strange. She spoke English with an Entirean accent. It slashed at him, somehow worse than anything.

She gazed at him with dead-eyed calm. There wouldn't be any recriminations, then. If she'd been angry, he could have begged her pardon. If she'd been sad, he could have let it cut him. But she had moved past him. There was nothing except to plod on and lay his offer out.

"The Tarig have a tie to the Heart, the place they came from. They return to it, perhaps to replenish themselves. I know they're altered beings. Pasted on to a living form. I'm going to cut them off from the source."

"Heroic," she said again, so cold and modulated.

"My God, don't you care at all?" It rushed out of him, misdirected and desperate.

"Care?" Sydney's face tightened, emotion in the corners. "I'd care if I thought you could cut them off. Then I'd care."

But not about Earth. Not about him. "I have a way. It's a gift given me from a Tarig lord."

"One of your friends."

After a beat he gave up the idea of arguing. "Yes, if that's how you want to put it. He gave me a key. I'll use it, and then I'll bring you to the brink of the Heart and you can do with it what you will." He watched her as she struggled to believe him. "In return, I want the Earth. I want Helice Maki. I won't let you burn the Rose, Sydney. I know you've suffered. But you can't help her kill the Rose."

"The only reason I'm listening to you is that you never used the weapon. You threw it in the river."

"What makes you think I did?" And how could she know that?

"We just know, that's all."

We. His mood fell grim. Helice knew. But by her silence, Sydney would say no more.

She looked out the orifice. The end of the bridge was coming into sight. "Yes, then." She rose. "You can have her. I'll trade you. Helice for the Ascendancy."

She stood on the brink of climbing down. She laughed, and she was bright and beautiful when she did. "I can't believe I'd trust you." Shaking her head, she crouched down, watching for her chance to descend.

"Mo Ti," he began, and her eyes flashed at hearing his name. "Mo Ti begs you to return him to service."

"Why should he hesitate?"

"He told me about Helice's plan—and, because I guessed the dreams of the Tarig were your doing, he told me of your plans as well. He's won me as your ally. If you'll have me."

"Mo Ti told you," she said. It sounded almost like an Eastern European accent. It made him sick that she was losing her hold on English. But it couldn't matter, it didn't matter.

"He may not return to service."

There, she had cut off Mo Ti, too.

"It might be hard to trust him anymore," she continued. "After he's been with you." She was casual with these cuts. She was an expert.

She looked closely at him. "They changed your eyes." He nodded, numb. "You don't look like yourself anymore."

"I hope I'm changed." That got a small reaction from her. But there was one thing more he had to say: "The Tarig lord. Lord Inweer. A few days ago he killed your mother."

She stared at him, still no expression.

"He beat her to death when he discovered she tried to help me destroy the engine at Ahnenhoon." She had a right to know that Johanna was dead. "You knew there is an engine?"

Sydney nodded, then looked down through the opening. Glancing back at him, she asked, "Are you coming with me, then? To take Helice?"

"Yes. Let me go first. I'll help you down"

"I don't need help." She descended.

They were coming in to the mansion. Quinn called up to Yat Pang in the Adda's sinus cavity. "We're ready!"

Yat Pang swung himself down. Sydney was already jumping from the ladder. Quinn scrambled down after her. The Adda was already rising to clear the balcony. Quinn grabbed onto Yat Pang, helping him jump safely.

They were on a large stone balcony, and the procession of Adda was sweeping by, returning to their staging ground.

On one of the Adda, Tai turned around to keep the people on the balcony in sight. They disappeared into the mansion. By the bright, he had just seen the Mistress of the Sway and Titus Quinn. He thought he had seen them. Other green-clad Adda tenders were also staring curiously at the scene of people climbing and descending the purple Adda's ladder. But none of them would realize what they had just witnessed.

Tai had been in the presence of Titus Quinn. He'd seen him help his daughter into the Adda and come back with her to her mansion. It was, at the very least, a conspiracy. And at its most significant, it was a glimpse of the passionate world that would one day be his: a world of heroes. Well, one thing he knew for sure. He wouldn't be able to question the tender of the Adda with the purple fringe. That man had debarked onto the balcony.

His heart expanding in his chest, Tai didn't long worry about that missed opportunity. He had seen Sen Ni. He had seen Titus Quinn. It was enough for one day.

On the great understructure of the bridge, blood dripped from Helice's hands, making her progress slippery and slow. She straddled a glass strut and, hunkered over, pulled herself along it, pressing with her hands lest she move too fast. The strut sloped down. The understructure of the bridge was smooth and empty except at the sides, where an enclosed trough conveyed what Helice imagined was waste water down to the bridge's footings on land.

The crystal edges of the trough tore at her fingers. She let herself rest when it became apparent no one was following her. She held on to a cross piece that joined the trough, hugging it. Halfway down now, she was closer to the confluence of sea and river, and could pick out individuals on navitar vessels. There was little reason to be on a vessel when the action was in the great Way, but one boat lingered. On its deck stood a massive Chalin man.

This one she knew. It was Mo Ti. He wasn't looking at her, but rather straight up to the pinnacle of the bridge. Then the ugly suspicion came to her, that Mo Ti and Quinn had formed an alliance. Against all likelihood, Mo Ti the faithful had become Mo Ti the traitor. Because who could he be waiting for other than Titus Quinn? Her soul darkened at the thought that Mo Ti had told Quinn secrets. Her secrets. Oh, the damage done, if Quinn knew! She carefully made her way around the cross-fret and straddled the trough once more, pulling herself along.

In the mansion the servants turned in unison as Lady Anuve burst out the doors and onto the terrace. Her face was terrible to look at. Everyone went to their knees.

"You will find her," she said in her low, even voice. "Now."

"Who, Bright One?" one of them managed to say.

"Sen Ni, your mistress."

The servant turned in the direction of the stairs. Sen Ni stood at her post, stopped in the action of throwing candy to the crowds. "Bright One?" she said. She kept her face calm, despite her desperate circumstance. Titus Quinn was on the premises. Helice, however, was long gone. This dark news had come to her as soon as she had led Quinn and his servant into Riod's stall to hide. She'd hoped to lure Helice to the stall, but those plans quickly collapsed. Riod was waiting with the news that Anuve had found Helice's little machine and had been stalking Helice through the mansion. Helice had fled.

Sydney watched as Lady Anuve strode toward her, raking the environs with a quick gaze. "You are here, ah?"

"Yes, Lady."

"And your servant Hei Ling?"

"I sent her to check on Riod. He's been ill."

"And left your post as well, hnn? Some time absent, so we are told."

"Yes, I threw up my morning meal. Too much candy. Or excitement."

Anuve paused for a moment, then rushed back into the mansion.

In his stall, questing his mind into Sydney's, Riod heard the exchange between her and the Tarig female. He turned now to Titus Quinn and his helper. *She comes. The fiend called Anuve.*

Quinn knew he'd failed. Helice was gone. And she had taken with her that very useful tool: an mSap.

"Riod, where has Helice gone?"

She is hiding. Amid the city.

"Where?"

She is there, with everyone in the Way.

Yat Pang was already opening a pack, pulling out the repelling rope. He opened the window off Riod's stall and scanned the outside balconies. "Now," he said. Yat Pang secured a loop around the railing.

Quinn went to the balcony door and turned back to look at Riod. "Thank you for caring for her when I couldn't."

She is Riod's heart.

Quinn heard this with a mixture of gratitude and envy. He nodded at Sydney's great protector. Then he motioned for Yat Pang to go first.

"Riod, can you sever the knot on the rope? Let the rope drop over when I'm down?"

Yes.

Quickly checking for anyone out on the porches, Quinn slipped to the railing. He noted the ship beneath him and Mo Ti holding the end of the rope, stabilizing it. Yat Pang was almost down. Quinn climbed over the rail, grasping the rope. He prayed Riod would untie it, erasing the evidence of their route. Down he went in a controlled slide, the rope jammed between his boots.

As Quinn reached the deck, Mo Ti signaled Ghoris to put the craft under way. The rope fell down next to the ship, coiling into the silver waters.

PART III
UNDER
THE
NIGH

CHAPTER THIRTEEN

Behave prudently to be considered wise; Act with decorum to be thought prominent. Thus you may enjoy the virtues in advance of having attained them.

—from *The Twelve Wisdoms*

R IM CITY CELEBRATIONS CONTINUED IN THE WAY, now spreading to side streets, squares, wine dens, and homes. Sometimes Sydney thought she heard remnants of the celebration, but confined to her quarters, she was shut off from the city.

With Helice exposed and Sydney blamed, all pretence of Mistress of the Sway had evaporated. Lady Anuve began her punishments by quartering Riod in an outbuilding, separated from Sydney. His sendings still came to her, but weakly, given his sickly state.

The other punishment she had been lucky to survive.

On Sydney's balcony Anuve had directed two Tarig to lift Sydney onto the railing. Below her, the sea, a thousand-foot drop. One on each side of her, the mantis lords had held her hands, keeping her balanced and facing Anuve, who sat in a nearby chair.

"One trusts the riding of Inyx gives you strong legs. Tell us, small girl. All your plans, each detail."

The wind off the sea had rippled Sydney's silks, causing her to shiver. She had never held hands with mantis lords before. Their bony grips were not as tight as she would have liked.

"You may begin."

Sydney admitted she'd hidden Helice under the guise of the servant, Hei

Ling. Admitted that Helice possessed a machine sapient, a piece of technology that seemed to disturb Anuve, by her close questioning on the subject. Sydney could not accurately describe the quantum sapient's powers, but she knew that at least at one time the mSap had created a nano assembler. Or the nano assembler had created the computer.

Anuve's aspect darkened. "My cousins tire. Perhaps one of them will rest, ah?" The lord on her right released her hand. Sydney wobbled. The other Tarig provided just enough balance, though his grip was not tight.

Sydney admitted everything. She admitted that Helice had performed a medical procedure on her eyes, removing the Tarig capability to see through her eyes. Their plan to spy on the Inyx thus had failed because of Helice, and Sydney felt a pang for offering to deliver her to her father.

She split her attention between Anuve and the long drop at her back. She was afraid, but loathing steadied her. To Sydney, Anuve was the same as Lord Hadenth who had blinded her. They were all one fiend, mingling their consciousnesses in the Heart. She wondered if individual memories of Tarig outlived their bodies. When a Tarig died and the body was not recovered, as was the case with Lord Hadenth, then surely those individual memories were lost. Despite such logic, she preferred to think of Anuve as Hadenth, to keep her hatred fired and her feet steady.

"Why has Titus Quinn not come to you?"

"He might still, Bright One. Maybe he suspected the celebration was a trap. But he'll come." He was reliable at showing up when it suited him.

Anuve failed to ask one question, however: *What is the Inyx role in the traitorous dreams?*

Some things were still secret.

After the questioning on the rail, Sydney had been confined in Riod's stall. Seeing it empty, she'd had time to worry that he was dead. After several hours the servant Deng had come to give her a blanket and tell her where Riod was. The doors of Riod's room were locked, but the blanket and the information led her to believe that Anuve would not kill her.

Sydney closed her eyes, remembering the great Adda approaching the balcony with their ladders trailing down. She saw her father sitting opposite her in the belly of the Adda. Things she would have liked to say to him! But the words wouldn't come, nor was there time. He should have spoken first, but when he asked for forgiveness, his words were of duties to the Earth. She wanted him to tell her *why* he'd left her. She wanted him to describe how he had been as much of a slave as she, no matter if he wore silks and drank Tarig wine—she knew a slave could be coddled—and how he had tried to come for her, even if he never could have.

Instead, he sat across the gap in the Adda's belly, saying *I can't forgive myself. I failed you.* And then it was all about saving the Rose. He'd give her everything, just help him save the Rose. That was their reunion.

And now he was her ally, she supposed. They shared an enmity toward the Tarig. But did they have an agreement, despite her inability to deliver Helice? And if he was successful in uncovering the Tarig doors home, would he want to keep control? Never mind: Despite all good sense, she had decided to trust him.

A noise at the door. Lady Anuve entered. Her metal skirt hung around her legs like a melted ingot. Her short jacket was a simple but elegant quasi-leather jerkin.

Sydney rose, brushing straw from her clothes.

"Does the stall please you?"

"I'd like it better if Riod was here."

Fireworks lit up the windows for a moment. Out on a navitar vessel, someone must have set off a display. The celebration would go on for days yet.

Anuve glanced at it too. "The festivities are much more than one anticipated. Rim City celebrates large."

"Lady, you told them to, I think."

"Not all Tarig rules are obeyed."

Well, yes. Was that irony in Anuve's voice?

Anuve went to the balcony doors and opened them, gazing out at the sea. "Where will the creature Hel Ese go?"

"She has no friends here; perhaps you'll catch her in the streets."

Anuve stood very still, letting the conversation lapse. When she turned around, she said, "We will send you home, small girl. We are ready to do so. Go, if you will."

Sydney stared at her. What was she saying?

"We do not lie to you. The Earth is your home place. One can send you there. But if you choose not to go, you may remain here as Mistress of Rim Sway. The condition is that you do not house fugitives or behave as a witless child from the furthest primacy. You must rule the sway in our behalf and with honor."

"Bright Lady, why would you send me home?"

"Hnn. Perhaps we tire of you." Anuve tilted her head, watching her carefully. "You create disorder about you, as does your father." Her expression hardened, if that was possible in such a spare face. "But this is not our primary motive. There is the matter of terrible dreams.

"In our perfection, we do not dream, but sleep in perfect calm. However, one's stewards and trusted counselors dream. Thus we know of things dreamt of. It is peculiar to us that when you sleep things come into your minds unbidden. Is that not an unwelcome intrusion?"

Voice steady, Sydney answered, "We are accustomed to it."

"But these dreams are different, so we are told. One wonders if this may be some ingenious scheme of the Paion."

"I do not know, Bright Lady."

"The dreams are constructed so as to make the Tarig appear, how would one say—evil? You dream thus, ah?"

"Everyone does."

"The dreams say that Tarig do not live as other sentients. That the gracious lords persecute the dwellers of the land, casting them, for example, into needless war at Ahnenhoon. You believe this, Sen Ni?"

Making an appearance of some candor, she answered, "I have wondered."

"So must others wonder. It is for this reason that we will free you."

Sydney was not following; the tension of the last hours had used up her reserves. She concentrated very hard as Anuve continued.

"The realm is tending against us. We like not to be seen thus, we who have been radiant lords for archons of time. Some days ago you, along with mother and father, came to us as intruders. As was our right, we kept you from spilling our secrets to the Rose. Now, however, the Rose has come into knowledge of the Entire. This cannot be undone. Therefore there is no harm for you to go home. And we wish for our subjects to know you have this freedom. If you choose to stay, it may offer a proof that you prefer us to the Rose."

Propaganda. They wanted her for propaganda. But, amazingly, it was still an offer of freedom, no matter which one she chose.

"We have caused you to suffer from time to time. But now is a different time. If you stay, you will be as free as any sentient." She lowered her already bass voice even further. "Now answer: Do you wish to go home?"

To Sydney's chagrin, she found her throat tightening, her eyes swimming. After all these years, she could return to the Earth? It was unthinkable to cry in front of a Tarig. She concentrated on being a stone.

"Do not answer with what you believe one wishes to hear."

Sydney thought of all the days when, as a child, she had dreamed of home and longed for it. Gradually her dreams became larger. But still: Earth. The word possessed a power that greatly surprised her. As to *home*, it had a different meaning. She might have lingered over this vital question. But she didn't need to.

"No."

Anuve turned her head to the side, fixing her with that awful one-sided Tarig stare. "No to what?"

"No to leaving. I will stay."

Anuve paused, absorbing this. Perhaps this was the lady's chance to redeem her failure in the matter of Titus Quinn. Sydney didn't care.

"In all truth you prefer to remain?"

Oh, yes. Even if just a rider in the roamlands. Even if just alone with Riod on the steppe. And if, at the feet of the Ascendancy, they wanted to give her a sway, still yes. She knew where home was: under the bright.

Sydney nodded her confirmation. There was no going back to a home that she'd already forgotten and where Riod couldn't follow. And there was still the kingdom to raise.

Anuve almost smiled. "My cousins will be surprised." Giving Sydney another moment to change her mind, she finally led her out of the stall and into the mansion's precincts.

As they passed into the corridor, Sydney thought she detected Riod's ghostly sigh of relief.

Quinn was alone in the city. Crowds still pressed into the Way, jostling and raucous. He moved clockwise against the current, knowing from Riod which direction down the underside of the bridge Helice had taken. Knifing through the throng, he watched. She was short: an advantage in a crowd. To conceal her dark hair, her head would be covered. Two other markers: a deeply scarred neck—surely covered up—and, less easy to conceal, she would be carrying something large.

He quelled the urge to run. She could be walking to avoid drawing attention, or holed up somewhere along this route. If she had found a place to hide, he would never find her. His only chance was to search in the Way, to locate her before she found shelter.

Down a side street he saw a wharf. A navitar vessel loaded passengers at the dock, and he turned down that corridor but stopped at the view of a Tarig inspecting passengers. Inconspicuously, he reversed his course. Helice wouldn't take passage; she wanted to be close to the Ascendancy to detect the Heart doors. Mo Ti had revealed this. Control the doors, control the Tarig. Unfortunately she was in the best position to find them. She had the mSap, and if it was a fully functioning one, it possessed nearly limitless computing power. In the hands of a brilliant machine sapient engineer like Helice Maki, it was the queen of chess pieces.

He clutched his knife close to him. He would kill her in the street. No more hesitation. Although he should learn the location of the Rose engine from her before she died, he wouldn't pause for that. He couldn't trust any-thing she told him at knife point, anyway.

He moved on, scanning, his senses alert for Helice, for the essence of Helice: small, dark, and vicious.

He'd had one chance to catch her off guard. Now he'd driven her to ground. Much as he hated to think it, this might be the time to call upon his one great unused resource: Lord Oventroe, the one who claimed he wanted to preserve the

Rose. The lord was devious and secretive, and Quinn still raged in his heart over his lies about the cirque; his claims that the chain had merely limited destructive powers. By this lie, he'd almost manipulated Quinn into destroying the Entire. So that it would have Quinn's signature on it. So that the lord could be blameless among his *cousins*. Oventroe was not merely a friend of the Rose, he was a fierce partisan on behalf of the Rose. Why, was the question.

Without knowing the answer, he couldn't get help from Oventroe. And Su Bei. Where was he? Did he labor at his reach, searching for the Heart? Even if he'd had success, the scholar would likely arrive too late, unless Bei was on the way at this moment.

There was no help; only himself. He paused, heart racing. He hadn't eaten for hours.

A foodery across the Way. His feet went in that direction, where he found an empty seat. He sat, bought food.

It was difficult to grasp that he had just seen his daughter. His new daughter. The one who had grown up beautiful and wild and cold. She had moved past him. In that, she was like her mother: *Find your own life, Titus*, Johanna had said. *I have.*

Johanna's face morphed into Sydney's: *Heroic*, his daughter said with that look of contempt.

After all the years of separation, it was ugly. After their shredded lives, he got a twist of a smile. *I can't believe I'd trust you.*

In the Way, the late floats lumbered by. A beku adorned with headdresses, bells. A contingent of Red Throne parishioners—banners showing a fat, misshapen navitar looking beatific. Well, Quinn himself had touched the mystery of the navitars and would have knelt to one right now if he thought a Nigh pilot could provide answers.

The plate before him was empty. He didn't recall eating.

In the street, a phalanx of Jouts marched by, their scales shining in the full bright, now freed of the low clouds that earlier had ghosted over the city.

He barely saw the Jouts. Instead: Sydney looked into his eyes and said, simply: *I watched for you.* That was the worst thing she had said.

On the other side of the marching Jouts, a green silk hat, just visible over the marchers; a glimpse of someone carrying a backpack.

He took a long drink of water. His muscles ached from the long shinny down the rope.

In another instant, he jumped up. The table clattered over, spilling plates.

Quinn rushed out the door, finding himself in the middle of the Jout formation. A woman carrying something on her back. Where was she? He couldn't see the green hat amid the marchers. He reached into his short coat and pulled the knife. Ramming his way through the Jouts, he found Helice—it must be her—kneeling on the pavement, adjusting a makeshift sling on her back.

Now to kill her. Don't think about it. He drew back the knife.

She turned in that instant. Yes, Helice. Incredibly, she had a gun. She fired.

He was on his back in the street, sprawling among heavy feet, dancing out of his way. After a few moments pain kicked him, hard and insistent. She'd got him point-blank. Where was she—amid the feet and the robes of the marchers—was she coming in to finish him off?

He dragged himself to the nearest wall, intending to stand if he could, to draw his knife before she came back at him . . . where was his knife?

A man dressed in a long sleeveless coat crouched down beside him. "What happened? Fireworks went awry?"

"Yes. Help me stand." The stranger did, putting Quinn's arm over his shoulder.

Quinn looked for Helice. There she was, lurking just a few paces off, gun hidden in the folds of her pants. The man was between them.

She walked toward him, raising her weapon.

Quinn's helper saw blood seeping out of the wound. Alarmed, he turned toward the street, calling, "Tarig!"

The shout froze Helice in place. Immediately, she backed up and disappeared into the crowd.

Turning back to Quinn, the man said, "We'll get you healing."

"No need for Tarig assistance," Quinn managed to say. "But I thank you."

"Nonsense, you are bleeding. Be assured, I am of the Red Society and will help you."

Quinn watched for Helice, but she was gone. "By the Navitar's Mind, will you do me a service?" At the invocation, the man nodded. "Find Zhiya of the godders. Ask her to come. I have no ill will against the gracious lords." Through a haze of pain, he forced himself to make up: "My father fell to their hands for his crimes. . . . I fear them still. You understand?"

A nod. The Red looked askance at the blood on Quinn's jacket. "You will need a healer."

"Find Zhiya for me and I will bless you."

The Red hesitated, not liking the situation, but at last he agreed and turned away to his promised task.

After a time, Quinn decided he was too exposed in the Way. He managed to walk, very slowly, to a side street. Within a few steps the crowd thinned. Leaning against a wall, he slid down into a sitting position.

By the time Zhiya came, a pink froth was collecting at his lips. A hit to his lung, then. Helice had proven herself a terrible shot.

CHAPTER FOURTEEN

He who rides a Gond is afraid to dismount.

—a saying

A SMALL AND INCONSEQUENTIAL SCHOLAR knelt before the high prefect in her audience chamber. Alone with the man, Cixi had heard his report with growing astonishment and distress. Now, leaving the scholar with his head pressed to the floor, she moved to her veranda, staring at the lords' hill of mansions.

She made sure her expression betrayed nothing of her inner turmoil. When Cixi stood on her balcony, a hundred functionaries watched from their own balconies and windows of the Magisterium. Her heart racing, she calmed herself by taking in the superb view of the fiends' elaborate city.

While complex, the layout of the Ascendancy could be reduced to a simple rule: The lords dwelled above, all others below. The floating city was a sphere cut in half, with the rounded bowl oriented down. In this bowl resided the seven levels of the Magisterium. In the upper realm, the Tarig had created a hill on one side. There, the lords' greater and lesser mansions clustered, looking down on the great plaza.

There was a chasm in the Bright City from which offices of the Magisterium could look up to the top structures of the city. Of course, the lower one's rank, the lower a functionary's level in the Magisterium, and the worse the view.

An enormous plaza footed the palatine hill, a space adorned with canals and small bridges. Punctuating its expanse were enormous uninhabited towers reaching almost to the bright itself. These columns were said to have a defensive function; one could not help but think they related to the bright itself. Among them was the tower of Ghinamid, named for the Sleeping Lord, the one who never woke in all the archons since early time.

Perhaps, given what Cixi had just learned, the lord would consider getting out of bed.

Out of the mouth of this man named Zhou had come a tale to stagger even the high prefect, who had heard one hundred thousand days of shocking things.

Zhou, it seemed, had been banished from the minoral where the scholar Su Bei lived. To be dismissed after such long service, when the two scholars had grown old together, was too much for him. His revenge was to bring intelligence to Cixi that would destroy his master. Zhou's story was that a lord of the city— one of the ruling Five, no less—had given away the key to the doors between the realms of light and dark. A messenger had come to Bei and put into his hands this great secret, one that Cixi had heard of but did not herself possess.

Su Bei obviously thought that the nature of the gift was secret. But the messenger had taken a cup or three of wine with Zhou and implied he'd come from a high lord. In fact, and by the fourth cup, *Lord Oventroe.*

It could hardly be believed. Was Lord Oventroe, then, a traitor to his own kind?

Zhou had found himself motivated to look at the redstones, and with great stealth used them, concluding that they were the fabled mathematical keys that could be used for going *to and from.* The correlates. Cixi had always assumed that they were myth. Perhaps they were not.

As she questioned the scholar, it became clear that Su Bei was in league with Titus Quinn. She learned how Quinn had hidden at Bei's reach when he had returned to the Entire the first time. Thus it might be concluded that Su Bei was holding the correlates for Titus Quinn. From there, it was a simple leap to understand that Lord Oventroe had allied with the man of the Rose.

Her mind wound in a tight skein around this shocking conjecture. If it was true, using this information would require her most delicate machinations. It was a story that should be brought to Lord Nehoov. But Cixi hesitated. Once Oventroe knew that she had moved against him, Cixi herself would be at risk. This would take a great deal of thought. She turned from her balcony's view and walked slowly back into the hall, her high-platformed shoes echoing off the smooth stone walls and floor.

Zhou was whimpering from the strain of the position of obeisance. She left him in that position while she considered.

If his accusation was true, what did the lord's support of Titus Quinn portend? What could possibly be Lord Oventroe's intention? If he was aligned with Quinn, he must secretly be aiding the Rose against the Entire, though how this could be was beyond Cixi's imagination.

"You may rise, Zhou."

With great effort he wobbled to a standing position. He had scarcely any hair left, and he was as thin as a dragon's whisker.

She should hurl him from one of the thousand balconies of the Magisterium. He was privy to things he shouldn't know, and now he could reveal to others that Cixi knew them. But murder was forbidden in the realm. She, least of all, could break the vows, laws, bonds, and clarities. Those of low status always got that piece wrong, thinking that the powerful could do what they liked.

"Zhou. I have a dilemma. Help me to resolve it, and I will thank you."

"Yes, Your Brilliance," he stammered.

"On the one hand, you are a repugnant traitor, helping the most virulent enemies of the bright realm. On the other, you have brought to the lords' attention a most foul crime that without you might never have been discovered." She leaned toward him. "What should the high prefect do with you, in all justice?"

"Advance me to legate. And punish Su Bei."

Yes, you want that faithless master to fall, don't you? She could empathize with such thoughts after all these thousands of days staring out at the palatine hill.

She sucked on her teeth, drawing the moment out. "I think I cannot trust you here in the Great Within after you gave refuge to Titus Quinn. The punishment for treason is the garrote. This you know, scholar."

"Great Cixi! Please. If it hadn't been for me, you would never have known." He fell on his knees. "I throw myself on your powers, your brilliance, your mercy, your—"

Cixi waved him to silence. "But such a late confession, after how many arcs? No, I think you will fall at the Tarig's feet. Yes, this seems fair."

"I am old to die such a way, Your Brilliance. By the Woeful God, I beg you."

"Mmm." She let him wait. Looking down at her index fingernail, she tapped it twice, blanking the scrolling words, her functionaries clamoring to talk to her. She tapped again, summoning her most trusted legate.

At the sound of the gentle hooves of her Hirrin attendant's approach, Zhou winced, as though hearing his executioners.

Cixi whispered to the Hirrin, "Give him a weight of primals and send him from the Ascendancy. He is never to repeat what he told me here. Make him understand that he is fortunate to have escaped my wrath. Make him love me, in other words." One needed a friend now and then, both the high and the low.

The Hirrin bobbed her head in obedience. Then she walked up to the cowering Zhou and kicked him with a hoof. The scholar was persuaded to rise and follow the legate from the room, leaving behind a puddle of sweat.

Cixi took her place on her chair of office, shifting her feet on top of the stool that kept her jeweled shoes off the floor.

Before all else she must have her spies bring Su Bei to stand before her and tell what he knew. Zhou also had said that Bei was harboring Titus Quinn's helper, Ji Anzi—a girl who styled herself a niece of Yulin, the disgraced former master of the Chalin Sway. A minor fugitive, this one, but perhaps a fount of knowledge about Quinn and his plans.

Likely both she and Bei were dead, however.

Bei's minoral had just been culled from the All. As had all the minorals of the Arm of Heaven primacy.

Reports were already flooding in to her of the collapse of the minorals. It was a tragedy of the highest proportions, naturally, and one the lords undertook with reluctance. It would take a long while for the news to travel, for the extent of the holocaust to be known. Cixi would declare herself as shocked as anyone, but in fact she had had advance warning from the Five. They had now closed all doors to the Rose. More to the point, they had closed all doors *to the Entire from the Rose.* To make sure of this, they had severed the minorals in the Arm of Heaven primacy. Minorals in other primacies were spared, since they did not access the Rose.

Maiming the primacy was an act of desperation. But the lords were alarmed. Ahnenhoon had barely averted a Rose attack; the evil dreams were now open knowledge; all sentients knew—or thought they knew—that the lords were not normal creatures of birth and death. These were anxious times.

While the Tarig were her enemies, Cixi certainly wished for them to succeed in securing the Rose as fuel. If Lord Oventroe was thwarting this worthy cause—as he must be if he thought the Rose had a future—then she must report him. All in good time. Meanwhile she must investigate whether Su Bei and Ji Anzi, against all likelihood, yet lived. She would dispatch her operatives to the city of Na Jing, near the minoral in question. A little quiet probing might quickly set the matter to rest. If the correlates were burned to cinders along with Su Bei and the girl, then it was all to the good

Sydney curled by Riod's side as he lay crumpled on the straw. She had decided to spend her ebbs with him in his stable at the far side of the crystal mansion. He was worse than two days ago when she had last seen him, and her anxiety mounted by the increment. She would have sent him home to the sway if he had been well enough; but it would be dangerous for him to travel in this condition.

He had been sleeping for several hours. When Deng came to bring him fresh water, Sydney motioned the steward away. Whenever anyone except Sydney came into the stable, Riod thrashed and sent chaotic thoughts to her.

Best mount, she thought fiercely, trying to soothe him.

Deng put the bucket down and backed away.

People had to obey her now. She was Mistress of the Sway in truth. She'd tested this a few times, once even going into the city without a Tarig escort. She'd bought a delicacy of goldweed thistles for Riod to eat, and he did nibble at them.

Her hand caressed the broad plane between his eyes and down to his nose. *What can I do for you, my heart?*

Riod's eyes came open. *No water*, he sent.

He really must drink, but he sent the message with such force, she sat up, alert.

The Tarig lady pours.

"She's in the house. I'll pour for you."

His head sank back onto the straw, trailing the thought, *Tarig lady pours bad water. No water.*

Sydney's mind began racing. Slowly, she came to her feet and walked over to the bucket Deng had left. "Is this bad water?"

Riod lay immobile. She waited, knowing he was awake but too weak to think straight. Then it came into her mind, that clear, familiar touch of his voice: *Water has poisons. Deng brings bad water.*

The bucket occupied the floor in the middle of the doorway. Sydney stared at it with growing fury. With a violent kick, she toppled the bucket, dumping the water out on the pavement. Then she hurled the bucket away, smashing it into a nearby tool shed.

A servant came running, looking at the spilled water and then at the expression on her mistress's face.

Sydney wanted to scream at her, wanted to raise the whole house, bringing them here to see the bad water. She wanted to force Deng to drink from the pavement. But it was not the fault of the servant standing before her.

"Bring me a clean bucket," Sydney asked in as even a voice as she could muster.

While the servant hurried off, Sydney went to Riod's side and knelt by him. *Oh, Riod. I will bring your water. No one will hurt you now.* Her hand trembled as she stroked his hide. *Beloved, I didn't know.* She hoped that he could pick up her thoughts, and in fact, he stirred.

Someone was coming. Sydney met the servant at the door and took the bucket. Dismissing the girl, she went outside to find a spigot. Deng was nowhere in sight, and that was just as well. She had to think carefully about how to handle this. Deng had received orders from the Tarig lady to poison Riod. But Sydney couldn't directly accuse Anuve, or even Deng, lest she push matters too far. Sydney might be Mistress of the Sway, but she was no equal of a Tarig.

Fresh, rushing water filled the pail. The execrable Deng had been poisoning Riod, under orders from Anuve. She should have guessed, should have paid closer attention. Thank goodness Riod's heart powers, though diminished, had not failed him. Deng must have worked skillfully to hide his intentions. And why had Anuve tried to kill Riod? It was obvious. The mantis lords—and ladies—were fearful of Inyx mind powers and wished to keep Sydney weak. That Sydney hadn't taken precautions against this possibility sickened her.

She brought her bucket of water into the stable and used her hands to form a scoop for Riod to drink from. He did so, feebly.

Her thoughts toward the steward were murderous, but toward Anuve, coldly calculating. She would wait her chance to punish Anuve. It might take some time, but Sydney would make her pay.

Tai bandaged the woman's hands as best he could. She wouldn't say how she had cut them, or if someone had done this to her. Huddled on the edge of his bed, ready to bolt at the first sign of treachery, she looked terrified.

As he bound her hands, he was shaking. If he was not mistaken, he thought that this remarkable being came from the forbidden place: the Rose.

There were clues. First, she spoke Lucent in a halting manner. Second, he thought that he had seen her in the home of the Mistress of the Sway, standing on the balcony. She kept a scarf wrapped around her neck and a tight skull cap that looked as though it perched on a bald head. It was said that those of the Rose began their lives with dark hair and moved to white, opposite to the All. So hiding her hair, or shaving it, was a clue.

He'd been watching the undercity for Titus Quinn. After seeing him riding the Adda yesterday, he looked for him in every crowd, in the face of every Chalin man. Then, instead of Titus Quinn, he had sighted this woman, the one he'd seen on Sen Ni's porch. Her expensive silks made her stand out—Tai knew his silks. Furthermore, these were torn. He followed her, noting her reaction when she spied a Tarig on the street. The woman shrank into a doorway, turning away. She was hiding from them. That was when he got close to her and offered his help.

She had a heavy bundle wrapped in a scarf. From the moment the woman had sat on his bunk, she had protected the package. It rested against her back, and by the look in her eyes, Tai thought she would attack him if he so much as touched it. Maybe she thought that since he lived in a simple burrow, he was some common fellow who might steal from her. He'd have to assure her, somehow. This burrow was one he'd enlarged by digging into the hard packed soils under the city. It had no portal to the Nigh and only a cloth over the door. It was hovel, but at least it was a private place where he could care for her.

"Water, please." A thick accent.

He brought her a drink in a clean cup, and it ran down her face as she drank, spilling into the scarf around her neck. She removed it, showing a patch of festering skin on her neck and chin. Now that he looked more closely, he thought she might be feverish.

"You need a healer."

She quickly snapped, "No." Her glance went to the door.

"All right. But you are sick."

"Not sick. No healers. No one finds me." She was wild-eyed and swaying from exhaustion, but afraid to sleep.

"I won't let the Tarig find you," he said. "I am honored to serve a being of the Rose."

At this, she moved back, drawing closer to the package in back of her. "If you tell about me, I will kill you." She gestured behind her. "This is a machine. I can make it hurt you even if you run."

She was desperate, and perhaps delirious. He humored her. "Some of us revere the Rose, did you know that?"

"I know some things. Not others. Who are you?"

"I am Tai. I am a mort. Do you know what that is?" She watched him warily. "My friends and I think the Entire is a place where people live too long. It makes them shallow and boring. We shun the bright, the upper city, so we will live shorter lives, and deeper. Like you do in the Rose."

She leaned against her machine, eyelids drooping. He wished she would lie down, but this appeared to be a woman who would sooner fall down than rest.

"Mort is a nickname for a Rose word meaning death. Morts aren't afraid of death, not like most sentients. The lords say life is better here. It isn't. I'm sure of that."

"You like the Rose, Tai?"

That seemed friendlier, and he was quick to answer. "It is my dream. To go there."

"I know how."

His heart crimped at this utterance.

"Your dream." She nodded. "Help me, and I will help you."

"I was going to help you anyway."

She asked for food then, and he spent his last minors on meat rolls and buns, bringing them back as fast as he could, afraid she would run away. But she was waiting for him.

He tried not to stare at her as she ate. He was so stimulated that he could hardly be still. At last he found the courage to ask, "Is Titus Quinn your friend?"

She swallowed a bite that looked like it got lodged halfway down throat. "Yes. Such a good friend. What do you know of him?"

"I know that he was at Sen Ni's dwelling on the crystal bridge. He took her up into the Adda, and after they were together a few increments, she came back down again. All very secret. I would never tell."

She stopped eating for a while, eyes narrow. Then she said, "That is good, Tai. Don't tell our secrets. You really don't want to tell. There are very big plans at work. You can be part of it. Then I will send you to the Rose. You can live the short life you want. You like that?"

He nodded, overcome.

That seemed to please her, because she said, "My name is"—he thought she said Hel Ese. "I'm on a . . . Rose mission. But I can't tell you about this. You have to trust me. Agreed?"

Tai began to relax. They were becoming friends. "If you have great things to accomplish, I want to be part of them."

She looked around her. "Tell me where I am."

"This is where I stay. It's a hole, but it's cheap. You're in the undercity. It's where we—us morts—like to be, because it's dark."

"Secret from the Tarig?"

"No, the Tarig built it long ago. They know we're here, but they don't come down among us very much. Morts like it here, since we don't fit in—" He pointed toward the ceiling. "—up there. No one will come here."

She lay down, keeping the machine between herself and the wall. "I have to sleep."

He brought her a blanket, a fairly clean one, he was happy to note. "Sleep, Hel Ese. No one will disturb you. Don't worry." He pulled the blanket over her as she lay down.

"Send you to the Rose," she murmured. "If you hide me well. If not . . ."

It hurt his feelings that she was still threatening him. He glanced at the machine covered with a scarf. Glimpses of metal showed through the wrapping. A picture formed in his mind of a machine sprouting legs and rushing after him like a Paion. He didn't doubt that she could be dangerous. There was something in her eyes that was flat and unreceptive. Once she knew him better, they would be friends.

She was already asleep, snoring lightly. Stepping close to her, he inspected the raw infection, oozing in places. He quelled a spike of worry. Counting out his few coins, he found he had just enough to buy medicinals.

Tai went to the flap on the door, slipping past it into the murky corridor. Elated and exhausted, he hurried to the market stalls. He kept an eye out for her good friend Titus Quinn.

CHAPTER FIFTEEN

Against the enemy, use a damning truth; to rouse one's own forces, a useful lie.

—from Tun Mu's *Annals of War*

"**O**NLY HIRRIN SERVANTS," Sydney repeated again.

Lady Anuve looked down at her with flat black eyes. It was a look Sydney was coming to identify as fury.

Of all the assembled staff, Sydney wanted only Hirrin, the sentients who could not lie. As the first test of her freedom, she banished Anuve's spies.

Riod stood by her side, distressingly weak but able to move under his own power now that Sydney herself fed and watered him. Today he was going back to the Inyx Sway, much as they both dreaded being separated.

Deng was the first servant to be dismissed, and if Anuve thought her poisonings had been discovered, then so be it. Because Anuve might overreact to a direct accusation, Sydney managed to hold her tongue. Clearly the mantis lords—and ladies—wanted no Inyx near the Bright City and its great secrets. In this regard, they would be surprised to learn how right they were.

Sydney pressed home her point. "I will have only Hirrin to serve me. And only Hirrin to escort us to the ship."

"Armed Hirrin," Anuve said, conceding the issue of servants. Hirrin made surprisingly good bodyguards. They could be equipped with ejectors in their mouths that would take down a sentient with a paralyzing stream at fifteen yards.

Sydney gave ground. "Yes, all right." She had to pretend that she'd use force to restrain her father if he attempted contact.

Waving her hand at the Chalin and Jout palace staff, Lady Anuve sent them from the foyer to pack their belongings. Earlier Anuve had said once more what the terms were, of being free: "You serve as Mistress of the Sway as long as you do so with honor. This means obedience to us, ah?"

"Yes," Sydney had answered. Thank God she wasn't a Hirrin and could lie pleasantly.

Still, she didn't trust even the Hirrin, not quite yet. She approached two Hirrin females Anuve had brought her.

"Do you serve me honestly, withholding nothing?" If she was truly free, then a Hirrin could answer a simple question.

The nearest Hirrin rolled her eyes and turned her long neck in Anuve's direction. "Have we leave to serve the Mistress of the Sway, Bright One?"

By gesture from Anuve: Yes.

Sydney locked gazes with the Hirrin. "Do you keep secrets from me?"

"No, Mistress."

Turning to the second Hirrin, she asked, "And do you?"

"I do not, Mistress Sen Ni."

Sydney turned back to the remaining figures in the foyer: all were Hirrin except for Riod and Anuve. "Every day I will ask this of each of you." That ought to clear the decks well enough.

Sydney turned to Anuve. "I'm going to the wharf. We'll keep watch for the man of the Rose." She wanted so badly to say, *And someday you'll eat my poison. Although it wouldn't much matter, would it? You'd just come back as another ugly fiend.*

Sydney and Riod left, along with the Hirrin guards. It was a slow progression, marked by Riod's uncertain steps. Sydney kept her hand on his flank: *I will miss you always, every minute, beloved.*

Riod concentrated on negotiating the palace steps. He would walk on his own down to the dock at the foot of the bridge. A short walk, but painful for them both. Riod had been at her side without pause for a thousand days. When he was gone, she would be alone. Mo Ti had left—oh, long ago, it seemed. Akay-Wat was in the roamlands. Helice had fled. Who was left now? With Riod's return home their goal of better penetrating the Ascendancy with dream probes evaporated. Helice still had her machine sapient; no doubt she still had her great plans of renaissance, within which she sought to control the Tarig at their doors. Perhaps Titus could find the doors to the Heart first. He said he had the means, though he hadn't confided his methods to her.

As they came into the Way, citizens bowed to Sydney, recognizing her from the celebrations of investiture. As she and her company went on, a small crowd followed them. Few people here had seen an Inyx, much less Sen Ni, up close. They hailed her, and it lifted her spirits. Above them, the glimmering crystal bridge lay aslant, as though leaning out to touch the Ascendancy. Despite the sad duty of sending Riod away, the sight was riveting. It was the largest glass slipper in the universe, and Sydney was the most unlikely of Cinderellas. She was walking free under the shadow of the Ascendancy. She was a child of the Entire, a mistress of a country, and the daughter of no man—only the friend of a horned mount. Looking out at the silver disk of the Sea of Arising, she had the feeling she would never be this free again. Surely it was just a bit of doubt and not premonition. But it came to her hard and fast like instinctual knowledge.

The navitar's vessel rested at the pier, with only a Hirrin ship keeper visible. No other travelers had booked passage yet, apparently. Riod watched the ship with loathing, remembering the trip out. But his agitation was not because of the pending Nigh voyage. He sent to Sydney, *The boy navitar. It is the boy.*

Sydney snapped a look at the vessel, searching. The navitar hadn't made himself visible on the deck, but if it was the same one they'd met before, that couldn't be a coincidence. Geng De was seeking her out.

I like him not.

Once on the ship's deck, Sydney looked down at her Hirrin servants. "Wait for me here, and don't interrupt us."

In back of the main cabin, a special billet had been constructed for Riod's transport. When Riod and Sydney entered it, Geng De was waiting.

His doughy face dimpled in pleasure. He bowed. "Mistress." Gesturing around the cabin, he said, "Everything for Riod's comfort, as you see. My ship keeper will wait on him, and if I do not care for him well, you may force feed me with river matter." The expression might convey the navitars' horror of drowning, a fear Sydney had heard of.

"Thank you, Geng De. Riod is very sick. Please go to the roamlands as fast as you can."

Exhausted, Riod sank to his knees in the straw. Kneeling next to him, Sydney felt incapable of a goodbye. *I will come home with you*, Sydney thought.

Riod snatched at the thought, always able to see her mind instantly. He reminded her that he would soon be well, once in the company of the herd and free of poisons. More important, Sydney must be in position to receive the gift her father might give her. If he found the doors.

Sydney reflected on these things. Titus might think he still owed her that much. Though she had not been able to deliver Helice to him, he still had promised her the kingdom, if it was in his power to give. He might believe a thing like that could make amends. And the truth was it could. She imagined that they would have a new alliance, a new relationship. She imagined that she might love him again.

In his boyish lisp, Geng De said, "I have come far to see you."

But *far* for a navitar was never much of a journey. "How are you, Geng De?"

"I am strong. In my largest powers."

Well, good for you. She pressed her face next to Riod's great head.

Geng De's voice came to her, needling: "I will help you, if you let me. We have ties, you and I. You remember?"

They would have to have a conversation. Wearily, she stood up, smoothing her silks. "I remember you said so. A lot of people say things to me. It's hard to figure out what matters. What's true." Riod was already beginning to drift off. *Stay awake, best mount*, she urged.

Geng De looked at Riod with concern. "I have a thing to tell the mount. Is he asleep?"

"Perhaps. Tell me, then."

"But it's Riod who needs to know. So he can infect the sleep of the All."

Ah. He knew about the source of the dream sendings. Sydney felt vulnerable now. She was on Geng De's ship, rocking on a sea that he commanded in ways she could not imagine. The room seemed dark and confining.

Geng De went on, "It is something I've only lately discovered, in the binds. Not many know this. Maybe only me. When it goes abroad into the dreams, it will make the lords unhappy."

She waited.

A dimple in the cheek. "It is a lot to tell you for nothing in return."

"What do you want, then?"

"Oh! I want to be your first counselor, your best friend, your religious guide. Co-master of the Sway. Regent of the Entire."

The list left Sydney breathless. "Anything else?"

"That's all you can give me. You might be Mistress of the Sway, but you don't own everything. Not nearly everything. That could change."

If he expected her to listen to this sort of talk, he'd have to do better than wild demands and claims. "Tell me, first." He had a whiff of desperation about him. She'd use that. She outwaited him.

"I know what the Paion want."

"Everyone knows that. They want the Entire."

"Did you think, Sen Ni, that the lords do not lie?"

No, she had never thought that.

Geng De's voice was very soft. "The Paion want to come home. This is their home."

She tried to grasp this idea, and failed. "This is home?"

"It used to be. They were expelled. If the lords would let them come back to their minoral—just one small minoral—the Long War would be over."

Geng De glanced at Riod, perhaps uncertain whether to wake him. "The Paion once had a minoral. This minoral was in the Long Gaze of Fire. It was cut off from the roamlands by a shield, and behind that shield was a murk of air only they could breathe."

"Shield . . ." Sydney had seen this shield. "In the Inyx lands."

"Well, they're not all Inyx lands. The primacy is vast. But you saw the Scar?" When she nodded, Geng De went on, "This was all back before anyone remembers. Then the Tarig cut it off. The Paion have been trying to get back ever since." He shrugged, as though it was just that simple.

"Why?" The idea of minorals *cut off* like dead fingernails was disturbing at a profound level. And yet, hadn't the lords done so again just now, in the Arm of Heaven? There were rumors that the minorals had all closed, like doors slamming. There were rumors that they had not just closed up, but vanished.

"The Tarig overreached. The Paion minoral was too expensive, for the energy it needed. To create special air. To keep it separate." He shrugged. "A guess. I am not in their counsels. But the lords need to keep the bright going. Every cut helps."

She let this story settle in her mind. It wouldn't. "So the Paion aren't from another universe?"

"Oh, now they are. After the Tarig cut them away. They learned to power themselves, but it's hard, and they want to come home."

Sydney's imagination went back to the time when she had seen the Scar. She was with Mo Ti then, the first ride she and Riod had taken after Tarig surgeries supposedly cured her blindness. A long ride from the encampment, there was an oval mark on the storm wall, the place where everyone thought the Paion had once tried to invade. But if Geng De was to be believed, it was only the imprint of the minoral where the Paion had *lived*; the shape of the junction between the minoral and the primacy.

"We have the Long War because the Paion need to come home. The lords could wipe them out of the next universe and end the war, but they like the war. It binds the sways in one cause. So they keep it going, though the Paion are nothing but fleas to such as the lords."

She thought of the slaughter of that war. "People have died. Sentients have died." She ran out of words.

"The bright lords find it useful. They might like to watch a nice war." The young navitar drew closer to her. "That is a fine secret to tell. Are we friends, then?"

Might like to watch. They keep it going. Geng De was right, it was very useful information. Perhaps explosive. If the lords were vulnerable in their image, this could fatally wound them. She bent down to touch Riod's forward horn, wishing he were awake.

The navitar looked down at Riod. "Are you two talking right now, mind to mind? Not very nice, in my presence."

"That won't ever change. Get used to it, or stay the hell away from me."

"But it *will* change. He can't be close to you if he goes home. You won't be talking to each other anymore. You could talk to me instead. I'd help you. You would be my queen."

She looked at him with an appraising eye. He knew some important things. Astounding things. His disclosures could galvanize her flagging rebellion. And—if he wasn't fabricating these stories—he might reveal further Tarig weaknesses. But associating with him might alarm Anuve.

"The Tarig watch me. How would I explain a friendship with a navitar?"

"I could instruct you, spiritually. The lords are used to sentients wanting religion. You could take on the religion of your sway: the Society of the Red Throne. It might be well to emulate your subjects, for political reasons. You could adopt an attitude of veneration of navitars, especially me." He dug into the folds of his red robe for something. "Here is my portrait."

Sydney took the picture from him. She had seen similar poses of navitars held aloft on the banners of the Society during the Great Procession. He looked like a chubby adolescent dressed up in a tent.

He beamed. "Do you like it?"

The cabin grew too warm. Outside on the dock, her attendants waited. Sydney would have to make up her mind. She hesitated. Riod was leaving, and this odd but intriguing pilot wanted to take his place.

"I don't know much about the Red religion. I wouldn't be convincing as a devotee."

"You don't have to convince the lords. They'd know it was for appearances."

"I won't worship you. And I won't pretend to."

"I don't want spiritual power, Sen Ni."

"You want the real thing."

"Yes. With you."

Geng De pulled himself to his full height, matching hers. "I will tell you the last thing to know about me. Then you can decide if we are to be brother and sister." He paused. "I have a gift for the future."

"A gift."

"Yes."

"To see the future? Then what is the future?"

He looked hurt at her scoffing tone. "It's more complicated than that."

"Tell me, Geng De, am I to be in the Ascendancy?"

His voice was perfectly serious as he answered. "Yes. If I say so."

She could only stare at him. Was he a madman? Certainly peculiar, but delusional?

Riod was present after all. He struggled, and his voice was weak in her thoughts. Still, he sent, *He speaks truthfully.*

Geng De went on, "Haven't you grasped it yet? I can control which strands combine. If the strands are strong enough, I can weave them together. Make you queen."

Riod's thought came: *That is against the navitar vows.*

"Against the navitars' way," Sydney murmured, her thoughts racing.

"Yes, the navitars pledge not to. But it's easy for them to give up what they can't have anyway. And some try, did you know? But I am the only one who can shape the strands. I've only succeeded in small things. The alterations are . . . complex. I only know that I feel the binds differently than others. I am from the river. I am of the river."

She wanted to dismiss his claims, as outrageous as they were. But he had already demonstrated knowledge of high secrets: seeing the chain cast into the river; knowing the cause of the Long War; discovering the motives of the Paion. But knowing and predicting were different—immeasurably different than controlling. Could he indeed, even in small ways, influence the future?

Riod, is this true?

He does not speak lies, my heart. But he can still be wrong.

She shook her head, overwhelmed.

Geng De put his hands on her shoulders. She pulled back, but he didn't let go. "You see that I am not like others." His voice was urgent, and the words spilled out quickly: "When I was barely nine hundred days old, my parents took passage on the Nigh, and as the press of passengers distracted them, I crawled up the railing. I fell. The water swallowed me. It was not water."

He released her from his grip, pacing to the porthole. "They pulled me up, but I had already gone under, again and again. By the time I was laid out on the deck, I was changed. 'Throw him back,' some urged, oblivious to my mother's cries. My father wrapped me in a blanket and took me to the navitar, but when she looked at me, she fell to raving, and the ship keeper sent us off. I was damaged, but my parents had no other children and were determined to make someone pay for their grief. Besides, my mother thought it was an omen that I survived. She thought me destined for some high thing. My father, though, went to the Magisterium to find a clerk who would draw up scrolls to bring action against the navitar for ruining me. It happened that the navitar of this ship was a great favorite of one of the lords, and to save the navitar from having to leave her ship and confront unpleasantness the lord, through his legate, offered a compromise: I could go for a navitar. No child had ever been created a navitar. The changing took time. When I emerged, I was as you see me. I am different *in nature* from the others. I am a child of the Nigh. When I am in the binds, and when I weave the threads, I control them. With difficulty and imperfectly. But, for example, today I brought you to my side. This is why we are brother and sister, Sen Ni, because I see you in my future days. To me, these days are already gone; I have seen them in the river."

He stood back from her, wiping the sweat from his face. The telling had taken something out of him: the arrogance, for one thing.

His story had moved her. His assertions and his upbringing were knitting into a coherent, if extraordinary, whole.

In a ragged voice, Geng De went on, "Are we not kin, Sen Ni? We were both dropped away. You by your parents, me by a stumble on the Nigh. Neither of us belongs anywhere, except together." He held out his hands, palms up. "Do you have the courage to hold the hands of a child of the river?"

Sydney hesitated only for a moment. Her counselors were all gone. All that was left was her father, and she didn't think he would be worth much in the end. This navitar might be a boy, a man, destined to help her. But he might be an unreliable, ambitious guide. Still, he was mistaken if he thought he could dominate her. She'd faced off with worse. She'd challenged Priov, the chief of the Inyx, when she was a slave. She'd survived Lord Hadenth. She'd keep Geng De in check, and if not, she would send him away.

She nodded her agreement. "Come with me, then. Be my counselor. Guide me." She would listen to him. She didn't have to obey. And if he could weave a future, then by the bright, let it be a glorious one.

Reaching for her hands again, he gripped them. "Kiss your new brother." He came closer.

He would be content with nothing else. She stepped forward and put her lips on his. Though she wanted to pull away, she knew this was the least of the penalties she would pay for his service. She kissed him truly.

Our brother now? Riod asked. He had been listening all this time, perhaps conscious enough to know that Sydney had turned onto a new path. Perhaps he discerned that she was tracing an urge she could not even name, except to align, bind, and gather those who were loyal to her. To provide recompense for things that kept falling away.

It had been a sexless kiss, as a brother's kiss should be. But Geng De was family now.

CHAPTER SIXTEEN

N A MISTING RAIN, CAITLIN LEFT THE FREEWAY and unlinked her car from the mesh system, cruising over the megabridge to the Washington side of the Columbia River. From here to the Hanford reservation the automated highway went to dark road: no dataflow on pavement conditions, no safety tracking of her car. In spite of the rain and the unfamiliar road, the moment she left the smart highway she felt a measure of relief. They'd need a satellite to see her now.

No reason they'd go to that trouble, though. Lamar expected her to be what she'd always been: the good trooper, the good mother. Doing what was expected of her. It was a role Caitlin had played her whole life. The dutiful child in a large family; the diligent student, rising as high as a middie could; the faithful wife—of sorts.

With typical savvy arrogance, Lamar didn't expect her to think for herself. Well, he was wrong on that score. As she took the steep climb up from the Columbia gorge, her anger rose. How gullible did he think she was? Titus had not sent for her, of course. Yes, he'd gone into another universe— this she'd known for years—but he wasn't asking for Caitlin by his side.

There'd been a moment yesterday when she'd let herself think he did. Back there on the deck of the houseboat, she had believed it for three or four breathless minutes. Jesus God, she had. But it wasn't in Titus's makeup to woo her away from his own brother. They'd been through that little scenario, she and Titus. *Even if you two split up, I can't be in line, Caitlin.*

So Lamar was lying. About Titus and her, and maybe a lot more. There were world changes coming. The *transform*, Lamar had called it. No doubt there was money to be made from the transform. She could not imagine what motive Lamar might have for involving her and the children it in, but she meant to find out. She owed Titus a look at Hanford, at this crossing-over site; there was something involved here besides a get-rich-quick scheme. And if it involved Titus, it could be critical.

At the top of the cliff she stopped the car at the old Maryhill mansion. A quick stretch here to steady her nerves. Playing the spy was new ground for her, and she was nervous. From Maryhill's cracked and windswept terrace, the gorge plunged a thousand feet, the Columbia River tracing a gleaming path in the cleft.

She looked around her at the decaying Edwardian mansion of Sam Hill, nineteenth-century railroad baron. Commanding the cliffs, the mansion slumped into ruin, its remaining windows cloudy, like cataract eyes. Three hundred years ago they'd called it Sam's folly, the palace Sam Hill built for Queen Marie of Romania as an ostentatious gift. Since then, it had served as a museum, an art gallery, and finally a hospital for the refugees from the Hanford phage outbreak, a nuclear waste solution gone wrong. Though the phage outbreak had been quelled, Hanford was still pockmocked from its incursions. A disaster piled on a disaster, given the original nuclear cleanup problem harking back to 1944. Despite all the tech that savvies could muster, radionucleotides still polluted the ground, and Cherenkov radiation yet curdled in mothballed reactors. All the reactors were cocooned now. A good place for secrets, then.

According to Lamar, a new group was pretending to take on the toxic waste problems: HTG, the Hanford Transition Group. From Caitlin's research, she saw evidence that the group had government contracts to test biomolecular remedies of some sort. HTG, with its Web site and white papers on experimental nuclear waste cleanup, established a convincing semblance of credentials. They'd gone to a lot of trouble to justify a presence in no-man's-land.

Lamar had said the compound would hold two thousand people and prep them to undertake the journey. When I call you, be packed, he'd said. He meant her, Mateo, and Emily. But not Rob. He assumed that Caitlin would leave Rob. She didn't want to examine how close Lamar had come to the truth. Nor did she want to think about how obvious was her infatuation with her brother-in-law. Was Rob the only one who hadn't guessed?

Why *was* Lamar trying to get Caitlin involved in this? At times, she thought she saw affection in Lamar's eyes. He was doing her a favor, by his lights. But she didn't trust him anymore.

A squall raced across the flats as she drove onto the reservation, pelting the blue hood of the Mercedes. Within minutes the shower was done, and sun reclaimed the Eastern Washington desert.

It seemed impossible for a conspiracy to be holed up in this open land. She left highway 240, turning into the new HTG road, surrounded by lupine, bunchgrass, and sagebrush. It was big country, dipping through low, rolling mounds all the way to distant hills. As she drove on through the desert, she began to catch up with the river's circuitous route once again.

Far ahead was a string of squat buildings, the old reactors built along what must once have seemed the perfect stretch of free-flowing water. Though the containerized waste products were long ago encapsulated and sunk to the bottom of the Mariana Trench in the Pacific, the ground at Hanford would be hot for twelve thousand years. Apparently HTG personnel weren't objecting to the location; they didn't plan to be there long.

Signs declared this road off-limits. *Passes required. Dead end.* She wondered if all the select personnel were already gathered here, or only those busy erecting the compound. The more people, the less she would stand out. But since she was part of the project, along with Mateo and Emily, it was logical that she might want to check out the accommodations. They might be in the compound for months, after all, and the kids needed a semblance of normalcy. She'd pretend to care about that.

The first checkpoint was a small glassed-in station breaking up a stretch of electrified fence. An unsmiling attendant wanted her pass; lacking one, Caitlin gave her name, waiting while he checked it against a database. He waved her on, saying there was another checkpoint ahead, a DNA scrape. Well, she could pass *that* test.

Where this group planned on going was still hard to grasp. Lamar claimed that as soon as Titus gave the signal, the people on the list would debark for a place called the Entire. She knew the place existed because Titus had told her it did, calling it *the adjoining region*. She didn't know how they would cross over; Lamar had said nothing about making the transition at one of the stellar black hole space platforms. Maybe this was the next generation of crossover stations. Those in the first wave of colonists were savvies, of course—the very best minds available to work on the issues of interface, settlement, and cultural integration. And they'd want their families along. Plausible enough. Yet Caitlin remembered that when Titus had left, he'd been filled with foreboding about things in the adjoining region. *There are dark things over there*, he'd said. *They can hurt us.*

Driving up to the second perimeter, Caitlin found a small group of buildings nested among idle earth-moving equipment and trucks. She parked where she was told and proceeded inside where she gave up her DNA sample; a slight stimulation of the tear ducts, and the blotter registered all her vitals.

"Your first visit," the pleasant technician said.

"Yes."

"We'll assign you a guide, in that case. It helps to call in advance."

Caitlin waited in the modest anteroom, paging through phony pamphlets about HTG and nuclear cleanup. All very bland and earnest, all making her deeply uneasy. Why was secrecy so necessary? Well, corporate espionage was big business, and Minerva had the biggest corporate secret of all: the adjoining region. And, she mustn't forget, EoSap or ChinaKor, or another of Minerva's competitors, had kidnapped Emily for one bad half hour not long ago . . . so there might be an understandable company paranoia. However, nothing in the brochures had Minerva's name on it.

But it could still all be legitimate. Lamar's story could yet be true. Titus could be waiting to sweep her into his arms.

Both things as likely as flying pigs. Caitlin stood up. Her escort had arrived.

Jess drove fast. A mousy, slight woman of about thirty, she didn't look like someone who lived for risk; but here she was, one of the two thousand—leaving for the universe adjoining.

Chatty, too. "None of us have time for tours," she said. "We're pushing hard." She gave Caitlin a rueful glance. "Then I checked your number and decided I had time. You're right up there. Your number's real high."

"That right? All I know is that I'm going."

"Yeah, well you're going before I am, that's for sure. I'm number one thousand eighty-seven." She shot a look at her passenger. "You're sixteen. Those are your kids then, Emily and Mateo?" She shrugged. "Numbers seventeen and eighteen. Somebody up there likes you."

Caitlin managed an apologetic smile. "I'm Titus Quinn's sister-in-law. Must be nepotism."

Jess grinned. "Oh good. For a minute there I thought I was going to have to make small talk with someone who talks in differential equations."

"Don't worry. Not my idea of chitchat."

They were coming up on the compound, a scattering of igloo-shaped huts in the shadow of the enormous, steel-encased reactor looming three stories high.

Jess saw Caitlin lean closer to the window to look at it. As they passed it, Caitlin felt a vibration through the car.

"Yeah," Jess said, "it's an abandoned reactor. Don't worry, the bad stuff's all buried."

The streets were empty of cars but dotted with pedestrians now that the sun was back out. As they drove into the company camp, Caitlin saw the requisite coffeehouse and soccer field, the former full, the latter empty.

"It's the kids that concern me," Caitlin said. "I think it would help to see the arrangements." She twisted the purse handles in her lap, putting on a show of temerity. "I just want the kids to feel comfortable here. We'll have enough stress as it is."

"We have one hundred seventy-five kids already, did they tell you that?"

"No. So you've got the educational stuff worked out? A school?"

She smiled. "Wait'll you see."

Before they went into the modular school unit, Jess turned to Caitlin and put her hand on Caitlin's. "I don't have kids, so I can't pretend to know what it'll be like for you. If there's anything I can do, let me know." When Caitlin nodded, Jess went on. "Must be tough, with the situation with your daughter. I know I'd be upset."

Caitlin covered her confusion by pretending to wipe at her eye. She wanted Jess to say more, but how to pry without exposing how little she knew? She mumbled, "How would you handle it, if it was your daughter?"

Jess looked surprised. "Well, all I can say is, you wouldn't stay *here*, would you?

"Maybe not."

A long pause. Jess was now looking at her more shrewdly. "Are you kidding me?"

Caitlin acted the distressed mom. "It's just a tough situation."

"Look. She's still young. She won't test for a few more years. And if she doesn't have the scores, you'll get your grandchildren from your boy. Better than nothing."

Grandchildren? What was the woman talking about?

Jess sighed. "It's our chance to get it right this time. Without the dreds pulling us down, diluting the good stock." She winced. "Sorry. Your daughter. Nothing against her. And she might be fine, she really might. She's got those good genes."

It was not as though middie or dred status meant you couldn't have children. Not yet. But was it coming to that? "Right," Caitlin responded. "Good genes. I'm counting on those." She managed a wobbly smile.

"I know you're anxious. But Emily will be fine. At least she'll survive."

Caitlin's thoughts stopped right there. *Survive?*

Jess's expression turned bleak. "I hate what's coming. We all hate it. It's our home." She snorted. "Gone. Just like that. I hate it."

Gone? Caitlin tried to match Jess's expression. Bleak. Wistful. Guilty. She sensed that they wouldn't stay on this topic. It was too unpleasant, But Caitlin needed more. "What will it look like, do you think? When it happens?"

The other woman paused. "You can't think about things like that. It'll make you crazy."

"Haven't you wondered, though?" She was pushing too hard, but she couldn't let it rest, couldn't back off. "I guess I'm just the nervous type."

"But you're committed."

Caitlin put starch in her voice. "Jess, we're all committed to this. You just said, you still hate it."

The other woman grabbed her purse out of the backseat, then stopped, hand on the car door. "Yes, I hate it. I dream about it. Fire roaring like a hurricane. You don't suppose they'll have time to see fire, do you? I imagine the river boiling off . . . I imagine . . . I imagine . . ." Her mouth trembled. "I imagine it. I can't describe it." She gathered her purse in her arms like a baby. "Let's go in."

The school had walls. A few tables for desks. Computers. Caitlin didn't hear a word of what the teachers said.

She was imagining the river boiling off.

When they emerged from the instructional module, the sky was darkening toward evening. Caitlin didn't dare ask to see the crossover place inside the reactor vault. She'd already gone too far with Jess. But then, as they drove back to the parking lot, Jess brought it up herself. The transition stage, as she called it, was off-limits. No one got in. It was a clean room, techs only. In the mothballed reactor vault. Well, actually, *under* it. The engine itself was on the ground floor of the old reactor vault.

What engine?

That was a little spooky, Jess admitted. To be so close to the thing. The stage and the engine were sited together so that HTG had no footprint on the land. Nothing an outsider could detect.

Caitlin took a closer stare at the steel-clad structure as they passed it this time. A deep thrumming sound came from it.

"We go in, we don't come out again," Jess mused. She crumpled her lips. "With the engine overhead, I think I'd rather be number sixteen. Get through it in a hurry. Last person out pulls the chain, I guess."

Caitlin could hardly wait to be rid of Jess. She waved at the woman and fumbled for her car keys. After several tries, she got the door open.

So this was the transform Lamar had been referring to.

Oh, Titus. Oh, brother-in-law, fuck me to hell. It was the end of the world.

CHAPTER SEVENTEEN

O, King of Woe, may your war last forever, may my sons be unworthy to fight, may I die disgraced in my bed.

—a prayer

THE HERD GATHERED AT SHADOW EBB, one by one and in groups, first to graze, and then to dream. They stood, heads held aloft, bearing the full weight of their double row of horns, or hanging low as though drowsing. But inwardly, they raced. Led by Riod, they joined above the roamland plain, circling, calling their herd mates, calling in that silent manner suited to the heart-joined.

Once Riod sensed enough were gathered, he led them in a communal act of will: the penetration of the dreams of the Entire. It was not difficult. All the Entire slept at the same time. All the Entire fell into Shadow Ebb at the same time, and therefore many were likely to be dreaming at once.

After his return from Rim City, Riod leached the poisons from his body by exhausting runs across the steppe. He was recovered, but riderless, a loss he felt acutely. But he was with Sydney in his intention as he led his fellow mounts into dream-space. There they told of the betrayal of the Long War: How for hundreds of thousands of days, the sons and daughters of the Entire had died on the plains of Ahnenhoon for a war that meant nothing. The Paion would have surrendered with a small concession: that the lords join their minoral back to the body of the world. But the gracious lords chose not to.

The Long War suited the lords. It united the primacies against an outside enemy. It deflected attention from the Tarig themselves, who ruled like gods, but who were pitiable, fearful creatures afraid of true life. At will, and over and over again, individual Tarig went home to the comfort of the Heart, a land of fire where all the Tarig melded into a singular consciousness. These were the beings who claimed to be gracious lords, who supposedly shared the life of the Entire. They were nothing but simulacra—a mode of being so removed from the general experience as to be no living thing at all.

Milinard the Jout tossed on his couch in the Magisterium. In his dreams he saw the Paion rap on the door of a Tarig lord. Let me in, for I am dying, the Paion cried. It was a small, weak creature, and a starving one. Though Milinard feared the Paion as much as the next sentient, he had to admit this Paion was to be pitied. The table of the lord was heaped high with food. Share with me but one meal, the Paion cried. But the lord turned away. In fury, the Paion set fire to the house of the Tarig. Out from the fiery house poured the inhabitants, but to Milinard's surprise, it was not Tarig who ran out, but Jout soldiers, bodies on fire. They died painfully, and their wives wailed at their demise.

Fajan slept on good silk sheets at his mother's dwelling in Rim City. He was tired from days of street parties, but his sleep alarmed him. He woke, sweating, heart racing. He'd had these dreams last night, too. And what dreams! Too crisp to be normal fugues of the mind, these dreams surely bore a message. The Long War must be resisted. It is not fought to save the Entire, but was needlessly provoked by the Tarig. Most of the morts refused service in the Long War. Now their instincts were proven right. Too agitated to return to bed, Fajan paced. Were the dreams emanations from a navitar? Who else would know such deep secrets? He looked around at his comfortable room in his mother's house. What was he doing, playing at mort by ebb and the good son by day? Maybe Tai was right, that there were bigger things to do. What had Tai asked him? *What if we had to risk our lives for something worthwhile?*

He wondered if the undercity shared this dream. Who could still love the Tarig after a night like this? He hurriedly dressed and slipped into the Way.

The dream of the severed minoral lingered in his mind. Had the lords really cut off the sway of the Paion? It might seem unthinkable, except that it was happening again. News had been arriving by pieces every hour from travelers coming to Rim City. There was no proof yet, only rumors—that many minorals of the Arm of Heaven primacy had collapsed in the last arc of days. Things were not what they had been. The All was changing. As disturbing as that might be, it thrilled him.

Zhiya dozed in a chair by Quinn's bed, keeping near in case his wound woke him. He'd been lucky. The gun pellet entered the right side of his chest just below the pectoral muscle, missing both heart and liver, fortunately for him. The healer had used a chest tube to drain the fluid, but Quinn still slept sitting up. Helice had very nearly killed him, though, and Zhiya dearly wished that her own operatives had earlier managed to assassinate the creature. With such murderous thoughts, it was perhaps no wonder she had violent dreams.

Quinn had told her that the Inyx sent the dreams, though. She watched his troubled sleep, wondering how close his dreams were to her own, and what he made of the current subject matter—nightmare matter. Holding her eyes open for as long as she could, she put off further dreaming, but ultimately sleep crept toward her from the corners of her mind. The dream came, stronger and more clearly, of the falsity of the Long War. One part of her mind evaluated the dream, while another part was swept away by it. Surely even the Tarig couldn't be so monstrous. Could the Long War be such a lie? And would the Tarig cut off a primacy, set it loose from the All? In her dream she was in her dirigible *outside the Entire*. It moved slowly, trying to catch the severed minoral, a tube of geography rushing ahead of her into the void.

Cixi did not sleep in the ebb. The high prefect had held court in ebb time for so long, it would not do to change her custom now. But she had learned, between audiences with petitioners, to meditate—to meditate so profoundly that she caught glimmers of the nightmare dreams of the Inyx. She paced in agitation, looking out at the palatine hill. From Mo Ti's former reports, she knew the Inyx stole into dreams. But how had Sydney and her band come into the knowledge of the false Long War? Surely Cixi with all her operatives would have known this first. She sighed, considering these swift changes. Sen Ni rose in power, thank the All. But the dear girl was doing it without her. Where was Mo Ti, and why had he not reported by now how Sen Ni fared? In all her spies' gatherings from Rim City, none had mentioned the eunuch being in her attendance. If he was dead, he had done his duty—to protect Sydney among the Inyx and to plant in her heart the seeds of power. Wherever Mo Ti was, perhaps he was no longer needed. Cixi remembered that once Mo Ti had gone for a soldier. She wondered what he thought of the Tarig now, realizing that he had fought for nothing.

Su Bei was weary of ships of the Nigh and bekus and the eternally late trains of the far-flung primacies. He was too old for this undertaking. It was one thing to journey millions of miles on the bilious ships and on the backs of bekus; but it was quite another to travel with many boxes of stone well computational devices, such as had to be set up at experimental minorals all through the All. He had to admit he could never have accomplished so much without Anzi. But still, he had found nothing in his relentless search, nothing that would help Titus Quinn.

Search for the Heart, the messenger had said. Titus will control the Heart. *Wanted* to control it, by the Miserable God. High time the man came into his destiny, though Bei well knew Titus didn't see himself that way. His vision was expanding, though: no longer just to save the daughter, now it was to save the Rose. Still, it brought Titus to the same place: control. And from there, the Chalin people had their chance to rise.

Yes, all to the good, but at the present moment, Bei could be no help to Titus. In this small, foreign reach set up by some long-dead scholar, he could see nothing. The Heart was not accessible here. So he and Anzi would be on the move tomorrow. He needed rest and hoped this ebb would grant sleep without nightmares such as the vivid dream of that nightmare rush down the minoral with Anzi, and the thunderous closing of the minoral. . . .

He threw the covers off and shuffled to the long-disused veil-of-worlds. The screens of the stone wells were dark. Not malfunctioning, but simply dark. Most universes were empty of light as well as mass. This certainly was not the Heart that the poor ship keeper spoke of. If the stone wells ever found a realm of bursting light, his alarms would wake the dead. He had made sure he and Anzi did not sleep through any discoveries. The stone wells would clang like the Ascendancy falling from the sky.

Instead of sleeping, Helice gazed at her image in the mirror. She hardly recognized herself, with her scabs turning spongy and seeping. Her eyes simmered with an unnatural intensity. It was quite possible, she now allowed, that she was dangerously ill. Trying to recover in this dingy underworld was proving impossible. It had been—what?—thirty days now since she'd arrived in Tai's nasty little burrow. For a while she had seemed to improve with the ointments Tai brought her. Until today. The infection was back with a sudden ferocity. This should not be happening.

Amid the squalor of Tai's burrow, among the dirty plates and piles of clothes, Helice barely had room to sit and spread out her work. The mSap was in the corner, humming away, probing for fluctuations in the electromagnetic signature of the Ascendancy. In another corner lay a pile of soil from Tai's digging project, where he was tunneling out a back door in case of need.

Frankly, Tai had saved her life, and she'd been eager to promise him all that he asked. He deserved it, though his excavation raised dust that made her worry about her mSap. She kept it covered, although overheating was a problem too. But the tunnel was prudent; she needed an escape route. Anuve would be looking for her. The Tarig bitch would never forget how Helice had duped her. Helice wondered if, weeks ago, Anuve had figured out what the mSap was, or if Sydney had immediately capitulated and told Anuve everything.

In her present condition, Tai's hospitality was essential. Without this hiding place the Tarig would have found her by now. Also a concern: she suspected Quinn was still alive to stalk her. And Mo Ti was working for him. Mo Ti! How had Quinn won the big troll over? Mo Ti might have told him of her plans. Her renaissance plans that she had confided to Sydney, but that Mo Ti had been lurking around to hear.

Raising her chin, she inspected the wreck of her skin. She thought she had a fever.

How could so much be going wrong given her initial spectacular successes? Her colleagues in the Rose had calibrated their engine to match the outputs at Ahnenhoon. She had crossed over to the Entire, following Quinn through many difficulties. She'd managed to win over Quinn's daughter, who had a goal so close to her own it was breathtaking.

But now a small, vile bacterium had taken hold. Exploiting her lack of natural Entirean immunity, it might get out of hand. She pushed the mirror away on the bed so she wouldn't look at herself accidentally. The Entire—that place she had thought of as rebirthing humankind—might well kill her as though she were nothing but an ideal disease vector.

It was a thought she had not allowed herself to consider until his moment. Was that long life of the Entire to be denied her? She let the black thought do its worst. It penetrated her. As she sat, helpless before this strong possibility, as her mind grappled with the preposterous notion of its own demise, she came to a place of calm. A cold place, yes. But not paralyzing. If she knew she couldn't share in humanity's renaissance, would she still be here? Did mankind's resurrection matter if she was gone?

If the worst was coming, did she still give a shit about the plans?

From the cold place within, she extracted an answer. Nothing would change. She would still go to the Tarig and demand a sway for her people. It surprised her that she wasn't more cynical. She'd fought her whole life for recognition and advancement. Altruism carried the sour whiff of entitlement. Yet, here she was doing something for others. This great scheme had never been solely about her. It was about giving humanity back to the fittest, and if necessary she would die for the cause. So much nicer, of course, if it weren't necessary.

So much more palatable if Tai could just find some fucking antibiotics.

She lay down on her cot again, silently urging the mSap to succeed in its search for cross-over points—points surely in constant use by the Tarig. Hurry, little friend, hurry.

Closing her eyes, she tried to rest, but the thought surfaced, was she doing everything she could? Surely she could reprogram the AI to perform better, to screen out the perturbations of the chaotic environment. Or perhaps the problem wasn't so much the mSap as the hovel itself.

She began to think of needed improvements. Thinking was the one great skill of Helice Maki, the gift that made her practically a twin to any machine sapient. Therefore it was not long before an idea began to blossom in her mind.

The mSap should have solved this problem by now. Being underground was not ideal; it inhibited the search pulses. But what if she used the space-time foam on the other side of these walls? The exotic matter led from the Sea of Arising to the great glittering columns, straight to the heart of the Ascendancy.

As the idea formed, she stood up in her excitement. She'd use the Nigh as her conduit. It wasn't an impediment, it was a transmission pathway. It was worth a try. To test it, she'd need to do a little programming.

And Tai would need to find a room with a view.

It was late in the ebb as Tai wound his way to his burrow. He had spent his day's wages on food, wrapped in a paper bundle to bring home to Hel Ese. After all these days of providing for her, his savings were almost gone; but it was more than worth it, to befriend a woman of the Rose.

He hurried down the street, eager to be home, but also curious to see what was brewing. All evening the street outside the foodery had been crowded with sentients, knots of morts and others, talking furtively of the dreams. Up ahead, Tai saw that a small rally was under way in front of one of the wine dens. Someone stood on an overturned cart, exhorting bystanders.

The dreams of the Long War had touched a nerve. Everyone here knew someone who came back wounded from the war—even if healed by Tarig largesse, and most knew someone who had died. It was permissible not to go for a soldier, but it put you at a disadvantage for the Magisterial examination. The tests determined whether you could enter into the great meritocracy and, through higher levels of exam, how quickly you would progress through the ranks. So if you cared to spend your life in the civil service of the Radiant Land as a clerk, steward, or any manner of legate whatsoever, you had to pass the examinations. Former soldiers promoted as quickly as the brightest of scholars. The system, morts had long noted, put all sentients at odds with each other, striving to pass the tests and surpass each other on the scramble to the top. If your family had money, they could afford tutors to ensure their sons and daughters did well. For the poor and those lacking military service, on the other hand . . . well, morts had no intention of wasting their lives in the civil service in any case: the very emblem of a dismal, repetitive, haggish life.

Tai had heard it all before, and moved past the small crowd, watching for seven-foot figures, listening with half an ear to the orator . . .

By the bright, he knew that speaker. It was Fajan. Blue feathers. He stopped to stare at Fajan as he spoke with passion about how the navitars were sending visions of the great lie of the Long War.

Tai listened to him with amazement. Fajan the flash boy, Fajan the ogler at rivitars . . . here he was, talking of the Tarig and their deceptions. Their eyes met. Fajan nodded at him and paused, as though to say: You were right.

Moved and startled, Tai listened to Fajan as he gave himself to a cause. Young morts were murmuring, peppering his speech with shouts of encouragement. "Fajan!" the chant began.

Then someone was pushing through the crowd, raising his hands for silence, for a chance to speak. By his conservative dress, a Red, Tai guessed. He was older than most in the crowd, his dark-streaked hair bound in a clasp at his neck.

"No proof," he called out. "Dreams are no proof."

Though the crowd growled at this, the Red spread his arms, imploring reason: "Why trust a dream sent by traitors? Have you thought who might be manipulating the dreams of us all? Might it be the darklings themselves, the very ones the gracious lords search for?"

The crowd called out insults and Fajan tried to speak over his opponent, but the Red was a big man, and his voice carried. "Remember that you're guests in our sanctuary. You call it the undercity, but it is the sanctuary of the Society. You are here by our sufferance, not to gather in traitorous cells, and not to burn resin and think you have knowledge from heaven. . . .

The crowd surged forward. Fajan was hollering for restraint. A young woman threw a stone. Pandemonium broke out.

Coming down the street were three Tarig, moving fast. Tai backed up toward the building frontage and moved quickly down the street, melting into an alleyway. He didn't like abandoning Fajan; but these days, Hel Ese came first.

CHAPTER EIGHTEEN

The wise commander avoids the traps of hills, rivers, and narrow places, while inviting the enemy into their embrace.

—Tun Mu's *Annals of War*

"**W**E'VE FOUND HER." Zhiya had left the door to Quinn's room open. One of her spies, a powerful-looking Jout, waited just out of hearing.

Quinn was already on his feet. "Where?"

"She's in the undercity. Your madwoman of the Rose."

By the bright, they'd found her at last. Not that he could have acted against Helice before; after thirty-three days he was only recently able to move without difficulty. The wound was clean, though, with the slug passing through the edge of his lung and making a clean exit.

She's in the undercity, Zhiya said. His knowledge of the place came from former memories of the world, but he didn't exactly have a complete grip on those. "Underneath Rim City, then?"

Zhiya nodded. "You'll need an escort." She gestured at the Jout. "This is Gaulter." They exchanged bows.

She watched Quinn as he moved, perhaps judging whether he was ready for battle. "I know that area well. Maybe you should let me do this."

He pulled on his jacket. "Murder's no job for a godder." It got the smile he hoped for.

"But it's a Miserable God, remember?"

"I remember." After all that had happened, he almost believed in the frowning deity. "Is she alone?"

"No. She's holed up with a young man who's bringing her food. He's a mort. They like the undercity, and some live there. He shouldn't give you any trouble, even if you're carrying around a wound that could fell a Gond."

"He's a what . . . a mort?"

"Funny word. English, isn't it? It's a cult. Disaffected young sentients ducking life. They have a partiality for the Rose, so your Hel Ese chose a good protector."

"She's not mine." He wouldn't have her in any way be *his*. Good God, he remembered that once he'd felt sorry for her, when she got burned in the crossing. She'd given a little speech about being fascinated by the Entire, looking for something fine, and couldn't she just tag along since she had already followed him through the veil and she couldn't return? If he'd shoved her back into the crevasse then, she wouldn't be on the verge of mayhem now.

"Tell me about the undercity."

"The place is small, maybe two hours' walk from one end to the other. A hangout for the dregs of the city. Young men in particular hang out there, looking for sex and other pastimes their parents would shudder at. They're a death cult in some ways, because they shun the bright. I believe you have rather a nice reputation among them."

He raised an eyebrow.

"Man of the Rose. They think you darklings lead a better life. You have to cram all those Rose experiences into fewer days."

By the bright, Helice would tell him where the Rose engine was. The matching engine to Ahnenhoon. A monstrous vision; from the demon herself. He knew what he was doing: dehumanizing her so he could outright kill her. She might deserve it, but he had never . . . no he couldn't say he'd never killed. He'd killed Small Girl. And from that moment he had seen himself differently. You find that you are capable of certain things that were once unimaginable, and you became, if not a stranger, then at least more unwelcome to yourself.

He tucked his knife into his boot, thinking that he was becoming a killer. He tried to remember that at least one person still loved him. And more important, he loved her, proving that he had come some few steps toward decency.

Zhiya turned to Gaulter. "Take Ni Jian to the woman's hideout. And if the spirit moves you, help him kill her. I don't expect you to murder for me, but the Rose woman is a vile, depraved gondling whose life is an insult to the bright. Do I make myself clear?"

The Jout cracked a toothy smile. "Venerable." He ducked a bow, and led Quinn down the steps to the city.

Shadow Ebb had crept over the bright while Quinn and Zhiya had talked. Now, Gaulter assured him, the undercity would be at its busiest, and thus at its safest for them to make their way down. They quickly found their way to a ramp leading to the burrows. Quinn's disguise was a wispy mustache and torn silks. As they descended, smells of greasy food mixed with a whiff of sewage.

Quinn's eyes began to adjust to their new surroundings: a dim underground street, cramped but lively, sparkling with marquee lights and shafts of light from open doors spilling a clattering music and the pulses of drums. Portholes punctuated the walls, letting in the confused light of the sea depths. Waves of layered dark light shimmered behind the glass, barely illuminating the corridor. Three-wheeled pedi cabs and pedestrians shared the main street. While the press of bodies was decent cover, one thing could well give him away: his age. The denizens of this place were young and artfully dressed. Bright silks clad the men as beautifully as the women. On second thought, some of the women *were* men.

They passed a few older Chalin men dressed in long sleeveless coats. "Red Throne," Gaulter murmured, and led Quinn on, out of the commercial district into a dimmer and more neglected neighborhood. He was nervous, aware of the knife in his boot. He'd have to act fast. See her, kill her. Keep her from delivering her devil's bargain to the Tarig. Why she waited was hard to know.

Up ahead, a Tarig. No, a cluster of them. Trusting that the lords hadn't seen them, they swerved into a busy foodery. He and Gaulter watched as the lords passed by on the street. Then, slipping back out into the street, Gaulter led him in the opposite direction of the lords. At last they ducked down a narrower street. *This way*, Gaulter assured him. It was a darker region, one that appeared abandoned. A nice place for a Tarig ambush, too. Gaulter looked behind. No lords following.

"It's one of the last burrows," Gaulter said. Putting on his game face, the Jout drew out his knife, not bothering to hide it.

Quinn thought of the first time he'd met Helice, at Stefan Polich's Christmas gathering. It was long ago now, though it depended on which clock you used. At the time he'd thought of her as typical of that class of hyper-smart savvy who had never learned social skills or compassion. He'd noted her expression when Polich announced that she wouldn't be going with Quinn on his expedition. A stricken look. He did wonder what had brought her to this. It didn't matter. He'd hesitated over such things once: at Ahnenhoon, when, if he hadn't been thinking too much, he could have preserved the Earth. Now, he wouldn't pause when the time came.

Gaulter nodded at a dark wall. "There," he murmured. Just down the alley, barely discernable in the murky passageway, was a hole covered by a cloth.

Quinn reached down to his boot, withdrawing his knife, the one Zhiya managed to recover for him when she found him wounded. It had lain in the Way, a beautifully crafted knife, a present from his old fighting master, Ci Dehai. He was thankful to still have it.

He told Gaulter, "I'll have a question for her. First."

Taking a quick look down the alley, Quinn lunged through the door, swiping the cloth aside. Gaulter was behind him, flashing a lamp around the room. It was empty.

"Wrong room!" Quinn muttered.

"No. This is the place."

A sinking sensation hit Quinn. He kicked over the bed, searching. "Let's try the next one."

Gaulter found a pan of water and bandages. "Was she hurt?"

In a corner, a flash of iridescent color. Quinn picked up a small, green silk hat. He'd seen Helice wear it when she shot him. The right den. The wrong time. His gaze lit on the wall near the bed. There was a hole. "Over here," he said to Gaulter.

"A tunnel," Gaulter said, then jerked his head toward the doorway.

His companion moved quickly to the door, peering out. *Tarig*, he mouthed. He clicked off the lamp.

"They followed us," Quinn murmured.

Gaulter whispered, "Move the bed in front of the door." It would force the Tarig to come in single file, but that would be little advantage. Quinn had fought with two Tarig: Hadenth and Chiron. He'd won against Hadenth, but the creature had been half dead; he'd lost to Chiron in seconds. They rammed the bed into position.

Gaulter pushed Quinn toward the wall. "Go into the hole," he whispered. "With any luck, goes somewhere." Left unsaid was that the Jout himself was too big to fit through the hole. When Quinn hesitated, Gaulter pushed him toward the wall. "I give my life for Zhiya. I gladly do." He turned to the door, murmuring, "They won't interrogate me." More swiftly than Quinn could have stopped him, Gaulter sliced the knife across his own throat. Blood erupted from his massive body.

The door ripped open, and the Jout, still standing, fell headlong toward the crouching Tarig just preparing to enter.

Quinn scrambled into the hole. He couldn't travel on hands and knees, only by a scrunching movement of his spine, pushing with his toes and knees and grasping for the sides of the tunnel to pull himself along. The burrow was rough and very dark. This fact might hold the Tarig back for a moment. They despised the dark—one reason why the Entire had no night. He scrambled forward.

Behind him he heard the noise of scrambling. So, they'd come in, after all. He couldn't out-crawl a Tarig, and this one, he'd just learned, had a lamp.

Fajan crouched beside the fallen speaker. Even if he was of the wretched Society, he deserved a chance to speak without a beating. "Are you all right? Can I help you to get home?"

The Red managed to stand, wiping the dust from his clothes. "You have more courtesy than the rabble, I see."

"You have a right to your wrong opinions," Fajan said, smiling to soften the rejoinder. The Red nodded at his wit, then straightened and walked off.

Three Tarig stood by, watching the crowd disperse. Merely the presence of the lords stopped the proceedings. Showing restraint, the lords scanned the crowd for the ones they searched for. Two people now, by the view spray posters on the walls: a man and a woman. The man was Titus Quinn of course. The woman, one without a name. The Tarig were foolish to think a Rose fugitive would hide somewhere so obvious when they had the whole of the never-ending city, above, to hide in.

Fajan nodded at the lords as he passed them, murmuring, *Bright Lords.* They hadn't seen that he was one of the speakers, so they had no reason to detain him. He drifted down the street, agitated, needing to walk off his excitement. He watched for Tai, hoping to see him.

Down an alley he saw a rowdy group. He headed for it, needing company, hoping it was morts.

Quinn crawled onward through the tunnel, already feeling fatigue. Lungs not one hundred percent, he pulled in gasps of air. Behind him, the scuffling sound of pursuit. In desperation, he turned onto his back and kicked the ceiling of the burrow, trying for a collapse of the tunnel behind him. He slammed his foot again and again into the top of the dig. Nothing. A light flashed in his face. The lamp of the Tarig. He twisted around and clawed his way forward again.

Ahead was a faint light. Even if he made it to the end of the tunnel, he would still have to face his pursuers once out of the hole. A freshening of air told him he was close to the end.

Scrambling for the light, he pushed out, finding himself in a narrow alley. Before ejecting from the tunnel, he gave a last kick. A cloud of dust rushed forward to spill from the hole. Part of it, at least, had collapsed.

People were milling around him. Someone supported him, asking if he was all right. Incredibly, the tunnel had caught his pursuers, but not him. He gulped air, reviving slowly.

But there was another survivor of the tunnel. A Tarig appeared in the hole, and stepped out, unfolding his tall body. Quinn drew his knife. The lord, blackened with soil, stalked toward him, claws extruded, reaching.

The crowd bellowed as one. From behind, they swarmed the lord from all sides, raising boards, stones, bare hands to strike at him.

The lord's first swipe took out two throats, a move that, rather than demoralizing, enraged the young men. Some of them had taken up a chant of *Fajan Fajan*. A large female Jout came into the fray with a shovel, slamming the side of the lord's head with it. Encouraged, the crowd piled forward to bury the Tarig, who thrashed under their weight. Then, bracing his long legs under him, and in a massive heave, he threw the bodies off.

Quinn tackled the lord at the knees, avoiding the claws, trying to bring him down. The Tarig fell, but nimbly came into a crouch and then stood up. As he came up, someone's knife impaled an eye, digging deep, sticking solid.

The Tarig howled—a tone to shrivel eardrums. The piercing cry stopped the assault, as the mob backed off, watching the creature standing tall among them, streaming blood. The Tarig grabbed the knife and pulled it out.

Then the Tarig lord went to his knees. But he was already dead. Someone came forward and rammed a foot into the Tarig's chest. He toppled.

"Fajan!" someone cried.

Quinn turned to the group, taking closer note of its composition: young men, likely morts, each one armed with implements and makeshift weapons. "Go now, go quickly," he said. "Before this Tarig's cousins come. And thank you."

The one called Fajan turned from the body to look at Quinn. Quinn nodded at Fajan, then spun on his heels and ran to the end of the alley. There, he turned, seeing that a few morts still lingered, staring at the lord's body. Whoever that Tarig had been, he could return, presumably—if Mo Ti's tales of Tarig rejuvenation were accurate. Although the recent memory in this individual would never be recovered, an earlier version of this Tarig could take on a new form. Death, in the world of the Tarig, was complicated.

Quinn walked quickly down the street, wiping himself as clean as was possible. Tarig blood was red, he remembered, but it still wouldn't do to be drenched in it. He found a public wastery and stripped, rinsing his clothes. He thought of Gaulter. Zhiya inspired such loyalty, and it was good that she did. But Gaulter was dead, and it angered and saddened him.

Emerging from the wastery, he was wet but clean.

Exhausted, grimacing with the pain of his exertions, he put his mind to walking normally toward the access to the upper city. As he walked, he watched for Helice, knowing he would never again have such luck, to see her on the street. Still, he muttered to whatever god was listening: *Just give me one chance at her.*

From deep in the undercity came the sound of a growing tumult. Maybe the Tarig body had been discovered. Quinn put distance between himself and the scene of the death, climbing the ramp down which he and Gaulter had come just an hour ago.

In the upper city, he made his way home under the lavender ebb. Time enough to consider this bitter failure after he reported to Zhiya that her friend had died. In the midst of these considerations, the thought struck him with special force: he had just witnessed a mob murder a Tarig lord.

CHAPTER NINETEEN

The Heart. Ancestral home of the gracious lords, land of remembrance of the Sleeping Lord, the heavenly womb of the All.
—from *Hol Fan's Glossary of Needful Terms*

HELICE STARED INTO THE DEPTHS OF THE SEA OF ARISING. It was bloody amazing. If she weren't so intent on practical matters, she would sit here forever and study the foam of the sea. She was a kid in a candy store, an mSap engineer in particle heaven. She was a tad worried about gamma rays, but they didn't seem to kill anyone in the Entire prematurely.

Tai was nearby, studying. Busy little beaver that he was, he was memorizing a list of English words and phrases Helice had given him against the day he'd need them in the Rose. *Friend; My name is Tai. Where is the bathroom?*

She was happy to help him. Her mood had skyrocketed within an hour of setting up shop in this new location. It was so lovely when mSaps performed their feats. They had a grace, precision, and power she had admired since she was old enough to build her first simple computer. She'd been twelve.

Earlier in the day, Tai had brought her to a mort hangout where, he had assured her, there was a porthole to the sea. Although empty now, the place had once been a favorite of some of Tai's friends, but these same morts were now afraid of the old haunts. The lords were jumpy after a murder of one of their own.

It wouldn't be long now before she could send Tai on his new mission: to the Ascendancy. To get things ready.

Outside, voices from the street penetrated. She cut a glance at the door, anxious.

Tai looked up from his tablet, then went back to his memorizing, his lips moving to form the words, *foreigner*; *please*; *pardon me*; *hungry*.

For the first time in weeks, Helice felt a surge of hope. The little machine that she had smuggled into the Entire, that she had carried on her back down the torturous descent of the crystal bridge, had just proven itself worthy. By virtue of her move to a new burrow, and concentrating on the search pathway offered by the sea, her machine sapient had found in the Ascendancy a particular and peculiar interface point along two branes. This locus generated a high wind of particles, much more intense than the bright itself, for instance.

She believed this was the Tarig access point. The doorway to their home place. The thing that Sydney and her crew were desperately looking for.

Once in position along the wall of the burrow, it had taken the mSap sixteen seconds to identify the interface site in the Ascendancy. Fourteen of those seconds had been devoted to creating a new reference grid with which to identify a location in the cityscape.

This doorway was not a broad, permeable field. Instead, it was a junction point, a slit through which information passed; through which Tarig passed. In solitary and titanic fashion, the junction leaked its gravitational anxiety, requiring a monumental force to keep it open. It required all the energy represented by, say, a whole galaxy, to maintain itself. The Tarig would not likely produce a lot of them. Helice reasoned, therefore, that the Tarig had only one door. But it was a pipe bigger than any she'd ever heard of.

However, though she had the junction point coordinates, she couldn't translate them into an understandable location. For one thing, she didn't know what the Ascendancy looked like, or how it was laid out. But still. She was on the verge of climbing into negotiating position with the CEOs of the universe. After a few guarantees were in place. Such as: I can blow your door to kingdom come if you aren't nice.

In his corner, Tai formed his English words silently with his mouth, aware that he couldn't talk while Helice was working: *bed*; *love*; *thank you*; *clothes store.*

She smiled at him. So earnest.

One didn't approach the Tarig and ask permission for a contingent of savvies to come over, not without assurances. Therefore Tai would have to go and set in motion certain assurances. He had an excuse to go to the Ascendancy: a Jout subprefect had ordered him to be on the lookout for Rose fugitives. He'd tell the subprefect that he thought he'd seen the fugitive Rose woman, someone who looked very suspicious on the street. It would be fairly useless information, but it would be Tai's excuse to be in the Ascendancy and would provide the opportunity for him to put in place her little guarantee.

So much to lose. The stakes had always been great: the survival of humanity, her preferred version of it. The preservation of the Entire as the repository of many far-flung cultures. But there was so much more. The Tarig, never mind their tendency toward domination, had been around for hundreds of thousands of years. They'd had time to master higher-order space-time and create the Entire. Their scientific understanding was of incalculable value.

They'd made some strange choices with their knowledge. They'd created this tunnel world and made it a meeting-ground cosmos for intelligent species. They'd chosen to live in those frightening bodies—tall, thin, metallic-looking—no doubt intended to convey awe and menace, but they'd rather overdone the menace part. Furred or feathered might have been a better start. She missed her pet macaw. Why couldn't masters of the universe ever look like birds?

Nevertheless she was looking forward to conversations with the Tarig about so many things. For example, their truly ingenious products, such as the sea she was gazing at through the porthole. Structurally, it was indistinguishable from the Nigh. Helice conjectured that these geocosmic structures of the Tarig were all related. Beginning with the storm walls—those were indisputably gravitational turbulence. People even called the walls a *storm*. Then there were the water analogs to the Rose: the Nigh and the Sea. The Nigh, though key to so much of the workings of the Entire, was also merely turbulence, in this case, temporal and spatial. Ditto the Sea of Arising, source of all the Nighs. But the storm walls and the Nigh were secondary constructs.

The primary construct—from a physics standpoint at least—was the bright, the greatest of the Tarig creations. She theorized that the bright was generated by energy sucked from neighboring universes. The most efficient way to accomplish this was along the interface of branes. In whatever way the

Tarig drew down that energy, they chose to selectively perturb the interface to give off heat and light only across the vast sky of the Entire. It was a shame the Tarig hadn't come up with a more sustainable world, but of course, from their standpoint, it *was* sustainable. Supply-side solutions always came to mind first. The very crux of the Rose/Entire geogalactic differences.

Damn, but this was fun. She profoundly wished she had more time to think.

She glanced at Tai. Yes, still studying, now on rising inflection: *lonely? help me? job?*

It was time to redirect her energies. She was programming the assembler module of the mSap to create a cell with a smart detonator. In stage one, the explosive burst would create just enough damage and smoke to get attention.

Can do, Helice thought merrily. She was a sapient engineer. Just the right person for the job, as she'd tried to explain to Stefan not long ago, when he hadn't listened and had sent the wrong person to do the job she should have had. Well, Stefan's punishment was that he wasn't on the *list*.

So Stefan, you see? You aren't coming along for this jaunt. You aren't coming along to the future at all.

Tai interrupted her thoughts. "How do you say 'the Entire' in English?"

"You might not want to use that word over there."

"But they'll figure out I'm a . . . *foreigner*. I'll be honest."

"They don't think of this place as everything that exists."

He frowned, trying to figure out her point. "Neither do I."

Well then, you will all get along famously, she thought. She pushed away feelings of guilt. She wasn't going to admit to an admirer of Titus Quinn that she planned to make short work of the Rose. Tai would go, if she could arrange it. He'd have a short life. Likely it would be quite intense.

She gave him the translation, and he wrote it in his tablet.

The excitement from her day of discoveries was wearing off, and she leaned against the burrow wall, feeling nauseous. Just a little sleep, and she'd be able to work. Her throat felt like she'd swallowed thumbtacks. Best to get to the Tarig soon and have a look in their bag of medical tricks. Closing her eyes, she slept.

Tai woke her up, urgently. She snapped awake, thinking of pursuit, of giant, thin *mantis lords* . . .

"It's at the porthole!" he whispered.

She turned to look. Something . . . something was out there. She stared at it. Nothing could be in the sea.

"A rivitar," Tai whispered. At her look of incredulity, he continued, "I don't know what it really is, but morts call it a rivitar. I've seen it once before."

It was a cube about one foot square. Images flickered on every side of it; faces of the sentients of the Entire. Helice and Tai stared it, transfixed. The sides of the cube appeared to stare back.

Very slowly, Helice knelt down next to the mSap and touched the screen. The box outside the porthole was emitting a tight-beamed light stream of encoded data. She selected the mSap's decryption functions. The thing in the river had an unusual energy signature, with fundamental particles exploding from nowhere in what had the appearance of a sustained virtual light. So the thing was only virtually present and yet sending messages, a nice little feat.

The mSap had not yet made sense of what was surely a message. So far it looked very much like static. It could also be something that looked like random static: a perfectly encrypted message.

While the mSap worked, Helice lowered herself to the floor, propping herself up against a piece of abandoned furniture. Through the distortion of the exotic matter, the faces on the cube's sides were clear: a Hirrin, a Jout, Ysli, Inyx, Chalin. Tai identified a creature she'd never seen before, a Gond.

"Tell me what you know," Helice whispered, and Tai did: He called it a rivitar. It came now and then to portholes here. Some of his friends had seen it often. But he knew, essentially, nothing.

Whatever this was, it had made an effort to elude Tarig detections. That by itself made the object an item of interest. Perhaps it had been attracted by the pings Helice had been sending. She indulged her curiosity; she'd give the mSap an hour to decode the static.

A hot weariness fell over her. She let herself close her eyes. . . .

The mSap woke her up with a vibration.

How she could have fallen asleep under the circumstances astonished her, but she was wide awake now. "Don't let me sleep," she instructed Tai. He sat on his heels, staring at the thing in the river.

On the screen, a line of type.

She scrambled over to it, peering closely.

... PLACE SUFFICES. JINDA CEB HORAT CONCEDE TO ANY PRIME REGION. MESSAGE REPEATS.

It was a recording.

JINDA CEB HORAT ACKNOWLEDGE SENTIENTS. ONCE OF THE PRIME REGION, JINDA CEB COME AGAIN, NOW WITHOUT THREATS. YOU WILL FIND PLEASANT INTERFACE. DO YOU ACKNOWLEDGE?

On the same frequency, Helice sent a ping.

JINDA CEB HORAT, ONCE OF THE PRIME REGION LONG SIGHT OF FIRE, SEND PLEASANT QUERY. JINDA CEB REQUEST JUNCTION. TAR IG NAME US PAION. ONCE, IN LONG SIGHT OF FIRE, TAR IG WISHED TO DIMINISH ENERGY EXPENDITURE THAT SUSTAINED THE JINDA CEB HOME. THE DWELLING PLACE SEVERED, JINDA CEB BECAME ALONE. JINDA CEB APPROACHED WITH UNPLEASANT INTERFACE TO SECURE THE DWELLING PLACE AT LOCUS AHNEN-HOON. WHAT HAS BEEN THE CAUSE OF DYING IS UNNECESSARY. JINDA CEB SEND QUERY TO RETURN. PLEASANT DWELLERS OF THE PRIME REGIONS MAY DECIDE. TAR IG DO NOT DECIDE. JINDA CEB HAVE PROCEEDED MANY DAYS TO LIMIT ENERGY DEMANDS. JINDA CEB HORAT LIVE A BILLION DAYS BEYOND YOU OF THE ALL, IN A TIME STREAM OF HIGH VELOCITY. JINDA CEB ASK FOR JUNCTION. ONE SINGLE SMALL PLACE SUFFICES. JINDA CEB HORAT CONCEDE TO ANY PRIME REGION. MESSAGE REPEATS.

Helice pinged again. The message repeated.

Tai looked at her with barely controlled excitement. "What does it say?"

He couldn't read it over her shoulder. The message from the Jinda ceb Horat had been in English.

"It said—" Helice paused to gauge how much she wanted to tell Tai. This apparition in the exotic matter was a challenge to the Tarig, and no mistake. Undoubtedly, this was another highly technically capable species; one so advanced it knew to send the mSap a message in English. She considered telling Tai it was confidential, but that might not be wise. If he was going to risk even more danger for her, a little trust was in order.

"The message, it claims, is from the Paion."

He turned a dumbfounded expression on her. "Paion?"

Helice was still staring at the cube submerged in exotic matter, *diving* in it as though it were a real sea. How did it happen that the message came to her in English? Perhaps the cube had accessed her mSap. That was a troubling thought. She was nothing without the mSap and she'd have no one fiddling with it.

The cube winked out of existence.

Helice let go a breath she hadn't known she was holding. A Paion. It was trying to stop the war, and it was going around the Tarig to do so. She wished, she mightily wished, it had stayed longer.

She sat back against the wall, her mind racing. "It was an image bearing a message. It just repeats the same thing, over and over. But yes, it was Paion."

Tai ran his fingers along the porthole in wonder. "What did they say?"

"They claim to be very old. Their time—Paion time—has been going much faster than yours. They may be a couple million years older than your civilization by now."

"Time changes speed?"

She blinked at him. Didn't they teach these people anything? "Each universe, each dimension is different that way." She went on, "It sounds like they want some land. Land they once had in the Entire and that the Tarig took away." She went back to the mSap, rereading. "No, they want to *attach* to any of the primacies, not just the . . ." here she traced the words on the screen with her finger . . . "not just at the Long Gaze of Fire. So, attaching to a primacy would make them a minoral."

Tai was gazing thoughtfully into the pale light of the river. "They used to have a closed-off minoral, so the dreams say."

Yes, Sydney and the horses were busy again, doing their dream spam. How had she known, or how had the Inyx discovered, that the Paion had been cut off in their minoral? And what a fine piece of propaganda it was, to make the Tarig look ruthless! Apparently it was true, or the Jinda ceb wanted people to think so. The topic begged for resolution, but she had to put it away for a time. She was exhausted, and more immediate work lay ahead of her.

Meanwhile, it was important that no one know about this. No one must know she had an mSap.

"Keep this secret, Tai. Or the Tarig will come for me. You don't want that, do you?"

"Haven't I proven this?"

He was hurt. It was difficult for her to nurture him along, to know how much to tell him. She softened her tone. "Yes, you've proven yourself, Tai. You've been a good man. The Rose will thank you."

She closed her eyes, resting them, thinking. The Paion message suggested they were trying to stop the Long War. And that they wished to return to what they apparently thought of as their homeland. How could this be useful? But she didn't have time to figure the Jinda ceb into her strategy. They were, if anything, a distraction from her purpose. The last thing she needed right now was a game-changing new player on the field.

That being the case, it was lucky that she and Tai were the only ones who'd heard this message.

Renaissance was still on. Time to get back to it.

CHAPTER TWENTY

Galaxy. Theoretical construct said to exist in cosmic space. An aggregation of stars and associated orbiting planetesimals that is bound by forces of attraction, travels through the void, and rotates around a center.

—from *Arcane Nomenclature of the Dark Cosmologies*

SU BEI WAS TOO AGITATED TO SLEEP. He stared at the membrane that covered the veil of worlds as it briefly showed a series of wondrous scenes.

He and Anzi had been traveling for thirty-eight days, time enough to wear blisters into their feet and run out of food and primals. But here—finally *here*, in an abandoned Reach of a minoral in the Radiant Arch Primacy, Bei's old eyes had fallen upon a thing of legend: a third kingdom.

Scholars had known there were, or guessed that there must be, more realms than the Rose and the Entire, but never a glimpse, not even one ever reported to the Magisterium. No wonder that scholarship had kept to the Arm of Heaven and its productive minorals, viewing the richness of the Rose cosmos. But Anzi had said there were hundreds of realms, or so she had heard Lord Oventroe say.

Here was the proof. On the veil before him flickered a cosmos with structures like the Rose. But it was not the Rose. Bei was at this very moment face to face with a planetoid of the third kingdom. Using both the correlates and his cosmography studies, he knew the correspondence here was between the Entire and a third cosmos. He had the mathematical proofs. There was an isomorphic relationship between the Entire and the kingdoms it touched. They *mapped* to each other. The correlates, by their very existence, implied this. But to see it in evidence before him in a third kingdom! It made him young again, and it made him ambitious, for his cosmography work had just proven its immortal worth, when the many data points of his great map did not correspond to the data at this veil. It drove him to look for correlations beyond the Rose, and thus the hypothetical *bubbles of universes* suggested by Anzi had just been confirmed.

He gazed with rapt attention at the veil of worlds, that membrane over the crevasse that pierced the next realm. Here, projected onto the membrane were beings—by happenstance, very like the Hirrin. *Hirrin*, the progenitors of the Hirrin of the All, likely on their originating planetoid. One might well conclude that the correlates tended to search out places of interest; this could explain his luck in finding another cosmos and planetoid after so brief a search.

Upon first setting up their stone well machines in this particular reach, he and Anzi had found the planetoid quickly, and watched until their eyes could stare no more. She slept now, but Bei could not.

They had not found the lords' universe, the Heart. They had merely confirmed the conjecture that such a thing could exist, because the third realm did. Why not a fourth? A fifth? A fiftieth? Anzi had accepted such a possibility with ease, but Su Bei had grown old waiting to see miracles and perhaps wonder came easier to him, as light will be more noticed the darker the room. Already he was developing this realm's geocosmic placement in relation to the Entire and in relation to the Rose. It was possible—likely, even?—that some of the realms—if there were yet more—existed without touching the Entire. It was possible—was it not?—that such and such a realm might touch the Entire, and the next realm would touch only a further realm, so there were links outside the All. . . . Yes, it was growing into a dumbfounding but unified complex of . . . bubbles.

He let his mind roam. It was elegant. It . . . It . . . but what name could be found for *It*, this supreme complex of realities? It was a boil of realms, a froth of worlds. Bei wanted a suitable term for It. For the sum total of everything.

The scene on the veil of worlds showed the roots of titanic trees waving in the air, perhaps taking sustenance from the soup of the atmosphere.

His mood darkened when he thought how the lords *used* the realms. For fuel. Was that not a heinous crime? What was a nurturing land for a particular civilization was nothing but a lump of dried dung to the Tarig. The engine at Ahnenhoon was beginning to eat at the Rose, or so Anzi had explained. Nor were other realms the only casualties. Bei had seen his own minoral destroyed, chewed up like some bale of goldweed destined for a beku's trough. He grieved that loss, his home of eighty thousand days. He suspected it had not been destroyed to conserve fuel but to prevent inter-course with the Rose—in his mind, a greater sin. The lords had ended archons of scholarship and viewing of the Rose. If, that is, the rumors were true, and all the minorals of the Arm of Heaven were gone. If true—and he prayed it was not—then the days of viewing the Rose were ineluctably over.

Even the thought staggered.

Not only was scholarship of the Rose ended, but passage, too. The lords feared more assaults on Ahnenhoon. Moreover, they were no doubt deter-mined that Titus Quinn not escape home. In that, they were wrong to worry. Titus was here for the duration. He was here to sit bestride their passageway to the Heart. He was going to bar the routes to the lords' renewal.

And it was up to Bei to point Titus in the right direction.

Bei sighed. He was not on the trail of the answer Titus needed. He was striking blindly at minorals, those that possessed developed scholar-reaches. And this minoral, sadly, was not the right one. Well, they could try other minorals in this primacy, or move to the Sheltering Path Primacy . . . Bei rubbed his eyes. Perhaps sleep was best.

Anzi appeared with a candle at the archway leading into the veil-of-worlds room. "Master? Not sleeping?"

"Too much thinking, Anzi, that's my curse." Bei pulled on his beard, gazing at the veil, now showing a mountainous region of the same planetoid.

Anzi looked at the scene with him, perhaps fascinated anew.

In the silence Bei said, "What shall we call the hundred realms, Anzi?"

She settled into an agile cross-legged position on the floor. "Perhaps the Great Outside."

He shook his head. "No, because it's us, too. It's everything."

She seemed to accept his ruminative state and adopted it, gazing into the ancient veil. "Perhaps the Celestial All."

"Too grandiose."

She crumpled her mouth, thinking hard. "The foam."

"Too small."

They sat amiably for a few moments thinking of names. Bei murmured, "Sometimes I think that it's all falling into place, Anzi. The correlates are not just about the Rose. This we discovered from the ship keeper. But as we move from primacy to primacy, from minoral to minoral, I see that we are traversing the great scheme of all the cosmos. The Entire, Anzi, has an enviable position in the . . . in *it*. We abut many other pieces of the foam, of the bubbles that represent the hundred realms."

"I never meant exactly one hundred."

"I know that, girl. I know that. There's more than a lifetime of work to know even the smallest part of what can be known. But as for finding the Heart . . . even that is a staggering question. What universes have borders with the Entire? And where can they be seen from?" It was a rhetorical question, and they sat in silence as the scene on the veil moved on to galactic views and dark space. Only a few guttering candles pushed back the dark in this underground place. Above them was nothing but the fractured plains of the Gond homeland sway.

They had traveled by sky bulb from a major docking site on the river Nigh. The shrewd dock master had bargained an unconscionable price for his sky bulb, one that left Anzi fuming and their expedition impoverished. Using the decrepit airship, they had traveled for days anti-Nigh-ward across the endless forests of the primacy, seeing on their journey not one Gond, with the legless creatures tucked away beneath the tight canopy of the forest's upper story. Who knew if the famed nests of the Gond were numerous or rare? Few travelers came to this primacy, most never venturing beyond the settlements along the Nigh. Once though, as Bei and Anzi's airship motored over a rare clearing, the sound of singing came from far below, confirming an ancient story that the Gond had voices that could fill the Empty Lands and knock a Chalin off his feet.

Anzi interrupted his thoughts. "We could call it the Great Sway."

She was still considering names—and that one. . . . He squinted his eyes. He mouthed the words, *the Great Sway*. He slowly stood up. "Anzi, by a beku's balls." He looked down at her, sitting easily in a position that would stove him up for days. "Anzi, you have come a long way since your days of senselessness."

"Thank you, Master."

Snaking a look at her, he realized she was mocking him. Perhaps she had always deflected attention from herself with that calm and pliable act. By the Miserable God, the girl could be sarcastic.

A shower of dust fell from the ceiling.

Anzi jumped up to throw a cover over the stone well machines.

Bei looked up, listening. A shuffle of boot on stone. He shared a look with Anzi. It could not be good that someone had followed them here. Here, on Titus Quinn's business, he and Anzi could not afford to be captured. But they were trapped. The veil-of-world room in this minoral, like most minorals, was a dead end.

Above, more shuffling. Fortunately, in this veil, the lift was no longer in operation, and the stairs were difficult to find. It gave them a few minutes.

Bei fingered the redstones on his necklace. He glanced at the veil of worlds, that film covering the wedge that punctured the next world. They could go through. They would have to. He untied the cord holding his redstones, sorting them into his hand.

Anzi saw him do so, and her eyes widened. Neither of them had spoken a word, nor did they need to. He was considering sending them through the to-and-from-the-worlds-door.

With a nod at the veil, he indicated silently that Anzi should secure one of their stone wells. When she didn't understand, he whispered: "We're taking one. Hurry!"

She shook her head. She looked like a beku balking at a ride.

He hissed at her, "You want to see Titus again? I can't help you fight them, and we don't know how many there are. Now remove its conduits and wrap it in a cloth!"

Anzi hurriedly wrapped the stone well, leaving it at Bei's feet, and rushed to the doorway, piling crates in front of it to slow their pursuers down.

Bei fell to his knees and fumbled his redstones off his necklace. All his insights, all his discoveries. . . . He had to preserve them; the only way was through the veil. He'd seen departures through the veil; by the bright, he'd seen Titus Quinn leave that way, once. A globule would form around them, preserving some air. . . . And that was as much as he knew. About to find out more, by the Woeful God.

Taking one redstone onto which the correlates had been copied, he dropped it into the stone well receiving cup of their second computational device, still connected into the veil with conduits. It was a terrible gamble. Bei couldn't direct which scene would appear, but starting a new progression might attract something of interest. They had no choice, they had to leave. How would they ever return? But Bei had the correlates, and no one must take them.

He tapped the screen with a formula he had just developed, an outgrowth of the correlates, but more specifically related to mapping. No use, no use, it was untested, foolhardy. But voices outside the room drove him to finish.

Anzi heard them coming. She drew her knife. "You go, Master. You must."

He finished and stuffed the now loose redstones into his tunic. They were both standing next to the veil. As the boxes crashed under the assault at the door, he grabbed Anzi and shoved her with all his strength into the veil, shattering the outer film and not giving her even a moment to catch her breath.

A Hirrin lurched through the barricade.

Bei said, "Welcome. And what might your name be?" He picked up the stone well computer that Anzi had wrapped.

The Hirrin, momentarily confused by the reception from an old man, turned to look at the Ysli just coming up behind him.

In that moment, Bei threw himself into the veil after Anzi. The Hirrin was fast. He charged across the room and gripped Bei's trailing elbow in his mouth. Anzi's globule was close enough that she saw what was happening. Lunging, she jammed her knife hand through the gel of the veil and slashed at the Hirrin's mouth.

She overreached, falling into Bei's globule of air, but she'd managed to gash the Hirrin's face.

Bei just managed to pull his elbow back in when the transition began.

Now joined in one vacuole, they held each other like twins in a birth canal. Through the cloudy transitional matrix Bei saw a space-time distortion of a Hirrin's face: streams of blood twisted about his face like ribbons on a gift.

Stunned and panicked, he and Anzi huddled in the muscular little sac and abandoned themselves to the mercy of the Great Sway.

CHAPTER TWENTY-ONE

IT WAS FULL DARK AS CAITLIN SPED DOWN THE HIGHWAY, keeping the Mercedes under manual control, passing meshed transport, passing at eighty, at ninety. To one side, the Columbia River. Instead of seeing its familiar placid waters, she imagined a cloud of vapor flashing into the air. The river boiling off.

Jess had said, *I dream about it, fire roaring like a hurricane. Our home, gone, just like that. I imagine the river boiling off.*

Lamar had called it the transform. But it was a holocaust.

At least we'll survive. But to survive, you have to leave.

A half moon brightened the water, drawing her eyes when she needed to drive fast, drive very fast. Be packed, Lamar had said. Be ready. And when did he plan to end the world? She was losing her mind. Wasn't she?

Lamar had lied about Titus. Titus hadn't asked for a few people to join him in that place—the Entire. He had nothing to do with this. Lamar was behind it—with whom else, Caitlin had no idea. But Lamar was high enough in the group that he could change Mateo's test scores. So Mateo could go over to the Entire, with his sister and mother. So he could stand on—what had Jess called it?—the *transition stage* excavated under the old reactor.

Something terrible was going to happen, and only Lamar's two thousand were shipping out in time to avoid it. An apocalypse of fire. Our home, gone. Jess has nightmares.

She kept remembering a small, niggling thing, something Jess said about Emily not having children. Lamar's two thousand savvies were not coming back. The children would grow up and have children in the Entire. But if they didn't test well, they wouldn't be having children. Because the average person was dragging us down, and the *average* was about to become better. It sounded like eugenics. She had no proof, but at the same time she was sure. Ugly as that was, there was more: they weren't going to leave the Earth intact.

There'd be a good, savvy reason for that. They didn't want more people coming over to dilute the gene pool. They were creating an uber-colony of smartasses, just like the fanatics who'd threatened for decades to start colonies in South America—or Idaho, for that matter.

She was driving too fast. Slowing, she drew in gulps of air. At a legal speed, she voiced to her dashCom, "Audio contact, Rob."

She had no fucking idea what she would say.

He answered quickly. "Caitlin? Decided to come home tonight?"

"Yes."

"How are the roads? Where are you?"

"About an hour out." She passed a platoon of meshed cars, ambling along at sixty mph. "Rob."

He waited. "You OK?"

"Of course, OK. I've had a thought about that bad software glitch and don't want to lose it. I'm going to encrypt."

A pause. "Right. Go ahead."

She voiced, "Encrypt audio signal." The light flashed. You didn't survive in business without keeping your conversations to yourself, and Emergent's virtual educational modules were constantly poked at by their competitors. Now encrypted, she started over. "It's not the software, Rob. Something's happened. Can you get the kids over to Mother's?"

A pause for decoding. "What, tonight?"

She really had no idea how to begin. "I need you, Rob."

A very long pause. "That's nice to hear."

Amid her panic a thread of shame corkscrewed in. "I'll meet you at Emergent, back door. Please don't ask me anything. Just do it?" *Do we have enough of a relationship that you'd get the kids out of bed at 10:00 p.m. and drive over to Multnomah and wake Mother up, no questions asked?*

"You got it," he said.

Oh, steady Rob.

Rob at her side, Caitlin stranded the door code into the panel of the deserted office. "Lights off," she voiced, and they slipped inside.

Once the door locked behind them, Caitlin fumbled her way to the bathroom, keeping the light off. Rob followed her, not speaking, blessedly not asking her anything until she could relieve her bladder and wash the misery from her face.

When she joined him, she sank onto the floor, pulling Rob down with her. She rested her back against the wall.

"What, you murdered someone?"

"I wish."

Rob was so bemused he didn't even know what his first question was. His silence gave her the room to shape her story.

"Was Mom awake?"

"Yes. I told her we were having problems. She figured out it was marital."

He didn't elaborate. He'd said Mother *figured it out* because they *were* having problems. Of course they were, even if they'd never discussed it. Caitlin brushed past that topic, dwarfed as it was by events.

"I have some things to tell you that I'm not proud of. But the worst things aren't personal. They're . . ." her voice trembled. "Rob, they're something so bad." She couldn't see him in the absolute dark. Maybe that was best for what was coming. "I'm scared to death."

He put an arm around her. "I know. Just start talking, hon, let some words out."

"It's about Titus. It's about Lamar. And the kids."

"Whole family, then," he said with a smile in his voice, treating her like a panicked child.

She stopped, thinking that this was the last moment of peace Rob would know. She gripped his hand in a wordless apology. Closing her eyes, Caitlin tried to find a thread to pull on, somewhere to begin.

"Lamar changed Mateo's standard test so that he's shown as having advanced capabilities. As savvy."

Rob whistled.

Oh, baby, you think *that's* bad.

"He also changed mine."

Their voices took on a chamber resonance in the great space of the con-
verted warehouse. She lowered hers to a whisper, and told him, then, of
Lamar's offer to get them in on something, and that she grew suspicious and
drove, not to visit her friend in Goldendale across the river, but all the way
to Hanford.

Rob's arm came off her shoulders. "Why didn't you tell me?"

"I was ashamed of something." She wasn't going to soften this. It would
be so easy to make this part obscure, and she by God wasn't going to because
Rob deserved the truth. They'd been married a long time, and she'd been
treating him like shit for years. No, not like shit, maybe like something
worse. Like a clueless, pleasant roommate.

Maybe it didn't matter any more.

"Lamar didn't change your scores."

"I don't need . . ."

"No, don't ask questions yet. I need to tell you the whole thing. Lamar
is planning a crossover to the place Titus went. For a bunch of savvies. Some
of them are his friends. Like me and the kids. But not you."

A much larger silence hulked.

"Lamar has a staging ground up at the old Hanford nuclear reservation
where people are starting to congregate. I saw it. It's innocuous looking. Just a
bunch of modular dwelling units, a makeshift school—surrounded by the
decommissioned plants. They're getting ready for a mass crossing to the place
Titus went. Lamar said it's like a pocket universe, but enough like our own that
they can make a human colony. Lamar is trying to say that Titus is ready for an
advance team of scientists and their families to join him. And he's letting me
and the kids go out of some kind of pity. He's excluding you. Because he assumes
that I want to be with Titus." She paused, letting that statement sink in.

"And do you?"

Well, that was a nice, controlled reaction. "No. No, but that doesn't
mean I'm not guilty, Rob. I'm not saying I've been . . . a good wife."

"You've been." But his voice was tentative.

Now was the time for the thing she'd been trying to say since she'd walked into the warehouse. "I've been in love with Titus for a long time."

They sat side by side staring into the darkness, trying to see something, anything that would save them.

"I've fought it and reveled in it. I've pushed it away and wished to act on it. I would apologize if it wasn't so pathetic and self-serving. I just fell in love with him. I just, at times . . . it crept up, and I—"

"Don't, Caitlin. Just stop explaining. I know this."

"You know?"

A fringe of bitterness attached to his words: "I may not be Titus, but I notice *some* things."

Jesus. He knew. And all this time he forbore to say anything. It sounded miserable, even to her, but she said, "You didn't care?"

"I cared. You weren't sleeping with him?"

"No."

"He didn't ask you to?"

"No."

From the sound of it, she thought he put his head in his hands. Anger flared as she realized that it was more important to him to have his brother's loyalty than his wife's. She could have told him, but she didn't feel like it, that Titus wouldn't have been with her even if something happened to Rob, because he wouldn't *be in line*, as he'd said. So not only did she not have Titus, but she could never have had him. The whole thing was so fraught with layers of abstraction and longing that she couldn't decide, at this moment, how to feel. Goddamn Rob for accepting things, and goddamn Titus, too, for saying no. She was not thinking clearly, but what was new about that, after years of pretending, pretending that her marriage wasn't cracked down the middle?

"Caitlin," Rob began.

She turned on him, frazzled and desperate. "Is it just that we didn't have sex? Is that all that matters? Is it all just a game of who shags whom?"

"That's a lot of it." He didn't back down. "It matters to me."

How was she planning to make this Rob's fault? That he didn't love her enough to care who she loved? She stood up, pacing, bumping into a desk and painfully crunching her shin. "Shit, oh shit."

Rob found her in the dark. "Look. Caitlin. I don't blame you, and I'm not looking for an apology. There's just one thing I want right now, and that's you."

He said it so artlessly and without rancor that it caught her breath. She wanted to move toward him, but that was too easy, to receive absolution and then move on to the end of the world. But the thing was, she was relieved by his words. A drift of comfort settled down from above, like a blessing. "Oh Rob, I don't deserve this."

"I don't care about who's right, Caitlin. Can't you just listen to me? I want us to be good with each other again. I want you back." He put a tentative hand on her arm, or tried to, but touched her breast instead. He moved to her shoulder. "I'm not Titus, but can you love me?"

"I don't know," she whispered. "I'm so fucked up. Please let me try. Can you do that, can you let me try?"

They managed to touch hands.

"And Caitlin?" He gripped her hand. "Why are we discussing all this in the dark?"

"Because Lamar is trying to kill me."

"I thought you said he was trying to help you."

"He was. But I went to Hanford. He'll find out. He or one of those people is going to start worrying about me, especially after we hack his computer."

"Hack his computer?"

"We have to get some evidence for what they're doing. No one is going to believe me, and we might not have any time to wait for people to investigate. They're hiding everything inside an old reactor. That's where the transition platform is. If we can prove there's something strange in there, it would blow their cover story of a nuclear cleanup. So we need to raid Lamar's files."

She was tired, and rambling, and she hadn't yet told Rob about the hurricane of fire, and how the dreds weren't going to dilute the good stock anymore.

"I think we need to sit down for this," she began.

Just before dawn, they left the warehouse. It was still dark, so she still hadn't seen Rob's face, not clearly. It was surprising how much you could tell just by voice. He was sober, focused, and a little stunned. Still, he was working the problem. He was probably dealing with all this so well because he hoped she was wrong. And when he found out the opposite, he would feel exactly what she did: Quiet, sick panic.

They said their goodbyes and went to their separate cars: Rob to get the kids and Mother, finding a hiding place for them, and Caitlin to ferret out someone who was good enough to get past Lamar's computer security.

She settled into the driver's seat. If she couldn't find someone for the job, she'd return to the office and put her mSap on it. It would mean losing eleven million dollars' worth of quantum programming. She wasn't a sapient engineer, but she could handle savant programming, and she could jury-rig an mSap. It might leave a quantum mess behind, but it could be done.

Rob started the car, then shut it off again and got out, coming over to her. She rolled down her window.

"I love you," he said. By the streetlight, she caught him putting a finger to his lips.

She wasn't to answer, and she didn't.

CHAPTER TWENTY-TWO

All alone, he hides in sleep,
Missing home, he cannot keep.
Watching o'er his eyes so blind
He flees to dreams his Heart to find.
—Lord Ghinamid Watching O'er,
a child's verse

Despite his resolve not to be impressed by the Ascendancy, Tai stared at the great plaza before him, with its canals, artful bridges, and occasional towers of mysterious purpose. A Jout passed him, walking briskly on her business, smirking at the expression that must have marked Tai as a newcomer.

The Ascendancy was not so grand. It was a circular city resting upon the under-warrens of the Magisterium. Its grand plazas bore a few immense and narrow towers rising to nearly the bright itself. But there were not many of these. In the near distance, a hill upon which the lords' habitations clustered, those of the Five dwarfing the manses of the lesser lords. Behind Tai, the cut-away sector where the levels of the Magisterium were exposed to the sky.

So. Now he had taken in everything in one round glance. For all his adult years he had dismissed the lords and their works; he had lived by the Sea, he had gazed up at the Ascendancy. It was not so very grand, or if it was, one should not revere such hollow things.

But who was he trying to fool? The Bright City staggered him. The plaza before him could have contained the whole of the Rim undercity. The looming towers, topped with curved roofs, were the more wonderful in that they were said to have no purpose. Crisscrossing the plaza were the twisting canals of the city, crossed by graceful arching bridges. Petitioners of the many sways conversed in knots along the canals and pursued their mysterious errands. Above him the sky buckled in deep folds of lavender-gray in this, the second hour of Early Day. So close to the bright's essence, one felt oneself in the very doorway of heaven. Add to all this, the city floated high above the land, providing views out to the nearest storm walls, looking from edge-on like the dark legs of the Miserable God.

A shadow passed over him; it was a small flying creature. He had never seen birds fly, though he'd seen them run in the veldt. Momentarily he was disappointed. He thought the shadow might have come from a brightship. Not that he would gape at such a machine. But he would not pass up the chance to see one at close range.

He still had not moved more than a few steps from the receiving docket of the pillar. It had been staggering enough to ride up and see the Arm of Heaven laid before him, in its vast length, but somehow the city gripped him more fiercely.

However, Tai would not begin his mission here by cowering before towers and bridges. He reminded himself that this city was the home of those who were afraid to live, who walked into their bodies and left them as easily. This city was created by those who refused converse with the Rose. Who, if rumors were true, had just destroyed the ancient minorals of the Arm of Heaven. The lords were both ruthless and petty, destroying while at the same time promising life of one hundred thousand days, and in so doing, draining value from hours grown too long and too numerous.

As terrible a loss as the minorals were, Tai felt a personal grievance as well. If the to-and-from-veils were gone, Tai could not go to the Rose. Hel Ese, too, was worried about the fate of the veils. Although she had not yet confided in him, he believed she was hewing the pathway for her Rose compatriots to come here. With all her powers, perhaps she would find a way.

Blinking at the glare from the canals, he took several calming breaths. He'd come to place a weapon here, and, though he hoped it would never be used, he was determined to do it.

Looking around, he found himself in relative privacy. Withdrawing the smooth cylindrical object from his pocket, he held it concealed in his fist. Hel Ese had termed it a *finder*. She'd given him another mechanical device as well, the one containing the weapon. Standing in place, he let the finder do its work.

He began to walk toward one of the canals, but as he approached, the finder cooled in his hand. Not that direction, then. He chose another direction, all the while praying that the object would not heat up toward the palatine hill. If his destination was the lords' mansions, he had no idea how he could even enter those precincts.

After an hour, he was still walking along canals, crossing bridges, waiting for the vibration of the finder to show him his target. His skin flushed under the heat of the sky. He had been so long in the undercity, he had no tolerance any longer for the bright. Would Earth's sun be gentler? It would do no good to worry in advance. Entangled so far with the woman of the Rose, he was in far more danger here than he would ever be in the Rose.

He stood at the foot of a great tower. Its twisting sides rose far, far above him, making him feel as small as a mange nit.

Here, at the base of this great pillar, was his destination. The finder was throbbing heavily in his grip. He surreptitiously pocketed the finder and withdrew from another pocket the thing Hel Ese had called the *cell*. That so small a thing could threaten the vast edifice seemed unlikely; but he trusted Hel Ese's direction. The surface of the tower had valleys and ridges, almost like the bark of vine trees. Seeing no one else nearby, he shoved the cell into an indentation. Hel Ese had said it could be pressed and molded. Still, he hesitated to push too hard. As he stepped back to observe the effect, he saw that already the cell was darkening to the color of the tower.

Now that the most difficult aspect of his job was complete, he began to feel nervous. His next steps were to find subprefect Milinard and tell his Excellency that he had seen the woman of the Rose in the undercity. It was useless information, since Hel Ese had by now left the place, but providing intelligence to the subprefect was his excuse for being in the Ascendancy.

Inquiring of a litter-borne Gond where the nearest access to the Magisterium might be, he made his way to his interview. The Jout would be waiting, as no doubt the gatekeepers had informed him that Li Yun Tai had invoked the preconsul's name to enter the Bright City.

Just as he was about to descend the stairs into the Magisterium, Tai turned to gaze at the tower where he'd left the cell. Stopping a Hirrin clerk and pointing, he asked if the tower had a name.

The Hirrin puffed through her mobile lips. "Name? Of course it has a name."

"May I know it, most excellent clerk?"

She squinted at him, unsure whether the appellation was completely sincere. "It is the Tower of Ghinamid."

"Ah. The famous tower. My thanks." It was, he was able to note at this distance, taller than the others. To maintain his persona of simple-minded newcomer, he bowed to the clerk, though she was only a Magisterial flunky.

Lord Ghinamid's Tower. The ancient monument to the Sleeping Lord. Even with Tai's cynical view of the Bright City, the name of the Sleeping Lord invoked a sober awe. The fifth of the great Lords, Ghinamid slept in a great chamber across the plaza from the tower. Tai's father had once traveled to the Ascendancy and had seen the bier of the lord—which was an open bed where the great being slept. It was said that as one of the original five lords, Ghinamid had longed so much for home that he decided to sleep until the day came when he might return. Tai had always wanted to refute that story. After all, if you were one of the Ruling Five, surely you could choose to go home. Yet he had been sleeping for a thousand thousand days, since the Age of Radiance began.

And a new thought occurred: If, as the dreams said, the Tarig were constantly passing to and from their home to the Entire, then why was it that Lord Ghinamid could not? Not that anything the lords said could be trusted.

He turned to go. There was no grand entrance to the precincts of the realm's governing hierarchy. It was a modest entryway, a carved double door, almost hidden in a small but well-kept sunken garden.

As he approached the door, Tai wondered what Hel Ese would make of the sights of this city. He wished he could be with her when she arrived, because he knew she would be, in her own way, rapt. Though she was ill and completely focused on her mission, her eyes sometimes betrayed her curiosity about the All; in those few times she had asked about the wonders of the Entire her voice carried a recognizable longing. He'd heard that in his own voice, when he spoke to her of the Rose.

Unconsciously, he patted the folded paper in his pocket, his growing list of words to memorize. Then he went down the stairs, beginning his descent into the tiers of the Magisterium.

Sydney knelt in contemplation before the low altar.

She hoped her attendants would gossip to their friends about her new devotion to the Red Throne. She hoped they'd say that Sen Ni was not so much human, as Chalin. It would be the truth, even if her adoption of the Society's ways were mostly for show. Even so, she was a child of the Entire.

And perhaps someday, something higher yet. Geng De said *queen*, but that was too grand. A leader; a mistress to fill the vacancy created by the fall of the Tarig. Cixi might want her as high prefect; but the citizens of the Entire would say what they wanted. For now she was mistress of the sway— because the Tarig knew the realm was *tending against them*, and they wanted to look merciful.

Geng De worked very hard on the future, entering the binds and contending with them in ways she couldn't even imagine. Recently he'd told her that, while there, he saw a disturbing occurrence: her father would betray her.

She had a bargain with her father. It *had* been a bargain. But since Helice had escaped, would her father still honor it? He'd told her he was close to cutting the Tarig off from their source in the Heart. Would he then let Sydney come into her destiny? She thought it was still possible. After all, Geng De's vision might have shown him one of Titus's past betrayals, not future.

"Mistress." Her servant Emar-Vad approached. This Hirrin was swiftly becoming her foremost attendant. She turned to receive him.

"News has come. In the city. Murders." He hesitated. "And Tarig punishments."

Sydney rose quickly. "Tell me."

"A lord has been killed. As a consequence, many are dying." As Sydney absorbed this, Emar-Vad added, "A massacre. The lords are retaliating across the city."

Sydney pushed back a rising alarm. "How can they do this?"

His ears flattened. "A mob killed a lord, Mistress Sen Ni. In the undercity. It was an unthinkable public execution."

Her thoughts raced. *Riod, what shall we do?* But he was not here, nor could she share thoughts with him. *Beloved*, she thought. It rang hollow in her skull.

Sydney strode to the door, and Emar-Vad moved with her.

"Where is Lady Anuve?" she asked.

He led the way. As they hurried, they passed knots of Hirrin servants talking in hushed voices, bowing as Sen Ni passed. She gestured to one of them. "Geng De will be here soon. When he comes, bring him to me." The navitar slept in his vessel at the foot of the bridge, but had planned to see her this Early Day for a show of religious instruction.

At Anuve's quarters, she instructed Emar-Vad to knock. The door opened to a silent command inside, revealing Anuve in a chair in the center of the room, giving the impression she expected a visit.

A quick bow, as Sydney rushed to say, "What's happening in the city, Bright Lady?"

Anuve's long hand trailed over her skirt, adjusting it. "Retributions."

Sydney turned to the Hirrin. "Wait outside, please, Emar-Vad." When she was alone with Anuve, she tried to calm herself. This was her sway. She was mistress of the sway. If she hadn't learned long ago in the stables to fight for position, she would never have survived.

"You have no permission to kill here."

"Ah? Such permission is granted by whom?"

"By me." The mantis lady considered this claim and the tone with which it was delivered.

Sydney went on, "How many are dead?"

"Some hundred sentients. Morts who gather in the undercity, pretending to worship the Red Throne, yet not deceiving us. They hate us. We have withheld our hand until now."

Sydney could not suppress a growing outrage. *My sway. My people.* But she needed facts. "How can a lord have been murdered?" The thought of a Tarig's murder, though never far from her mind, still startled her. For one thing, they were practically walking weapons themselves.

"A crowd came at my cousin with a knife." Anuve added, "The lord pursued your father. Your father may have killed him, but if so, he was assisted by many sentients."

"My father? You have him?"

"No."

Sydney quelled any expression of relief. "We'll have no more killing."

Anuve rose, her voice lowering. "Mistress of the Sway, hnn? You think the Tarig are under your sway?"

"No. But if retributions happen, they won't be in my sway."

"The criminals abide in your sway. However, they are dying quickly, by Tarig mercy."

A rap at the door, and Sydney, in her fury, snapped, "Enter," though it was Anuve's apartment.

Emar-Vad stood in the open door. He bowed, nodding in the direction of Geng De, who stood in the hall.

Anuve's voice came low and smooth. "Perhaps spiritual sustenance will calm you. Let the navitar teach you."

This pushed too far. Sydney swung around to the creature, saying, "No more deaths. One Tarig has died. In return, you took a hundred. Enough."

"It is enough when Rim City achieves calm. It is not calm. Citizens have smashed property, people chant in the great Way. It shall become calm."

Sydney advanced on Anuve, to make her words more forceful. From behind, a hand grabbed her. It was Geng De. Swinging around, Sydney jerked her arm away from him.

He pinned her with his gaze. "It does no good to provoke a gracious bright lady, Sen Ni. Come with me now."

"The lady and I aren't done."

"Sen Ni, you must come away. Walk into the city. See for yourself." He bobbed a bow to Anuve. "It is allowed for the mistress of the sway to walk abroad?"

Anuve could not object, nor did she.

Geng De's fist closed around Sydney's arm. The firm grip and a few moment of consideration had allowed her black anger to abate. She responded to the urgency in Geng De's eyes.

She bowed at the Tarig. "Bright Lady." Geng De pulled her from the room.

As they walked down the hall, Emar-Vad some paces behind them, Geng De murmured, "One future I saw last night is that Anuve slit your torso from throat to waist." They headed to her quarters, as servants bowed very low indeed, avoiding her gaze. The palace staff had perhaps understood that when Sydney went to Anuve's room with that look on her face, she might not emerge alive.

"I rushed to find you this morning." Geng De cut a glance at her. "You should dress the part of the mistress of the sway. Hurry."

Geng De had done well to restrain her display of temper. They had jockeyed over the last forty days for mastery of each other; both of them were stubborn and sure of themselves; she trusted that he had learned that he couldn't control her. Today, his restraining hand had been welcome. She only wished that, if he could weave the future, he had woven one without a massacre of her people.

Outside her apartment she paused. "Are they still killing, Geng De?"

"Yes. I have seen blood, cries, and death. Here is our best chance."

"So you're glad of all this?" She gazed at the navitar, rotund and soft, and perhaps cruel as well.

"Wear something pretty," he suggested, pushing her through the door.

Emar-Vad didn't like the roughness and moved in on Geng De, shoving him.

The two faced off. Emar-Vad's lips folded back to show the ejector in his mouth.

"Emar-Vad," Sydney said quickly. "Help me dress." Her attendant relaxed his lips and passed Geng De, entering her room. Sydney closed the door behind them. She rushed to her clothes chest for something to wear. Out came jade green pants and a heavily embroidered jacket, garb rich enough to proclaim her position.

Geng De had said such a day was near, when she would go into the Way at his side, and must look every inch the mistress of the sway. A day when many would die. *Will I die, Geng De?* she had asked. To which he responded, *I do not permit that future. But the binds make no promises.* The answer chilled her, but she liked that he was honest.

Four Jouts bore Sydney's litter into the city. At her side was Geng De, tipping the conveyance in his direction.

They sped down the ramp of the crystal bridge, plunging into the Way, strangely deserted at this waning hour of Early Day. A few people peered from behind curtains at windows.

Geng De was nervous, watching the side streets, alert. "The Tarig are overreacting. Now you can show your mercy."

"What mercy can I give?"

"Whatever comes to you, seize it. But hear me, Sen Ni: Do not provoke any Tarig lord."

Faintly, voices came to them. Angry shouts, at first muffled, then growing louder. Geng De pointed to the avenue leading to the Quay of Heaven. A wave of citizens was rushing down this side street into the Way.

As they stood milling, a Tarig appeared from a nearby habitation. The sentients turned as one to confront him. He advanced toward them with long strides.

A woman shouted, "No! Our street! Our street!" As she moved forward from the line of the throng, the Tarig slashed at her, ripping open her arm. She fell. Not pausing, the lord lunged into the crowd. In the confusion of the milling sentients, Sydney couldn't see the confrontation, but she knew by the sounds that the lord attacked viciously.

Ignoring Geng De's murmurs of warning, she instructed the bearers to move closer. When they were some fifty feet from the mob, she jumped to the ground and shouted, but her voice was lost in the screams of the melee. Nearby was the hulk of a leftover float from the Great Procession that had been dragged into the Way by the protesters. She called a Jout attendant to her side, and using his help, scrambled to the top.

Geng De had told her to express outrage and compassion. She needed no coaching. "Stop!" she shouted. No one heard. She ordered her four attendants to shout, and they did so. Sentients on the edge of the crowd turned to her.

"Stop!" she called again. "I am Sen Ni, Mistress of the Sway. You *will* stop. No more killing."

A pause came to the fight. The crowd parted, revealing the Tarig lord among them. He walked toward her.

At the foot of Sydney's perch, the lord looked up, his face smeared with blood. Holding out a fully clawed hand, he boomed, "Come to us, small girl."

Geng De was on the other side of the float, standing amid the Jout attendants whose terrified faces were all turned up toward her. "Do not, Sen Ni," Geng De pleaded.

The lord was Hadenth, that half-mad, paranoid prince. The lord was not Hadenth. But, again, he *was*. They were a combined swarm, dipping in and out of the Heart, sharing their experiences, mingling themselves in each new body.

"Come and get me," Sen Ni said. "Come and kill the Mistress of the Sway, then. But I'll be your last kill. Then it . . . will . . . be . . . enough."

The lord reached up to climb.

She prepared to die. Geng De screamed, urging the Jouts on the lord, but at that moment, the lord paused in his climb and looked behind him, distracted for a moment.

Approaching them from further down the Way was a massive crowd of sentients: Chalin, Ysli, Jout, Laroo, and Hirrin. They bore lengths of pipe, hammers, and butcher's knives and whether propelled from behind, or fueled by rage, they advanced on the lord.

With these overwhelming numbers, Sydney knew that another Tarig would die. That must not happen, or the city would suffer.

"Come up to me!" Sydney urged the lord. She hardly knew what she was doing, only that the lord must not die. This war could not be won by hammers and kitchen knives.

The Tarig lord cocked his gore-spattered head to her, and for the first time in her life, she saw a Tarig grin. It was the most awful thing she had ever seen.

Then she knew why he had no fear. From the direction of the quay a line of Tarig advanced. Twenty or thirty lords strode forward, coming into the Way.

They stopped, standing quite still, murmuring among themselves and watching the mob.

Then, as one line, they turned their backs on Sydney, the float, the bleeding lord, and the pile of bodies in the street. They advanced on the larger crowd.

Before she knew quite what she was doing, Sydney had scrambled down from her perch, racing past the bleeding lord, rushing to outflank the Tarig line. She was faster than the advancing lords. She stood now in the middle of the Way, halfway between Tarig and non-Tarig. For some reason, the street had gone quiet. The silence, suffocatingly hot, was pierced by Geng De wailing, "No, no, no, no."

The line of Tarig stopped, eyeing her.

"I am Sen Ni," she said, her voice sounding like a butterfly's wing scraping a leaf. "We are done dying today."

A hiss came from one of the lords. His stride brought him to her quickly.

From one side, Geng De ran toward her, his caftan hampering him, causing him to stumble. His voice warbled, "She is the Mistress of the Sway; no one must touch her! Mistress of the Sway!"

Geng De fell into her arms, bringing them both onto their knees in the street.

The lord raised an arm, and his fingers pointed to the bright with yellow, extended claws.

Geng De sobbed.

Then, one by one, the claws on the lord's hand snicked in.

The lord said, "We have finished retributions." He looked past Sydney and Geng De, toward the hushed crowd of sentients. "Ah?" He turned from one side of the mob to the other. "Ah? One of you wishes to die?"

No one spoke. The bright fell in hot gouts on the Way, the slicks of blood, and the wailing injured. The lords surveyed the scene, finding no further challenges. Then they retreated down the side street where Sydney now saw a brightship waited to take them away.

Geng De urged Sydney to her feet. She staggered on legs gone limp with terror, but he was right, she needed to be here, still needed to assure that the mob would not lose control.

Once upright, she walked toward the crowd. Moving down the edge of the throng, she put a hand on a shoulder, on an arm, on the head of a youngster. "Enough sorrow," she murmured to this one; and to that one, "No more dying, let this be enough." She continued on, tears in her eyes from the exhaustion, from the relief of being alive. "I will help you." She moved into the depths of the crowd, talking to some, consoling others. She began to see that some wanted useful employment. She nodded at a few. "Bring the wounded help. You and you, go forward. There are people in need, lying in the street. The rest of you, go home. For now. Enough for now. But we will not forget."

The crowd began to thin as a few individuals obeyed her, followed by most of the others. Turning back into the intersection of the Way and the side street, she found citizens tending to the injured. She saw Red Throne healers and litters bearing the dead away.

Geng De stood in the midst of it all, watching for her. When she approached him, he bowed deeply. Then a few from the crowd bowed to her. A healer, hands full of gore, nodded in her direction.

She went to him. "Tell me how to help."

"Mistress," he said very kindly, "the helpers need water."

Sydney sent her attendants for buckets and dippers and clean cloths, which they asked for at doorways along the Way. Once they returned, Sydney brought cups of water to the healers and the wounded.

A Laroo sat propped up against a store wall. He wasn't bleeding, but only stared out at the Way.

"Drink," Sydney urged, offering him a cup.

"Their claws," he said, holding the drink, staring past her. "Terrible claws."

"Yes," she whispered, though he wasn't listening. "I remember."

When she at last returned to her litter, she looked once again down the side street toward the Heavenly Quay. She saw a small individual standing on a pier jutting into the Sea. It might not have gained Sydney's attention, but something made her pause. A group of Tarig stood in a knot in front of the pier.

Geng De leaned in to her. "She's been waiting there for quite a long time."

Sydney turned back, looking more carefully. "Helice."

"Yes."

Sydney noted that none of the Tarig near the dock moved toward Helice. Then Sydney knew why. A Tarig lady was pushing through her cousins, moving toward Helice.

"Anuve," Geng De whispered.

Helice stood her ground as the lady approached.

Sydney couldn't see how Anuve hurt her, but Helice screamed. Then Anuve, nearly twice as tall as her captive, pulled her from the dock, with Helice staggering to keep up with the lady's long strides.

The group of Tarig parted ranks, and Anuve dragged Helice to a nearby brightship. Sydney was too far away to object, nor could she hope to stop what was happening in any case. But the Tarig finally had what her father feared the most: Helice and her plans to sacrifice the Rose.

The ship leaped forward over the water, rising rapidly into the sky on a steep path.

CHAPTER TWENTY-THREE

Drop a child on the ground and he will fear holding. Drop a child in the Nigh and he will fear nothing.

—a saying

QUINN DREAMED OF THE PLAINS OF AHNENHOON. Soldiers lay on the open fields, some sleeping and some dead. The slumberers occasionally woke up and tried to rouse their dead compatriots. Because of the number who had died over thousands of years, the recumbent forms covered the wide and shadowed plain. The wind stirred their hair, clothing, tack, and flags. The wind moaned, *To no purpose, to no purpose.* In his dream-knowledge, Quinn understood that if the Tarig would only give the Paion their home, the war could be over.

He came awake with a start. A noise outside his door. It was Between Ebb, what would have been dawn on Earth. He found his knife in the dark before remembering where he was: in Zhiya's compound. The sounds here would be her courtesans. Then his visitor announced herself. "Zhiya."

She came in, bustling past him and throwing open his curtains for the meager ebb-time light. Turning, she said without preamble, "She's been taken to the Ascendancy. I'm sorry."

By the distressed look on the godwoman's face, he knew this was very bad news. "Anzi?"

"No, not Anzi. Worse. Hel Ese gave herself up. She got herself an escort . . . up." Zhiya raised her eyes to the ceiling.

He swore. "When?"

"Second hour of Prime of Day, so my operatives guess. She went to the

Quay of Heaven, and according to those who saw it, she waited for the Tarig. They beat her. Then they took her."

Panic streamed into his veins. Helice had found the Heart. By the Miserable God, she had found it first, she must have. He sat to put on his boots.

Zhiya murmured, "She's already there, Quinn."

He swore again, but didn't slow down. All right, she was there. He'd go after her.

Helice was going to tell the lords that she'd help them burn the Rose. She was going to tell them that their plan to burn it a little at a time over the next hundred years was a bad one, since the Earth would keep launching assaults. The Tarig wanted to stop assaults; they weren't used to serious attacks; and they were vulnerable to them. The Entire was fragile. If the lords wanted to keep it, they had better make their strike once and for all.

Zhiya regarded him. "What do you propose to do? She's already in the floating city."

He didn't respond. She wasn't going to like his answer.

Zhiya went to the door and ushered in one of her girls. The courtesan Ban entered with a small tray of oba and a few skewers of meat.

Ban opened a small basket filled with steaming dumplings. He nodded to the woman and she left the room flicking a bold glance at him, closing the door behind her.

"I'm going after her, Zhiya. Now, before she has time to establish a relationship with them."

"Perhaps she already has."

He shrugged. Then what difference would anything make?

Helice had forced his hand. By the Miserable God, she was in the Ascendancy. The world on this side of the veil was changing. A second Tarig lord had been murdered, and they'd come into Rim City to punish their subjects. His own daughter had stopped the reprisals. His daughter had stood up to a platoon of Tarig. All this he and Zhiya had heard from her spies who had run back and forth with reports most of the previous day.

The Entire was shifting. Dreams undercut the Tarig. Ahnenhoon had almost come undone, and they had not yet found the man with the lethal cirque. So the Tarig world was tottering. They had maimed it themselves, cutting off the minorals of the Arm of Heaven.

How would they react to Helice's proposal of a fine, clean end to the Earth?

He put on his jacket. "I'll let Sydney take credit for my capture. At the bridge." Zhiya's compound, in the center of the lower Rim, was within minutes of the crystal bridge.

On his bedside table lay Akay-Wat's Paion hoop. He picked it up, looking at it for a long moment. "Give this to Anzi. When she comes home."

Reluctantly, Zhiya took it. "Quinn, think. What good will you do from a Bright City dungeon?"

"They won't put me away. I'll be in the middle of it. I always am." Her droll stare got through to him more than a voiced objection. "I have a contact in high places. Time to call on him."

She knew whom he meant. "He's no friend. He'll use you, as before."

He ignored her caution. He wasn't fool enough to think Oventroe a friend, just an enemy with mutual goals.

"Eat something, by the Woeful God."

He obeyed, taking a skewer and chewing quickly. "Is Lord Oventroe at the Ascendancy?" This lord was his strategy of last resort. Oventroe could silence Helice, and would silence her—for he wanted the Rose preserved, seemingly at any price.

"Yes, in residence. But the Five have changed again. Now one called Lady Demat is among them, replacing Chiron."

He nodded. There were always four high lords, five including the Sleeping Lord. Now the Tarig chiefs were Nehoov, the longest serving lord next to Ghinamid; Inweer at the Repel of Ahnenhoon; the newcomer, Lady Demat; and Oventroe, friend of the Rose.

Zhiya had turned subdued. "I have a litter waiting in the street."

He glanced at the hoop that she held. "I don't know what that thing is. Akay-Wat's mount kicked it up in the sand. They think it's Paion."

"It looks like a child's toy."

"I keep thinking it's a mirror with the glass missing." He was postponing leaving when he should be rushing. It was time to go. "You'll help Anzi, if something happens?"

"I will."

Quinn paused. "I want her to know that . . ." He stopped. That what, that despite walking deliberately into the Bright City, he truly cared for her? "Tell her that I wish . . ." Damn it to hell.

Zhiya coughed, covering the moment when Quinn had run out of words. "As though I even know where she is."

"She knows to find you. She can find the Venerable Zhiya."

"I do live large," Zhiya said, trying to rally her mood. "I'll watch for her."

"I love her. But I don't think I get to."

"No," Zhiya agreed. She walked him to the door. "Go, and do the thing you have to. We'll do the same."

She put a hand on his arm. "Mother wants to say goodbye."

"I've delayed too long."

"Please. She's agitated, awake. It doesn't happen often."

He followed her into the hall and down a long corridor to a parlor where Zhiya had a bed set up.

The last time Quinn had seen Zhiya's mother, she had been in the dirigible, the Most Venerable's airship heading for the Nigh. He remembered her poor, distorted face, and her expression when she learned he was going to Ahnenhoon.

Zhiya led him to the sickbed. The woman lay on spotless silks, her hair combed out on a pillow. As to the rest, it was ghastly. Her skin, though smooth, had sagged dramatically away from the center of her face, almost flowing onto the pillow. Her eyes, elongated and large, had slid to either side of a hatchet-shaped face. Her mouth had closed to a small hole.

She was that rare creature, an old navitar.

Most navitars chose to walk into the Nigh when they were beyond their piloting work. They knew what awaited them otherwise. Why had Zhiya's mother chosen this? Zhiya held her mother's hand, a small cup of flesh that no longer had fingers. Surely the Tarig could have rewarded her service on the Nigh with something better. But the lords didn't want old navitars around; who knew what capabilities they might accrue.

Her eyes had been closed, and she now opened then. Strange how her eyelids fit perfectly, even over these distorted orbs. "Titus," she whispered. "Where bound?"

"The city of the lords, Madame."

The line of her lips moved as though it remembered the old shapes of words, but the utterances were forced through the small remaining slit. "Time, time comes." Her voice, barely a whisper.

"I hope, not too late."

She closed her eyes. Zhiya put her hand on her mother's brow, murmuring something to her. She bent low to her mother's lips, because the old woman was speaking again, a sound like mewling.

Zhiya stood up, frowning. "She says a baby fell in the river."

He blinked. "A baby?"

Zhiya looked down. Her mother's eyes were open again, pleading with her daughter to interpret. "She wants you to know that you have to protect yourself. From the child."

The litter was waiting for him; he mustn't stay. "What is she talking about, Zhiya? What child?"

"A grown child, I think. Mother gets times confused. She's talked about this child before. I didn't know the child was your enemy."

"Name? What's this person's name? A Chalin?"

Zhiya's mother struggled to speak. "He is—" her mouth worked, but nothing came out. Finally, from deep in her throat came the croak: "—a navitar."

There was no time to try to learn the name. Perhaps she didn't know it. "Thank you, lady, I'll watch for him." He turned to go, but her hand shot out from its position on the bedcovers and grabbed his arm, holding it in a soft cuff.

"Navitar weaves," she mewled. Too weak to say more, she closed her eyes and appeared to sleep.

With this strangely mauled word, *weaves*, still on his mind, Quinn bid Zhiya goodbye.

In the street outside, he took a seat in the litter. Her strongest and fastest servants bore him quickly away.

A hot calm lay over the city. In the deserted Way, the bearers avoided piles of refuse and hulks of burned-out carts. Down a side street to the sea, Quinn glimpsed a blur of cleaning fabbers foaming through the street. Soon all would be tidy again.

Amid this eerie peace, his mind went to his hoped-for meeting with Oventroe—somehow the lord would arrange to see him alone—but plans slipped away. Nothing held up against the thought that he was giving himself up. His long flight from the Tarig would presently end.

Before he'd met with Sydney in the Adda, he'd hoped that he could restrain the lords with the idea that he possessed world-shattering military nan. That Anzi had it, and would use it if any threat to the Rose loomed. But Helice would put a doubt into his lie. Sydney had told him that both she and Helice knew he had no chain. A navitar had seen him throw the cirque away—*seen* in that sense navitars had of knowing realities.

So he'd lost his primary deterrent. Then his new strategy, to find the doors, failed. He'd set Su Bei on that quest, making it a contest between an old man with the correlates and a young woman with an mSap. Every day he'd hoped to hear from Bei, but the truth was, he didn't even know if Bei had received his message.

His litter sped past an old Ysli woman sweeping rubbish from her storefront, where the street cleaners had not yet reached. She waved her broom at the conveyance and screeched, "It should be clean!" Perhaps she thought the fabbers would always arrive. Strange, how unthinkable change was in a city, in a universe, that had not changed for ten thousand years.

The bearers sped up the ramp of the crystal bridge. He would see Sydney at any moment. Beyond what lay before him with the Tarig was the keen awareness that his daughter was just inside those crystal doors.

Quinn sent the bearers away. Standing in front of the mansion, he looked for a twelve-year-old girl. Despite all he knew, he looked for that child. He'd spent so many years remembering her that way, it was hard now to think of the beautiful, harsh young woman he'd seen here.

He stood in front of the steps leading to the mansion. It was not as imposing as Yulin's palace, but grand enough. Formed from both clear and opaque crystal, it gathered light and reshed it on those about to enter. The portico surrounding the recessed door bore delicate tracery. If he looked close enough, he knew it would be Lucent words from the books favored by the

Lords: their admonitions, pronouncements, and lies. The three vows always made good decoration: Withhold the Knowledge of the Entire from the non-Entire. Impose the Peace of the Entire. Extend the Reach of the Entire. In his years here, he'd learned what those vows meant, and what they hid.

Hirrin guards near the door eyed him warily, and one of them moved forward to meet him on the stairs. "Servants enter at the side door." When Quinn didn't respond, the guard said, "Have you matters here?"

"I would see the mistress."

"A matter concerning the city's troubles?"

Quinn plunged in, revealing it all. "Tell Sen Ni that her father has come."

Another Hirrin came through the central doors. The others turned to this one. The guard who had first spoken said, "He says he is Sen Ni's father, Emar-Vad."

The new Hirrin flattened his ears. "You are Titus Quinn?"

Quinn confirmed it. "Before telling a lord, please let Sen Ni know I'm here."

"Escort him," the Hirrin told his associates, and then Quinn was flanked on three sides by guards. They ascended the steps until they stood before the doors of the mansion. There they bound his hands. They brought him just inside the door, where the lead guard now hurried off.

A minute passed, and then another. Quinn thought that Sydney was some distance into the mansion, and it would take a moment to bring her. But Tarig were closer. Two lords approached from down the corridor.

After being told the situation, they took custody. He was made to kneel.

One of the lords crouched down beside him. "Prove you are he. You do not look like the one we seek."

Zhiya's surgeon had altered him, but it was easy to prove who he was. He could cite a thousand details unknown to any but the Tarig and he. "I know that the Lady Chiron was burned to death at Ahnenhoon by her own Hirrin servant."

The lord hissed at this recitation. "She gave you many privileges."

"I was her pet. An animal you keep for your amusement."

Even in that stark face Quinn saw that he was having difficulty restraining himself. The Tarig said, "You will amuse us, be sure."

A rush of footsteps to one side drew his attention. Sydney ran into the hall. Seeing the group, she slowed and walked up to them with dignity. Wearing bright orange, she looked startling in this pale hall among the silver-clad Tarig and the plain brown Hirrin.

She wore her hair pulled back, a severe look, perhaps regal. Her eyes were made up in the Chalin style. "Titus," she said.

He had this small gift to give her, that he would give himself up here. He hoped it would serve her purposes, give her credibility with the Tarig, for however long she needed to deceive them. "I'm here, Sydney. Sen Ni, if you prefer."

"I prefer." She stood there, uncertain, looking down at him as he knelt. Her voice wavered until she brought it under control. "You must have had surgeries on your face, then, if you are who you say you are." There, she'd covered that detail, for the sake of the listening Tarig.

"Why did you come?"

He had an answer ready for this question. "I was sent by the Rose. I'm ready to talk." It could delay things to claim he had something to say. He needed delay. Anything to sow doubt around Helice. "I hope you can restrain these minor lords. They make me nervous."

"I don't command them." She glanced up at the Tarig, but it was clear she didn't fear them. She had faced down worse than these. "They can kill you later, perhaps, after you have given your messages from the Rose."

Ugly words. Part of her act, he hoped.

"You'll take him to the Ascendancy," she told the Tarig, who were preparing to do just that. "But I don't want a brightship in Rim City. It could cause panic."

"We have done with panic."

"Then take him by Adda."

"Perhaps."

She looked at a servant. "Prepare an Adda to come for the prisoner." The Hirrin left at her bidding.

"Most Adda do not rise so high," one of the Tarig said.

Sydney raised her chin, staring at the creature. "Some do. I've seen them."

Quinn marveled that she could speak in this manner, and wondered what power she had over them. Perhaps her quelling of the riots made her useful to them.

She turned back to him, softening her voice. "They've found Helice." She made sure he heard that piece of information.

"I know." Now they understood each other. Helice was pressing her agenda forward; and Quinn would do anything to stop her.

Heads turned to look in the direction of someone approaching. A man in a red caftan hurried toward them. Rotund and bland, he came to Sydney's side with the air of someone accustomed to privilege. His face was strangely unformed, with a small nose and mouth, almost like a child's, though he was Sydney's height.

As the newcomer bent close to whisper to Sydney, she leaned toward him, sharing a private moment. They whispered together, giving the impression that they knew each other well. It stirred a pang of jealousy in him. Belatedly, he realized this person must be a navitar.

At that moment the Hirrin called Emar-Vad approached, and Sydney left the group to confer with him on the other side of the hall.

As she did so, the navitar spoke to one of the Tarig. His voice was high and smooth as he said, "You should kill him before he escapes again. It would solve a lot of problems. I predict he will escape. You definitely should kill him."

"Hnn." The Tarig considered Quinn.

He was still kneeling. Sydney rejoined the group. "We know of an Adda that can journey high. Emar-Vad will arrange it."

The navitar bowed, "Well done, Mistress. No brightships, then. Well done."

She glanced at him, pleased.

A Tarig pulled Quinn to his feet in a lunge of effortless power. The Tarig said, "First a ride by Adda. It may amuse us to see you fall from the beast, ah?" Quinn had goaded the lord. Perhaps not wise. The Tarig lord nearest him guided him forcibly out the door.

Out on the broad porch of the mansion, Quinn was made to wait. A small group of Hirrin servants had gathered to watch, but Sydney wasn't in their midst. After what felt like an hour, he saw an Adda in the distance, winding its way slowly toward them in the slight breeze. Next to him, the Tarig lords stood like pillars.

It took a long time for the creature to tack to the verandah.

Sydney went to her apartments, shutting Geng De out in the hall. Perhaps he'd been right that she mustn't seem to care for her father, but she still wanted to be alone right now.

Her apartment looked toward the sea, not the primacy, and so she couldn't observe the proceedings on the verandah where they waited to convey her father to the Ascendancy.

She paced, trying to discharge her agitation. Ever since Helice had given herself up yesterday, Sydney had been vulnerable. Helice knew all her plans. The woman's ambitions could easily push Sydney aside. Would Helice expose her and the dream insurgency? It was a dark conjecture, but she could do nothing to prevent it. They weren't friends. Any early hopes for that were long dispelled. They had used each other when convenient. Now, Sydney doubted Helice saw much convenience in it, but perhaps she was preoccupied.

Walking the perimeter of the room, Sydney noticed how empty it was. The bed was, in the Tarig custom, in the center of the room. A carved chest at the foot of the bed contained her folded wardrobe, her book of pinpricks, a scroll with a likeness of her mother, and little else. Sydney owned almost nothing. Her life had focused on beings who were loyal to her, who loved her. In her mind there was no difference between loyalty and love. Riod. Akay-Wat. Mo Ti. Cixi.

She paced. There was another name to add to that list. Who was it? Stopping, she considered. Wasn't it the man she had just turned over to the mantis lords?

Oh God, she thought, thinking in English. *I gave him to them.*

She wandered to the doors to the balcony, and threw them open, walking into the pale light of Early Day. No, she hadn't given him over. He'd done that to himself. But she saw herself telling the lords they could have him. The Tarig listened to her; she had helped them control a mob; she acted the part of their Mistress of the Sway. They wanted to show themselves gracious, and she helped them to do so.

How had it come to her, this being in the mansions of the enemy? When

Riod was here to spy on them, she'd had a reason. What was her reason now? What was anything now except a corrupt and sickening dance?

A shadow passed over her.

The Adda. Its trailing membranes almost touched her head. It moved beyond the balcony, slowly floating over the edge of the sea. Titus was on board. The ladder from its orifice hung down, beckoning her. But the creature was already rising in the sky, puffing out its bladders until it rounded into a floating moon.

I think you loved me, Titus. It was never that you didn't love me. It was that you couldn't meet my proofs. You couldn't be pure enough. You couldn't be with me when Priov whipped me in the dorms, when Hadenth used his claws on me, when I had to trap my own food though I couldn't see it, and when the riders told me you ate off crystal plates. But I think you would have traded places with me.

Perhaps the Adda would turn around. Perhaps the lords would say to each other, we must take all the Quinns, not just the father. Let them be here together as the prisoners they once were. Let them start over again, and see if it can be different.

But the Adda rose and rose higher.

She watched a long while until the Adda was merely a speck in the sky, like a planet far away.

PART IV
THE DRAGON'S EYE

CHAPTER TWENTY-FOUR

CAITLIN SLEPT IN HER CAR IN A DOWNTOWN PARKING GARAGE. When businesses opened, she purchased a briefcase, then paid a visit to her bank and withdrew $300,000 in cash, a transaction that drew the attention of the bank manager. The manager made polite inquiries about her need for such an amount in cash. Scams and swindles abounded, she must be aware.

Yes, she was aware.

She faced him calmly. "We may be making another withdrawal in a few days. Let us know if this is inconvenient." It would not be, the manager assured her.

She ate a fast-food breakfast, wolfing down something that a half an hour later, she couldn't remember having eaten.

Highway 26 to Beaverton, meshed to savant control that kept each car a few feet behind the one in front, and then, unmeshed, onto side streets. Her destination: a run-down neighborhood with intentions to do better. Planter strips by the curbs held well-meant flowerbeds on the turn; a few houses had seen recent paint.

Kell Tobias's had not. The former Minerva savant tender had let the yard go to weeds, but she liked that he bothered to mow them. Parking out front, she knocked on the door. No answer, though she heard music inside. After several tries, she was back in the car again, deciding to wait. Maybe he'd gone out, would be back. Her nerves started to unravel. Who else did she know who she could bribe into an act of computer piracy? No one.

Compulsively, she checked her message center. No word from Rob, but there wouldn't be. They'd agreed not to communicate until she had a file to send him. Even encrypted, every data strand made her movements traceable.

And Rob's. He wasn't telling her where he'd taken Mateo and Emily. Everything about the last two days felt like someone else's life, someone who needed to hide. Someone like Titus Quinn's sister-in-law.

A half hour passed. She'd go back to Emergent, try the hacking herself . . . no, it would take all day; she didn't have time to waste. Kell, just come home. Sitting quietly in her car made her want to scream. Deep breaths. She'd wait until noon.

At ten minutes after, a beater of a car pulled into the driveway. Kell. With a sack of groceries. Caitlin's heart kicked at her, hard. Propelled by adrenaline, she got out and approached him.

Kell had changed little. Still the three-day growth of beard. As skinny as ever, but a more wary look in his eyes than the old days when she'd seen him with Rob at Minerva. Then they'd been two aging savant tenders hanging out. From there, Rob had spiraled up and Kell down.

He squinted hard at her, and she had to remind him who she was. He nodded. Handing her the groceries, he stranded his code into the house lock.

Watching Kell work his data rings, she drank coffee from a stained cup. The living room wall was live with scrolled code. From time to time Kell shook his head to get the hair out of his eyes. Between Caitlin on the couch and Kell in his chair lay the briefcase containing his down payment for accessing Lamar Gelde's files. If he failed, he kept the briefcase. If he succeeded, another similar payment in a week. It felt like a swindle to Caitlin. If her intervention succeeded, he should have a payment in the millions.

After a half-night's sleep, Caitlin was marginally more clear-headed. Panic had receded, replaced by nagging doubt. She was operating on more instinct than proof. What would she tell the police? There's something inside a reactor at Hanford. . . .

Kell had asked no questions. To his credit, he seemed relieved when she told him Rob knew what she was doing. Left unsaid was that if caught, they both could spend time in jail. All these considerations were pushed aside by the prospect of six hundred thousand dollars for two hours' work.

"Holy Jesus, Lamar's got himself a sweet piece of optics."

What did he think, a former Minerva board director would be working off a minor optical computer? Lamar had a savant, absolutely. She wouldn't have been surprised if he'd had a personal mSap, but that would be like using a hypersonic jet to get groceries.

Caitlin didn't bother to comment. He wasn't talking to her, anyway. She strolled to the window and kept watch on the street. If they'd been following her, they'd have been here by now. She just hoped that didn't mean they were following Rob, instead.

When she turned back, Kell was frowning. "He's pretty good," he mumbled.

"Meaning?"

Data rings flashed; windows tiled up. Kell was mired down.

Caitlin knew better than to interrupt. She sat down, waiting, feeling the coffee cup in her hands go cold.

"Can you please hurry?" she asked, knowing how obnoxious that sounded.

An agonizing fifteen minutes later, he mumbled, "Trying something else. This should work."

It didn't. While Caitlin digested her stomach lining, Kell continued a single-minded and increasingly bitter struggle with Lamar's firewalls.

From across the room she heard Kell mutter, "Okay, in."

But the news wasn't good. "Encrypted tighter than a virgin's twat . . ."

She was ready to push him off the chair and have at the encryption herself.

An hour later, he finally broke through. Caitlin was facing Lamar's file names on the wall display.

"Now it's your turn to hurry," he mumbled. "Get in, get out. Go."

As the file contents ballooned onto the screen, Caitlin shook her head no. No, not that. Not that. Keep going.

"Personnel," she said, spying another name to try. "Open it." Squinting up at the smart wall, she said, "Scroll to the bottom."

He went to the end.

"How many names?"

"Exactly two thousand."

"Scroll up to number sixteen." He did so. She read: Caitlin Quinn. Number seventeen, Mateo Quinn. Number eighteen, Emily Quinn.

"That file. Strand it to me. It was small enough to save onto her smart-Suit. "And print it."

As he backed out of Lamar's savant, he bragged, "No footprints." Kell mopped up after himself. "I was a butterfly."

CHAPTER TWENTY-FIVE

In war, destroy the enemy's soldiers. If you cannot, diminish his supplies. If you cannot, disable his allies.

—from Tun Mu's *Annals of War*

THE HIGH PREFECT WAS OUT OF SORTS. Cixi would give no audiences, hear no reports this ebb. Her chamberlain closed the great doors of the hall, the doors that when shut showed only the tail of the dragon inlaid into the audience chamber floor. The chamberlain, a Ysli who'd been in her service so long he was almost as old as Cixi herself, now stood in front of those doors, sending her supplicants away until the fourth hour of Prime of Day.

Petitioners, legates, preconsuls, and stewards—those who had hoped that by staying up late into Deep Ebb they could find the high prefect with perhaps a few moments of idle time to hear their briefs—went away unfulfilled.

Behind the great doors, inside the hall, nine figures gathered in the lavender shadows. One was Cixi. Of the remaining eight, three were Hirrin, two were Jout, and three, Chalin. Cixi stood by a small carved table, her finger resting lightly on a pile of scrolls.

"These are your paroles," she said.

A stirring among those gathered here. Hirrin nostrils flared. A Chalin man, lately a soldier of the Long War, narrowed his eyes. Each of them knew what parole was his. For six of them, the parole was for a high crime that until now Cixi had held over them in case of need. Tonight she had need. For the soldier Yinhe, the parole was for a crime of his daughter, as he well understood.

"After tonight, each of you is freed forever of vow breaking in my eyes, and therefore in the eyes of the Magisterium. You understand? You have absolute pardon. I erase not only your guilt, but the crime itself. Where there were victims, they are forgotten. Let any sentient remind you of the sin, and they will quickly know my displeasure. Your grave flags shall say only heavenly things, may the Miserable God not look on you early, of course." She eyed each of them in turn. "You understand."

They did. They also understood that something large would be asked of them.

Cixi nodded at the scrolls. "Let each of you take the scroll inscribed with your name and read his parole. Come forward."

As they did so, Cixi went to the verandah doors and with great effort—she being small, old, and wearing elevated shoes that made most movements difficult—closed them. A further gloom descended on the hall.

Lord Oventroe would arrive in thirty increments. They must be ready.

For the first time in her long life, she trembled. Soon she would set in motion an action that could never have parole.

Titus Quinn had just come into Tarig custody in Rim City. Earlier, a fugitive woman of the Rose had also given herself up. This individual, known as Hel Ese, was now sequestered in the furthest cell of the Magisterium, the Dragon's Eye. She was said to be sick. Perhaps that was why she came, for the lords' healing.

Why Quinn gave himself to the lords, she could not know, but she guessed that he wished to have access to the Ascendancy. She didn't know his plans. But she was quite sure they were coming to fruition. He had the correlates. He'd given them to the scholar Su Bei in order to effect some great plan. Her minions had almost caught the old meddler. Following him across the Gond primacy, the incompetents had let him slip into the veil. And he'd taken the correlates with him. So the key to travel to and from was still loose, and in the enemy's hands. She would pay dearly to know what Quinn intended with those correlates. But what was it likely to be, except to open the Entire to the darklings? Why else have the correlates? Why else, indeed, would Lord Oventroe have given him the correlates, except to open the Entire to the Rose?

That must never happen. Rose billions would descend, and they would corrupt the All, eschewing the traditions, undermining the Magisterium, and bringing their warlike ways to the realm of peace. Another hard kernel of misgiving was at the center of it all: Titus Quinn rising in power would mean Sen Ni weakening. For thousands of days Cixi had watched her plans for Sen Ni unfold. One man could ruin it all.

He would soon arrive. Then he would have access to his ally, none other than one of the Five. Who knew but that by Heart of Day tomorrow, he might be High Lord of the Ascendancy? He would put his own partisans in place of her subprefects and preconsuls. He would cast Cixi down, replacing her, perhaps with Su Bei. Or with the detestable Yulin.

These thoughts put iron in her bones, and she walked with a steady gait back to the reprieved criminals. Finished perusing their scrolls, they had placed them back on the table.

"Now I will tell you," she said, "what you must do for the sake of the All. We have in our midst a great traitor. He is one who has given the keys to the Entire over to the Rose, those who hate us. I have separately told each of you how the darklings sent Titus Quinn to Ahnenhoon to destroy us. His goal was to attack the engine of the Repel, that great mechanical so needed to generate wardings against Paion incursions. That attack, had the lords not foiled it, would have pulled apart the realm.

"This is the man whom the traitor has aided. Titus Quinn is now on his way to the Ascendancy, supposedly as a prisoner, but soon to prevail with the help of our traitor. Tonight we will stop that traitor. Tonight we will kill Lord Oventroe."

She waited as they absorbed this news. "Among you are three who will watch if any of you hold back. Those who hold back will die with the lord." Watching them carefully, she waited. They must get over the shock now, but not wallow in it. Too much thinking would make cowards of them all, even Cixi.

"At my request Oventroe comes by a secret route. No one will know he came here. When he disappears, there will be no trace. On this floor I have created a barrier line, a perimeter over which the lord and I will pass. I will call you to me, and then enliven the barrier. It will not hold him long. It must happen quickly. Sounds will die inside this circle. It will repress even a Tarig bellow." She knew from former reports from Mo Ti that the Tarig did not die in the ordinary way. But she would take Oventroe off the stage at a critical time. It might be many arcs before he returned. By then, with any luck, Titus Quinn would suffer the Tarig execution he so deserved.

"Now that you know the night's work, you understand there is no turning back. None of you can be innocent of this." She saw that one of the Jouts looked ill, but the Chalin assassins, especially Yinhe, were stalwart, and the Hirrin could be depended upon.

"Have no doubt, you serve the Entire. Heaven will shine on you."

They heard a sound from the far wall.

"Go into the shadows, all except you Hirrin. You are my attendants. Stand by my chair." The group quickly dispersed, each one armed with his best weapon.

Cixi had no time to settle herself on her dais, so she turned to watch Lord Oventroe approach. He moved warily toward her from the far wall where the access lay to the passageway, one that only Cixi and the Tarig knew. *Was* he moving warily? No time to be imaginative, she chided herself. Bowing just deeply enough, she murmured, "Bright Lord."

"Prefect." He stopped some paces form her. "Such secrecy, and at such a time."

"Yes. You will not regret the effort, my lord."

He nodded at the two Hirrin. "They share in your secrets?"

"Absolutely to be trusted."

"Yet it is your secret, not mine, and I am eager to be among my cousins for what is to come." He had not yet come close to her. As a courtesy, he held enough distance that she needn't look up at an undignified angle to see his face. However, tonight she wished him closer.

"Walk with me a few paces from my attendants," Cixi murmured. "Some things I will whisper, Bright Lord." When he made no move, she felt sweat forming around her hairline. She made her face stern. "We have only these few increments before the woman Hel Ese may say what she knows. Even now she has sent word to me that she will tell what she knows. It will change everything, you must understand." The lie was flimsy and could not hold for long. She turned and walked toward the side of the hall, crossing the barrier line, praying that the lord would follow her.

"You do or do not trust the Hirrin servants?"

"I trust them. Yet some things are private."

With that, he began moving toward her again. In what seemed a life-time, Oventroe crossed the threshold.

When he had joined her in the middle of the corral, she said, "The Rose woman knows about the correlates. In fact, she has the correlates." These lies need only seem credible for a few more heartbeats.

Oventroe raised his chin just a little. She had his absolute attention.

"You may not believe me. I did not think my word alone would suffice. I have brought two witnesses." She turned from Oventroe, saying, "Come. He will hear you."

Two Jout came from deep shadows where they had been standing along the wall. In their wake, three Chalin.

"You said two witnesses." Oventroe was now troubled and alert.

"Two who saw the correlates. These others—they saw how the correlates were delivered. Most strange, my lord. Most troubling. Worth your hearing."

"How delivered?" Oventroe asked. He turned at the sound of Hirrin hooves on the floor.

"Yes," Cixi murmured. "How delivered. Let me whisper."

Oventroe bent down, but he took hold of her arm as he did so, in an unbreakable grip.

When his face was beside hers, Cixi whispered, "By you, great fiend." The eight were within the circle. Cixi broke a small stick in her hand, and the air crackled into walls of invisible force.

Oventroe spun at the sound of the barrier snapping. Charging against the nearest wall, he fell backward from the shock. In that moment of surprise, the first blow came to Oventroe's back, a short sword driven in, sending him staggering against the wall again. Still holding Cixi in his grip, he thrashed, sending her flailing off her feet, shoes hurtling away. With an agonizing grip on her arm, the lord spun around, kicking high, catching a Jout in the neck with a blade extruded from his boot. The Jout fell, spraying blood, but now the Hirrin grinned, sending darts into the lord's chest from spring-loaded mechanisms in their mouths.

It was a silent dance. No one shouted or cried out. The blows came too fast. Yinhe darted in, slashing at Oventroe's hands with a sword. The lord, though now gravely wounded, was upright and still able to kill. He jumped into the midst of them with sickening speed, delivering a massive blow to the nearest Hirrin's muzzle. From behind Oventroe, Yinhe found the leverage for a mighty blow that took off Oventroe's left arm. It was the one that held Cixi. She fell to the floor, blood-drenched, with the gripping Tarig hand still attached to her.

Then it was Jout, Chalin, and Hirrin, stomping and thrusting, grunting at the work of killing a powerful animal. The sounds of tissues rending.

Cixi thought how quiet killing was, even this melee. And how fast. Only a few increments had passed since she whispered in his ear, *By you, great fiend*. Now Oventroe lay on his back, pumping blood onto the floor. It was finished. True, he might come back, if Tarig never died utterly. But Oventroe's cousins might wait a very long time before giving him another body; after all, they could not know where he was. Cixi would make sure he was never found.

Through a growing slick of blood, Cixi crawled toward him. She pulled herself over a Hirrin body to get to the felled lord. Drawing the stiletto knife from her tall coiffure, she knelt on Oventroe's chest. Despite his grievous injuries, he remained conscious.

"It does no good to kill us," he whispered.

She knew that. But it would slow him down. And she would kill him again if he came back.

She sat on his chest, heart hammering, mouth so dry she could hardly form words. He was dying, and Cixi still knew little about his conspiracy; by the looks of him, she had only a few moments to find out. "Why did you give him the correlates?" When he didn't answer, she leaned forward, bringing her face close enough to his that he could not avoid hearing. "You are dying. Tell me, my lord."

He burbled through a gashed neck. "The correlates do not matter. Going to and from. It does not matter. You love a worthless thing, old woman."

He closed his eyes, and she feared he would say no more. But now she was adamant to know: could he really want the Entire's destruction? She pressed her hand on his neck to staunch the frothy blood.

His eyes flashed open. "Only one may survive."

"But *our realm*! You would destroy it?"

He whispered, "I want . . . the Rose . . . instead."

She had never heard a lord use the word *I* before. "Want it?"

"Lord of the Rose. They would call me lord."

"They would fight you."

"I would give them knowledge . . . they would worship me. I would rule them; I would give you a high station. Do not oppose me, Cixi. Give my body to my cousins, and I will return for you."

When he came back, he wanted to know his enemies; he wanted to know how he died; she would be a fool to let him know a thing like that.

Still, she could not fathom the enormity of his defection. "You already have worshippers *here*. Is the Rose better?"

He looked past her as his vision failed. "I grew tired of . . . *here*." He said the last word with clear contempt.

Cixi took her hand from his neck. Still sitting on the lord's chest, she contemplated a creature who would betray a kingdom out of boredom.

"My cousins . . ." he pleaded.

"But it would be rather hard to explain your body . . . to your *cousins*," she sneered. With enormous satisfaction, she drove her knife into the side of his eye.

Afterward, there were three bodies: Oventroe's, a Jout's, and a Hirrin's. They were all wrapped in tapestries and taken to the crematory through the secret ways, down five levels, to the catacombs.

The clerks tending there had been excused for the evening.

The three dead found their resting place in the alcoves. They each had a grave flag. Oventroe's said, at Cixi's order, "A bad death. Instead."

Finally, the Tarig lords let Helice sleep. After hours of questions and terrorizing, the tall beings looming over her, bending at the waist to peer at her, threatening her with strangling, at last they abandoned her to her cell.

Fighting for emotional control, she reminded herself that the lords' great city had been her destination since the first day she'd sat in Minerva's boardroom and seen a spike of Entire grass. Despite the awful interrogation, she was nearing the end of her quest. She clung to her intention; to renaissance.

She slept intermittently, dreaming of the Tarig and their swarm minds. Sydney and her horse friends thought most sentients would despise this style of consciousness, but to Helice, it made the Tarig more imposing. Each one bore the collected wisdom of thousands of years. The swarm, as Helice imagined it, was like a luscious hive of honey, with the bees constantly bringing home the nectar of experience. The Tarig weren't disgusting; they were splendid.

After taking her clothes and searching her, they'd given her a long sleeveless shirt to wear, made of the finest soft cloth. So, here in this hellish prison, she wore silk. The room, small but not confining, had a toilet and nothing else. They called it the Dragon's Eye, they'd told her when they brought her here.

Mustn't look down.

As she lay on her back, staring at the ceiling, her whole face ached. The putrefaction stank. She wanted to sleep again, but terror kept her awake. Their rumbling voices stuck in her mind, replaying. *Where is Titus Quinn?*

I don't know about him, but I control your going home place, she'd told them.

They became very quiet. She had time to marvel at their excellent English. Their interrogation had been fluent. At least language was no barrier to her plans.

What place? they wanted to know.

She couldn't describe the location; only the mSap and Tai knew that. She had grid coordinates, but they meant nothing to her or to them.

The place where you go home, and where you come back, entering new bodies. That place. I don't know the name, only that it's here and that my machine with artificial intelligence marked it by the energy signature. A very big one, so we could hardly miss it.

You will die now.

I have said: I control it. I've planned how to destroy it if you hurt me. But I don't want to destroy it. I need you for something. And now you need me.

All this time, she had only looked down once. She was proud of that self-control amid the powerful draw of the sight. Soon she'd have Tarig respect; when they learned to fear her, when Tai set off the demonstration at the junction point between the Ascendancy and the Heart. As soon as the Tarig saw a little destruction, they would come back to her, prepared to talk.

The demonstration would prove she could threaten the Heart door. She'd tell them that the ability to completely destroy it lay with her mSap. That it was preprogrammed to do so unless she intervened. They might stoop to torture; but her frail health should give them pause. And one thing more: she would rather die than give up. After weeks of consideration, there was no doubt in her mind: she was fully prepared to die.

The mSap lay safely hidden. After Tai had left for the Ascendancy, Helice had taken the mSap and gone into the city, finding an old God's Needle. There, she'd climbed the circular stairs and hidden her machine sapient amid the refuse at the top where devout sentients left offerings. The mSap sitting atop that God's Needle could bring down the great door of the Tarig, a transfer point requiring so much power that, once destroyed, it might be impossible to rebuild.

However, some aspects of her scheme were pure subterfuge. She had not programmed the mSap to act on its own. That was too important a decision to automate. Sick as she was, she might lose consciousness at any time. The threat of it was enough, she reasoned.

Destroying the door to the Heart depended on actuating a command on the device that Tai held in safekeeping. He thought that the finder was a simple mechanism to help him locate the door. It was not that simple. Finding a way to retrieve it from him would require some ingenuity.

She needed to use the toilet. But that meant getting up. Turning over, she crouched on hands and knees first. Not being able to stop herself, she looked down. Her stomach felt like it was dropping out of her body. She was standing on nothing, high over an ocean. Here, in the bottom-most section of the Magisterium, she stood on a small concave section of the floor, like a giant eye staring down.

Yanking herself away from the view, she crawled to the toilet and vomited. Her face and neck burned from the stomach acid splattering up. She put a hand to her throat, something she usually avoided for fear of breaking the scabs. Her fingers came away sticky. She didn't know whether to hope for Tarig healing, or mistrust it.

She allowed her thoughts to stray to comforting things: to her stay among the Inyx and her first excitement about being in the Entire. Everything had been before her then: that pure vision of humanity renewed. Earth cleansed of its imbeciles and entitled commoners. Earth cleansed of every ancient burden and unworthy desire for ease. Now came the final steps, no longer abstract, but solidly real, washed clean by fever, pain, and vertigo.

She would hold on. Hugging the little commode, she rested her face on its cool side.

Tai stared as the giant celestial's face rose over the edge of the city. Those sentients in the great plaza of the Ascendancy turned and pointed as the gas bag creature appeared on the horizon, lifting on warm currants from below, blinking at the greatness of the Tarig royal seat.

The Adda hovered for a moment at the edge of the plaza as though reluctant to come near the spires puncturing the city's sky. Nearby, an astounded Laroo commented to a Ysli steward that Adda could not float so high—because nothing living could rise so near the bright—but the celestial beast moved serenely toward them, oblivious of the Laroo's declaration. Functionaries rushed out of the Magisterium, pointing at the beast. Tai stared with the rest of them, hoping to see the Adda come to ground in their midst, but it sailed over them toward the mansions of the lords.

"It is Titus Quinn," Tai heard a legate say. Through the crowd shouldered six large Chalin men carrying a sling bearing a Gond—by his silver-capped horns, a preconsul. Gap-mouthed, the Gond watched with the rest of them. Tai heard him say to a clerk that Titus Quinn had been captured in Rim City, but the sway's upstart Mistress would have no brightship in the city and commanded an Adda for conveyance, and to the preconsul's evident disgust, she had been indulged.

But Tai's only thoughts were, *Titus Quinn, Titus Quinn.*

More denizens of the city came streaming across bridges and up from the Magisterium at the fast-spreading rumor that the man of the Rose had been captured. Titus Quinn, the one whose exploits were on the breath of every sentient in the Entire—who had killed Lord Hadenth, who had stolen the fleet of brightships, whose daughter was now queen of the Rim.

Tai wondered what they would do to Titus Quinn now that he had been captured. The lords hated him, but Hel Ese would protect him. They were friends. Though she didn't tell Tai what her mission was, he felt sure that she and Titus Quinn worked to open converse between the realms.

Tai sat on a low wall next to a canal, watching the Adda disappear behind the slanted roofs of the lords' palaces. At his side the canal bore its stream of water flashing here and there with mottled carp. He was in a strange city, great and despised. He had done things and hoped for things that had split his life into before Hel Ese and after. The last arc of days traced a new Tai— one he admired but did not know very well. The things he'd seen! The man of the Rose, the clandestine meeting with his daughter climbing into the Adda, a Paion missive, the halls of the Magisterium. And the things he'd done! Hidden a fugitive, defaced the Tower of the Sleeping Lord . . . lied to Sublegate Milinard. *Excellency, I saw her in the undercity, but she slipped away. She's probably hiding there.* Milinard, at first excited to have news, soon dismissed Tai as sincere but of little interest. Hel Ese had already been captured. The sublegate bid him stay in the city for a time in case further questions occurred to him.

But Tai's mission was done. He was glad of that. He could sit here for days, watching carp, watching for Hel Ese. Soon she would be powerful among the Tarig, and when that happened, she would send him to the Rose.

Something moved on the lords' hill. Squinting against the glare of the bright, Tai saw the narrow avenues moving, filled with some dark material. He tried to make sense of it. Then he saw what it must be, a surge of Tarig through the streets. Every lane, every pathway, avenue, and even the terraces and overlooks, brimming with Tarig.

Now he noticed that the plaza itself was devoid of the lords. They had withdrawn from the public spaces. It made him uneasy to think that the masses of Tarig crowding outside on the hill might be due to Titus Quinn's arrival. Perhaps some plan of Hel Ese and Titus had gone astray. He watched the Tarig stream through the streets in the shadows of the mansions, a splash of silver from their garments sometimes catching the light.

Too nervous to sit, he wandered toward the Magisterium, thinking to find news. He closed the door behind him, taking relief from the cool interior, away from the press of the bright. Hoping to learn what was going on, he went down to the precincts of the clerks where he had waited yesterday for a summons from Milinard. He listened to what gossip he could overhear. The clerks, the lowest order of magistrate, were the easiest to talk to. They carried their computational boards with them wherever they went: the broad, backward sloping hats. By this means they could always be productive, and by this means too, they seemed to know the latest gossip.

Posing as an interested newcomer, he began asking questions about the man of the Rose and his capture. It was no more than everyone was doing. On the great stairways, in the covered galleries, in the immaculate corridors of the Magisterium, he heard the man's name whispered by legates, clerks, factors, understewards, and sublegates.

Titus Quinn. Titus Quinn.

CHAPTER TWENTY-SIX

Seek you the Hirrin in the Sheltering Path,
A finer primacy no sentient hath.
To meet the fierce Inyx or most noble Jout,
The Long Gaze of Fire you must seek out.
Chalin and Ysli together reside
In Arm of Heaven and exalted abide.
Far travelers roam Laroo and Adda to find,
The Bright River holds them, and no lesser kind.
The Radiant Arch, the last of the five,
Guards nests of the Gond, may you safely arrive.
—Shanty of Five Primacies

SU BEI CURLED INTO THE SAC, abandoning himself to the veil-of-worlds, to the Miserable God and to his own untidy fate. He had no idea how long he and Anzi had been crossing, or *what* they were crossing. There was no sensation of movement. The sac, holding enough air to sustain them, was both tough and yielding, adjusting to their movements.

They were out of the world, at the mercy of the veil and Bei's own benighted understanding of how to direct the crossing. His stone well computer had gone dead. Powered by the bright, it had lasted long hours, but now lay useless. Nevertheless he was in a state of high mentation. He had never felt so capable of thought and insight as these last hours. Was this how one died, the mind showered with brilliance at the last?

He and Anzi stared at the walls of their conveyance where visions had been appearing, visions of alien places, far from the Entire. Bei felt sure the scenes were representations of worlds, much like the representations that appeared on the veils-of-worlds.

He looked at Anzi, tucked next to him in the sac. "Anzi, girl. How are you?"

"Master Bei. I'm well. Do you know where we are going?"

"No, girl. We'd have been there by now if my efforts had worked."

"Lost, then?"

"We are in the Great Sway," he said trying to be reassuring.

"The Great Sway," she said, accepting this with equanimity. They whispered, partly because they sat so close, and partly for the awe of what they were looking at. They stared at the scenes coming before them.

Landscapes hove into view, stretched by the curvature of their cell, but clear enough to rivet their attention. If he and Anzi were in the next realm, then these were images—sometimes brief, sometimes lingering—from the third kingdom. They saw cities of organic bone grown from an egg; a single mountain as high as the Ascendancy; an endless chain of creatures hooking nose to tail in a line of migration; a submerged generation ship carrying travelers at the bottom of an ocean. After the first hour they saw yet more.

At the beginning of their crossing, Bei had immediately set to work to study what he was seeing, using the correlates to set data points with reference to the Entire, though it was problematical given that they were not *in* the Entire. Still, before the stone well gave up, Bei had his theory.

The Entire, he conjectured, might well lie at the conjunction of five kingdoms. Each of the primacies might burrow into a different realm, as this Radiant Arch primacy did into the third kingdom. Another kingdom—so Titus must have thought—would likely be the Heart. He could picture it all as a schema. Five primacies penetrating five realms. Overhead, at the center, the Heart, small, hot, and wicked.

His mind raced. Here was a grand schema that so far surpassed his life's work that he could hardly contain his excitement. He had begun his cosmography of the Rose fifty thousand days ago, thinking to map that kingdom. The correlates greatly accelerated his accomplishments, and had it not been for Anzi's arrival at his reach, he might still be working out that worthy—but woefully minor—map of the darkling universe.

Oh, the girl had been right. The correlates were so much more; the Rose was only one of many.

He calmed himself. His instinct was to rush to inscroll his findings. His reach would be a center of learning; scholars would come from far and wide. . . . He had to stop short, remembering that his scholar's reach was gone. And he was adrift.

Still, he had not just one astonishing theory, but two. A corresponding theory to his schema of the kingdoms related to *views* of the kingdoms.

The veil-of-worlds—and in some analogous way, the sac they were in—reflected scenes from the respective kingdoms because everything that was in the kingdoms, all points within, had corresponding points on the perimeter of that kingdom. It went against logic, but it might well be the case.

He theorized that he and Anzi were not traveling *in* the next kingdom. They were traveling on the perimeter, on the surface area, perhaps skimming along the outside of the bubble. Though they might be traveling some real distance, they could not encompass all the worlds and views that they had been vouchsafed on these sac walls. How, then, in this brief excursion, did they see the wonders of so many planetoids, surely separated by vast distances?

His insight staggered him. Bei surmised that everything in the kingdom had a correspondence on the surface area. The reality inside the bubble was inscribed on the surface, in an isomorphic relationship. *This* data point on the *surface* related to *that* one in the *volume*, in a complex system of equivalences! This might well imply that the inside was an illusion, and that only the surface was real. But that was playing loose with his data, and giving vent to imaginations. Still, wasn't this how great discoveries were made?

He sat back, breathless with his summary. If this was how the Woeful God had designed the Great Sway, then perhaps they owed the deity an apology for hating Him. It was only a theory. But the grandeur! He thought of the first name Anzi had suggested, the Celestial All, and thought that it might not be too flowery, after all.

Bei felt he could now die without curses, except for the maddening awareness that no scholar's library would be likely to see his thesis. Authorship aside, he would gladly fling his necklace of redstones to a waiting hand. . . .

"Su Bei."

He looked at Anzi. Though close enough to bend down and touch, she appeared indistinct to him.

"We are separating."

"Eh?" Looking around him, he saw a seam had formed at a midpoint on their enclosing sac and a thin membrane had grown between them. He punched at it.

It held.

"Anzi, poke at it." He shoved his hand uselessly against it. "Cut it with your knife!"

She did so, but the knife slid away. Looking more closely, Bei could now see what Anzi already had noted, that their bubble was in the process of splitting in two along the plane created by the new membrane.

"No," Bei whispered. "Take the stone well. Don't take her . . ." But the splitting proceeded.

Anzi stood up, leaning toward Bei. "Su Bei," she said, in a tone that he would never forget. "Master."

"Anzi, Anzi . . ." He forced himself to say: "There are five realms touching the Entire! Six if the Heart is among them. The Entire makes seven. You must tell someone!"

He saw her face, darkly visible through the thickening wall. She fixed him with an open, full look that left cosmology and realms behind. "Remember me, Su Bei. Will you remember?"

He had no time to answer. Jiggling and pulling, the bubble calved. Anzi was gone.

After that, he cared less about what he saw. A profound weariness came upon him, and he mourned. He had the sense that he was going somewhere, and that Anzi had been lost, although it might as easily be the other way around.

He dreaded telling Titus this. Perhaps he would never need to do so, because he would be lost among the seven kingdoms.

It would surely be better than explaining to Titus how he'd lost the man's wife.

Quinn was in darkness. A light clung to his body so that he could see his hands bound in front of him, his hobbled feet. By a faint brush of sound, he perceived movement around him. Oventroe, he hoped.

He guessed he was somewhere in the depths of the Tarig mansions. He had been brought into these subregions of the palatine hill immediately upon his debarking from the Adda. But now they had left him waiting when his need for haste was great. Helice might even now be bringing forth her monstrous plans.

"Titus-een."

His skin prickled at the term of endearment. It was Chiron's style. Could this be Chiron returned? The memories of her death would be gone, but any return to the heart before the events at Ahnenhoon might have preserved her memories of Quinn.

A second voice came to him. "My cousins clamor to kill you and be done with it."

"Well, here I am." Neither of these voices was Lord Oventroe's.

The second voice continued, "My cousins are in the streets, saying you must have the garrote. We are content for now. You may speak, ah?"

"I've given myself up. Do you want to know why?"

A hiss from the first Tarig. "You have missed us, perhaps."

"Who shall I address, Bright Lord?"

The first speaker, the one who had called him Titus-een, said, "My cousin is Lord Nehoov, one of the Five."

"And you?"

"One's name? Oh, Lady Demat. Of the Five."

So this lady had assumed Chiron's empty chair. But Oventroe was not here; either that or he hung back in the dark chamber, not revealing his presence. Perhaps he had not been in residence, though, and was now hurrying home.

Pushing aside his disappointment at Oventroe's absence, he addressed them: "Lord Nehoov, Lady Demat, I brought a weapon to Ahnenhoon. You know about that. I didn't trust it. Even though I was at the foot of the engine, I withdrew the weapon. I still have it. You can threaten my land, and I can threaten yours. Maybe that's peace. Is it, Bright Ones?"

Lord Nehoov said, "We found no chain of molecular destruction. You have it elsewhere, perhaps hidden. Perhaps useless."

"It *is* elsewhere. With a trusted friend. She can forge its power into one packet, and the Entire will be gone."

More movement outside the range of light. They were watching him intensely, and he tracked the sounds of their movements.

"Hnn, a trusted friend," Lord Nehoov mused. "Would it be Hel Ese of the darkling realm?"

"You know better, Bright Lord. We are enemies."

"Another friend, then. One who would destroy the All of All?"

Nehoov was skeptical that Quinn could have such an accomplice; he'd need convincing. "She knows it's not everything," Quinn said. "The Entire never was the whole of it. She's content that the Rose will live, at least."

Lord Nehoov said, "She will give the Entire up to ruin? Hnn. One does not credit such a thing."

"But she will."

A long silence. They weren't moved. He would have to say more.

"She's my wife."

He heard noises around him. Then silence. It took several moments before he realized that they had left. Anxiety spiked. Was Anzi already in custody? Were they in Anzi's cell right now, demanding she give over the chain?

Oh, Anzi. He didn't know how to weigh the two levels of his life. He was a man, he was the last hope of the Rose. He was a husband. Did that matter? A moment ago, he'd had the choice whether to mention the cirque and his wife. She could have been safe from them. So he'd chosen his role. Never mind doing a good thing. He had to do the great thing, and it made him sick of himself.

His only hope was Lord Oventroe, that he would intervene.

Quinn waited. As he did, there was time to consider who Lady Demat might be; who she might once have been. The voice wasn't hers, but the cadence was, and the irony. This was a high distraction. Might Chiron and Demat be one and the same? If so, then he had a powerful personal enemy to contend with.

The detonation, when it happened, shook the plaza, sending shudders radiating out to all points of the Ascendancy.

One who saw the unthinkable event was Yinhe of the Long War. He had been crossing a canal, and thus from the center of the arched bridge he had an unobstructed view to Lord Ghinamid's Tower. First, the piercing squeal, a sound that disrupted the peace of the Bright City like a dragon in a sitting room. Whipping around to face the noise, Yinhe saw a spray of fire and smoke jetting out from the tower. An incandescent glow coursed up the side of the edifice as though reaching for the bright.

He rushed off the bridge, drawing his sword, ready to act the part of the loyal soldier.

A breeze lifted the smoke away, and the Tower of the Sleeping Lord slept again. Yinhe was relieved to see that it yet stood.

As he ran toward the tower, he wondered if the ancient tower was protesting the massacre of a lord. Was the tower sparking in anger that he, Yinhe of the Long War, had raised a military hand against one of the Five? Unconsciously, he felt for his scroll of pardon. It still resided in his belt, but doubtless the High Prefect Cixi had no rule over the tower and its stony judgment.

He'd had no peace since the murder. Over and again he played it in his mind. The lord's missing arm. Yinhe had taken it at the shoulder. The high prefect scrambling on the blood-slicked floor. The lord kicking toward Yinhe, the blade on his boot nearly taking his face off. He had never been in a worse fight. He had killed a Tarig. The high prefect had ordered it for reasons he only dimly understood. The lords bled a crimson hue. Since that day, his dreams—despite sharing the universal dreams against the high lords—tended toward blood.

Taking his place at the entrance to the tower, he stood poised if something should exit from inside. He waited long minutes. He expected to see masses of Tarig descend into the plaza. But none did. Taking his attention away from the tower door, he saw some lords standing on the mansion rooftops, looking down. No, *hundreds* of lords stood on the rooftops, and also on the balconies, avenues, and lookouts. Their dark forms were still, like trees in a sentient forest. He wished they would come forward or show some sign of disarray.

They watched but did not come down.

In the plaza, emptiness. Everyone had fled the public spaces; they hid where they could, hid from Paion attack. Or was it an assault from Titus Quinn once again?

The tower was silent. It loomed over him, intact. There was damage just at eye level, where the projectile had pierced. If that was what had happened.

It was very quiet in the heart of the palatine hill. It had always been quiet, Quinn remembered, but not like this. In the time before, brightships had come and gone, their thrusts and breaking a dull but familiar cadence to the day. Voices had arisen in the mansion, the low rumble of Tarig conversation, punctuating the silence like the occasional barking of dogs. But now. So calm and blank.

The lights came up suddenly. A Tarig female swept through a door, charging for him. A net over her close-cropped hair, sparkling. A slit metal skirt, a jeweled vest. She grabbed him by the upper arm, yanking him savagely to his feet. She dragged him from the cell. Now in a corridor, she rushed forward with him in tow, his arm nearly pulled from its socket. He scrambled to keep his feet under him. She must have cut the binds off his ankles, but it happened so suddenly: the lights, the lady rushing toward him, he couldn't remember. Demat, he guessed.

She hauled him to a place where the corridor widened into a rotunda. The place was full of Tarig. When they saw him, they muttered deeply, a basso profundo of derision.

The lady dropped him, making sure he fell to his knees.

"This—" the lady said, "—this is the darkling who would take the Entire and all our joy." The crowd surged toward him. From the floor, he looked up at them. A lord kicked at him, slicing open his cheek. Bleeding now, he put his hands to his cut face, but Demat grabbed him again before others could join in the savaging. She pulled him to his feet; his face was streaming blood.

"No one kills him but the Five," she said. She stopped in midstride, and held him still for a moment, her nostrils flaring. "No one kills him but me. Would that be just, Titus-een?"

Oh, it was Chiron.

"Justice looks different where I come from." Blood came to his tongue. He spit it out, and inadvertently hit Demat's vest. It pearled away. No soiling from crimes. The Tarig imperative.

She drove him down corridors and ramps, all downward. The Tarig lords followed, and their rumbling voices sounded like a rock slide behind him. His thoughts were catching up, thoughts of Anzi. Had she convinced them she had the cirque, and had they put her to the question of its location, and had she refused? What else could enrage them so? If they showed him her body, he would kill Chiron again. It was too much, to always save the Earth, and never grieve, and never care who was lost to him. He was no *hsien*. Just don't kill her, he thought, and I'll be what you want. Even a prince again, and my soul gone then.

A door flew open and Demat pushed him through it into the shattering day. A narrow street deep in glarish light. Along its length, Tarig, in numbers he had never seen before. Solitary creatures, they did not care for congregations, not even of themselves. And why should they? They were all one thing, or almost. It would be like versions of yourself populating your life, mirroring and mocking. They drove him through the narrow street then, with masses of Tarig raising their arms, making them taller yet, creating a canyon of hate.

He smelled smoke in the air. Something large had happened. And he was going to pay for it.

The lords crowded into the street, leaving only a narrow passage for Demat and him. The shock of a cut to his side. Then one to his back. They were clawing him. Pain burst from all his nerves. He felt the cold slap of blood-soaked fabric against his skin. Maybe they would have killed him by now, but Lady Demat moved swiftly through the gauntlet.

A searing gash to his free arm; it dropped to his side, useless.

By the other arm, Demat yanked him close, whispering, "Where is this gondling, your wife? Have you a voice left?"

"I don't know where she is."

"Tell us."

Filled with relief, his eyes clouded. They didn't have her. They didn't have her.

"I don't know. She left on a navitar vessel. I didn't want to know."

Hissing with rage, she pulled him onward, down the street. The cousins were dashing out to strike at him. Little cuts. To make him last. Weak and in shock, he let himself be dragged. At his side, his arm hung uselessly. He looked up at the bright, wondering why it had seemed so right at Ahnenhoon to save it.

CHAPTER TWENTY-SEVEN

*One is welcome in all sways, but in two be watchful: the forests
of the Gond, the mansions of the lords.*

—a saying

ELOW HELICE THE ENTIRE LAY FLAT AND SILVER. Thousands of feet down
was the sea. Pillars of frazzled light fell from the city, and she could
see—in the nearest one—things riding up and down in it. It took an hour to
reach the bottom, as nearly as she could judge. It was very difficult not to
watch. Forcing her gaze to the perimeter of her view, she caught glimpses of
the storm walls, mere smudges at this distance. The city was at the center of
everything, as though she could forget, as though anyone could.

Tai, did you do what I asked? Did you bring the nan cell to its proper
place, or did you disappoint me, losing your resolve here in the Tarig city?

At times, lying on her back for relief from the view, she stared up at the
ceiling. She forced herself to think of other things. Guinevere, her pet Macaw.
The good beku that had pulled the cart carrying herself, Quinn, and Benhu
across the midlands of the Entire. The cart was bright green and decorated
with the face of the Woeful God. She thought of Titus Quinn, and wondered
if she had killed him that day on the street of Rim City. Soon after that came
the riots; maybe his murder would have gone unnoticed.

Tai, have you kept faith with me? Tai, you must understand: The Rose
was once great—the Earth, that is, was great. But the world grew timid and
gluttonous, breeding indignities great and mundane. You wouldn't like it,
Tai. They would give you a wall screen and feed you stories of happier people.

A sound at the door.

Only one Tarig entered the room. This one was imposing: his long garment looked like poured mercury. He wore a black choker around his throat that shimmered more than his skirt. His hair was formed into little knots on his head. He had long nails. No, his claws were out.

She rose, standing in the center of the dimple. Now it begins, she thought.

"Lie down," the being said.

She knelt and was beginning to lie on her back, when he strode forward, coming into the dimple. With a powerful grip, he flipped her onto her stomach. He held her there on the concave floor, with her back arched in the wrong direction. Pressure on her neck kept her motionless.

His voice was low and eerily gentle. "This is the Dragon's Eye, darkling. Look, or I will take your eyelids off." He murmured: "It blinks, this Dragon's Eye."

She tried to speak, but the hand around the back of her neck pushed down, silencing her.

"It opens."

His meaning registered in her stomach, and though she tried mightily to prevent her gorge from rising, bile rushed up her throat. He let her spit it out, a small kindness.

"If you hurt me . . ."

The voice came, more menacing. "You will not speak, hnn?" His voice droned above her. "We created the Dragon's Eye and all that it sees. You have created nothing. Your world builds with stone; we build with forces. You languish in darkness, stumbling with weapons. We have the bright forever. You are nothing. But you come against us, ah?"

"I don't . . ."

The hand on her neck pressed harder.

"The Radiant Land existed from the dawn of all things. Your land was an accident of cosmologics. The Radiant Land grew as the many universes grew. We are a *universe*"—he said it as though it was a word he seldom used—"but your world is a node of matter in a universe. Against the Entire, the Earth does not signify. Yet you come against us."

Tai! The demonstration had taken place. She had come against them, he said. Well, yes. Take a good, unblinking look, you gangling freak. Tai had done it. Oh Tai, I will give you anything now.

Outrageously, she felt pulled to sleep. Maybe it was her brain turning off so that she didn't have to think about the dimple beneath her opening.

"Eyes are open?" he asked as though reading her mind.

"Yes."

"Now, darkling, tell us of the door."

Forced to speak with her face pushed up against the glass, she whispered, "You go home through a brane interface. You go home frequently, some of you. At home, you exchange information and come back."

Savagely, he pressed her face down. She could hardly breathe

"The door," he hissed. The hand relented, giving her room to suck in a breath.

"I found it. I brought a machine sapient from the Rose. I looked for all the doors, but there's only one. I won't hurt it if I don't have to. I gave you a demonstration that I know where it is. Just a demonstration."

The Tarig slowly lifted her from the floor. He sat her up, holding her to prevent her falling over. Gazing at her with terrible, steady attention, he said, "Sen Ni brought you to Rim City for this purpose?"

Helice had decided not to implicate Sydney. She might have to make nice with the girl sometime, if the dream rebellion paid off. "No. I used her, plying her with stories of her father in the Rose. I wanted to come near the Ascendancy with my machine sapient. She's ignorant."

Softly, he continued, "Now again, the door."

His face was long and planed, but not so much as to be deformed. If he'd been sculpture, he'd have been beautiful, but as flesh . . . at close range, she shuddered.

"You may speak."

"When the nan cell burst, it sent parts of itself all over the vicinity. The next time the pieces actuate, it'll eat through the tower. The whole brane interface will likely collapse. Given your resource issues, that's bad for you. It doesn't need to happen, if you'll listen to me."

He looked at her sideways, fixing her with one eye. "Titus Quinn brought the device?"

"No, please listen. He and I aren't for the same thing. He wants to preserve the Rose. I don't."

"Yet, you, Hel Ese—" he used her name for the first time—"are from the darkling realm. You come with Rose machines, Rose thoughts. You attack us. We see no difference between you."

"Oh, there's a difference." To her horror, she felt faint. "I'm sick," she said. "Get me out of this place."

"Hnn. Sick. We have seen this," he said, utterly flat.

She had to keep going, she had to say it all. But from days of raging infection and lack of sleep, her thoughts were growing muddy. She blurted, "I have friends in the Rose. They've built an engine. Similar to Ahnenhoon. We can match the engine to yours, immediately. That's how we can stop the assaults on the Entire, assaults like Titus Quinn at Ahnenhoon. All we want is for some few of us to come here; not many." She slumped to the floor. God, this wasn't how she'd imagined bargaining with them. "Don't you see? Then you can be done with assaults. And burn it all now. But I have to have water. If I die, you'll die."

"If you die, your threat dies."

"No, it's all preprogrammed. I can turn it off. I'd rather let you kill me before telling you how. I'm already half dead. You see?"

"And Titus Quinn?"

"Is nothing! Why keep bringing him up? He's alone here. He has no plan, no commission from the Rose. He threw away the cirque. He threw it in the river!" God, she had planned to say that at the very first. They didn't need to worry about retaliation anymore. They could act at any time. If they acted immediately, it would forestall the Rose devising any new cirque. She fought to stay conscious.

"I'm your ally. I could be your proud servant, the same as any person of a sway. I ask for a sway. A small one. And for my people to come across, and then your door is safe. Do you see?"

The lord regarded her with a feral gaze.

Quinn stood on a small balcony overlooking the city. His right arm hung limp and bleeding at his side. The right side of his face was hot and leaking blood. Around him, hundreds of Tarig crowded. Standing, determined not to fall in front of them, he staggered, turning in every direction, taking the measure of his surroundings. On one side, high balconies and rooftops formed perches and viewpoints for them; they gathered in judgment of him. No, judgment had been delivered long ago. They stood to watch him die, to say they'd seen it. Behind him was a long railing; far below it, the great plaza of the Ascendancy. He stood, swaying.

A tinge of smoke in the air.

Lady Demat left him alone to stand if he could. Whether she did it for her amusement or to give him a last measure of respect, he didn't know.

The crowd turned toward a side street as something drew their attention. He had a moment of calm to gather himself. He had time to wonder if Demat/Chiron would kill him. She had loved him, once. She had showed him kindness when others had only curiosity. Even Su Bei had been at first only curious. In those days Chiron had been his only friend and they'd taken their pleasure of each other. He long ago had decided that although he'd been typical of a man locked up, he had still betrayed others. Nothing could change that except forgiveness. Sydney had not given it to him, but Johanna had. He would have taken her home; he would have died first, before abandoning her to Ahnenhoon. Then events had turned, maliciously. The Miserable God had given Johanna the mission to destroy the Entire. It was the only way to save her beloved Rose. She had been willing to kill the All. And he had not been willing. So she fell at the site of the engine and he left her there. Because if he hadn't slipped away he wouldn't have been able to contain the compromised cirque. Thinking the Rose's demise many decades off, he'd disposed of the cirque, the only deterrent to the lords.

It was a miserable recitation of his performance in the Entire. He mightily wished for a chance to do better.

Someone was approaching. Lord Nehoov. The executioner?

Quinn looked at Lady Demat. "I'm ready," he said, in case she cared.

Nehoov come near and leaned in to Demat, whispering. Then Nehoov turned to several of the lords who came forward, voices angry.

During the next interval, Demat took his arm, the one that still worked. "No, Titus-een," she said softly. "Not yet. It is not yet."

The bright shed its glare on them, but it wasn't enough to cure him. He toppled.

Lady Demat caught him, lifting him up like a rolled rug.

The lord had been absent for some time. Around Helice in her delirium, the room spun. She no longer cared if the Eye opened, if only she could sleep.

Someone pulled her up. She had drifted off. The lord was back.

"If you hurt me," she whispered, "if you hurt me, I won't stop my sapient from hurting you back. And I'm sick. If you try to hurt me to get information, I might die. You shouldn't hurt me."

"Yes. We have understood you." Not ungently, he helped her hobble from the middle of the Dragon's Eye, up the sloping sides to a place where she could sit propped against the wall.

Woozy, but fighting for consciousness, she heard the cell door open. A Chalin attendant holding a tray came to the Tarig's side.

"No medications," she murmured. "If you give me medications, I'll make my sapient kill you."

"You are full of infections," the Tarig said.

"Need water."

The Tarig brought a cup to her lips. She drank, though it stung her lips. When she finished, she noted that the attendant had something large on the tray.

"One's name is Lord Nehoov," the Tarig said. "We will listen to you. First we will heal you. You should wish us to."

Fever made her confused, but she hung on to her decision. "No."

Lord Nehoov gestured at the servant to come nearer. "Here is a picture of health, what we can do. You are healthy here." He flicked a wrist at the attendant, who pulled a cover off the object.

It was a bell jar. Inside, a small person pressed hands and nose against the glass. A miniature human on a plate. The human was as tall as her hand. It moved inside, just a little, pushing against the glass, looking up at her.

It was Helice herself, under the bell jar. A very small Helice.

Helice began to cry. "I . . . can't . . . don't . . ." she began to wail. "Take it away. Go away from me!"

The Tarig cocked its head. "This small Hel Ese is free of infection. She can be disposed of. It is just a . . . how do you say it? A *demonstration*."

"Take it away. God damn you, get it out of here." She was shaking now, horrified to see the miniature of herself.

"Among us in this cell, darkling, we think God has damned *you*."

The attendant placed the jar on the floor and left.

Sitting on his heels, the lord looked down on her. "You do not wish healing? It can sustain the conversation that you wish to have."

The little figure walked over to the edge of the jar. It looked out of the glass toward the Dragon's Eye, a look of profound horror on its face. It fell to its knees, head against the glass.

Helice looked at the little golem of herself, sickened. "I do not wish . . . your healing. Only take me out of here."

"Stand then, if you can."

She managed. Helice waved at the bell jar with its awful prisoner. "Cover her," she rasped.

The lord did so.

Anzi tried to look through the shell of the sac, pressing her hands against its concave sides, peering at the noises. Since separating from Su Bei, her journey had been silent. These new sounds were very close, just outside the shell.

Something was trying to get in. She could see shadows outside. The sac walls were becoming transparent, no longer showing scenes from the third kingdom. She had finally arrived somewhere. Half-starved and weak, she felt ready to welcome whoever or whatever was out there.

The sac rocked, throwing her against a wall.

The assault on her conveyance finally succeeded, as a puncture wound opened at the top. A sharp object slowly drew down the wall, splitting it. The sharp object looked very much like a claw. Miserable God, let it not be a Tarig, she thought. There would be no fighting a Tarig. In her present condition, perhaps there'd be no fighting anyone.

The rupture of her little shell continued. Beginning again at the top of the sac, the creature slit open the other side.

Keeping well away from the moving claw, Anzi held her knife ready.

The walls on either side began slumping away. She glimpsed a dark thing waiting for her. "Oh, Frowning God," she murmured, "do not look at me, do not see me, do not note my small life. Oh counter of sins, look on this attacker, so worthy of Your notice, but do not notice me . . ."

However, it was too late to escape God's notice. He had already singled her out. "Then may You be damned," Anzi muttered. She rose to defend herself as the two halves of the shell fell heavily to each side.

She sprang to her feet, kicking away the remains of the wilted sac.

What waited for her was not a Tarig.

It was a being she had never seen before. A being of the third kingdom. Though not large, it looked fully able to slash her to pieces.

Anzi went to her knees.

CHAPTER TWENTY-EIGHT

C AITLIN LEFT KELL'S HOUSE, leaving the briefcase with the money behind. It had taken Kell an hour and a half to access and rip off Lamar's savant. It was 1:30, and Rob must be wondering what the hell was taking so long. Hang on, Rob, she thought. Give me some of your steadiness.

Rain pelted down as she locked the car doors. Pulling the printouts from their folder, she tried to focus on the names. She'd already scanned the sheets, seeing her own name, and Mateo's and Emily's. Now she'd look more closely. So who are your fellow mass murderers, Lamar?

A shadow moved over her windshield. Caitlin jumped, and the papers fell around her feet.

It was Kell, hovering by the passenger-side window. She jerked her head around to see if someone was with him.

He made a roll-down-the-window motion to her.

She hesitated. Why would he come outside? He looked beady-eyed and unhappy, especially the longer she hesitated to open the window.

Oblivious of the rain, Kell held up the briefcase and said, "I think you'll be needing this empty case."

He meant, don't forget to refill it. Rolling down the passenger window, she snapped, "Throw it on the seat."

With a smirk, he tossed the case in.

Up went the window. Caitlin nodded at him, trying to smile. He'd get his money. She started the engine and pulled away from the curb, heart still blipping from the moment's panic that the computer intrusion had been discovered.

Titus, she thought, am I doing the right thing? She heard his voice in her mind: Raise hell, Caitlin. Tell everyone you know. No, he wouldn't say that. He'd say, go underground, Caitlin. Don't let the bastards find you. . . . It settled her, a little, to imagine what her brother-in-law would say. And despite the end of the sweet green world, she still thought she'd give anything to just have him hold her. For comfort. For . . .

Jesus, she'd forgotten to send Rob the file. He needed it immediately; she couldn't be the only one who had it. She'd only driven two blocks. She pulled over. Hands shaking, she stranded the file to her dashCom. The load/send took three heartbeats.

The papers were still scattered on the floorboards. My God, she thought. I'm hardly operating on the few neurons they give me credit for. She gathered the papers, putting them in order.

Then she began reading the names. Oh, she knew some of these people: Booth Waller, Development Manager for Minerva; Peter DeFanti, Minerva board of directors. Here was Lamar's name, number three, she noted. The list contained no one else besides her own family that she knew. Something about that didn't click.

Then she pounced on it: The list named only one Minerva board member. And it wasn't the chairman, Stefan Polich. Could it be that Minerva was clean on this conspiracy?

Strange. She'd been so sure that the odious Stefan Polich was among the two thousand. The man who'd threatened her when he started to lose confidence in Titus Quinn, the man who'd threatened her family if Titus Quinn ever reneged on his promise to come back from the Entire—that person was *not* on the list.

He didn't even know, then. If he'd known, he'd want to get off the sinking ship, wouldn't he?

Caitlin stuffed the pages under the driver's seat and tried to drive normally out of Kell's neighborhood toward the highway.

Lamar waited for Booth Waller in his car near the pier, engine off, the air inside the custom ZWI 600 cooling rapidly to match an unseasonably cold September. A rain squall cruised through Portland, peppering the windshield. He tugged at his pigskin driving gloves, nervous. It was overdramatic to meet out of the way like this.

Booth didn't trust anyone anymore. It was getting on time to bring the new renaissance to the world. The engine was finished; they waited for Helice, now, for her signal that it was time to start the voyage. So near to their goal, Booth was getting antsy. Renaissance had put him in charge of logistics, and logistics was all that was left now. Well, not quite all—there was personnel: getting people to HTG, holding hands with those getting cold feet, running interference for them; and for those judged unreliable, making sure they were on a side rail. They had a good man, Alex Nourse, in charge of that. Lamar's end of it was compiling the list of two thousand. That part was finished. Two thousand exactly, with a few names in mind for fill-in. If, by this meeting, Booth was thinking of getting some of his friends in on this . . . well, he could forget it. The list was done.

A car approached down the frontage road. Lamar voiced: "lights on, and off." The ZWI shot a wad of light at the incoming vehicle as it approached. Lamar was sweating in the cold. He was too old for these shenanigans.

The car stopped close by and the passenger door opened. Booth.

Lamar voiced the locks off, and Booth slid in, shaking water off his good suit. "Fucking weather," he muttered by way of greeting.

Lamar shrugged. "Not for long."

Booth barked a laugh. It was all going—bad weather and everything with it. They used black humor to get through the end times; they all did.

Lamar's ZWI was a two-seater. Cozy, for whatever secret conversation Booth had planned. He hoped it wasn't going to be about Caitlin and her little spy trip. She'd gone to Hanford, she'd met the folks. It was against her instructions, but she wasn't going to blab even if she learned anything. Mateo and Emily were on the list. What mother would doom her own children? If she even learned about the engine.

"It's Caitlin," Booth said.

Lamar shifted irritably in his seat. Booth was fussy as an old woman. Why was he haranguing about Caitlin at a time like this?

Booth turned to him, "You've got lousy security on your home machine. I've got to say, I expected more from you."

"What, my optical?" It was a dumb machine, no controlling mSap. Now Booth wanted a fortress around it? "For Christ's sake, I use it for banking and e-mail."

"And for keeping the list, apparently."

Lamar stared at him.

Booth left a pause for emphasis. "You keep it there, right? The list?"

"Yes." Goddamn. Someone had unlocked his computer and accessed the list. "It's without context, Booth; it's just a list of names. It doesn't *mean* anything." He couldn't stop himself from sniping: "How do you know what's going on with my home machine, anyway?"

Booth shrugged. "We're monitoring *everyone*. No one's exempt."

"It was Caitlin, then?"

Stonily, Booth stared out at the patter of rain. "She's sent the list to her husband. Love to know how she got it, but it doesn't matter now. So she knows something. Probably everything. She must have gone to a lot of trouble to break your encryption—even as inadequate as it was."

Lamar was getting sick of this superior attitude. He didn't work for Booth. They were equals in the project. Renaissance had been Lamar's damn idea—all right, Helice's idea at first, but massaged by Lamar, with all the key players recruited by Lamar. No, Booth wasn't getting by with the condescending attitude.

"She won't talk, not Caitlin. She's got the kids to get across. She lives for those kids."

"The kids have disappeared, Lamar. So has the grandmother. That's the first place we went."

"Went!" They'd gone looking for her without consulting him? "Went, you son-of-bitch? Why wasn't I told?"

"Alex Nourse has personnel. He was gathering the facts."

Lamar felt sick. She'd sequestered the children. She was on the run. Holy mother of God. Caitlin, why didn't you come to me? Lamar put his head in one of his gloved hands. Caitlin. Now Alex Nourse would silence her. God, it was unthinkable.

She'd learned that it wasn't going to be a nice little advance guard of scientists going over. It was a lifeboat of survivors. And she hadn't liked that.

Without understanding the context, she'd freaked. She didn't understand the
principals, the logic of it . . . oh Christ, they were going to kill her.

"Don't," Lamar murmured. "Let her be. We're so close now. Let her be.
I'll talk to her, I'll force her to come along; let me handle it."

"That's what I'm here for. To let you handle it."

"No one would believe her. She's got no evidence. Even Hanford isn't
proof of anything. The engine is useless without a matching one next door.
They'll never shut us down. And if they did, they'd never do it in time. We're
just waiting for Helice. Any day now. Any *hour*."

Booth nodded. "That's why we can't afford a loose cannon." He reached
inside his coat lapels, patting for something, then went for a side pocket. For
a moment of sheer panic, Lamar thought he had a gun. But he brought out
a little box, longer than wide, about three inches high.

"We don't trust her anymore. We don't want her along."

"Who's this fucking *we* all of a sudden? When did I get shoved to the
side?"

"When? The day you altered her test scores, and her son's. That day."

"It didn't hurt anything. Titus will thank us . . ."

"Titus is irrelevant. You trying to buy his favor?" Booth shook his head
in disgust. "You've strayed a bit from first principals, Lamar. You're still on
board, we decided. But only if you get rid of her."

Booth was inspecting the outside of the little box. "You need to get rid
of her, and you need to do it now. Today." He handed him the little box.
"We've had her car rigged since the day you fucking altered her Standard
scores. She was always unreliable. She's a *middie*." He pointed at the recessed
button on the box. "We'll strand her coordinates to you here. Then you hook
into the highway mesh, find her, and press the little button. You have to be
within about two hundred feet. If it doesn't work the first time, get closer.
The closer you get, obviously more risk for you. But then, you're the one that
created this mess."

Lamar was shaking. Caitlin, oh Caitlin. Like a daughter to me. Titus, like
a son. Oh God.

"Why me," he whispered.

Booth opened the door of the sports car, then paused before getting out.

"We just don't want you blaming *us* for the next three hundred years. You're going to do it Lamar. If not, Alex will, but then you're not coming."

Booth slammed the door and transferred to his own car.

Lamar hardly noticed the car leaving. He started the car after a few minutes. The dashboard lit up with an incoming strand signal. Staring at this noxious light for a full five minutes, Lamar finally accepted the data. She was on I-5 heading south.

Hands shaking, he drove slowly away from the pier, from the river, from things recognizable.

CHAPTER TWENTY-NINE

More bitter than a sip of the Nigh, one's faithless friend.

—a saying

SYDNEY PRESSED THROUGH THE CROWD, her best Hirrin servant, Emar-Vad, by her side, and another attendant just behind. Hands reached for her, to touch her or to hail her. She told Emar-Vad not to prevent them. They were her charges now. She recognized one or two of them and smiled in recognition. With the insouciance of typical Rim City dwellers, they weren't overly impressed with titles. She belonged to them, and they pressed as close as they liked.

This high station of Mistress of the Sway wasn't all sham. A thread of loyalty had woven itself into her heart on that day of the Tarig massacre. Sentients of the Rim, she thought, this city is yours. And the Entire is yours. When my father gives it to me, I will hold it for you.

She looked up to the Ascendancy. It had been tightly closed for six days, with no one coming or going. Wild with uncertainty, she wondered what her father was facing. And what Helice had done. Helice had given herself up, and would have done so only if she was ready to act. If she held the fiends' access doors hostage, it would shock the Tarig to the soles of their clawed feet.

As her party moved down the ramp from the bridge to sea level, the crowd grew. She asked how they fared, received their petitions, and listened to tales of hardship—of relatives dead or recovering from the Tarig incursion. The citizens of Rim City weren't criticizing the lords—they didn't trust her that far—but a new and darker view of the Tarig lay behind every utterance.

Anuve wisely stayed behind; the crowd was in no mood to see a Tarig lady, and Sydney claimed the right to walk into her city in relative freedom.

Her destination: the wharf and Geng De. He had not come to her since the massacre in the city—too long an absence for one who wanted to be her advisor.

From the wharf she saw that the sea had fallen to an amethyst hue, reflecting the bright in Deep Ebb. As she boarded the navitar's vessel, her followers milled on the dock, waiting for her. The ship keeper met her at the main cabin door, leading her to the companionway.

But as the ship keeper began to ascend the stairs, Sydney placed a restraining hand on the Hirrin's back. "Alone." The ship keeper retreated as Sydney climbed the stairs.

Geng De sat at a small writing desk. Turning at her entrance, he spread his arms in welcome.

She went to him, exchanging the kiss that, for Geng De, sealed their bond. "My Sen Ni," he said. "You should be resting, like me—after your triumph in the city."

"But where have you been? It's been six days." Her tone was more blameful than she had planned.

His expression turned pained. "No. That is not how it will be between us. You will not chastise me for what I do. I have kept you alive. I have dissolved the bad strands." His youthful voice had an odd rasp. Perhaps he wasn't well.

He went on. "The binds showed me a future: you on the junked float in the street. I saw how the lord climbed up and drew a handful of claws across your neck. You slumped against him, and before any of us could climb to your side, you were dead. Then, all who came to your aid were slaughtered." He gazed at her until he judged she had absorbed that vision.

"Instead, Sen Ni, you turned the Tarig line away from massacre. You brought help to the injured. These sentients now love you." He gestured toward the pier where the crowd waited for her. "You did well. You did what I knew you were capable of. But *I* wove that future in your strands. *I* did that. I am still protecting you."

She hadn't thought clearly how the things that were happening might be separated into events that were bound to occur and those that were altered. It stunned her to think that the confrontation with the Tarig soldiers had been orchestrated by Geng De.

But there were immediate matters before them, serious ones. "What about Helice? We have to know what she's doing. Have you . . . seen . . . anything?"

Agitated, the navitar struggled to his feet. "No. Do you think me a magician? Performing for a carnival?"

This was a new tone of voice, and she didn't like it. "She needs watching, Geng De. I had hoped to find the doors. Now, maybe she's done it first."

It was then that she noticed a cane leaning against the bulkhead. He took it for support, shuffling to the nearest porthole.

"That's not who needs watching," he murmured, staring out.

"If you're tired, then rest," she said, trying to soften the tension in the room.

He turned to her, looking bemused. "I will. I will rest when I must and follow the binds as I can. Neither you nor I decide, but it comes to us. By all that's bright, sister!" He waved the cane at her. "No one has ever done it before—to take the day and make it conform. No one else is a child of the river. But even for such as me, it takes from me. *Takes* from me."

His lecturing tone grated, making her push harder. "What about my father? Surely you've seen *him* in the binds."

"Oh yes. Him I've seen." Standing with his back to the light of the portal, his shadowed face was impossible to read.

"Must I beg you to tell me?"

"That was the vision I wrestled with, the one that sapped the strength from my limbs. I *wrestled* with it." He leaned on the cane, as though just the memory of it made him weaker.

She waited, suddenly fearful.

"I see a thread that floats almost in my grasp, where he acknowledges you. A beloved daughter. The wronged child. And he lays the Entire at your feet."

The simple words undid her. Her face heated up, and she turned away. *Beloved daughter* . . .

"And then," Geng De went on, "I've also seen . . . other things." His gaze slid away.

Her father would die. The navitar was going to tell her that he would die in the Ascendancy. She stood frozen. A glint of the ebbing sky struck the porthole as the vessel rocked at anchor.

Geng De's voice was low and soft: "I've seen him cast you down."

"No, he would not . . ."

The navitar's voice rode over hers: "I've seen him king himself."

"That is not a true vision," she snapped.

He only gave a small, insufferable smile. "Now *you* are the navitar?"

"I . . . I am his daughter." It was feeble, embarrassing.

"Daughters can be sacrificed. As surely you recall?"

She spun around, throwing out the words with venom. "Have better visions, Geng De."

Now a silence came between them, cold and prolonged. What was she saying? Geng De didn't decide what to see. *Neither you nor I decide, but it comes to us.* What she'd first feared he'd say—that her father would die in the floating city—was now preferable to *I've seen him king himself.*

Her voice faltered. "King, you say?"

He limped closer to her, his face showing a trace of compassion. "It is a thread. Hope for a different one. But be prepared, Sen Ni, for the worst."

For years she'd been prepared for the worst from Titus Quinn. Why did it hurt so much now?

Geng De put a hand on her arm and said, his eyes pleading: "Learn to trust me, as I do you."

"Trust is a hard thing." When she thought of *trust*, it was only Riod who came to mind.

"Hard things are just beginning." He sagged against his cane and made his way to the closest chair, where he eased himself down.

Ashamed to take so little note of his condition, she brought him a cup of water from a pitcher on a nearby table.

Holding the glass without drinking, he looked up at her. "When will you call me brother?"

She tried to control her voice, but it was husky in her throat. "Don't ask me today." She went to the stairs and turned back. Geng De was her advisor now; without him, who did she have?

"Come to me soon."

"Yes."

Cixi went to her secret meeting in full view of the world. She might have taken a secret passage; there were passageways everywhere. They riddled the floating city, ancient, between-the-walls routes, some so old even Cixi could not remember which high prefect had had them forged. But some things were more reliable in full daylight.

She was accompanied by a procession of legates and consuls snaking through the great plaza and over the bridges. Her formally clad entourage made its way toward the hill of mansions to pay an imperial visit to the dark-ling in his cell. Parasols up, the attendants shielded the high prefect from even the ebb's bruised light, and carried scrolls so that work could be done in progress. The outing took a very long time, a grand sight, even in Deep Ebb.

Civil servants and visiting petitioners who, at the first sign of trouble, had run in confusion to their chambers below crept back when the dragon court's delegation was sighted. They craned necks to make out the smallest personage, the one who wore the dragon icon on her jacket. Cixi hobbled onward, looking regal, she presumed, whereas her pace was dictated solely by the God-blasted platform shoes.

She was attended by the clerk Shuyong, should she wish to compose mes-sages or have a minion on hand for errands. None of the legates with her this ebb knew the clerk; he was new and coached by Cixi how to act.

Subprefect Mei Ing bent close, murmuring, "The lords are everywhere, Your Brilliance. Will they let us pass?"

Without deigning to look at Mei Ing, Cixi muttered, "I'll see the gondling."

Mei Ing fell silent then. By the expression on Cixi's face, no words were welcome; Mei Ing could not imagine that even the Tarig would question her mistress in such a mood.

Cixi noted Mei Ing's cowering aspect with satisfaction. They must all understand that she went to the darkling to bid him fry in the bright. Even the lords could understand that High Prefect Cixi would demand to see the man who had made a fool of her. On his infamous return to the Bright City the time before, Titus Quinn had pretended to be someone else. The traitor had gone so far as to brazenly seek an audience with Cixi. And she had let him pass. Even the lowliest clerk knew Cixi's fury over this humiliation. And they were not wrong.

A bird flitted close over their heads. Cixi didn't allow herself to look up. Of course the fiends would have their spies about. In the last few days the loathsome flying vermin had even swooped down into the Magisterium, taking in views of the balconies and windows there. No, she would not take note of them. Most people thought they were favored creatures of the Tarig, and they *were* favored, the vile little spies. Well let them peek. All they could see was the prefect and her entourage.

The procession of the dragon's court reached the palatine hill. Through the steep and narrow avenues, the functionaries passed throngs of Tarig who waited and watched in their silent manner. Cixi looked to neither the right nor the left, affecting single-minded purpose, despite her deep disquiet.

She was a woman in desperate need of news. For the first time in a reign of one hundred thousand days, she was bereft of information. The lords had not summoned Cixi, had not sent word, had not *informed* her of any details regarding the astonishing events of the last days: The damage to Lord Ghinamid's Tower; what would be done with Titus Quinn; what they had learned from Hel Ese, and why they had taken her from her prison cell in the Eye.

Her spies had learned that Titus Quinn had been tortured in the street. But he still lived, they said. That might prove useful. She needed him for information and guessed that he had some pieces she lacked. Oh, how it galled.

A Tarig lord blocked her path.

Cixi bowed. "Lord Echnon, my life in your service, I will see the darkling."

"High Prefect," the lord acknowledged. "Which darkling?"

"The creature who wormed his way into my court. The gondling who came in disguise and caused the death of our beloved Lord Hadenth. The darkling who stood before my throne and lied." She bowed again, not so low this time. "That one."

"Ah."

"May I pass?"

Standing aside, he waved her forward.

"He is caged where, Bright Lord?" She said this pleasantly enough, but she had lost face by having to ask what she should have been already told.

The lord pointed to the mansion of Lady Demat, and the line of legates got under way once more.

Quinn's jailors brought him water and small, tough bricks of food. They might be poison, but he ate them. He slept what seemed like long hours, perhaps induced by the food. A Tarig came in once to clean his wounds, but Quinn was in a stupor; all he knew was that it was not Lord Oventroe.

The lord had abandoned him.

He sat on his pallet and leaned forward with his bad arm braced on his thigh. If Oventroe was washing his hands of him, then the whole strategy of coming here had failed. The lord might have reasons for delay, but Quinn could no longer rely on rescue from that quarter.

There remained another angle. Ugly beyond bearing, the idea had been wheedling into his consciousness over the last hours. It was time to use every scrap of leverage he had.

He managed to rise. Staggering over to the bars of light that separated his cell from a small antechamber, he shouted for his guards.

A Hirrin appeared in the outer door. He was impassive and cold-eyed, like all his Hirrin guards.

"Tell Lady Demat I have to see her. I've got something important to tell her."

The Hirrin blinked. "Next time I see her I might mention that."

And she might slit your long, ugly throat, too, he thought. "Tell her, if you value your career in the Magisterium."

The door slammed.

He had not handled that well. Next time he would try a more diplomatic approach.

But at his next opportunity, it was the same Hirrin guard, and he responded no better to flattery than he had to threats.

Quinn tottered back to his bunk. Once the whole Entire had been on the lookout for him, combing the cities and midlands for any sign of the man of the Rose. Now that they had him, no one was impressed, not even his guards. He slept, cradling his bad arm, hoping to be wakened by Oventroe's voice, fearing to hear Demat's, instead.

Cixi saw the darkling asleep on a pallet by the wall. She half expected him to stink of blood, but the fabbers had cleaned him up, no doubt. Even prisoners did not escape Tarig fastidiousness.

She nodded for Shuyong to hold well back. The clerk was the only other visitor allowed in. He carried a box of pens and scrolls, standing ready to record anything of note that Cixi said. That, however, had been for show. He would hear nothing.

She leaned toward the bars of light that stretched from ceiling to floor. "So, bastard son of Yulin." He sat up. Swaying slightly, he struggled to his feet, squinting toward her.

She growled, "So you come among us again."

"Cixi . . . High Prefect." He bowed.

His address was presumptuous, but she ignored the lapse. He had done worse. "If you touch the bars, your hands will burn, bastard son of Yulin. Do be careful."

A crooked smile. "Thank you, Your Brilliance, I will."

His wounds were healed, those that she had heard about. But when he approached, she saw that his right arm hung stiffly.

She noted that his face had changed once again. Would the man never cease transformations? It was so much easier, over time, to hate the same face. "Before they kill you, I would know Yulin's part in your lies at court." She needed no confirmation of Yulin's treachery, but listeners might expect her to ask.

A long pause. "Yulin knew."

"And his supposed niece, Ji Anzi."

He smiled again. "I assume her greater sin is having married me."

"True." She gestured for him to come closer. When he did, she spit in his face.

Slowly, he wiped his face on the sleeve of his good arm, his expression turned as cold as any she'd seen from a Tarig.

Having performed the necessary drama, she brought her hand to her belt and activated a small jewel. The prisoner followed her movements with extreme focus.

"For a few moments we have privacy, darkling." She hoped that was true. Such engines of science as she had were small and carefully hoarded. The Tarig bestowed little knowledge, but they couldn't keep it all. "I would know why you've come; why Hel Ese is here. Tell me the truth and I will give you a small reward. Tell me lies, and I leave you to the lords."

Hesitating only a moment, he said, "I followed Helice here to stop her." Then, with growing openness, he told more; and why not? He was in desperate circumstances. Confidences might appeal.

"She's come to offer the lords a quick burning of the Rose. In exchange, she wants them to allow her to live here. Her and a group of her human friends."

She saw him teeter. He was weak, and his right arm looked immobile. Had they taken the arm off during his march through the streets? Cixi thought it had not come to dismemberment. In any case, the arm was attached now. "The lords would never allow it."

"She's found their access to the Heart. The way they go home." He snaked a look at her as though checking to see if she understood what he meant. "She wants to control it. Maybe she already does."

By the bright, the door was at the Tower of Ghinamid! "Did you know, Titus Quinn, that the Tower of Ghinamid suffered a small fire? Hel Ese's doing, then?"

He nodded.

The Tower of Ghinamid stood the highest of any of the pinnacles in the Ascendancy. Of course no one saw Tarig moving to and from it . . . it would all be hidden in passageways. Despite this portentous revelation, she must focus on her questions. One was terribly dangerous to utter. "How does Sen Ni fare?"

"My daughter?" Frowning at this unexpected question, the man of the Rose said, "She's Mistress of Rim Sway. You knew?"

"Of course I knew! Tell me what else."

"She has done well; she faced down the Tarig in the streets."

Cixi snorted in disgust. He would not divulge secrets unless she did so first. Very low, her lips barely moving, Cixi whispered, "She is my daughter. My daughter of the heart. I have . . . comforted her." She let that ultimate secret settle on him.

By the look on his face, he doubted her.

Cixi hissed, "Why would I give you proof of my treason? I do not lie. She is my dear girl. We have been united against you. Take no offence. You brought it on yourself."

"If you were her friend, why did you let them put her in slavery?"

"Why did *I*?" She decided to let that despicable comment pass. "No one could have stopped them. There was an advantage for her to exploit with the Inyx. I sent a warrior to protect her."

He seemed stunned. "Mo Ti?"

"Where is Mo Ti, darkling?"

"In hiding." He came very close to the bars, speaking rapidly. "Mo Ti was helping Sydney to raise the kingdom. And you, Cixi, I think you were helping them. If you are, I'm on your side. I'll give her the kingdom; I've already told her I will. But first, I have to eliminate Hel Ese."

"She's with the lords; too late, I expect."

"Help me, Cixi. Helice has a controlling device brought over from the Rose. She's using it to threaten the doors to the place where the lords go to renew themselves. I need to take control of those doors. You should help me, because if I control the lords, I'll give them to Sydney. If Helice does, it will be for herself alone."

She stepped back, fending off the idea that she would ever align herself with this man.

"Cixi, listen! I've promised the Entire to Sydney. I don't want it."

She snorted at this claim.

"I don't want it, I've never wanted it. It's all to protect the Rose."

Cixi sucked her teeth, considering. But, no, it could not be done. "I cannot help you, darkling. Hel Ese is welcome here. The Rose must die for us to live. I am not opposed. She is already released from confinement, conferring with the lords."

That brought a grim look. "She won't let Sydney raise a kingdom of sways. She won't share power. She'll betray Sydney to the lords."

Well, perhaps she would. But Cixi didn't trust either of them. "Leave that, darkling. Our time is done. I cannot save you or your Rose Earth, nor could I bear to see you rise high." Cixi put her hand over her belt, waving her clerk forward. "I have not the power to save you. We are done."

He blurted out, "Send Lord Oventroe to me, Cixi. I beg you for a last favor."

Ah, so they *were* in alliance. Or had been. "He is suddenly out of the city." The man's chagrin was easy to read. "But I will give you a small favor; a visit from a friend."

Shuyong approached. Cixi went on, "If this man is your spy, you may work your strategies through him. He will have a few minutes with you alone. I have instructed him to write down—for promulgating to the Magisterium—your abject apology for your degradation of the court when last you came among us. Use your time wisely."

She backed away from the cell. "Goodbye, Titus Quinn. I have hated you too long to change now. Do not expect I have esteem for you."

"I would never presume on your esteem, High Prefect." As she reached for the door she heard him say: "Please! One thing more. A favor, High Prefect, easy for you to grant. The life of a steward named Cho. They say he is interred."

The steward Cho had long outlived his usefulness. "Dead, I regret to say." Quinn nodded slowly.

The clerk, whose real status was mort, and whose real name was Li Yun Tai, came up to the bars of Quinn's cell.

Cixi bowed, just the slightest tip of her chin. Titus Quinn was a worthy adversary. Unlucky, perhaps, but worthy.

For the second time in his life, Tai looked on the man of the Rose. Tai's artless question in the Magisterium had drawn attention, and before he had quite understood his mistakes, he'd found himself answering to the High Prefect herself. Although he admitted nothing, she had deduced that he was an operative of Titus Quinn. To his surprise, she said she might help him.

Standing before Titus Quinn now, Tai was exceedingly nervous. This was politics well beyond him, and beyond his instructions from Hel Ese.

"I am Tai, a servant of Hel Ese."

Titus Quinn's eyes grew wary.

"Hel Ese is here, too, of course! It is all arranged, Master."

"Call me Quinn."

Tai wasn't sure he could manage that, but he nodded, pretending to write on the scroll, in case anyone was observing. As he did so, he said, "It is all arranged. Hel Ese is working on your mission. A great enterprise of the Rose, she said. She's been sick, and I cared for her. I can't talk to her because she's with the lords, but she'd want me to help you. If I can, I will."

"Do you know how to get me out of here?"

"No. The high prefect gave me nothing. Only permission to see you."

Titus Quinn came closer, fixing Tai with a riveting gaze. "Helice has lied to you. She and I aren't together. But I'll tell you the truth, if you want it."

Dumbly, Tai nodded. Hel Ese had lied?

His Excellency—Quinn—went on then, telling him a profoundly different story than the one Hel Ese had related. As the awful words slid out of the man's mouth, Tai grew sick with shock. Could he have been so wrong about the woman of the Rose? Was he to believe Hel Ese or Titus Quinn? But could there really be a doubt? In his heart, Tai admitted he didn't like Hel Ese, that she had always treated him with contempt. He had been duped.

Quinn's mouth quirked in sympathy. "She's fooled the best of us. You couldn't have known." He continued, telling—oh, telling such terrible things—how Hel Ese wanted safe passage to the Entire for a few, and then the Rose would be gone.

Gone. Tai's throat felt glued shut. Gone. Was it possible that the Rose could die? That he had been helping it die? He broke into a sweat beneath his heavy clerk's robe. It was monstrous. She'd used him. Promised him a terrible promise: to go to the Rose. Which would be dead.

A steward appeared at the door to the anteroom of Quinn's cell. The Chalin steward fixed Tai with an authoritative gaze. "You are to leave now, Shuyong."

When he received Tai's nod, he departed.

Desperately, Tai leaned toward the activated bars. "How can I help you, Master Quinn? I will do anything, even if I die for it."

"Give me a parchment, Tai. And something to write with."

Though Tai worried they were being watched, he obeyed. He fumbled among his box of supplies and retrieved a small paper and an inked pen, passing them through the bars.

"What will you do, Master?"

Quinn tucked them in his jacket.

"Tai. Take a message for me to Zhiya the godwoman. Ask for her in Rim City, and her people will eventually find you. Tell her that I'm going to try to go home. That I found no . . . help . . . in the Ascendancy, and that I'm going home to stop Helice's plans. Would you do that for me? I want someone to know what became of me. I want my wife to know."

"Yes, Master Quinn, anything. I'll find her."

The man of the Rose glanced toward the door. "Do you know the names of the Tarig who are currently among the ruling Five?"

Tai shook his head. He had never paid attention.

"Are they all assembled here? Do you know if they're all in the Ascendancy?"

"I . . . don't know, Master. I'm sorry." Tai was now experiencing a growing horror as his past actions began to sink in. "There must be something more I can do!"

Titus Quinn murmured, "If you believe in God, pray for me."

Reluctantly, Tai left the room. He wondered if Titus Quinn was a religious man, or if he was just that desperate.

As he hurried to join Cixi's entourage still winding its way through the great plaza, he stifled little moans of dismay and terror. He considered his foolish, rash actions. Hel Ese had used him without pity, if the man of the Rose was to be believed.

And oh, Tai believed him.

CHAPTER THIRTY

It is impossible to snare a dragon cub if you do not enter the lair of the dragon.

—from *The Twelve Wisdoms*

HELICE LAY ON A BED SURROUNDED BY A DOZEN OR MORE TARIG. Out of the Dragon's Eye at last, she had come to what Lord Nehoov said was his habitation. In the oversized room, the small bed felt adrift on a sea of pain. The walls exuded a harsh light. For the sake of her raging headache, Helice had asked them to dim the room, but they had not.

Here in the fortress of the Tarig, the scene she had imagined so many times was unfolding, but in a nightmare way. She was bargaining with them from a bed, because she could no longer rise. She was dying.

Undoubtedly she could save herself if she chose. But if she submitted to their ministrations, she might lose her will, her power, and her goal.

On a table nearby she spied the thing that the Tarig had made, the creature she thought of as a golem. It was still captive under the glass bell jar.

Lord Nehoov was there, and others just as magnificent. Lean, sculpted, and clad in silver, they possessed the beauty of powerful animals. Or perhaps it was just the beauty of power. They had come to hear her, and had been listening for the past hour. Only Nehoov asked questions. They had been probing about the attack launched against Ahnenhoon, no doubt fearing that others might come.

"How do you know there are not molecular attacks under way? You do not control the Rose."

They were speaking to her in English. She kept forgetting it wasn't their native language. She was forgetting things, struggling to remain competent. "You're right, I don't know. The sooner we act, the sooner that can be prevented."

"When you die, who speaks for your contingent?"

They spoke so matter-of-factly about her death. "One named Lamar speaks for us. Another named Booth."

The bell jar drew her gaze. Was the golem really her? Did it contain all her knowledge, all her true self? How would the Tarig be able to judge whether it did or not, even if they were sincere? Could they create a normal-size reproduction of her? And then, too—and this was the worst conjecture—what if the small Helice had gone mad during the transformation?

The one thing the Tarig hadn't reckoned on was how facial expressions could convey a state of mind. The golem was terrorized. Its eyes were glazed and feral.

But it was true she looked healthy. No scabs. Good skin color. Helice wished they had put clothes on her double. It was a small thing, but Helice didn't like seeing her naked form on display. It was so tempting to close her eyes and trust that she was captured in that miniature form. But she didn't believe it.

She breathed deeply, fending off a wave of pain. "Can you bring my people over? You should do so quickly. It'll go badly for you if I die before I signal my computer to cease its countdown. Do you understand?"

"One understands. But Titus Quinn still claims to have his weaponry. We must hesitate if he has such a power."

The damn cirque. Didn't they realize how lucky they were that Quinn was such a weakling he hadn't dared to use it? She had already told them to kill him. But clearly they had some residual fear that the cirque still existed.

Summoning her strength to continue, she whispered, "The longer you wait, the more likely it is that more people will come with molecular weapons, nuclear weapons. You have a fragile world. You should get rid of enemy states. I can help you. Our engine is ready now. It'll take you years to do what we can effect in a few hours, joining with you. Do it, Lord Nehoov. Bring my people through."

She frowned. "You *can* bring them over? People say you destroyed the crossover points in the Arm of Heaven. Can you find another place?"

"It is no barrier to us."

"Where will they find entry if not at the Arm of Heaven minorals?"

Nehoov paused. "If they begin an insertion, we will find them. We will bring them to our city. Directly here."

One of the Tarig, a female, hissed. She looked around at several of the lords. So they were not in agreement. Helice dearly hoped that Nehoov didn't need a vote.

"Then do it now. The engine will prevent further attacks from the Rose. That's why I came here. To protect you. Remember that. Bring them over, Lord Nehoov. Do it now."

The female Tarig whispered to Nehoov, and they bent toward each other, in discussion. When they separated again, the female, by her expression, had lost. The other Tarig murmured angrily.

The female stalked from the room, and several Tarig followed her. It reminded Helice that there were factions.

Nehoov turned back to Helice. "You have an engine. It can be useful. For this reason, we will grant favors."

Helice remembered a crucial question. "When you bring them, you need to fix the time differential. I have to see them here now. Not in ten years. Not in ten thousand days."

"It can be done."

Incredibly, the decision had been made. Nehoov had said yes. *It can be done.* The four best words of her life. She forced herself to stay on track: "We'll live anywhere. Give us a small sway. We'll be your Rose subjects. You might even find us interesting." Tears collected on her eyelashes. She wouldn't be a part of it. It would be the new world, and she wouldn't be there.

"We will bring them," Nehoov said

In her exhaustion, tears coursed down her face, stinging her scabs. "Send them a message, Lord Nehoov. Can you send a message so they can begin? Is there a way?"

"Yes. The engine is easy to find."

She nodded. "The message is: 'From the dark to the bright.' They are waiting for that."

Gradually, the remaining lords dispersed, leaving her alone with Lord Nehoov. Her people might have enemies when they came through, but they would be here. And their protector, the mSap, would be nearby.

"A favor, Bright Lord." Thinking of enemies, she couldn't forget Anuve. "I don't want Lady Anuve around to cause trouble. Send her back for . . ." she was going to say recycling, but caught herself ". . . back to the Heart. She wouldn't mind, would she? To be frank, she hates me."

Nehoov said, "She has already gone. In disgrace that you escaped her. If she returns, perhaps she will not care about you."

Helice was starting to long for that nice little renewal system they had. And she did wonder what pure mentation would be like. Alas, it was not for her. The present circumstances were as strange as she could bear.

She nodded at the bell jar. Fixing Nehoov with her coldest gaze, she said, "Take it away and kill it."

"But she can be useful."

That put chills into her. "No. Destroy it."

"You will change your mind."

Helice lurched out of bed. "No! I won't . . . change my mind. It makes me crazy." She stood there, swaying and desperate, all the horror and stress rushing into her limbs, trying to get out.

Nehoov watched her with a maddening calm.

She rushed to the bell jar. Lifting it from its table, she used all her strength to raise it over her head and hurl it onto the stone floor. The glass shattered, splintering, screaming. The base rolled into the room's far corner. Amid the glass fragments, a still, bloody form.

Helice tottered back to the edge of the bed. "Never . . . do such a thing . . . to a human again, ah?" Those words took her last strength; she sank back onto the bed.

Nehoov looked down on her. "Are all the others like you?"

No, they weren't. She was unique. They could have never done the things she had. They could never have killed their own golem, for instance.

As Quinn had paced in his cell during the last few hours, he'd struggled to come to terms with Lord Oventroe's absence. If Oventroe was going to intervene, he would have done so by now. So the lord was not going to help him.

The lord might still have some plan, but his silence was ominous. Oventroe had once risked everything to save the Rose, saying that his cousins' intention to burn it was rash, wasteful.

Not the words Quinn would have used; nevertheless, the lord was his ally. Or had been.

All that remained was to return home to try to stop Helice's conspiracy. He'd start with Stefan Polich, given Helice's link to that company; or he'd start with Lamar, who, in retrospect, might be the most afraid of dying. *Remember that I'm an old man,* he'd once told Quinn. Remember it when, Lamar? Today, when you planned to come across to the Entire?

There were obstacles. Su Bei hadn't come to him; the ship keeper might never have given him the message. Even if Bei were here, how could the old man help him? They had no minoral, no scholar's veil for a transit point. Even if he found a way through, where was the engine? What if Lamar and Stefan had already gone to ground? But he'd go home if he had a way; he'd expose Helice as quickly as he could.

The penalty was that he might not be able to come back—for many reasons. He was dependent on Minerva for the crossing, and if he did return, time in the Entire could have left him behind; Anzi could be aged, or dead. Crossing over established a time relation between the traveler and the world, and unfortunately, the insertion point was random. Each time he left or came back, time twisted. It was the best argument for never doing it.

Nevertheless he was preparing for it, determined. It was all written down, all he knew about renaissance. He'd scrawled it with his left hand, since his right hand lacked fine motor movement. If he managed to make it home—then even if he died in the transit, it was possible the information could still be found.

A jolt of pain coursed through his shoulder and arm. In these four days some of his cuts had begun to heal, but the gash to his arm was still raw. He counted himself lucky that they hadn't killed him that day in the streets, though he still didn't know why they hadn't.

A noise at the outer door to the cell unit. Someone entered the short hall giving access to his cage.

Demat. In poker, you seldom get the card you pray for.

She came to the light bars, and he did, gazing at her. "We will leave you lame," she said. "It makes you pliable."

"I'm at your disposal anyway."

Her face was broader than Chiron's. Demat had prominent cheekbones and wore her hair shaved very short. Her vest was plain linked silver, her long skirt jet black. Altogether, she was not as imposing as Chiron. Disappointing. He was counting on them being the same, on their seeming the same.

"I have the cirque. I'm growing impatient. I'll use it if I have to."

She cocked her head as though confused. "The pilots saw you throw it into the Nigh. So you do not have the cirque."

"The navitars see what they want to see."

"So you might think, Titus-een. But they all saw it, all the navitars."

Titus-een, she'd called him. Chiron's term, once again. Chiron might truly hate him, but hate was no barrier to an interesting relationship. "If you believed that," he said, "you'd ask the navitars how to solve all your problems. They're mad."

"In a few hours, the Rose as you know it will be gone. We think it is pertinent to tell you."

So, the lords had gone over to Helice. Bitterness flooded him, nearly spilling out. He held it in. *Woo her*, if you remember how.

"Then I'll have to use the cirque in revenge."

So he didn't remember how to deal with women. Threats were not a good start.

"No, Titus-een, you will not." She seemed very sure. Her voice, like melted pearls. He remembered how self-assured the Tarig could be.

"You could have killed us at Ahnenhoon. You will never do it. The Entire claims you now, admit it. But even this will not save you."

"My wife—"

She interrupted him. "You have no way to tell her what to do. And if you did, she would not destroy her home." After a pause she added, "My cousins give no credence to your threat."

He saw how it was. How pathetic his threats were. What remained was this last measure. Pausing, he wished for something to happen that would stop him from speaking. The silence between them lengthened. Drawing closer to the light bars, so close his face almost touched them, he whispered, "Save the Rose, my Chiron, and I'll stay with you. I'll stay forever and it'll be as it once was between us."

"You have a wife."

"I've had wives. They come and go. There's only one Tarig queen, Chiron. Why should we have less than each other?" He had her attention. "Spare the Rose, and I will love you."

Her gaze didn't leave his face. "And give us the cirque, ah?"

"No. But it won't matter between us."

"Say again, Titus-een, why we would do this."

"Because the Rose is of interest to you. Because you don't love the Entire enough to commit genocide. Because you love me."

Slowly, Demat raised her fingers to the light bars, banishing them. She touched his face, pressing his skin as though testing him in some way, or commanding him. At length she said, very softly, "So the Entire will fade, Titus-een. Without burning the Rose, we would have so little time."

"It all vanishes. It's why life is so sweet, Chiron. Sustain the Entire as long as you can, and then let it go. At the end, go back to the Heart."

"And you will come?"

He considered this only for a heartbeat. "No. But you'll tire of me by then."

"Perhaps we have tired of you already." Dropping her hand from his face she backed away. The bars flashed into place.

She left him alone. He tried not to think about what he had just set in motion. But the vision came, of a life with Chiron/Demat. From what he knew of the Tarig now, how could he even treat them as real beings? The definition of life was malleable, he had learned in the Entire. But when he thought how they sometimes went blank and insensible, he thought they were only semi-alive. They turned off in some way when they were bored. To stay involved with the world they needed the stimulation of other sentients. For that task, other Tarig would not do. Other sentients were their favorite sparring partners. Quinn wished that, in his past life with Chiron, he had not been quite so interesting.

Pranam the Ysli steward performed his circumambulation of the bier every day. It was considered odd, but Pranam took great comfort from the ritual and cared little for others' opinions. He walked up from the sunken garden of the Magisterium, as he had so many ebbs before, pausing at the pool of the carp, then made his way to the great hall of the Sleeping Lord.

Pranam had been in service to the Magisterium for seven thousand days. He found happiness in small accomplishments and in devotion to the lords. His piety waxed all the stronger these last few days as he'd watched with dismay the lords' very home suffering indignities. No doubt it was all due to the traitor Titus Quinn. Pranam remembered the darkling when he had lived among them. He had been seen everywhere on the plaza, sometimes feeding carp, or staring at the bright, and other times in the company of the great lady, Chiron, or some other high figure. Now the miscreant was back again, said to have defaced the tower, among many previous crimes. Pranam and many of his friends expected a public execution. Though the Ysli had never witnessed a garroting, and did not look forward to it, he would be there when justice was finally done.

Entering the hall of the Sleeping Lord, Pranam climbed the back stairs to the gallery surrounding the hall on the second floor. In the center of the spacious room below was the bier itself, the only furnishing of the great mausoleum. Properly speaking, it was not a bier. It was the very bed of Lord Ghinamid, the lord who missed his home in the Heart so dearly, but stayed in the Entire for love of the land over which he reigned with such graciousness. Even if he was asleep. It was a fabulous mystery, and a comfort to those who toiled in the Magisterium and seldom left the Great Within even to visit loved ones.

Lord Ghinamid had lain there for two million days. The mystery and miracle was that the lord still breathed.

Pranam walked beside the railing, the only sentient in the hall that ebb. It was often thus, and his excursion was more peaceful for the solitude.

Continuing his circumambulation, Pranam glanced down on the hall below. And stopped. Moving closer to the rail, he peered down.

Pranam's peace vanished. How could this be?

He heard a cry issue from his lips. Then he rushed back to the stairs, pounding down them and hurrying to the center of the galleried hall.

His heart kicked heavily in his chest as he looked at the bier. The stony coverlet that had draped over the lord's lower body lay crumpled on the end of the bier. The lord's pillow lay askew.

Lord Ghinamid was, unthinkably, gone.

CHAPTER THIRTY-ONE

C AITLIN SPED TOWARD HER MEETING WITH STEFAN POLICH, passing the
meshed cars in the other lanes. The list of two thousand in her hand, she
finally had evidence, weak as it might be, to show him. He'd agreed to meet
her. It was only two o'clock, and he couldn't meet her until five, the bastard,
but better to wait for him downtown than risk being late, especially in this
rain.

The list was no proof, but in Caitlin's mind, it was the last, damning
clue. The evidence that had begun with Jess's words: *It's our chance to get it
right this time. Without the dreds pulling us down, diluting the good stock. I hate
what's coming. We all hate it. It's our home. Gone, just like that.*

On her way to meeting Stefan, she ran over in her mind the way she'd
approach the bizarre topic of what Lamar was up to at Hanford. For starters,
she'd show him the list. Maybe he wouldn't believe her. That's why Rob would
take a copy to Minerva's competitors: EoSap and TidalSphere. But it was Stefan
Polich on whom her hopes rested. There were Minerva names on that list. Plus,
he and Caitlin knew each other. She was the sister of the man he depended upon
for benefits from the Entire. Stefan would have to listen to her.

Oh Titus, she thought. Come home, my dear. Now, more than ever, you
must come home.

As she drove, her thoughts for some reason went to Johanna. The
woman's ghost seemed to touch her for a moment. Oh, Johanna, to have died
so young. And Titus loved you so. What was that like, to have had such a
man? In the end, was the marriage like most—comfortable and plain?

No, Caitlin decided. It was good, it was very good.

She thought that Johanna was very near to her, and why that should be, was both strange and comforting.

I envied you, Johanna, but it didn't stop me from liking you. I hoped you were alive, but I feared it wasn't so. You know that, don't you?

Yes.

I can't help but love him.

Yes. It's what we can't have that we always want.

Lamar drove through the light rain, feeling half dead, unsure that after today, he could stand himself. It didn't help to think that she was going to die anyway. He wouldn't think about it. It had to be done; if he didn't do it, Alex Nourse would step in.

Coming up the on-ramp, he put his hand on the small box next to him on the seat. Don't think about it. Oh, Caitlin.

At least they hadn't asked him to kill the children. They were sequestered somewhere. Until the end came. Oh, Caitlin, like a daughter to me.

He found the blip on I-5. To his dismay, he found that by kicking up his speed to 75, he was gaining on her. What was he doing? Lamar, you evil son-of-a-bitch. What was he involved with, anyway, that he should be sent onto this freeway to . . .

Don't think about it. It's all dying, it'll make no difference. But somehow, it did matter, and it was breaking his heart. He urged her to pull off, abandon the car, take a cab. Run, Caitlin.

The mapping on his dashCom showed the blip, the target, practically next to him. She must be close enough to see. He felt relief that he didn't.

But then, in the next lane, he did see the blue Mercedes.

God in heaven. He slacked off, letting some distance come between them, so that when the explosion happened, he would be well clear. No, that didn't make sense. He'd be driving into mayhem. He needed to pass her.

Speeding up, he sped past her car, gripping the wheel like death, driving with one hand, putting his free hand on the box, looking in the rearview mirror. Just enough room.

He pushed the button. And sped away, hearing the explosion like a brief, ugly cough, like the preview of the detonation to come. Smoke billowed behind; cars skidded, rammed into each other.

Pieces of her car floated on fire and smoke, spiraling away, adding brilliance to the rain-soaked day.

PART V

THE
SLEEPING
LORD

CHAPTER THIRTY-TWO

NED ISLINGTON WAS USED TO BIG NUMBERS. As an astronomer, he dealt with them all the time, thinking nothing of distances measured in the megaparsecs, for example. Conversely, specializing in black holes, he dealt with very small numbers, such as those needed to describe the amplitude of black hole–generated gravitational waves originating far away. Such detections were the specialty of the Super Massive Gravitational Telescope, the SMGT, near Sudbury, Canada.

Therefore, on this Saturday morning at the beginning of his shift at SMGT, he was staggered by the size and frequency of the incoming wave. The amplitude was too big, the frequency too high, to be ascribed to any astrophysical phenomenon. The detectors were designed to pick up extraordinarily small effects, since the amplitude of a wave fell off as the inverse of the distance from the source. This reading almost kicked the detectors off their hinges.

Add to that, the source of the wave was no longer producing it. The wave was gone. Preserved in the passing, but whatever was out there had ceased to radiate. Even while it was coming in, it registered no sidereal motion whatsoever, suggesting that whatever its source, it was fixed in relation to the motion of the stars.

They'd never seen an anomaly like this one before at SMGT, ensconced as it was in the midst of the Canadian Shield, one of the least geologically active landforms on Earth, one of the least likely places to perturb the quantum interference devices.

With calls in to the senior staff, Ned took a closer look at the readings and waited for the quantum gravity folks, the ones whose research grants paid the lion's share of SMGT, to descend.

In most respects the reading had the properties of a gravitational wave. It did not, for example, register in the electromagnetic spectrum. Quite a lot was known about gravitational waves, and thus it was easy to spot a bogey like this. It had been a major breakthrough in physics when gravitational waves had been directly measured for the first time in the mid-twenty-first century. Since that time, gravitational astronomy had become a major field. So unless it was a malfunction of some kind, it was a bogey, and he was quite interested to know what could have caused it.

His fingers were sweating on the keyboard as he ran a few analyses of the problematic data. Could the source be close by? Nobel Prize kept tickling the back of Ned's mind.

But that prize was likely going to the lucky devils studying the star extinctions. Incredibly, Sirius was the latest disappearance. It had vanished without a whimper—no outburst of stellar material, no fluorescing gases—and its extinction had been confirmed on observatories throughout inhabited space. The astronomical community had been calling them *occlusions*. But the public and the newsTides were calling the phenomenon *lights out*.

Sometime later, when Ned was rather far back in the circle now crowding around the mSap control board, they found themselves with quite another issue, causing—incredibly—the complete sidelining of the question of *source*.

The sapient engineer had detected very small waves riding on the gravitational wave. In other words, there was information hitching a ride. The wave had an embedded signal.

Hearing this, the group of astronomers and quantum physicists generated a silence that spread out in its own stupefying wave. If this was an extraterrestrial message . . . but Ned was getting way ahead of things. Then again, what else could it be, but an advanced communication method, a method not even contemplated by those searching fruitlessly for messages from galactic civilizations?

"Try to decrypt?" Program Manager Laurel Friedman said, her voice showing the steadiness that Ned was fairly sure he couldn't have mustered.

The quantum engineer nodded, leaning in to the keyboard.

It took him longer to type in the command than it took the mSap to unlock the code. Sitting back and staring at the screen, he said, "You're not going to believe this."

The signal was in English.

From the dark to the bright.

With the message on the screen still lit up in his mind, Booth Waller furiously drove his all-terrain rig off road, sending up clouds of dust. The quickest way between the detector facility and the transition camp was straight across the flat scrub-steppe. This was a message he'd deliver in person.

From the dark to the bright.

The fact that Booth happened to be present at the detector module when the signal came in was nothing short of miraculous. Now he drove like a madman, windows open, the sage wind hurtling through the car, the last of the sun beating on his elbow outside the cab. It felt like the last ride he would ever take. Likely it *was* the last ride. The transform was just a few days away. He pushed that thought aside. There were too many last times to endure; it would make you crazy.

He would never forget the image on the screen: six innocuous typed words carrying the freight of a permission to launch. A full year in development and assembly, their small-sized detector was viciously accurate and cooled to a few microkelvins above absolute zero. It was enormously expensive to run. They'd spent half the combined resources of renaissance to run the thing in the last few months.

It was a phenomenal success. The message had come through just as Helice and her crew had originally predicted: by gravitational wave. The Tarig wouldn't use radio waves to reach Earth; the brane interface would form an impervious barrier. Helice was counting on gravitational waves, and she had been right. Even more critically, she'd secured their right to cross over, or demanded it. *From the dark to the bright.* The exact words contained another message, previously agreed upon: *Expect difficulties with the Tarig; bring no weapons.* It gave him some pause about what they would face when they got there. But, come over, Helice said.

What must the rest of quantum gravity research be making of this message? They'd be picking it up in Japan, Italy, Sudbury, Hanover. . . . It didn't matter that there was no way to keep others from reading renaissance's private communication; at first they'd be astonished; by the time they'd finished conferencing about it, it would be too late. Damn shame though. Those who were even now puzzling over messages riding gravitational waves were the very people who should be going along.

Booth shook that thought. Only a small number could go—the minimum likely to carry a sufficiently varied gene pool. Tarig paranoia would prevent a much larger group from migrating in. A damn waste.

As he came to a halt in front of the reactor building, the cloud of dust he'd stirred from the sage flats caught up with him, and he stepped into its sun-fired presence, squinting at the obscured surroundings as though he were already fading from the Earth. A few people were waiting for him, no doubt having seen his trail as he came barreling over the desert.

Peter DeFanti was foremost among them, but others were hurrying to join the small knot that converged on Booth's ATV.

Booth caught DeFanti's sharp gaze and nodded. "It's started."

"Holy shit," someone said.

"Yes," Booth murmured. That about summed it up.

CHAPTER THIRTY-THREE

To begin anew, destroy the old.
—Si Rong the Wise

IN LORD NEHOOV'S COOKING ROOM, WENG WAS NERVOUS. These were uneasy days in the Bright City, with Tarig gathering in the streets and outlaws captured. But today was worse. She had never accustomed herself to the silences of the mansion with its changing rooms and reconfigured paths, all empty, or nearly so. Once lost in a Tarig lord's habitation, one could not count on meeting another servant to show the way. The lords preferred solitude and favored mechanicals to perform needful tasks.

Lord Nehoov, however, was particular about his food, and he liked Weng's cooking.

For this reason he had graciously created special path lights for her to follow down the halls to the cooking room and to his dining platform. She need never worry about getting lost, no matter how many times the mansion altered itself.

In the midst of scraping plates, she heard a sound nearby. She stopped and looked behind her. It had been a definite thunk. A normal-enough sound among normal sentients—but she was in the house of a lord. Still, it did not repeat. Her hands, for some reason, were sweating.

Something was wrong in the city; everyone felt it. It would have been best for her not to go abroad in Shadow Ebb, but Tarig must eat twice a day, and evenly spaced meals were their preference. She would just serve the lord's after-dinner skeel and leave, letting the mechanicals clean up after the last course.

The noise again.

Wiping her hands on her apron, she walked to the end of the chopping table and peered into the corridor behind the cold boxes that held Tarig delicacies.

A shadow moved behind the last box. Or had the lights dimmed for a moment? Weng saw nothing further. But she followed the line of cold cabinets down to the very end and swung around to face that part of the cooking room she'd just been working in. Empty.

"Bright Lord?" she called.

He never came into her cooking room. Perhaps what she had glimpsed was a mechanical, although they were small and could not have cast a shadow as large as she had seen. Or thought she'd seen. Sighing, she went back to her station, resolving to leave quickly this ebb.

Placing the decanter on a tray along with a filigreed cup, she gathered her self-possession and carried the heavy tray toward the dining room. Halfway down the connecting hall—and following the light path, showing faintly but clearly in a mansion already light-filled—she considered how it might have been well had she put two cups on her tray, in case Lord Nehoov had company. But she would be late if she turned back to the cooking room, and the lord expected things on time.

The lords had little use for doors. Often, when they wished for an opening, they ordered one. Thus, when she came to her accustomed access to the dining area, she was only mildly surprised to find it gone. It was a long walk around to come in from the far end of the dining hall, a passage usually left open.

Arriving, she turned into the room. Lord Nehoov was alone. However, there appeared to be a broken container on the table. It had leaked. Crumpling her face in worry, Weng approached the table. As she did so, Lord Nehoov slowly fell forward. His forehead crashed horribly into the table, and he sat immobile in that impossible position. Weng rushed forward, skewing the tray, losing the decanter in a crash onto the floor, followed by the cup. She still held one end of the tray as she stared at the lord, bleeding robustly from the neck. "My lord, wake up!" she whispered. He must sit up and heal himself, he must . . . "Bright Lord, please!"

He was a Tarig. One of the Five. He could not be struck down, could not be hurt. A Tarig lord, oh, a Tarig lord.

He didn't move, his proud, giant form bent over at the waist, and his neck bleeding onto the tablecloth as it hung over . . .

Weng opened her mouth to scream. Even in this extremity she hesitated to scream in front of a Tarig. But scream she did, a wail that frightened even her. She called out, "Help! Oh Woeful God! Help!"

But who was there to hear? None except the murderer. Weng spun around, searching the room. As she looked toward the doorway that had disappeared, she saw that it wasn't a solid wall after all. It was open again. She glimpsed a swath of fabric that glinted before disappearing down the hall.

She looked back at Lord Nehoov. The table, set so formally a few minutes before, was now smashed, with a gout of blood darkening the white tablecloth.

Weng put the table between herself and the door. She screamed again, unable to contain herself. She still held the tray. Bringing it to her breast, she held it over her vitals like armor. Something had hurt the lord, woefully hurt him.

Lord Nehoov had not moved. He would never move again. Oh Frowning God, Lord Nehoov was dead.

Helice came awake suddenly.

The walls glowed with a feral light; skylights stared up at the gilded sky. A little dusk would be welcome in this too-bright house. In her sick bed in the middle of the outsized room, she felt exposed and uneasy.

Far down the mansion corridors someone screamed. It was the screaming that awoke her, horrid, foreboding screams.

Struggling to rise, she managed to dress and slip her feet into soled slippers. She staggered against the bed, then breathed deeply, mustering her equilibrium. Although fevered and weak, she made her way to the door opening and peered out. Another cry, louder, and then one fainter, as though the person in distress was not always moving in the same direction.

Helice expected someone to come for her, but no one did. No caretaker, no Tarig, no healer—she had banished those. Without someone to guide her, and since she would not be able to go far in her condition, her instinct was to hide. Turning into the hall, she headed opposite to the direction of the screams.

The precincts of Lord Nehoov's house were strange. The halls were sometimes tubes, round on all sides but the bottom; at other times they were absurdly wide corridors, filled with artifacts like statues, fabric hangings, and tables displaying jewelry and what might be tools or weapons. Worse, the halls changed. She didn't know where she was.

Behind her the wails occasionally pierced the silence. As she hurried down the odd corridors, she wondered how long she had slept and what could have happened that a person could scream for so long in Lord Nehoov's mansion and not attract notice.

When she found a corner that was obscured by an imposing and incomprehensible sculpture, she crept into the space behind. It was a good hiding place, so long as she crouched down. She shrank into the little space and put her head on her knees, exhausted.

After a time, the screaming ceased.

Perhaps the person in distress had left, or found someone to help her. It was a she, Helice felt certain. The longer the silence stretched, the more ominous Helice found it. Something was dreadfully wrong. It was the worst timing for bad events and screaming women. After her meeting with Nehoov and his council, things should have proceeded calmly and directly to renaissance. She feared that anything else was profoundly counterproductive.

Lord Nehoov, get it together. Just fucking *handle* it. Whatever it was, he must smooth it over. So close now.

After a very long wait, during which time Helice was dismayed to find she needed to urinate on the floor, she decided that no one was in the building. Determined to find Nehoov or one of his companions, she hauled herself to her feet and began to hunt for the way out. The mansion lay icy and silent.

Where were the Tarig? Surely they had servants, guards, flunkies of some kind. How could the palace be so utterly empty?

She had noticed a thin line of light along the wall; unconsciously, she had been following it. Keeping to the light trail, she passed what looked like a kitchen. Then, within a few steps a doorway gave onto a room with a table covered in a cloth. . . .

There, a Tarig lord lay bleeding, head on the table. She froze in the door opening, heart pounding.

Without a doubt, it was Nehoov. Immobile, a puddle of blood around him, he looked quite dead. A small robot was busily cleaning up around the lord, cleaners fizzing in the blood. The sight appalled her. Nehoov, her ally. His enemies had killed him. And his enemies were her enemies.

Adrenaline fueled her rush away from the room and its body, down the hall, following the line of light. As she hurried, she shrank from doorways that might reveal the conspirators. Nehoov, dead, oh God. Didn't they know she could cut them off, dispose of the Heart door? Hadn't Nehoov explained this to them? Or had she threatened too much? Would it all unravel so easily? If so, then she wanted to die. But it was not a release she could give herself, not yet.

Ahead of her, a lumpish form on the floor, in the middle of the corridor. A body. An older Chalin woman in an apron lay in a heap. By the angle of her neck, dead. No cleaning bots had found this one yet; so she'd died after Nehoov. The screamer. The conspirators were ruthless, killing even servants. No doubt they were just working up to the main murder they had in mind: Helice. She was determined to make it cost them.

At last she found a vestibule she thought she recognized, and the door to the outside. Slowly opening it, she peeked out, then slipped into the empty street.

Anzi watched with increasing anxiety as the Jinda ceb showed her scenes from the Ascendancy. She would have to decide soon where to insert, but with Lord Ghinamid on the loose, she had better choose correctly.

The Jinda ceb were masters at maneuvering their field of vision. They worked in tandem with Anzi as she suggested places to look. The problem with the lords' mansions was that they revised themselves, and thus any previous paths the Jinda ceb found were irrelevant as guides. Anzi watched the shifting views on the veil: old Cixi staring up from her balcony at the empty plaza; masses of Tarig in the upper streets; flights of bird drones over the city. And just now, Ghinamid's swift and sickening murder of Lord Nehoov.

But where did the lords keep Titus?

Although she had been among the Jinda ceb a long time, just an arc of days had passed for Titus. She vividly remembered her dismay when the time difference became clear to her, and she'd thought for a terrible moment that the time discrepancy would be the cruelest separation of all. But realignment was possible. They had done it, unless what she was viewing was history. It was too perplexing to hold in mind. She was going back, whatever it meant.

A new scene: Lord Ghinamid had entered a different house. There he rounded on a group of Tarig and, being larger than they, and quicker, he cut them down. A few fought, while others actually knelt to him, but whether asking forgiveness or welcoming destruction, she couldn't tell. Some Tarig lords, he didn't harm. Then Ghinamid lurched away.

Anzi's Jinda ceb companion explained: "Lord Ghinamid is designed as a soldier to guard the interface. He has more skill in fighting than other Tarig."

She nodded, realizing that Ghinamid was indeed imposing. He appeared to be looking for someone, and it made her frantic to think that it might be Titus.

The veil drew her attention again. Here was a glimpse of a small woman with a deformed face racing down a side street on the palatine hill; had Lord Ghinamid attacked her, leaving her face in shambles?

And there! Deep in the underbelly of a lord's mansion, it was he. Anzi moved closer to the veil. Titus. In his cell, Titus. She had no idea how she would get him out of there, but she must not waste a moment.

"Now," she said. "If you please, now." Then a tardy thought came to her. "No, wait! Set me outside the cell, not in it."

With that adjustment, they sent her.

The insertion took the wind out of her, and she went to her knees, accidentally touching the light bars. Jerking backward, she was left with a painful scorch on the back of her hand and the smell of burning skin.

When she looked up, she saw that the cell was empty. But he'd been there only a moment ago! Were the Jinda ceb wrong in how they aligned the timeframes between their realm and this one? Had they erred? She stared into the cell, staring past the bars of hot light.

Titus had vanished.

Tai stood in the recessed porch of a closed foodery watching for any sign of Hel Ese. He was as close as he could reasonably get to the palatine hill. If she was in the Tarig confidences now, she might be given free reign to move about. From the foodery, he had a clear view up to the lords' mansions. Scanning the porches and such avenues as he could see from here, he waited.

No one was in the streets or the great plaza. Occasionally he noted a Tarig on the hill, but those great massings of lords in the streets had evaporated.

He could not help Titus Quinn. The great man had asked for prayers, but Tai couldn't recall one. His mind was focused on one thing alone: Find Hel Ese and strike her down.

Tai had been working to destroy the Rose. She had known his great desire to be in the Rose, and she had used him without mercy, making him complicit in a crime so large it left him stunned. But it wasn't for his own humiliation that he would kill her. It was for the Rose. Maybe he could make right what had gone so terribly, unthinkably, wrong.

From the corner of his eye, he caught a movement. A figure came down the street, walking like one who was lame and furtively looking around. He drew himself further into the shadow of the portico. By the bright, it was she. She didn't look triumphant, or even healed. It gave him a spike of hope that perhaps the lords had spurned her. This changed nothing of his plan.

Then, behind Hel Ese came several Ysli whose short legs hampered their panicked run away from the palatine hill. Others followed: a Jout in company with a Chalin legate; a gaggle of clerks. By their haste and troubled expressions, all seemed to be fleeing something.

Tai moved into the street, mixing among the other sentients, following Hel Ese.

Quinn felt his way in the dark, narrow passageway, with Lady Demat just behind him. They crept with as much silence as they had in them. Lord Ghinamid had wakened. He stalked them, Demat said.

Quinn stopped, whispering, "There's a split in the tunnel."

"Go to the left," Demat's voice wavered in her terror of the dark, though it had been her idea to come into the tunnel, leaving it dark.

"Do you have a weapon?" he whispered. "If he finds us?"

"No weapon will help you."

He shuffled on, Demat behind him, like the ghost of his previous life, still trailing. He would end in the Entire where he began, in an alliance that confounded and mesmerized him: a bond with a Tarig female.

"Another split."

"Still left."

They crept on, trying to hear any sound besides their own. Quinn knew from Demat's report that Helice had forged an agreement with Lord Nehoov. Now Ghinamid was here to be reckoned with. What did he want? Quinn profoundly hoped he wanted Helice dead.

Demat pulled on his shoulder, stopping him. She knelt down and he heard her fumbling at something along the wall. A crack of light sliced at his eyes. With a push, they were through a wall. It pearled closed behind them.

There were on a terrace.

"Too exposed," Quinn said, squinting into the ebb time sky.

"We will locate Lord Ghinamid. Perhaps from this high view."

Dead birds littered the terrace.

Seeing them, Demat hissed, "My cousins want no spies."

Quinn stepped through the birds to join Demat near the railing overlooking the great plaza. The city was deserted. On a lower terrace, a Tarig body lay sprawled. How many had Ghinamid killed?

Demat pulled him down to a crouch and pointed through the balustrades to the canals below. "Do you see the small form there?" she asked. A body lay there. "It is the first of those who crossed over from the Rose. Killed by Ghinamid. He does not allow the migration."

Quinn squinted at the crumpled form. The thought staggered him. It was someone from the Rose. Though Helice's plan depended on people coming over, the sight of a dead human was grim. A bad way to die, to come into the Entire and face an executioner like the Sleeping Lord. "What does Ghinamid want?"

She surveyed the plaza carefully. "Nothing that you want."

"Tell me."

Still scanning the environs, both in the plaza and on the hill of mansions, she said, "To control us, as is his right. We no longer wish his control."

It was the first Quinn had ever heard of a schism among them.

She went on, "A million days ago, when we first came into form, it was agreed we would meet in the Sleeping Lord as a plenum. As occasion showed it needful, we would mix in this way, both the solitaires here and the congregate of the Heart. In the Sleeping Lord we would mingle in pure thought. It gave us comfort, to have our consensus near, in the great hall of the Sleeping Lord."

"You meet in Ghinamid's form?"

"At first, very often. In recent times, rarely. We grew to prefer autonomy, even if it put us at conflict. We found this interesting, that we could be separate from each other, becoming utterly single with particular desires. Even going back to the Heart, we maintained our strains of particularity, and any Tarig who met physical death in the Entire could be brought forth again. But our congregate state became a convenience, a secondary thing. Some of us loved to be solitaires and went home seldom, utterly abandoning Ghinamid." She nodded at the body of the Tarig on the veranda below. "These Ghinamid kills now."

Ghinamid was nowhere in sight, now. But Quinn wished for a weapon, even if it meant wielding it with his left hand.

Demat narrowed her eyes at the body in the middle of the plaza. "This person of the Rose was the occasion that awakened him. Lord Ghinamid noted the door from the Rose opening here. The violation awakened him. We must blame Lord Nehoov for this calamity."

"What will you do, Demat?"

Turning to him, she looked at him without expression. Had that been Chiron's look as well, all those years ago? It seemed he had lost his ability to read the Tarig.

"This lady will kill him," she said. "He has no usefulness and is a danger to us, slaying indiscriminately. When we have accomplished this, it may be that we will send you home, Titus-een, to do your own killing."

He heard these words with a shock of hope.

"You must return to us, in that case."

She might allow him to save the Rose. The Earth might live, after all. In return he would pay the price. His heart was deadening by the moment. He would have to return to her.

"Do you swear to love us then?" She rested her jeweled hand on the railing, her arm, sinuous and strong, her hands, slender, despite the sheathed claws.

"Yes, I swear."

"Hnn, Titus-een. But would it be true?"

She was not stupid or blind. He had to answer with care. "We would have to find each other again." He would keep his word. It would be a permanent bargain, he knew.

He looked down on the plaza. "If you're going to save the Rose, it must be soon."

"You do not command us."

Something caught her attention. Snapping her head to the side, she watched, utterly still. He strained to follow her gaze, but the Ascendancy lay under the most profound composure. She shrank back from the stone railing, making a small hissing sound. "Hide," she whispered.

Quinn crouched next to her, watching where she watched.

Whispering next to his ear, Demat said, "He is in the street below."

They huddled together for a moment, making themselves small. Quinn caught a glimpse of a very tall Tarig, moving purposively below, carrying a sword. He wore a silver helm. A warrior of great size and determined pace.

After a moment, Demat pulled him to his feet. "Go," she whispered. "Hide yourself."

"Where?"

"Go where we could not imagine. Think like the Roseling you are, then we will never guess your location. When you see him dead, then come to the center of the plaza. This lady will find you. Go!"

"Let me help you kill him."

She seemed bemused. "Help us, ah? You are crippled and have no knife."

Well, she knew how to discount a man. "How will you kill him?"

Demat was already retreating across the veranda. He thought he heard her say, "With my army."

CHAPTER THIRTY-FOUR

WHEN LAMAR TOOK THE CALL, he heard only a tinny, almost deadpan voice: "From the dark to the bright."

Just one simple sentence, it had the ability to make his heart race and his mind freeze. No need to answer, it was a recorded message, now going out to 1,999 others. He sank into a chair, hearing in his mind that plain, flat sentence, "From the dark to the bright." He looked straight ahead as the wan afternoon sun silvered his houseboat windows.

Events had eclipsed his ability to process them. The lords of the Entire were killing the universe. He'd betrayed Titus, a man who was like a son to him. When he looked up at the sky at night he confirmed for himself what they said: Sirius, the brightest star in the sky was gone. All this paled before the fact that he'd just killed Caitlin Quinn.

An hour later he took a sweater off its hook and put it on over his shirt. He washed up the few dishes in his sink, setting them on the drain board. Checking his refrigerator for perishables, he threw them into a plastic bag. He shut off the gas valve, then went into his bedroom to fetch the small satchel with his change of socks and underwear. Calling up the time, he calculated he could be at Hanford in about three hours. Road conditions on I-5 southbound would be disastrous, he had cause to know. He decided to head north, taking the Washington side of the river.

On the way out, he picked up the garbage sack in the kitchen. Stepping out onto the deck, he voiced the houseboat door locked. Hanford, then. Oddly, he found he had tears in his eyes. Not for the general demise of the world, but for the particular end of Caitlin Quinn.

On his way to the car, he dropped the sack of food in the garbage bin.

A crowd had gathered outside around the reactor building. They stood talking, singly or in knots, staring at the door to the vault containing the engine, and below that, the transition stage. Children ran freely, their shouts and squeals making the adults seem grim by comparison. Maybe they *were* grim. They really should have waited in the dorms until their number was called, but Lamar couldn't blame them if they wanted to gather together, now that it had begun.

In the press of bodies, Lamar saw Booth Waller near the reactor door. He was with Alex Nourse and Peter DeFanti. Lamar thought that the crowd was too large, might draw attention. But what attention? Satellites? Spies? Their one apparent spy had been dealt with. He had avoided newsTide accounts of the ball of fire on the freeway; no need for the news—he'd been an eyewitness.

The mothballed reactor towered above him, its steel encasement looking molten in the Eastern Washington sun. The steel dome encased the first mothballing of concrete and lead shielding. That pathetic sarcophagus lasted barely two hundred years. Now, even clad in steel, the beast looked nondescript, nothing like a nuclear reactor, much less a launch platform to other universes. From Lamar's vantage point on the edge of the crowd, he saw Bechtel's enormous vitrification plant in the distance. It was very nearly the largest building in the world before it was abandoned. Strictly low-level waste, that place. The aluminosilicate glass tubes could only hope to hold the easy material. The hottest stuff—the cesium and technetium—went into the big trench in the ocean, ignoring the screams of the whale lovers and other paranoids. But despite technical problems that had stymied generations of physicists, the thorniest problem at Hanford was record keeping. As generations of cleanup projects started up and broke off, the reservation filled up with failed, only partially characterized projects. When it was time to leave, contractors simply walked away, sometimes not even locking the doors.

And wasn't that what renaissance was doing? Normally Lamar would kick such a thought away. Now he let it sit in his mind. Because he had no heart for the thing anymore. It struck him squarely, without doubt: he really didn't care. He didn't want to live with himself for the centuries that might lie ahead of him.

He turned around looking toward the access road, wondering if anyone would notice him slipping back to his car and just leaving.

But Booth was walking toward him, Alex Nourse in tow. The three of them nodded at each other, a quick acknowledgement that Lamar had earned back his right to be here.

Booth said, "We've begun. First one gone, Lamar."

Lamar was confused. "Gone? But *you're* number one, Booth."

Alex spoke up. "We're starting a little further down the sequence. For practice."

The sons of bitches were afraid of screw-ups. They were afraid of their own systems.

Alex looked around at the crowd. "Most everyone's here. We're up to 1,989. Some are going to be too late." An eloquent shrug.

And some died before getting here, Lamar thought. "Well, how did the practice crossing go?" He tried and failed to keep the contempt out of his voice, but they didn't notice anyway.

"Looks good," Booth said. "Solid contact. The strongest on record. We locked on—and here's the exciting part—we've stayed locked. We think she's managed to stabilize the interface from the other end."

No need to say who *she* was. Goddamn, to think of that annoying youngster pulling it all off! But he didn't begrudge it to her. It just surprised him that everything was working. Perhaps somewhere deep in the compost of his being, he'd hoped it wouldn't.

Booth went on, "We don't lack for volunteers to move up the list. People are anxious to go." He nodded at the superstructure of the vault building. "The engine. Hear it?"

Lamar listened. Yes, a few decibels higher. Now that he focused on it, it threw an ominous, thrumming net over the day. No wonder people seemed grim.

"I'd like to see the pond." Despite his ugly mood, he wanted to see with his own eyes the migration under way.

"Trent Phillips is going next."

Lamar hesitated. He was already letting himself get sucked back in. "Okay, then." He had liked himself better under the cloud of despair. At least that had showed a little conscience. He followed Booth and Alex toward the access door. Already, Portland seemed a universe away.

The crowd reminded Lamar of shoppers waiting for a sale. They looked enviously at Lamar and Booth as they headed to the door. Alex stayed behind to marshal the list, jockeying people, kids, luggage—didn't they remember, no luggage? Lamar's thoughts, though, were on Titus Quinn. What was he going to say to him?

The cement corridors were cramped, cold, and feebly lit. It was like walking through the passageways of an Egyptian pyramid, pathways few were meant to use. The engine's throbbing pulse was louder here, like the heartbeat of a nuclear beast. But there was no reactor inside. The whole thing had been disassembled and buried in discreet pits around area five of the reservation, pits hot enough to kill sagebrush in three days. All to make room for the engine. It pounded at Lamar's chest, as though demanding access. Wasn't there some bible verse? *I stand at the door and knock. If any man hears . . .* What was the next part? *If any man hears . . .* How did it go? It seemed important to remember. But if he remembered, would he be held to account for all that he was doing? And if he'd forgotten, would God forgive him? An old man, after all. He glanced at Booth Waller. So what was this young man's excuse?

Here on the main floor were the makeshift showers and dressing stalls so that people could suit up for the crossing. Don't want to contaminate the pond, or infect the Entire with disease vectors. We'd arrive as clean as possible, and what needed cleaning up later, the Tarig would no doubt attend to it.

They descended a staircase, entering a region of yet colder air but brighter illumination. Down a narrow hall they crammed into the tiny control room. The transition stage itself was a clean room, so no idle observers there. At the boards, John Hastings and Isobel Wu nodded at the brass as they entered, then turned to their work. Isobel's witlessly reassuring voice came over the speakers: "It'll take twelve picoseconds to move you out of the water, Trent, you understand? That's twelve trillionths of a second."

For God's sakes, they didn't need to explain picoseconds to a particle physicist, but Isobel didn't know anybody this far down on the list. She went on, "Don't think of it as holding your breath, but don't suck in material as you go under. When you feel your hands come to the end of the railing in the matrix, just pause and remove your hands from the grip. It'll be over in a blink. Ready?"

In his clean togs, standing by the pool, Trent looked uneasy. He stood at the head of the short flight of steps leading into the transmission matrix. Dressed all in white, he looked like a man about to undergo a total immersion baptism. Sometime in the last few months they discovered that the probes worked better in a high transmission-induced colloidal mixture. People had been prepped about this, and Trent looked stalwart, if eerily pale.

"I'm ready."

Isobel voiced to the mSap. "Entering the bright." Now the sapient would take control.

Trent walked down the stairs, bravely, Lamar thought. His hair, spreading out on the surface for the moment, looked as though it was reaching for a last moment of air.

The mSap controlling the connection initiated the quantum implosion and inflation, a daunting process that essentially reduced matter to fundamental particles and reconstituted so quickly, the body didn't even noticed that it hadn't, for a moment, existed. Best not to think about it. Everyone knew that Titus Quinn had come and gone that way; he was the only proof it could be done, and it calmed the nerves of even the quantum theory guys.

"Done," Isobel said.

Already another person was entering the transition room, suited up and eyeing the pool like an electric chair.

Booth glanced at Lamar. "Do you want to go after him?"

"I thought we were going in order."

"Not having second thoughts?"

"Of course I am, you stupid fuck." Lamar was sick of them all. "I'll wait my turn."

Lamar stared at the surface of the gel. He moved closer to the control room window, straining to see into the vat. It was empty. There'd been no light show, no zapping sound, just a . . . he didn't want to think *silent dissolve*. It sounded too much like oblivion.

At Pioneer Courthouse Square in the middle of downtown Portland, Caitlin felt reasonably safe. A crowd might be her best protection, both for anonymity and for security, if Lamar's group decided to come after her. She worried that her two-hour wait would attract attention, though. Stefan had claimed he couldn't possibly get away from the office before five. The transform was coming, and Stefan couldn't be bothered to hurry.

She tapped her coat pocket for the dozenth time, feeling for the list of two thousand. She wished she had her other documentation with her, but the letters from the Bureau of Standard Tests were sitting on the coffee table at home where she was afraid to return.

Damn Stefan anyway, for making her wait. But if anyone could marshal serious opposition to Lamar, if anyone she knew *personally* could do it, that would be the head of the fifth-largest company in the country. He might not like her—she and Stefan had clashed before—but he couldn't afford to disregard Titus Quinn's sister-in-law.

Her phone vibrated in her pocket again. It had been ringing over the last few hours, but the only person she would take a call from right now was Rob. She looked at the incoming. Her mother again.

No calls. It was too dangerous. Lamar could find her if she used her phone, if they were tracking her.

The damn phone again. This time, instead of *Call Mother*, the message said: *Emergency. Call Mother.* It could be a ruse, someone using her mother's phone. She ran a typeprint check on the message, seeing that it had an eighty-seven percent chance of being her mother's typing, her digital signature.

Then, without making a conscious decision, she placed the return call. "Mom?" she said when her mother answered.

"Oh my God. So I was right."

In the background, Emily's voice, and Mom shooing her to her room.

"What *emergency*? The kids all right?"

"They're fine, but . . . Oh honey. The police called."

"You answered the phone? You're not supposed to answer. You've got to stay hidden." Jesus, her mother was being reckless, answering the phone, placing calls. . . .

"It's Rob. It's about Rob."

"What are you talking about?"

"There was a car accident this morning. A blue Mercedes—they think it was a Mercedes—piled up on the freeway. It's yours."

She wasn't driving the Mercedes. In a bout of trembling, Caitlin found a half wall to sit on.

"They traced the car to you, hon. I've been trying to reach you for hours. The police thought you were okay because your phone was still working."

Caitlin couldn't speak, couldn't even think.

Her mother went on, "Someone died in the car." Her voice wavered, but didn't break. "It was Rob, sweetheart. I'm . . . so sorry. He brought us here in the Mercedes, so I knew he had that car." Silence, as Caitlin tried to absorb this. "What can I do, hon? Where are you?"

"It could have been anyone's Mercedes, it could have—"

Her mother interrupted. "They found a piece of the license plate."

The reality began registering. She held the phone in her lap.

"Caitlin?" came her mother's voice.

She had traded cars with Rob; she was driving his sports car, he was driving the Mercedes because he had to transport the children and Mom.

Horribly, she felt relief—relief that the children hadn't been with him. Shock was there, too, a staggering weight of it.

Caitlin spotted Stefan Polich. Tall and thin, dressed in his signature jogging suit, looking stiff and out of place in the public square. He saw her, waved.

She threw a bleak wave back. "Mother, call the police. Tell them someone has been threatening our family, and I'm on the run. I'm going to hang up. Promise me. Call the police."

"Honey, what—"

"Just do it. Don't call me again, I can't answer." Caitlin hung up. The Mercedes, crashed. They'd murdered Rob. By mistake. They were trying to murder *her*.

Pushing her emotions into a firm, small hole, she took a deep breath. It shuddered when it came out. Then she stood up and started walking toward Stefan. Looking around, she scanned the square for signs of Stefan's security people. She'd asked for no goons, not trusting Stefan yet.

Caitlin, they go everywhere with me.

They drop you off, and they stay away, Stefan. You'll be in a public square. You'll be fine for twenty fucking minutes!

They'll stand across the street, that make you feel better?

She saw them, standing with a clear line of sight to Stefan.

As she crossed the square, she jammed her fists past the corner of her eyes, wiping away tears of pure, overwhelming panic. Rob was dead.

As she stood in front of Stefan, he took in her expression. "God, what's the matter?"

"We have to get out of here. Hurry." An enclosed, hidden place was best. Keeping moving was best; don't let them close in.

She charged out of the plaza, checking to be sure Stefan was following her. Making her way to the curb, she dashed across the street into the recessed entry of a mall. Stefan waited on the other side of the street, watching for traffic to clear.

Just run for it, she urged. He found a break and hurried across. Grabbing him by the arm, she pulled him through the door and into the hubbub of a super mall. She led him around a media kiosk and found a bench out of sight of the glass front doors. She sat, pulling him down with her.

"Caitlin, what the hell is going on?" He looked at her reproachfully, as though there was little that could justify *running* in a public place.

She had to summon her argument, but instead she was just realizing what Rob's death meant. He was on his way to EoSap, the biggest competitor Minerva faced. EoSap would have listened to Titus Quinn's brother. They knew someone had gone over to the Entire; one of their flunkies tried to kidnap Emily to apply pressure. They would have listened to Rob. Stefan was her last chance.

Two of his guards came through to the mall; he waved them back. They took up posts beside the cheap diamond outlet a hundred feet away.

She chose her beginning point and asked, "Where is Booth Waller? He works for you, right?" She paused, waiting for him to answer. Then she went on: "Where's Peter DeFanti?"

"Booth? He's on vacation. I never see DeFanti." Stefan waited, eyebrows raised. The shoppers were young, carrying purchases in fancy bags, chattering, laughing.

"Booth isn't on vacation." She lost her train of thought almost immediately. After planning what to say for hours, now her thoughts vanished. She made a new beginning. "Booth and Lamar and DeFanti have a plan. The plan involves the Entire, and going over to it. Rob and I found out, and they've just killed Rob." She saw his expression of disbelief, and despaired of telling him even more preposterous things. "Have you heard about a crash on the freeway? They demolished my Mercedes. Rob was in it, and now he's dead."

"Rob?"

She sneered. "My husband. The one that used to work for you. Never mind. He's dead, and now they're hunting *me*. I just talked to my mother. She and the kids are in hiding, Stefan."

He was starting to look around as though for people he could pretend to know so he could get out of this increasingly unpleasant conversation. Across from the goons, a mall security man chatted up the barista at World Bean, armed with a pathetic tangle gun. He'd be ready to take down anyone threatening America's merchandise.

"You think Booth is killing people? And Lamar? He's your uncle, for Christ sake."

"He's Titus's uncle." It sounded defensive, and it was irrelevant.

She charged on. "They have two thousand people they're planning to send over to the Entire; I've been to the place where they're congregating. It's on the Hanford Reservation in Washington. Near one of those big abandoned reactors. It's *in* the reactor. I mean in the shell of the reactor." She stopped in frustration. "Stefan, they're *hiding*. Hiding what they're doing, because they plan to leave this place in ruins when they go so no one else can follow them, because they hate the rest of us and want to keep the race pure."

Stefan watched her with the blankest look she'd ever seen.

Bringing the papers out from her coat pocket, she handed them to him. "That's the list of the ones who're crossing over. I'll bet not one of them is at work today. You should check."

Stefan was shaking his head. "I don't know these people." Wrinkling his forehead, he muttered, "I know a *few* . . ."

"They're not all Minerva people. They're all savvies, though." When he dared to shrug at her, she snarled, "Look at it, read it. I almost got killed getting this, so you can damn well read it."

But he wasn't intimidated. "Caitlin. This isn't making any sense. Why go over, why go over secretly? We're waiting for Quinn to report back. And the Hanford thing . . . I . . . I'm sorry, it's nonsense." He looked at her with some discomfort. She was Quinn's sister-in-law. She could be influential with their man in the Entire, so no doubt he realized he owed her a little time, but it was coming to an end.

She plunged on, talking fast now, trying to pull together the evidence for him, so he could see, so he could believe. "Lamar got my scores altered at the Bureau, Stefan. He moved heaven and earth to get my scores changed to savvy so I could join his damn group and go over too, because he knew Titus would be pissed if I was left behind. In the ruins."

"Ruins." Stefan challenged her with silence.

She took a deep breath. "They're going to blow up . . ." She had planned a small lie, to be more convincing. "They're going to detonate a nuclear device. To hide their transition place, their crossover platform that has all the new technology that they don't want anyone else to have, so that they're the only ones going over. That bomb is going to go off about two hundred miles from here. And very soon."

"Lamar is going to detonate a nuclear device? Are you listening to yourself?"

"I know what it sounds like! But you—"

"Why didn't you call the police, then?" He gestured at the security cop, as though this lone, beefy guy could stop what was coming.

"The police wouldn't believe me, would they? The only one who would is someone who knows about the Entire, and that's you."

He reached over to touch her hand. It turned into a pat. "You've just lost your husband. You're in shock. Anyone would be."

Jerking her hand away, she said, "I have two letters at home. The Bureau of Standard Tests has said it made a mistake on my scores—from twenty-five years ago—and also on my son Mateo's scores from a few months ago. We're now both savvies, isn't that nice? And we were invited to cross over. When I refused, they came after us, so I wouldn't tell anyone. You want to see the letters?"

Stefan stood up. Reaching for his cell phone, he said, "I'm calling someone to come down and drive you home, Caitlin."

"No!" she jumped up. "For God's sake, at least investigate. All those people on the list"—she waved at the papers he was still holding—"all of them are at Hanford. Call work, ask your people who's there and who's not!"

The cop was now watching them.

Stefan hesitated. "Caitlin." He paused until he had her attention. Speaking quietly, he said, "I don't believe you. I'm sorry. You're falling apart, and I'm going to get you some help."

"You son of a bitch," she murmured.

As he directed his attention to his phone, Caitlin backed away. "If you don't do something, I'm going to make sure that Titus Quinn never deals with you again. We're bringing everything to EoSap. Every ounce of every damn thing that Quinn learned over there is going directly to EoSap."

He was talking on his phone, ignoring her. The goons, now concerned, were walking toward her.

She turned and rushed toward the door to the street. Barreling past people just entering, she chose a direction, and hurried away from Pioneer Square. Rounding a corner, she saw an empty cab and hailed it. Mercifully, it stopped.

"Just drive," she said as she clambered in. Just drive. Where to go? She had no idea.

The driver looked at her in the rearview mirror as she moaned. It had just struck her that she had left her only evidence—the list of two thousand—with Stefan Polich.

CHAPTER THIRTY-FIVE

Shed no tears until you see the grave flag.

—a saying

IN THE FIELD, TEN THOUSAND INYX GRAZED AND SLEPT under the Deep Ebb sky. It was a peaceful scene, observed from a distance by Akay-Wat, Takko, Adikar, and the other riders, but they knew the mounts were vividly awake. No tendrils came into Akay-Wat's mind from Gevka; her mount was pressed into the service of the herd, led by Riod, and directed at the city of the lords.

In the midst of the herd consciousness, Riod felt himself swept along, faster and higher than he had ever flown. They knew the path to the minds gathered in the Ascendancy, and sped there each ebb, spying for Tarig weakness. Although never able to penetrate the mind of a Tarig, the mounts sensed them as streams of light. One frazzle of light was much stronger than any other. This lord had been of interest to Riod for many weeks, but not even a concerted effort by his combined forces could penetrate the being's heart-thoughts. This ebb the creature grew stronger. The signature of its consciousness grew incandescent, spraying into the dream realm like a beacon.

If Sydney were home in the steppe lands, Riod would tell her what they witnessed. But she was far away. Over far distances, their hearts were silent to each other. Only Inyx to Inyx could leap past such barriers. In the field, his fellow mounts soothed his mind, bringing him back to their purpose. They surged on, dipping now and then into the dreams of Titus Quinn, whose mind was also a bright flame. But the man slept little, and his heart was as chaotic as the lord's.

Geng De stood at the prow of his ship as his vessel sped out, leaving the quay and Rim City behind. At a time when ordinary sentients slept and when Geng De longed for rest, he ordered the ship under way. And now, into the binds.

He nodded at his ship keeper, who moved to his bed to wait out the journey. Taking one last look at the floating city in the distance, hanging like a pendant fruit from the tree of heaven, the navitar gathered his caftan about him and climbed the companionway, leaning on his cane. The stairs were steep to his enfeebled legs. Each time he dove down and wrestled with the strands, he paid a price. But it must be paid! A mad lord loose in the Bright City; Titus Quinn seeking kingship; the lords themselves divided; the world contending with the Rose for precedence.

He prepared for the plunge into the binds. Now the strands would come to him: red, the color of the Rose, gold, the color of the Entire. Only one could thrive. The possible futures were complex blends of colors. Pulling on them—oh, so gently—he would knit them into one vast plait. Why had this weaving been given to him, of all the navitars? It granted him large and frightening powers. It made him a slave to the Nigh, his life an offering to the Entire. As was Sen Ni's.

Was she strong enough to thwart her father? Oh, but she must be. She was the beloved land's only hope. The binds had taught him that the Entire could die. First the bright would pale; then flicker. The Nigh would leave its banks and surge across the midlands. The Empty Lands would pull down the storm walls. He saw the Ascendancy sucked into the Heart. Perhaps at the end, the lords, and they alone, would endure.

The ship plunged down. Geng De stood up on his platform, ready to weave.

Zhiya sat by her mother's bed, unable to sleep while her mother was in such distress. She dipped a cloth in the pan of water, dabbing the old navitar's face and arms to cool her.

"Hush, Mother. All will be well." She didn't believe it but said it anyway. It expressed a hope and was perhaps a worthy prayer.

"Nooo," Jin Ye moaned.

Then it would *not* be well. So much for God listening to a corrupt godwoman. "Sleep, Mother. That is best." Over the last days her mother's mutterings were again and again of a baby—also a navitar—whose mouth was stopped with river matter and who had become deformed. Mother feared this child because he was breaking—or would break?—the immemorial ship vows to navigate and never tamper with fundamental things. Zhiya hadn't known that tampering was possible.

She had asked her mother: "What is the worst that will come of this child?"

"The world, devouring everything."

But what could this mean?

Zhiya put her head on her mother's shoulder and rested. Sleep tugged at her. But her mother's hand came up to touch Zhiya's hair, bringing her daughter awake.

She looked steady and clear, her eyes bright. With great deliberation, she enunciated her words. "Each . . . universe . . . is . . . sovereign. Leave the Rose to the Rose . . . and the All to the All. This is the *law*, my daughter. You remember?"

"No, Mother. Should I?"

"Geng De . . . forgets."

"Sleep is best, Mother."

Her mother moaned. "Do not sleep. Not this ebb, do not . . ." But then she closed her eyes, appearing to sleep.

Geng De. That was a name Zhiya knew. It was a navitar who had been visiting Sen Ni, according to her spies. A fully grown navitar, but one who left his vessel, one who walked about and did not appear to rave. Zhiya's mind circled darkly around this thought: the baby had grown up. He was tampering, devouring.

Sleep was out of the question, now.

Anzi tore the hem of her tunic to make a bandage for her hand. It had bled from the fiery bars of Titus's cell. From this side of the bars, she saw little in the cell that indicated he had ever been there, only a blanket thrown at the foot of the pallet and a water cup.

How much time had passed? Had he set down that cup, cast aside that blanket, only increments ago—or a much longer time ago? She pushed away some of her darker worries. He was gone, and she would have to find out where.

A sound at the door to the anteroom leading to Titus's cell.

The door pushed open. In the opening stood a Tarig carrying a short sword. Anzi backed up a step.

The Tarig lord was muscular and tall. He wore long pants made from a metal mesh that scraped as he strode into the room. A cloak over his shoulder fell to his calves, making him seem enormous. On his head, a metal helm with flaps covering his ears and neck.

Lord Ghinamid.

She'd been watching him with impunity through the veil. Oh, that she had stayed on that side!

His gaze flicked to the cell, then back to Anzi. While it might be proper to greet the lord, nothing would come out of her throat. Her attention focused on the sword.

When he spoke, his voice was a low growl, a terrible sound. "Titus Quinn. Where?"

"I . . . do not know, Gracious Lord. I came here. He was gone."

With a few paces he came close and put the sword at her neck.

She managed to whisper, "I swear by the Bright. I do not know."

The growl again: "Released him, did you?"

Anzi was acutely aware of her windpipe and her small voice, all at risk of severing by the sword. Faintly, she eked out, "I swear. I did not."

Slowly the sword moved down and away from her neck. The lord grasped her hair with his free hand, bringing her close to him. She thought he was going to kiss her, as bizarre as the notion was. Bringing his face close to her neck for a moment, he held her in an immobilizing embrace. Then, stepping back from her, he said, "You are Chalin. We can smell the others."

He moved to the fiery bars and they evaporated as he passed through. In a mighty kick, the lord toppled the pallet, as though Titus might have hidden under it.

Anzi thought of a dash for the door and abandoned the idea. The lord could easily close the distance between them.

Then suddenly, he moved out of the cell in her direction. She closed her eyes in dread, but in a moment he was past her. Turning, she saw that he had opened a hole in the wall behind her. Light burst from it as he ducked into this opening, turning into a passageway.

He was gone.

Without thinking, she rushed in the opposite direction, out the door and up a stairway leading away from Titus's prison. She was in an arched corridor, sparkling and empty. Choosing a direction at random, Anzi ran.

Despite her brush with the Tarig's sword and his grotesque voice, Anzi was harboring a kernel of relief, if not outright happiness: she hadn't come too late; she and Titus were back in the right harmony of time. Though she was older than the last time he saw her, *he*, at least, was the same age. She gave thanks to the God of the Rose. Then, as she ran, she put two fingers by her left eye to ward off the usual bad luck of prayer.

Quinn had just left the balcony after taking leave of Lady Demat. Climbing a narrow flight of stairs that curled around the outside of the mansion, he sought out a better viewpoint of the hill itself. Demat had told him to find a hiding place that no Tarig would think of. But he had no intention of doing so. Helice might have done her worst, but he still needed to discover the site of the engine she and her people had created. He still needed to find Helice.

Demat might help him. She had strongly hinted she might. He had promised her his life; and that it would be *true*. Among the many—perhaps endless—differences between Tarig and human, here was the most chilling: that she could accept his promise to love her at some point in the future, although he did not love her now. She obviously believed such a bargain was possible.

Anzi, he thought. Anzi. What will we do?

Noises from the city caught his attention now and then as he climbed higher on the hill of mansions. He heard an occasional closing of a door, a shout of Tarig voices. All other sentients must be cowering in the Magisterium. He thought of the questions he should have asked Demat: Can you send me home quickly? Is there a *way* to go home from here?

If he had ever doubted Helice's renaissance scheme, the human body lying on the plaza put an end to skepticism. Helice's people had started to come through. If they crossed over in groups, their intentions could be realized in a few minutes or hours. Then they'd match cycles with the engine at Ahnenhoon and the destruction would proceed. No time remaining now. But he couldn't just wait and hide. If he glimpsed Helice in the streets of the palatine hill he'd confront her and extract the information from her. Of where the Rose engine was. Then Demat would help him. That was his plan, if an unlikely one.

He wandered upward, choosing paths at random, watching for Ghinamid, who would surely kill any human he found. Did Quinn pass for Chalin? He'd counted on that during his days of hiding in the Entire, but today he felt exposed, as though his true self was obvious to anyone who looked.

Ahead was a dark archway overhung with black vines glistening in reflected lavender sky. It looked familiar. While his head had pondered things to come, had his feet followed a course he'd used before?

He knew this place. The tall facade of the mansion surrounded a garden on three sides. On the ground, bird drones lay scattered like fallen black leaves. Over the corner of the pond in the center of the garden, a plant trailed drooping limbs. The sky was amethyst, darkening quickly into Deep Ebb, but he could see the garden clearly.

He moved inside the archway, staring at the water, empty now of toy boats. Because it was *that* garden, of course. Glancing up at the dense shrub on the far side of the pond, he imagined someone hiding there. It was something a child might do, peeking at a stranger, afraid to come out in the open. His mouth felt dry. Not wanting to be here, his steps nevertheless led him to the very edge of the pond.

She would not be hiding. This was now, and she had been dead—how long? In his own time frame, about two hundred days. His throat caught. A breeze lifted the leaves of the vines, rattling them and the feathers of the fallen drones. The Tarig had no children, Mo Ti had said. Small Girl was a decoy creation, fashioned to be childish. He had killed that malformed creature to keep her from bringing the lords down upon him when he had the world to save. Anyone would have done the same. He had said this to himself many times, but the thorn still remained in his side. He had tested savvy at thirteen. Didn't his mind grasp that he had . . . not . . . killed . . . a child?

But that day when he brought Small Girl the toy boat, he had thought her a child. And wasn't she, in some sense? They had created a being something like a Tarig, but with less developed intelligence. He stood staring at the pond. What, by the Miserable God, *was* a child, what was the very definition, what was the quality of life and years and cognition that made a creature a young sentient?

He had taken her into the pool. She had fought with ferocious power. Under the water, her screams had been silent.

The darkening bright glowered down on him. Sitting on the lip of wall around the pool, he let his injured right arm hang down, his hand breaking the surface of the water, sending out small carnelian waves.

Despite all that he had told himself of reasons and logic, he wept. He had become a man who could do terrible things. Titus Quinn must have his way; let nothing get in his way, but he would do his job, the thing that fell to him to accomplish. He couldn't take back what he'd done. Worse, he didn't want to take back what he had done. He would make the same decision today. It was all mixed together in a poisonous brew. Why was his life always about the child?

Removing his hand from the water, he tested his range of motion. He could raise his arm, if slowly; he could make a fist, but not grip a pen. The Tarig cuts had severed the muscle down to his tendons in his upper arm. Other slashes might have gone deeper, and as Demat had implied, they had done a sloppy job of mending him.

"She won't fix this," he whispered. "I promise, Small Girl. When I come back, Demat will not fix it." He would keep his body just as it was. He knew how it sounded: like he was crazy. But it gave him some peace to have decided this.

When he stood up, a motion at the garden wall caught his attention. Something gleamed. It was someone walking on the other side of the wall. It was the top of a helm.

Ghinamid.

There was only one way out, through the arch. But Ghinamid was headed straight for it. Quinn rushed to the entrance of the mansion. The door yielded to his push, and he slipped inside. Too bright and empty; no place to hide. He ran through a large, echoing room and into a wide corridor, also empty. The place was abandoned, perhaps had never had occupants. He ran down the corridor, turning into a side hall.

In the distance, the outside door banged open.

He ducked through the nearest doorway, closing the door behind him. The room was furnished with a few large chairs against the walls. A window gave onto the garden below. Rushing toward it, he looked out to see the garden empty. He grabbed an object from a table nearby, a hand-sized cube of filigreed metal. Then, opening the window casement, he hurled the object through the window, aiming for the archway. It crashed outside. He hoped the noise would attract Ghinamid; hoped the lord's hearing was keen.

Positioning himself behind the door, Quinn waited. From the hallway he heard footsteps; he guessed they were retreating.

A movement at the windowsill startled him. He half expected to see that Lord Ghinamid had climbed the outside of the mansion in his zeal. But it was a small, dark thing: a bird. It shook its wings in a remarkably accurate display of preening, then turned to the clear glazing of the window and pecked.

It was pointing at him. *Titus Quinn is here, here, here.* If Ghinamid had gone into the garden, he would hear this pecking. He turned to the door, putting his hand on the latch handle. Was the corridor empty? He couldn't be sure where Ghinamid was.

Turning back, he saw that the window was melting away where the bird pecked. A small aperture had now formed in the midst of the window. The bird hopped through.

It gripped the edge of the melted glass with its feet, head turned to the side, one eye fixed on Quinn. In a voice like the smoothest silk, it said, "Hel Ese is on Magisterium. Fourth level, Titus-een." It nuzzled its beak under a wing.

Demat had sent the drone, and its message was spectacular: the Magisterium, fourth level. Helice, at last. The talking bird might be helping him, but it was also marking his location. He ducked into the hallway, and seeing it empty, turned down the corridor in a direction away from the garden entrance.

Now he'd have to cross the plaza. And he wasn't the only one who had been watching it, he was quite sure.

A sound behind him. Quinn whirled. Flapping past, the bird drone sped to the end of the corridor, then waited for him. He followed the creature until it led him into a foyer that had oddly frozen in place in the midst of one of the mansion's transformations. The ceiling was domed but too large. Walls jutted up to different heights, while doorways sagged. The bird pecked at the floor. As Quinn watched, a hole melted open on the floor. Expanding rapidly, it revealed a passageway beneath. Now it was large enough for Quinn to pass through. The bird fluttered in, and Quinn followed it, jumping down into a cramped passage. The bird worked at knitting the hole back up and then flew ahead, glowing phosphorescent in the darkness.

"Demat?" Quinn asked the bird. He didn't know if some part of her consciousness might ride in that drone.

The bird flew on, not answering.

The drone left him when they reached the Magisterium. Quinn would apparently have to find Helice on his own. As he stood in a small chamber with a bed and washstand, he considered his chances of passing unnoticed among the stewards in their fourth-level province. Searching through a chest in the corner, he looked for a uniform, finding nothing.

Soon he was rifling through the rooms and apartments nearby, all deserted. When at last he emerged into the corridor again, he wore the humble uniform of an understeward, with the backward-sloping hat of the room's occupant and a jacket bearing the image in back of a white carp. The hall was empty, but he heard voices from a gathering nearby.

Helice could be hiding in any of these rooms. He could begin searching them, but it would take longer than he feared he had. Approaching the source of the voices, he saw a mass of sentients gathered in a large hall. A legate addressed them, urging calm. They remained surprisingly professional. They were of the Magisterium; the lords would protect them. Except the lords were killing many, and some who served the Great Within had already been slain.

Quinn scanned the crowd. He would never find Helice if she was among them. But he doubted she would risk mixing with the stewards outright. As he turned away he remembered the drone's words. Something odd about what the bird had said, that Helice was on the Magisterium. Not in it. On it.

She was *outside*. That would have been a place that a bird/drone might have seen her, and was a good hiding place. He quickly made his way to the nearest egress door.

A cold breeze confronted him as he stepped outside. He stood on a long balcony overlooking the flat, five-armed world. A ramp connected the balcony here with one above, on the third level. Ignoring the view, he moved to the end of the balcony, looking over to the ramps, viewing platforms, and balconies jutting out from the fourth level. They were all empty. Even if she was on one of them, he'd have to approach her from the inside, guessing which door led to her.

The viewing platform where he stood was littered with the bodies of birds. Who had grounded them? Lord Ghinamid might be one who didn't want to be tracked. Still, Quinn wished his guide bird would return and make a circuit of the outside walls, looking for a small, Chalin-like woman with a scarred face.

The underside of the city was in the shape of a bowl, making it impossible for him to see levels above, where overhangs obstructed his view. He, could, however, look to the level below by leaning out.

Pressing against the railing, he pushed his upper body past the resistance of the field barrier, which assured a modicum of safety on the outside decks.

Helice was there, below him, on the fifth level.

Huddled into a ball in a recessed alcove of a balcony, she sat with her head on her knees. Oh, sleep, Helice, he thought. Sleep.

But she was on level five, not level four. How could he find her again, once inside the Magisterium and trying to guess which door led where? He'd have to try. Turning to leave, he paused. He would lose her. Going inside the Magisterium he could easily become lost. He knew the Magisterium only slightly, and these lower levels not at all.

He leaned over the rail again, looking below the jutting balcony on which he stood. His stomach contracted at the view: a drop of thirty thousand feet into a blinding mirror of water, reflecting the high bright. He would not look down again.

Moving to the very end of the balcony, he squinted down at the wall, seeing protuberances he might use for handholds. The wall curved inward, dropping away from his sight. It was impossible. But on closer inspection, he noted more jutting features of the skin of the Magisterium: nozzles, vents, spars, and moldings. He had no more time to evaluate; Helice was in his sights.

He climbed up to the rail, gripping it with what strength remained in his right arm. With his left, he reached out for a grip, spied his footing below him, and pulled himself out onto the outer wall of the Magisterium. The air was cold beyond the field barrier. Feeling with his feet for the next foothold, he discovered an indentation that gave him a tiny ledge to balance on. He lowered himself, willing strength into his right arm. Moving with what efficiency he could, he sought his next foothold. With his face next to the crenellations of the wall, he found his handholds, using his left arm and hand to lower himself, and his right to hold fast to the protuberance nearest his chest, to keep himself clinging.

Lower, now, and unable to lean out for a view of where he was going, he continued his blind downward creep. It had only been a minute, and already his good arm was losing strength. He hooked his right elbow around a large, jutting bar, resting his impaired hand. Without that bar, he might have fallen. Hanging thus, with a shallow foothold barely a help, he rested for a few seconds. But he had to keep going, or his body would give out.

Resuming the climb down, he found, of all things, a window. The deep reveal provided a tiny space for him. It was, blessedly, a flat sill. He rested there for a long time, but his hands were growing cold in the sharp air. He had forgotten the cold outside the field barrier. That might be a fatal miscalculation.

Crouching on the sill, he peered below. There was his destination, curved under and away: the rail of Helice's balcony. Setting out once more, he willed his hands to by God hold on, because it was only another minute, and he would have his feet on the solid world of a balcony. He was now just a machine on a puzzle of a wall; there were only feet and hands—good hand, weak hand—searching, praying for a handhold, for the next foothold, . . .

The railing was just below him. With an urgent command to his trembling legs, he persuaded them to reach for the railing. He swung his leg, feeling for the rail, finding it. Now with one foot precariously planted, he clawed his way to an upright position. He felt he couldn't move another inch. His body had gone beyond its strength, held together by will alone. He felt like a block of ice. Somehow he managed to slide down from the rail; he didn't allow himself to fall and collapse. Silence was important.

She was just around the curve of the wall.

Crouching and shivering, Quinn recovered. He tried not to gasp for air. Quietly he stood up and leaned out enough to see the rest of the balcony.

She was still there. But now she saw him.

Jumping up, she turned to flee. Quinn raced to grab her, reaching her and pulling her back. He jerked her against the wall, his hand at her neck.

She looked ghastly, sores oozing, hot blue eyes looking at him with feral panic.

"Don't make me kill you," he said in a whisper, all that was left of his lungs.

As she struggled against him, he noted with relief that she was not stronger than him in his exhausted state. He kept her pinned to the wall, his thumbs on her windpipe. "Now, Helice, you're going to tell me. Everything."

"About what?"

He struck her. To do so, he had to release her with his good hand. She fell away from his blow, stumbled, and fell. Following her, he fell on top of her, too weak to drag her up. Her face bleeding, she spat out the blood that ran into her mouth.

Sitting on top of her, he grabbed her hand and brought it forcibly in front of her face. "I'm going to break each of your fingers, starting with this one, unless you tell me where the machine is." He leaned over her, ready to murder her, ready for anything, nothing held back.

"Go to hell."

He pulled her index finger back in a jerk, breaking it.

She screamed. Then she clamped her mouth shut against the sobs. Her defiant eyes met his. Perhaps she didn't understand that he was going to break them all.

He spat at her, "Don't try lying to me, because I'm going to take you with me, back to the engine. If it isn't there, I'll kill you."

"Go . . . ahead. I don't care, I don't bloody care. In fact, you can . . . kill me now."

"Nobody wants to die," he hissed. He climbed off her and pulled her to her feet, looking at her with loathing. They stood in a mutual embrace, each leaning against the other, each wounded, sick, exhausted. "You don't want to die," he said.

"Quinn," she whispered, her eyes alight with a calm madness. "I don't care what you do. I'm already dying. Didn't you notice?"

He stared at her.

She smirked at his hesitation. "It's too late for you. And it's too late for me. I'm free of you. A dead woman already."

"But you have an engine that will kill the world." Now he needed to hear that there *was* an engine.

She grinned at him, cracking the scabs around her mouth. "Yes there's a bloody fucking engine." She held her hand with its broken finger next to her like a claw. "We're already bringing people here, and they're going to start over again. Start from a clean slate. Clean up the mess you've made. Your precious malformed Rose. Yank it out. Replant, as it were."

Enraged, he dragged her to the rail.

As he hauled her, she gasped, "I won't live to see it. But it was worth it, just to stop insufferable, self-righteous crusaders like you."

He held her at the rail, forcing her to look over. "Look, look down. Tell me where the engine is, God damn you to hell. Before you die, do one decent thing."

With far more strength than he'd guessed she had, she yanked away from him. Then with a quick jerk, she rammed her knee into his crotch. He crumpled, and as he did so, she kicked his damaged arm, sending him staggering against the rail, down to one knee.

Someone rushed at them. Suddenly someone else was between then, grabbing Helice, wrestling with her. Just as Quinn managed to haul himself to his feet, he saw Tai holding Helice balanced on the rail on her back. They struggled. Helice reached her knee back for a kick.

As she did so, Tai pushed hard against her, heaving her over the rail. She fell, the expression on her face startled and puzzled.

"No!" Quinn rasped. He reached for her as she fell. He clutched at her tunic, got hold of it, gripping it fiercely. His hand didn't work, nor his fingers. The material shredded away from his grasp. She fell, dropping away, falling like a lost soul from heaven.

"No, no," Quinn said, leaning over, watching as she fell, watching her grow smaller.

At last her form vanished into the platinum brilliance below.

Tai turned away from the sight, his face ashen.

Quinn was leaning his hands on the railing, letting his defeat settle around him, dark and brutal. She'd taken the information with her. My God, she was still falling, somewhere below, had not even hit the water yet. It would be minutes yet. It made him sick.

Tai croaked, "She would have pushed you. I tried to help, but she fought, and then . . ." he turned back and looked at the railing, as though he could see the progression of events more clearly, staring at it. ". . . and then I pushed her."

Quinn still stared down, but he couldn't see her anymore. "Yes. You pushed her."

After a few moments Tai whispered, "I wouldn't have pushed her, but she pushed against *me*." When Quinn didn't speak, he went on, "I tried to help you. She would have killed the Rose, wouldn't she?"

"Yes. Perhaps she still will."

Tai looked confused. "She was evil, wasn't she?"

"I don't know. I don't know what she was."

But she was the only one who knew the location of the engine.

CHAPTER THIRTY-SIX

Guide the journey, O pilot mine;
Show the path, O clear-eyed one;
Keep me near, O wayfarer;
Bring me home, O navitar.
—*The Red Book of Prayer*

QUINN HAD FALLEN INTO AN EXHAUSTED SLEEP, more like unconsciousness than rest. Tai wakened him gently. "Food," he said.

Rousing himself, Quinn let the memory of the last hours rush back. He groaned.

"You need to eat," Tai said, spreading out fried tubers on a clean plate. He had water too, and Quinn drank it all, wishing for more. His right arm felt like it'd been flayed open, and his left hand, the one that had borne most of his weight on the climb down to the balcony, would hardly close.

"How long have I been out?"

"An hour. It took a long time to find food." Tai explained that the Magisterium was oddly silent, with clerks huddling together in great rooms and few sentients abroad in the corridors. He watched as Quinn ate.

After a time, Tai ventured, "She was trying to kill you. She was, wasn't she?"

Quinn looked at Tai, wondering how much of a burden to put on the young man. Helice couldn't have thrown him over the rail. Perhaps it had looked like that, the way they were struggling. He decided on mercy. "She'd been trying to kill me for some time."

Quinn heaved himself to his feet. "To the plaza, Tai. If you're coming with me?" Tai nodded. Quinn would watch for Lady Demat there. She was his only hope now. Maybe she could send him through the passage that Helice's people were using, but going the other way. He didn't know what was possible, only that he was running blind, trolling for some good fortune, somewhere.

He and Tai made their way up the ramps and stairs of the Magisterium toward the plaza. Watch for me in the plaza, Demat had said. After Ghinamid is dead. Demat needed to handle her own enemies before she would let Quinn handle *his*.

When they reached the outer door of the Magisterium, the one in the sunken garden, they walked through a packed layer of bird drones, their wings fluttering in useless attempts to rise. The steps to the main level of the Ascendancy were also littered with trembling birds, a black carpet that heaved and quivered. As they ascended the stairs, they heard shouts from the plaza. Scrambling to the top of the steps near the Hall of the Sleeping Lord, they found that the center of the plaza was the stage of a gruesome fight.

Covered in blood, the Sleeping Lord commanded the space. Quinn and Tai stood beside a pillar of the hall and tried to make sense of the scene. There were two individuals still standing in the scene of carnage, like a battlefield, with bodies strewn. One of those standing was Lord Ghinamid; the other a man dressed all in white. The clothes didn't look like a clerk's. The man had dark hair. Sickened, Quinn realized it was someone from Earth, crossing over, being murdered. It was an execution. Ghinamid followed the man's staggering form, hacking at him. He had already taken his arm off. . . . Mortally wounded, the man fell to his knees. The lord drew closer and raised his sword arm. Standing over the man, his helm gleaming, his jacket spackled with blood, Ghinamid brought the sword down on the man's head, splitting it in two. The body fell, pouring blood onto the paving stones.

Beside Quinn, Tai crumpled, vomiting.

Out of nothingness, another person emerged into the plaza. Dressed all in white, the young man took in the scene of bloodied corpses. He backed up, but nowhere to go.

Tai groaned. "Oh no."

Ghinamid advanced. Already there were dozens of bodies. It was a massacre, and Quinn had no way to stop them coming.

As Ghinamid strode toward the next sacrifice, Quinn saw something in his peripheral vision. A lone figure standing at the base of the palatine hill, wearing dark green silks and white hair pulled back. It was Anzi. By God, Anzi. *Go back, hide*, his mind shouted at her.

Anzi had seen him where he stood beside the pillar and was trying to cross to him. Quinn waved her back, but she didn't acknowledge him.

In the center of the plaza, the cry from a blow. Ghinamid made short work of the murder.

Meanwhile, Anzi darted to the bridge nearest her where a covered roof provided a hiding place. The other gaps in the plaza would not be so easy to cross, and she was getting closer to Ghinamid, who was just pulling back from his killing thrust.

"Tai," Quinn said, "Find me a weapon. Something long: a knife, a staff. Anything. Go into the Magisterium. Hurry."

Tai, looking pale and wretched, caught the urgency in Quinn's voice, but hesitated. "Are there weapons?"

"I don't know. Go into the cooking rooms. There will be knives." Could he wield a knife in his left hand? Yes, maybe clumsily, but even in an unpracticed hand, better than no weapon.

Tai hesitated. "Where will you be, Master Quinn?"

"Here," Quinn said, still watching the covered bridge, already forgetting about Tai.

Anzi hid in what cover the bridge afforded. Her dark clothing gave some camouflage, but she was inching toward the opening. Quinn put out a hand to restrain her, to keep her from revealing herself; it was just pushing back air, it was pushing against a will that had always taken as much risk as Quinn. *Anzi. Stay.*

Ghinamid's attention stayed on the spot where people were materializing, where his victims innocently appeared, perhaps expecting to see Helice with a delegation of Tarig. . . .

Anzi made a dash for the next bridge, one bridge away from Quinn.

The awakened lord turned toward her, seeing her completely in the open.

Quinn prayed for another sacrifice to come over from the Rose. Prayed that three would come at once, prayed that the Ascendancy would tip to one side, or the bright would fail. Instead, the worst: Ghinamid rushed toward Anzi, and Anzi, seeing him, and not wanting to lead him to Quinn, ran back to the first bridge.

Quinn moved out from behind the pillar. He didn't ask himself what the Rose needed of him, or what the trade-offs were. There was no time for distinctions. He called out to Ghinamid, and the lord halted, swerving to look at him.

Ghinamid walked toward him without haste. He wore a helm of metal that protected his neck with flaps of steel. His pants were of metal mesh, and his vest was blood-soaked padded silk. Over his shoulders, a heavy cape was thrown back to reveal enormous shoulders. He was large, even for a Tarig. Perhaps the lord knew who Quinn was. His measured steps seemed to reflect the gravity that he might attach to the killing of the man who had started everything.

At that moment, Quinn heard someone shout out: "Bright Lord." Another person had come to the plaza: a figure in black on the periphery near the palatine hill.

Ghinamid stopped, eyeing Quinn, but perhaps undecided which was the more important antagonist.

But this second figure was a Tarig, and was rushing forward. Ghinamid turned to face the newcomer.

The individual moved with long strides, dressed in adamantine black, a suit of armor hugging the body: tall boots, hair sparkling with a diamond cap catching the bright like a halo. It was Demat.

Reaching the covered bridge where Anzi hid, she strode through it, ignoring all distractions.

Now there were three figures on the plaza: Quinn, Ghinamid, and Demat. Quinn understood that he'd be dead now if Demat had not come forward. She was dressed for battle.

As she approached Ghinamid, she raised a weapon, something short that snugged into the palm of her hand. A gun of some sort. She fired. Ghinamid staggered back, swaying for a moment. She fired again, and then again at closer range. The lord went down on one knee.

It gave Demat time to glance at Quinn. She nodded at him, once. She intended to be his savior.

But Ghinamid had recovered. Slowly, he rose to his feet. Demat fired again, but it had no effect. The first shot had doubled him over. Perhaps now he had strengthened his armor. Demat threw the weapon away. She pulled a narrow sword out from a scabbard behind her back.

From the plaza some thirty yards from where Quinn stood, Lord Ghinamid spoke to Demat, his voice like rocks scraping together. "Come to our arms. Mingle with us."

"Go home, warrior. We are safe here. Go you to the Heart, if you love the congregate state. I do not."

He shook his head. "Do not remain solitary too long, Chiron. It must ruin you."

"Let each Tarig decide, my lord."

"We are all one."

Demat raised her sword. "Perhaps not this one, ah?"

She looked to the towers of the plaza, the tallest places, and past them to the hill of mansions. Nothing stirred. No phalanx of cousins, no surge of an army such as might come from the loyal Magisterium.

Lady Demat had no army. Not even one.

She advanced on Ghinamid, who stood on the plaza, solid as a bull. Was he weakened by the wound she'd been able to deliver? Quinn fiercely hoped so. He looked back toward the garden, watching in vain for Tai.

Demat circled around Ghinamid. She looked small compared to him. She must not die; that must not happen. He had sold his soul to her, for good reason.

Diving forward like a loaded spring, she lunged for Ghinamid. His sword met her with ease. The lord flashed two quick strokes against her, driving her back. She staggered under the weight of his blows. It gave him time to kill two more travelers who had emerged from the Rose; his sword made a deep path across their chests as they stood clinging to each other. He turned back to Demat, but too late to avoid a hit, marked by a bright spike where she'd pierced his armor, whatever sort it was.

Behind the circling fighters, Anzi emerged from the bridge, edging away from them. The fighters paid her no attention. Then she was racing toward Quinn. He ached at the sight of her. He opened his arms.

She came to him, and they held each other. "My love," he whispered, "I can't stay. I have to fight."

Hearing this, she pulled back, searching his face. "No, he will kill you."

Her hair was pulled back severely, making her look different. He let himself drink in her face, her presence, but he couldn't stay. Turning toward the fight in the plaza, he noted that Demat had taken a cut. She pivoted away from Ghinamid, protecting a leg.

"I have to help her." He saw Anzi's alarm. It broke his heart that he had found her at this moment, and they had no time, no time at all.

"You have no weapon!"

He looked toward the Magisterium. Where was Tai? Surely in all the Magisterium there was one long blade.

"Then I'll distract him."

She moaned. "This can't be your fight! Why is it yours?"

They both turned at the sound of someone approaching. Tai was racing up the stairs from the Magisterium, bearing a long, slightly curved sword. He gave it Quinn, who grasped it with relief.

Out of breath, Tai panted, "I stole it from a wall of a prefect. A ceremonial . . ."

Quinn stopped him with a gesture. There was no more time. Turning to Anzi, he said, "Some people hate the Earth, Anzi. Helice did. She's dead, but her people are coming over. As soon as they do, they're going to kill the Rose, so their enemies can't follow them." He looked at the mayhem proceeding on the plaza. Ghinamid was still slaughtering people coming through, as though fighting Demat was no barrier to efficient execution.

"Demat said she'd help me. Without her, we have no chance."

Reaching inside his jacket, Quinn brought out the paper on which he had written everything down; everything that Helice had done, everything that had happened since Mo Ti had come to him to say that the spider would abandon the Earth to a very bad death. He thrust the note into her hands. "Anzi, I wrote it all down. This is all I have to give you, to tell you why."

"No, Titus . . ."

But he was backing up, moving into the plaza. "I love you forever." Then, balancing the weapon in his left hand, he turned from her and raced toward the fight.

Ghinamid caught sight of him, but did not pause in his pursuit of Demat.

Quinn rushed forward to attack from behind, to force Ghinamid to turn his back on Demat. He caught the lady's glance; there was relief there, and fear, too. His ceremonial sword; his crippled state. How could he help her?

Instantly, he learned that he could not. The lord, sensing a new opponent, spun mightily on his heel, and raising his sword, became a blur of muscle and steel. The weapon circled and took Demat's head from her shoulders.

Ghinamid roared. The lady crashed to the ground.

The lord held his sword up and turned toward the palatine hill. His voice carried well and far. "Cousins of the Heart! Now come down. We are finished with Tarig blood. Let the Rose die, let it warm us and keep us as we have always been! Come to me."

It was all ashes now. *Oh, Chiron, so nobly dead.* Quinn stood on the plaza, exposed. Ghinamid would make short work of him now.

Ghinamid regarded Quinn as he stood awkwardly before the lord, carrying a jeweled sword. "Come to us, Titus Quinn. We have slept too long. We are awake now. Come."

Quinn might have harried Ghinamid from one side had Demat still been in the fight. Now he couldn't win. But did it matter? He couldn't go over to the Rose now. Demat would have sent him, but she was dead. Renaissance would proceed to its awful conclusion. No one on Earth could know that the Entire was lethal for them, that their enterprise had failed. Now would come the inevitable conclusion.

Quinn faced the Sleeping Lord. Bluffing, pretending he had the same deterrent that Helice had, he said, "We will destroy your door."

He stood in the middle of the plaza, sweat streaming down his face, the bright spread in a smoldering lid over him. Doggedly, he went on. "We'll destroy the path to the Heart. Wherever you have a door, wherever you create a door, we'll destroy it. Your time is over here. You can go back. But you can't stay."

He was bluffing. He didn't have whatever means Helice had devised to threaten the door. It must have been the mSap that she was using to control their door. But he didn't have her infernal machine sapient. He had nothing except a jeweled sword.

And Ghinamid was a chaotic, unbalanced Tarig, barely capable of thought. He wasn't deterred. He advanced, sword ready.

Anzi looked at the paper Titus had given her, but it was in English, useless. She spoke some of the darkling tongue, but had never learned to read it. She tucked the paper into her jacket. "Who are you?" she asked the young man next to her.

"Tai. I helped Master Quinn. But he will die now." His face betrayed his anguish.

In the plaza, Quinn and Ghinamid seemed to be exchanging words.

Titus should have slipped past Ghinamid and gone over to the Rose. But she'd had no time to suggest this. She knew the door was open—both ways— the Jinda ceb had told her. Now it was her job to stop the destruction of the Rose.

"Tai. You must tell him that I went to help the Rose."

Anzi and Tai watched helplessly as Titus backed up, staying out of reach of Ghinamid, who stalked him at a leisurely pace.

"Tell the man who is going to die out there . . ." Her face ran with tears. "Tell him that I crossed to the Rose. If he has a breath left when Ghinamid strikes, tell him. Will you?"

Tai was crying, too. "Yes."

Clutching the paper, and stuffing it into her tunic, Anzi ran into the plaza. She crossed the distance in a desperate sprint, racing past the two fighters. Her target was plain to her. She'd seen it through the veil as she'd watched with the Jinda ceb at her side. She dashed into the nexus point of the great geometry of the plaza, defined by the orientation of the canals, which were not canals at all, but tunneling channels of power. Lord Nehoov had bound the two worlds together, spatially and temporally. This the Jinda ceb had told her. The doorway drew in the wayfarers, but it could as well serve to send a wayfarer, too.

As she plunged into the center of the transition point, the place where the Jinda ceb had told her a crossing could be made for a few increments more, she breathed a goodbye to Titus. She hadn't the luxury of hoping she would die, but if she had, she would wish—with all her heart—to die at the very moment that he did.

CHAPTER THIRTY-SEVEN

IT WAS 9:00 P.M. when John Hastings came back on shift at the transition stage, what everyone was calling the pond. After dinner and an hour's rest, John prepared to take the first evening shift, relieving Isobel Wu. Beside Isobel in one of the three chairs in the control room sat Booth Waller, who had taken refuge there, watching the transitions, too nervous to wait outside.

When John entered, Isobel gave him a weary glance, finishing up her last crossing. "From the dark to the bright," she voiced to the mSap. Upstairs, the engine thrummed hard enough to jangle John's teeth.

Isobel and John would both be awake for the last transition; they'd cross together after activating the renaissance engine for the transform: Isobel to make sure John didn't have a change of heart; John to make sure of *her*.

In the transition room, Chitra Kamath had just entered. She balanced her toddler son on her hip, adjusting his face mask that supplied oxygen for those too young to hold their breath.

"Get some sleep, Isobel," John said as he settled into his chair.

"Who can sleep?" Isobel muttered.

Booth looked up from his crossword puzzle. "You can. Take a pill, we need you fresh tomorrow."

"Chitra's all yours," Isobel told John, and left the control room, heading for a sandwich and a sleeping pill.

Leaning into the pickup mike, John instructed Chitra on the immersion process, feeling a bit like he was drowning a mother and child. But it was life, not death, they were headed for.

Chitra's crossing was controlled by the mSap. The AI controlled it, moni-

397

toring the connection with the Entire; that part had to hold steady, and was. In the back of John's mind curled a disquiet over how they'd been changing the order of the list, with the head folks holding back, letting others precede them. He guessed that neither Lamar nor Booth trusted the other to be left behind. Maybe at the last, the two of *them* would turn the lights out. That was fine with him. Who wanted to have such a thing on his shoulders? All the mSap engineers had drawn from a hat for the responsibility entailed in the last slots. But the world would undergo a *transform* of sorts, anyway. The Tarig made sure of that. Speeding it up was no crime, nor was saving a few good people.

The mSap registered a successful crossing. The pool cleared. Chitra and son and were at this very moment in the new world. John wondered mightily what would be the first thing they would see.

Outside the crossover vault, people were still gathered, sitting in huddled groups, giving support to the next ones lining up to go. A few people had already bailed out. They were allowed to go to the back of the list to settle down. John didn't envy Alex Nourse's task of managing them. When John had come on shift, he'd seen Alex with his clipboard, looking official as he chatted with people and organized the line. He'd also had a gun clipped to his belt. No one missed that little addition to the tech array.

John turned in surprise at a noise at the control room door. Lamar Gelde poked his head in. "Booth."

Looking up from his crossword puzzle, Booth rose to his feet and joined Lamar in the corridor outside. He shut the door, leaving John to concentrate on his migration task.

Lamar looked every bit of his seventy-seven years. Booth had often wondered why Lamar even wanted to go over. Who would choose to be *old* for the next two hundred years?

Lamar glanced up at the stairs. "Folks are getting restive. Alex is having a hard time keeping them steady. It's taking too long. It's the waiting."

"We all knew how long it was going to take. Can't people go to bed?"

"They're all out there. Nobody is sleeping, Booth. I think we should double up. The longer this takes . . ." He shook his head.

"Your nerves shot, Lamar?"

"Bloody fucking right."

Booth bit down on a retort. "I'll come up and talk to them."

Lamar snorted, "You'll talk to them? They hate you, Booth. You were supposed to be the first. How do you suppose that looks to everyone that—"

The control room door slammed open. "Jesus, get in here," John shouted, lunging back to the control panel.

Booth and Lamar jammed in after him. Through the control room window they could see someone lying on the floor near the pool. Someone had collapsed. "They just came through," John said, looking ill. "Came through, came up. My God." He pushed past Booth and rushed into the corridor.

Alarmed, Booth ran after him to the transition room.

When he got there, he saw a woman covered in slime from the transition matrix, her white hair pulled into a clasp at the back of her head. Kneeling, she coughed up fluid. She was wearing dark clothes. That couldn't be right.

Crouched down before the woman, John stared at her in dismay.

Booth looked at Lamar who had just come in the door. "Get Alex down here, fast!" They needed to control this situation, and Alex was good in an emergency.

Struggling to rise, the woman coughed up a wad of pool fluid. Then she sat up, leaning against John, who held her like she was contaminated with radioactive trailings.

"Who the fuck is this?" Booth asked John, who was supposed to be in charge of the transitions.

"She came *through*," John whispered. "Up from the pool."

"Dressed like that? Dressed in—" then Booth realized what John was trying to say and hadn't quite put into words: The woman covered in slime and coughing her guts out had come *from the matrix*.

John wiped her face clean with a hanky. After a moment she pushed herself up into a sitting position, sopping wet and starting to shake. "Give her your sweater," Booth snapped at John. She accepted it, looking puzzled by the garment. John put it around her shoulders.

At a sound from the door, they saw someone entering: a white-suited figure. The next in line for crossing. Booth waved him away. "She fainted," he said, standing up to block the view of the visitor. "Wait upstairs. We'll come and get you."

The door closed behind him.

Shakily, John helped the woman onto a bench next to the vat. It was hard to tell who was shaking more: John or the visitor.

The woman spoke, looking directly at John. "No more," she said, her speech heavily accented. She spoke English, so maybe she wasn't from the other place.

"Who are you?" Booth asked her. Her age was impossible to guess. She didn't look old enough to have pure white hair. . . . Then, Booth remembered Quinn saying that some of the people in the Entire had white hair while young. His heart was hammering hard enough to jump out of his chest.

The woman said, "He killing all. All are to dying."

Booth exchanged glances with John. "Who is killing?"

"The Tarig lord dying persons in a pile of blood."

"Oh God," John whispered.

"Shut up!" Booth leaned down to her. "What are you talking about? Who the hell are you?"

The woman looked up at him with clear, yellow eyes. She spoke again. "I called Ji Anzi. From where you call Entire."

Booth seemed to have stopped breathing. Gulping in a lungful of breath, he struggled for calm, wrestling with the improbability of a *reverse* crossing. But yet, with the connection established between here and there, maybe it wasn't so outrageous after all.

The newcomer looked around her, noting the pool, the control room, the men gathered around her.

The door crashed open. It was Alex Nourse, with Lamar right behind him.

"Shit," Alex said, seeing their visitor.

Booth nailed Alex with a stare. "Did you tell people to wait?"

Alex nodded. "We've got one in the dressing room, but we told him we're taking a break. He'll go back to the dorms."

John blurted out, "She says they're killing us as we go over. Everyone is dead. Everyone."

Booth silenced John with a look. This wasn't his lead.

Alex and Lamar joined the circle around the woman.

Booth thought it likely, almost certain, that the woman had come to them from the very place they were all bound. He would have been more impressed by this fact if she hadn't just told them that the Entire would kill them. *In a pile of blood.*

He got down on one knee to look her in the eyes. "What's going on over there . . . Jiasi . . . what is your name?"

"I Jianzi."

"Jianzi. What's happened there?" Unconsciously, he had glanced at the pool, as though that was the direction of the Entire. "Tell us."

Hugging the sweater around her shoulders, she said, "Tarig not wanting humans. Tarig killing all coming into our land. Hel Ese, she dying too."

Worse and worse. "Helice Maki is dead?"

"Yes, sorry. Very much dead. They kill she. Now they kill you."

John looked like he had just drunk a quart of pool matrix. He put his hand to his head, whispering, "Oh God, oh God."

"Why should we believe you?" Booth spat at her, realizing that she could unravel everything, that John could blather this and no one would go over— that they would *all* lose their nerves. It nagged at him, that this might be a counterstrike. She looked harmless, but she had already derailed them, if temporarily. "Jianzi, do *you* want us to come over?"

"No. Lords killing you."

"I mean, do you welcome us, personally?"

"In my person, do I have welcome of you?"

"Do you?"

She paused. "You should take welcome, certainly. Sadly, they not liking you."

Alex burst into the conversation. "Who sent you?"

"No person sending. I always want be in Rose. Now door open—you open it, or lords do? But door open, I see dying, and I run for warning you."

Booth and Alex exchanged glances. Deep shit. And she was maybe lying and maybe not. Alex shouldered closer to her. "Who's doing the killing? How are they doing it?"

"Lord Ghinamid using a—how you say, knife sword. Then with thrusting and slicing, he killing everyone to die."

"Why the hell doesn't someone stop him?"

The woman pursed her lips. "They Tarig."

Alex whispered at Booth's side. "Anybody search her yet?"

"Do it."

Alex pulled her to her feet. "We're going to make sure you aren't carrying a weapon. You understand?"

The woman nodded, allowing Alex to pat her down. In her jacket he found something. Booth thought it looked like a heavy flexible cloth. Alex pushed her back down on the bench and began to read it.

Lamar knelt down beside her. "Why? Why are they killing us? Why not just shut down the crossover link?"

The woman looked at him, at his white hair, his face, maybe trying to make sense of a situation as bizarre for her as it was for them. "Tarig, they hating of the Rose."

Lamar frowned. "But they sent us word we could come."

Having finished reading, Alex nodded at them all to go out into the corridor. They left the woman and regrouped in the corridor.

Alex passed the piece of writing around. Booth got it first. English, of course, or Alex wouldn't have been reading it. It was an account of the renaissance project from the viewpoint of someone inside the Entire. From the viewpoint of Titus Quinn, for Christ's sake, who'd signed it.

Lamar looked at it next, swearing under his breath.

John said, "Why is she carrying the note? Why bring it *here*?"

Alex had grown very quiet. "Because Quinn hoped to alert someone here to what we're doing. Unfortunately, for him, it's *us*."

John looked confused. "So she's lying? They're not killing us?"

Booth said, "That could be one interpretation. Maybe a damn good one." This Jianzi was against them and making up a story to disrupt everything. If Booth didn't manage the situation, John Hastings could go off the deep end, killing the group's confidence in the project.

The men leaned against the cool walls and tried to get a grip on what they were facing. Booth threw out: "I think she's lying."

John looked panicked. "But what if she's not!"

"Why would Helice have sent the message that we could go over unarmed? We had it all worked out which message to send in each circumstance. She indicated *unarmed*. There were some issues, but not critical ones."

"To be fair," Lamar said, "that could have changed." His hand was resting on a gun he wore in his waistband. Booth hadn't noticed before that Lamar had started wearing a gun.

Booth snorted. "Quinn's behind this, he signed the paper. We knew he had to be kept out of it. Maybe Helice failed to do that."

John shook his head. "She said everyone's lying in a pile of blood. We've got to stop the transitions. It's too dangerous." He flicked a glance at Alex with his clipboard.

"Shut up," Booth said to John. "You don't give orders. You don't make decisions."

Alex Nourse frowned. "Why didn't Quinn come himself, then? Why send a woman to stop us? She might be for real." He nodded apologetically at Booth. "I'm not saying stop the crossovers. But I'm just asking."

Lamar rounded on him. "You stupid scumbag. We've come all this way, and now you're backing out?"

Everyone was talking at once, but Lamar had drawn a gun, and he faced off with the other three men. "Let's be clear," Lamar said. "There'll be no defections. None."

"Lamar, come on . . ." Alex moved forward with a placating gesture, but as he did, Lamar shot him in the face. At the impact, Alex jerked backward and sprawled on the floor, pieces of bone and blood clinging to the wall that had been in back of him.

With the roar of the gun still reverberating in his ears, Booth looked in disbelief at Alex's body. "Fucking hell! Jesus fucking hell."

Lamar licked his lips and pointed his gun at John. "You clear where we're going with this? We've come too far. We're going on."

Booth felt like his legs might give way. Beside him, John was moaning, head in hands. Booth managed to say, "Lamar, put the gun away."

The old man did, reluctantly. "I'm just saying. We stay the course."

Booth took John's elbow and shoved him toward the door to the transition room. "Go keep her calm. And get a goddamn grip."

When John staggered through the door, Booth and Lamar faced off with each other. "Why the *fuck* did you kill him?"

Lamar's lip curled. "He was wavering. He was influencing John. We've got to be steady." He bent down and picked up the clipboard that had fallen from Alex's hands.

Booth looked at that calm gesture, and shook his head. "You're out of control."

"Well, if I made a mistake, I'm sorry."

"Sorry . . ." He'd just killed Alex. And he was *sorry*. Booth thought of the next people that would come down the steps. "Help me drag him out of here." He pointed down the corridor. "Around to the back."

The two men bent to their task, depositing Alex's body in a dead end around a corner. Booth took the gun from Alex's body and put it in his pocket. Then they came back with rags and water, and cleaned up what they could. There were stains; it couldn't be helped.

When at last they'd finished, Lamar said, "I'm going up. I'll keep things moving."

Booth couldn't shake the picture of Lamar shooting Alex point blank in the head. "I never knew you were such a bloody son of a bitch."

Ignoring the jibe, Lamar glanced at the door to the transition room. "And her? What are we going to do with her?"

Booth had been wondering the same. On the one hand, they needed to know everything that she had to tell them. But it could take hours to find out all she knew, maybe days. Could they afford to delay? Maybe this was exactly what Titus Quinn intended: Send her to slow them down, then Quinn comes through with a larger force. . . .

Booth said, "Let's bring her up to the engine vault. I'll question her there. If there's anything else we need to consider, I'll fetch you."

Lamar shook his head. "No good. We need someone to watch John. He's going off the tracks."

Booth nodded. Their mSap engineer was freaking out. They couldn't let him out of the control room now, to spread this news.

Lamar offered, "You stay with John. I'll get someone to handle the line out there. Then I'll come back and see if there's anything more to learn from her. That way, there's only the three of us who know anything."

Booth hesitated. "Maybe. But the next person who crosses over goes with a weapon."

"Good."

"Whoever's next, give him yours, Lamar. You've got no business with a gun." In the back hallway was a cache of weapons under lock and key. Booth was astonished to realize that this once far-fetched precaution was now proving needful.

They went into the transition room, finding the woman wild-eyed, crouched in the corner. John still had flecks of blood on him, which wasn't helping the visitor's panic. They managed to calm John down, bringing him into the control room and explaining the plan. People would have guns going over—those who were willing to carry them. But nothing would be said about Tarig killing people. It wasn't confirmed. The woman could have been sent by Titus Quinn.

John balked, but saw reason when Lamar threatened him again.

"I'll be waiting at the top of the stairs, John. Nobody comes back up. Especially not you."

Jianzi, or whatever her name was, pressed herself firmly into the corner, not wanting to go into the hall. It took two of them to get her up the stairs. Through the antechamber, they dragged her to the heavy doors into the engine vault. Long ago, people used to take tours of this very room, back when it gave access to the front face of the reactor core. Superceding the reactor core now was the renaissance engine, two stories high, sprayed with cooling foam and thrumming mightily.

Once inside, they left the lights off, searching by flashlight for something to tie the woman's hands and feet. Here, the engine's relentless drumming sounded like the pounding of ocean surf, further stressing Booth's ragged nerves. Dragging Jianzi along with him, he found some copper wire coiled in a box in the corner. As he bent to retrieve it, his prisoner bolted for the door, but Lamar caught her, and the two of them managed to bind her. An oily cloth served as a gag.

They left her there, parting in the upper hallway. Its walls were still mint green from the old days, and a sign, fresh as in 1945, said, "Evacuation Route."

Booth had by now gotten his determination back. He told Lamar, "As people come down to the transition room, I'll give them a gun from the cache. I'll talk to them before they go over. You just find someone out there who can take charge of the list and keep people coming. Can you do that without murdering anyone?"

Watching Booth slip back down the stairs to the transition room, Lamar considered drawing his pistol and getting rid of the bastard. But Booth was armed too; he had Alex's gun.

Lamar had only a few minutes—a brief window when Booth would be rummaging in the weapons cache and waiting for the next victim to suit up and come down. Lamar's first move was to handle the people outside; then he'd handle the girl inside.

The moment that he'd seen the Chalin woman on the bench near the vat, he'd known that their enterprise had failed. She was saying that their colleagues were all dead, and whether she was lying or not, he knew that things had gone far enough. He'd almost quit after killing Caitlin. Now, with Titus Quinn fighting back and the Tarig possibly on his side, Lamar knew that renaissance was in shambles.

The Tarig were welcome to the Entire. Let them have it. The Earth was good enough. It would have to be good enough; it was all they had. Lamar was simply too disheartened and too tired. He was a murderer twice over, but Alex Nourse didn't count; only Caitlin counted, and he'd have turned the gun he had in his waistband on himself if it weren't for the fact that he bloody well was going to stop Booth and crew if he could.

And he thought, just maybe, that he could.

Smoothing his hair down, he took a calming breath and opened the door to the waiting crowd outside.

Anzi looked around her at the cavern prison. It was cold and dark here, just like the songs said. But of course she was inside.

She had made one terrible mistake. She carried the note from Titus. He'd meant it for her alone, or at least never meant it for his enemies. By carrying it on her person, she had revealed that she was against them. They didn't believe her about the lord murdering their people. At least they didn't act like it. And therefore they were still going to kill the Rose.

It was at times like these that she wondered why the Jinda ceb couldn't have given her a decent weapon, something a thousand thousand days in advance of anything that the Roselings *or* the Tarig had ever dreamed of.

But the Jinda ceb had their own agenda, and unfortunately, it was not to save Titus Quinn's universe.

Left alone in the dark, she thought about Titus and his adversary in the plaza. It was clear who would win that fight. And perhaps he already had. The Jinda ceb had told her that the orientation of the two universes had been firmly fixed for these hours by Lord Nehoov. So, in the same moments she was breathing the air in this cold, hollow place, Titus might be taking his last breaths in the Ascendancy.

This seemed impossible to her. She felt her breath coming in, going out. It was as though she was breathing for him, of him, through him.

Oh, Titus.

Under a heavy mantle of stars, in a dark broken only by hundreds of flashlights, Lamar stood in front of the groups camped out in front of the vault building. The 1,947 remaining Earth-side members of Project Renaissance stood in small knots of friends and co-workers. Anchored by one or two flashlights, the groups looked like an army around its cook fires. And they *were* an army of sorts. An army of self-styled rebels, determined to salvage the human race from its inevitable regression to the mean.

Some of them had clustered by profession. On his left, a gaggle of astrophysicists; directly in front, the biologists. They sat on the ground, or on folding chairs, or stood in tight circles, offering each other comfort or just plain company. And although they were savvies—each one of them—they were all dumb as stumps. *Did you really think we could pull this off?*

Yes, and he'd thought so, too. But no longer. The decision, when it had come, had brought him an acute relief. It just hadn't been clear until a few moments ago what he could do to set things right. Killing Alex Nourse was an ugly prelude to all that came next. Although he'd intended to shoot him in the chest, in his panic he'd got him the head. Fatal either way, but, Christ, to see that carnage on the wall! It had shaken him to kill Alex. But everything depended on geeks like Booth being in control. They had no idea how to be ruthless. Alex Nourse had.

Lamar held up his hands and called for attention. People moved in closer, but he could really only talk to those closest.

"We've run into some trouble with the mSap, I'm afraid. We're running some diagnostics. Nothing to worry about, but we need to take a break and do a little cleanup." He hushed people when a few started to speak. "Look, we're going to start up again in the morning, once our readings stabilize. We'd like you all to head back to your dorms and try to get some sleep. We'll be fine, but move along now. No point in drawing attention to our location with all the flashlights. Really, people, let's call it a night. We begin again at first light."

A dozen questions hit him all at once. What was the problem? What did he mean, readings? Why weren't they sharing the problem with the other sapient engineers?

He answered as best he could, while shooing people off. The mSap engineers were another matter. They had to be dealt with.

"Those of you who've been working on the sapient engineering, John wants to meet with you in Dorm B. Please assemble there. John will be over in a few minutes." He delegated a few people to take the message into the crowd and get people to go back to the dorms.

That had taken what he judged to be five minutes. Booth might be just settling in down there, ready with a supply of weapons to hand out and wondering when the next person would show up.

People were moving along, heading back to their dorms or the coffeehouse. Lamar ducked back into the vault building through the steel access door and along the corridor between the old concrete cocoon and the outside wall. He was wasting precious minutes coming back for the woman, but he was tired of being responsible for death, and this woman would die if Booth concluded she was sent by Titus.

She looked up in alarm as he entered.

He hurried over to her and began removing her bonds. As he worked the wires binding her ankles, he said, "I'm helping you, you understand? I know you want to stop the engine, but there's nothing you can do from here. That takes an engineer. You understand? We have to go for help. All right?"

"Yes." She stood, rubbing her wrists. "We going outside?"

He gave her the jogging outfit that had belonged to Chitra. "Put this on, and hurry."

Once the woman had discarded her wet clothes and dressed in Chitra's too-small garments, Lamar led the way by flashlight to the door. In the corridor, the sparse working lights showed that they were alone. Looking at the woman, he realized he'd forgotten that her hair was pure white. God almighty, she stood out like a fox in a hen house. With his flashlight tucked away and gun drawn, he dragged her quickly by the elbow toward the nearest dressing room.

"Help me find something to cover your head." He searched the piles of clothes. Nothing. Jesus, why didn't anybody have a bloody hat?

She left the dressing room. He charged after her, but when he got into the hallway she was just emerging from the next dressing room with a scarf tied around her hair. It didn't cover it completely, but it didn't need to. Enterprising girl. It would have to do.

Here in the corridor it was a straight shot to the outer door, but they'd have to go past the stairway entrance. He hoped Booth wasn't getting impatient. All he needed was just a few more minutes.

"Quiet, now," he whispered to the woman. *Jianzi* she called herself. "Step quiet, Jianzi. No foot noise."

Careful not to clank on the metal floor grating, they hurried past the dressing rooms and the stairwell. At the door, Lamar whispered to her, "Say nothing, you understand?"

"Yes. Sky is outside?"

What kind of question was that? "Yes. Just be quiet, and when I start to run, you keep up." He opened the door.

A group of people were walking purposively toward him. God almighty. It was Peter DeFanti and some of his cronies. He tried going off in the other direction, but Peter hurried up to him.

The Minerva board member confronted him. "What the hell is going on, Lamar? We can't stop now. People are worried sick. Why wasn't I notified?" He slid a glance at Lamar's companion.

Lamar snapped, "For one thing, turn the goddamn flashlights off." He rounded on Peter's friends. "I said off. Now!"

A few lights clicked off, but Peter kept his on. "Why?"

Lamar affected an exasperated sigh. "We never wanted people out here lighting things up. Everyone was supposed to wait at the dorms. I was just coming to get you. We're having a meeting in Booth's office. Booth is coming up. We can't talk here," he enunciated, glancing at the others who weren't in the need-to-know loop.

"Who's she?" DeFanti asked, snaking another look at Jianzi.

"Jesus, Peter, we're in a hurry. She just got here, a late arrival. Can we meet at Booth's, please?"

"Then why are you headed over there?" he glanced in the direction Lamar had been going.

Jianzi cupped her hand over her mouth and made a few gagging sounds, bending over as though she'd throw up.

Lamar took the welcome cue. "Shit, she's already thrown up twice down there. Just trying to get a little fresh air."

"Christ," DeFanti said, looking at her with disgust. "I'd like to know how she got in line before me, Lamar. What, you guys are changing everything on a whim?"

"I said we'll explain," he said, sending another meaningful glance at DeFanti's pals. *We're not going to talk in front of them.*

DeFanti stared at him. Finally he said, "Okay, I'll be at HQ. Just get your ass over there."

Jianzi continued a show of retching as the group turned away.

Lamar led her away into the dark, blessing her quick thinking. He looked around him. There were still hundreds of people milling around, but the cluster was thinning. Taking Jianzi by the arm, he made his way through some of the outlying clusters of people, which he was relieved to see were breaking up and heading in the direction of the dorm huts. Continuing in a wide arc around the gatherings, he headed on a trajectory that he judged would eventually bring him to the parking lot in front of the mess hall. After a hundred yards or so, he flicked off his light.

He'd forgotten how dark the nights were on the Hanford reservation. The moon was rising over the hills to the east, but it was just a sickle. They stumbled along blindly to get distance from the vault.

"Good thinking back there," he told Jianzi. DeFanti didn't know all two thousand of their group, so he couldn't expect to recognize her, but there was something about Jianzi that drew DeFanti's attention. Remembering this, he quickened his pace.

Switching on the flashlight, Lamar took a quick reconnoiter. He was without landmarks—nothing but grizzled clumps of sage and bunchgrass. Behind him, he saw pinpoints of lights near the vault building. That would be his reference point then; move away from those. Before he switched off his light, he noted Jianzi staring up at the sky.

"Stars. So small?"

"Yes." Christ, to think that she'd never seen a night sky! She might be quite unused to the absolute dark. With the flashlight off again he asked, "You all right, Jianzi? We have just a little way to go."

"I fine to hurry, please."

Whatever that meant. He patted his pants pocket, assuring himself that he still had his car keys. Out of decades of habit, he'd brought them along. Car keys. He snorted. He was back in the world now, after so many months of projecting himself into the Entire. *Where they were killing people in a pile of blood.*

As they trudged on through the cooling desert, he asked her, "Titus Quinn sent you?"

"Titus. Yes, but no time to tell me how to do. No time, he fighting Tarig murderer."

God. Poor Titus. "He's a brave man."

"What your name?" she asked him as he flipped on the flashlight again. There were no buildings within range of the light stream. They had overshot his target. "Shit." He realigned himself to the distant lights of the gathering by the vault, lights barely visible now. He led her on a new tangent toward the parking lot.

"Your name Shit?"

He snorted. Yes, from now on. "Just call me Lamar."

"You Titus uncle?" After a moment she said, "He trusting you."

Well, good. Now where was the damn car?

"You hurry for killing engine, though."

Using his flashlight recklessly, he washed its light over the parked cars, quite forgetting where he'd left his own. Jianzi was pulling away. "You hurry for killing engine."

"I don't know how to kill it! We have to drive for help." Collecting his wits, he remembered that he was parked at the very back of the lot, having arrived later than most. He rushed on. At last, with exaggerated relief, he found his own vehicle.

He yanked open the passenger car door. "Get inside. It's a car. You understand car?" When she didn't answer he said, "Can you trust me?"

"Yes. I trusting you, for Titus's uncle."

"The car will be noisy, and it'll go fast."

"We needing fast."

Rushing around to the driver's side, he slid in and fumbled for his keys. Turning on the engine, he backed up and tried to keep the direction of the road firmly in mind. He looked back in the direction of the vault. Were there more lights than before?

Finding the road, he drove slowly enough to drive by the parking lights. Now was no time to end up in the ditch, stuck on some ancient sage root.

"Jianzi, look behind. Tell me if you see people following us."

She turned in her seat, watching.

Before them, the road dove into the night. He traveled at a good clip, watchful for tumbleweeds and elk. "Is Helice Maki really dead?"

"Yes, I told so. She dying of bad wound from to and fro."

When he judged they had gone about a mile, he turned the lights on full and gunned it.

Helice was dead. The enterprise was over, indeed. Except for the engine. Booth might not believe that people were being killed as they went through to the other side. He still might just go last and pull the plug. Maybe when he discovered the girl and Lamar gone he'd figure out that Lamar had gone for help. He'd double people up—triple them up in the pool, if that was even possible, and keep the stream going, trying to get as many across as possible before intervention. He drove on.

"Stars so small," Jianzi said again. "I thought they bigger."

"Far away."

"Yes. Far away small."

Lamar wished she'd keep quiet. He listened for cars in pursuit, maybe following them at this moment, lights off. But at the same time, he was fascinated to be sitting next to her. Who was she, really? And the sheer marvels of what she'd known and seen . . .

His thoughts turned to the man he had most betrayed. Though he had killed Caitlin, his harms against Titus harried him closely now as he thought of whether he could make amends, could even get away from Hanford at all, and when he did, if he could hope to bring in law enforcement help. The woman with her strange yellow eyes and white hair would be a big help.

"How has Titus fared in the Entire? He didn't destroy the Ahnenhoon machine, did he? Did Helice stop him?"

She turned around from her perch on the car seat to look at him. "Ahnenhoon still there. Titus gave chain to river where lie down quiet."

"Good man. We never meant to blow up the Entire. The chain was a mistake. Is the chain why they hate us? Why they're killing us?"

"No. They hate Hel Ese. Hate door open. Bringing you. Door shut to be best. So thinking they."

"Helice thought they'd let us come."

"I confused why. I gone some time. Come back, and Titus fighting, Hel Ese dying." She paused. "I fearing Titus dead."

The way she said it, he thought she was close to Titus. Maybe his lover. "Too many people dying, Jianzi. You were good to help stop it. Thank you." He thought he saw lights in the distance. Lights coming toward him from up ahead. His gut tightened.

"If anything happens, I want you to know—that I'm sorry."

She turned around in her seat to face the front, peering through the windshield.

"Stars getting bigger," she said.

Had Booth called in backup, backup that no one knew he commanded?

Or had they circled around through the scrub and come at him this way? He turned out his headlights and slowed to a crawl. He considered getting out of the car and hiding in the desert, but what good would that do? Without a car, he had no way of getting help. The nearest city was still forty miles away.

Pulling off the road, he cut the engine.

"Wait in the car."

The September evening was still pleasant here on the hot side of the state. It was a land that nurtured grape vines and apples trees as well as engines of ruin. He took a deep draught of sage-filled air, savoring a last look at the stars. He'd done the right thing in the end. That wouldn't save him, but it made him like himself a little better.

He thought of the Entire, and how Titus's friend had just said he'd thrown the nan-filled chain away so it would *lie down quiet*. Titus, he thought, you were always a good man. He wondered what that felt like.

The lights got bigger. It looked like a convoy, but when it got closer, Lamar saw that it was only five cars. They stopped a ways down the road, lights still on, blinding him.

Car doors slammed. People got out.

Lamar stood with his hands at his side.

A burly-looking man came into the light. "Throw your gun on the ground. Easy and slow."

Lamar did as he was told. Shadows milled next to the cars. He squinted at them, wondering who this was. Not renaissance, unless Booth had hired some thugs. The big fellow was patting him down.

One of the others was striding forward.

Lamar knew him. Christ. His heart began beating again. It was Stefan Polich.

"Enough," Stefan said to his man, who backed up a couple paces.

Stefan had, of all things, a gun in his hand. Lamar shook his head. "Stefan, put that away before you shoot your foot off."

Stefan didn't budge. From behind Stefan and his bodyguard, he heard, "We're going to need a few guns, Lamar."

Caitlin moved into view. The shock almost took him to his knees. Wonderingly, he stared at her. Caitlin.

She sized him up. "Where were you going, Lamar?"

"To hell," he said, realizing the joke was bad, but feeling suddenly giddy. But who was it that he'd blown up in that car, then?

"Besides that," she growled.

"I was coming for help. To stop them."

"And I'm the sweetheart of Titus Quinn." She strode forward and slapped him hard across the face.

He took it. It was just the beginning. He didn't dare ask her who was driving her car. Was it Rob, then? Thank God, no matter who it was.

Lamar tried to focus on their immediate danger. "I ran from them, but they'll be coming after me. So get out your big guns, Stefan. You did bring some?"

They were quiet on that score.

"The engine," he said, looking between Stefan and Caitlin. "You found out about the engine, and you've come to stop it. Yes?"

Caitlin sneered. "Not exactly. He doesn't exactly believe me. Or didn't until maybe now." She glanced at Stefan. "But he's willing to go in for a look."

Lamar's stomach dropped. "For a look? A look?" Incredulous, he turned to Stefan. "They'll shoot you down, Stefan. They're leaving, crossing over. And shutting us down here with the engine. Where are the fucking marines?"

Stefan gestured behind him. "It's all I brought with me. I can call in some favors. I can make some calls. First you tell me what the holy hell is going on." He told his security to turn off the car lights. That done, they stood in the dark.

"Who's in the car with you, Lamar?" Caitlin asked.

He wanted to say, *Titus's sweetheart.* And knew not to. "Her name is Jianzi. She's from the Entire."

He looked behind him into the distance, to the spot where the crossover vault crouched in the darkness. And there, yes, headlights coming this way. Stefan was too late. All he had was five cars full of security. To stop the transform, he'd needed the US Army, and he'd brought his goddamn bodyguards.

"Make your phone calls, Stefan," Lamar said. "Whoever needs to get woken up, wake them. These folks are going to blow up the world."

CHAPTER THIRTY-EIGHT

Where the enemy creates noise, look in the opposite direction; there your doom comes softly.

—from Tun Mu's *Annals of War*

IN HIS PERIPHERAL VISION, Quinn saw the city's denizens gathered at the edges of the plaza. Lords assembled too, on balconies on the hill of manses. The slaughtered dead lay in red heaps on the plaza as though fallen from the sky, sacrificed to a horrid god. Deep Ebb cast a purple, gloaming light.

And the Sleeping Lord, no longer asleep, was stalking toward him.

Alone, Quinn faced the ultimate Tarig, designed as a warrior, created as a protector of the Heart—and of the Entire. And Lord Ghinamid saw the darkling in front of him as a threat to both.

Quinn could only wish that he was. Deep in his crippled arm surged a will to fight, but the arm that had taken the cuts of the Tarig gauntlet would last only a few parries. The jeweled sword he bore in his left hand was glittering sharp. Still, it was no match for the short, heavy sword of Ghinamid. Quinn noted that the lord wore a traditional-looking leather-and-mail vest, but, once pierced by Demat's bullets, it had become more impervious, he knew.

Anzi had rushed past him a moment ago. Where was she? Stay away, Anzi. I love you, but this is my fight, and it would break my will to see you die.

He backed up as the lord approached. Delay was his strategy. Let Ghinamid size him up. He might suspect that Quinn had a weapon of the Rose. Damn him to hell, he thought, damn him for killing Demat, his last hope. Damn him for everything that the Tarig had taken from him, one beloved person at a time.

Quinn silently prayed to deliver one good wound. *Miserable God, let me at least draw blood. Look on me, you son of a bitch, and help me deliver woe.*

Moving behind a crumpled body, putting the dead man between him and Ghinamid, he taunted, "You can't keep them from coming." It was the same thing he'd said to Master Yulin long ago. *They will come. It can't be stopped.* "We'll come over, no matter who you kill." Old Suzong had seen the truth of that and had urged him to find the secret of going to and from. Much good it had done him when he desperately need to do the journey.

The lord rumbled, "We will kill you first, Roseling. Shall we prune the arm gone bad?"

Ghinamid took off his helmet and threw it away. No doubt he'd see better in his peripheral vision without it. He stormed forward.

Quinn had been waiting for that. Now he paused a long second. Then, left-handed, he swept up his sword to meet the charge, bracing it with all his strength. Ghinamid's short sword was in the air, coming down, but Quinn's blade bit through a chink in whatever armor he had, piercing him, letting out a sonorous bellow. At the last moment, Ghinamid's sword went wide, allowing Quinn to snake away.

The lord's wound was solid, but not deep. Worse, the blade was stuck in the mail of his vest. Quinn scrambled farther out of reach as the lord grasped the blade with gloved hands and pulled the sword out of his gut, cutting his hands as he did so. He flung the weapon aside.

At the sight of his bloody hands, Ghinamid roared. He stood between Quinn and the jeweled sword, preventing Quinn from retrieving it. Advancing, the lord's face was a bronze and predatory mask.

Ci Dehai had been Quinn's fighting instructor those first days with Master Yulin, when he had to learn to fight Chalin-style. The general's words came to him now: *When overmatched, conserve energy, watch for openings.* He watched, backing up on the great plaza, retreating over bodies sprawled, darting to the side just enough to avoid the blows. Ghinamid had slaughtered the others because they froze. He had to keep moving. That day in Yulin's fighting yard, the old general had beaten him well and good, teaching him how to win even against such as Ci Dehai. *When overmatched, be content with small harms. Small adds up to large.*

But there was nothing to strike with, and his opponent was not allowing him to circle back toward his fallen sword.

Quinn retreated through the obstacles of bodies, but the Tarig, having taken stock of his wound and regained his purpose, abandoned caution and attacked. His sword circled and lunged. Quinn twisted away, sliding dangerously in blood slicks. Up came Ghinamid's arm again and down, the blade cutting fabric, notching skin. The lord, however, moved slowly, as though his blood had thickened in his million-year rest. Even so, his strength was likely to last longer than Quinn's.

In a heart-stopping moment, Quinn slipped on a patch of blood, falling to one hand. He regained his stance as Ghinamid moved swiftly in, ready to finish the business. The lord's feet slapped into the spill of blood, spattering it over both of them.

A great shadow cut across the square. As Ghinamid looked up, Quinn lunged to the side, taking refuge in a heap of bodies. He didn't spare a glance for what had flown over them, but far away he saw the flash of a brightship descending to the landing bay on the edge of the city.

Ghinamid's pivot was instantaneous. He followed Quinn, closing the distance, thrusting over the barrier, snagging Quinn's jacket, slicing it from waist to neck. He charged over the bodies, but faltered as a shadow came at his face.

Something hovered near, diving for the lord once more. Ghinamid stormed through the shadow, but now there were two shadows, fluttering and diving.

Birds.

They circled and flapped around the lord's face. More appeared, aiming for his hair and eyes. They flew silently, circling and flapping. The lord stopped in his tracks.

Staggering backward, Quinn slipped on the outflung arm of one of the bodies, and he toppled. Ghinamid was quick to notice. Turning his attention to this advantage, he moved in for the final thrust, but birds were in his face, flapping outspread wings, obscuring his sight. He shoved at them with his non-sword hand, giving Quinn time to regain his feet.

As Quinn stood up, the plaza darkened. Overhead, a wedge of birds sailed in from the palatine hill. The formation circled once, then speared down at Ghinamid.

Birds. So this was Demat's army. Another sortie of wings cruised darkly from the direction of the Magisterium. The plaza was awash with inky feathers and the eerie rustle of thousands of wings. Quinn was in the midst of a fluttering melee, but the drones were moving past him, not touching him. It was Ghinamid they wanted.

Demat had reprogrammed the birds, overcoming whatever powerful block Ghinamid might have put on them. His purging of the Tarig ranks earlier in the ebb had required secrecy, and he'd made sure the spy drones were disabled. It must have been on Demat's orders that they had struggled mightily over the past hours to rise from their grounded state. Was it Ghinamid's wound in the gut that had weakened his control? Or was it the work of the lords who now watched from the balconies of the hill and hoped to remain solitaires, as Demat had once hoped?

When Quinn won a clear view for a moment, he saw the lord blanketed in a rustling black cloak. The Tarig flailed his sword at the air, striking some birds, instantly replaced by others. Ghinamid staggered to and fro, his tormentors following.

The lord bellowed as his face became the focus of pecking and diving slices. He went to his knees, trying to cover his face with one hand while stubbornly gripping his useless sword in the other, stirring the black brew boiling around him. It had become a soundless battle, with the lord not daring to open his mouth and the drones mute even when cut.

Quinn came up to Lord Ghinamid. A shroud of black, pecking feathers mantled him. Ci Dehai had been right. *Small adds up to large.* A presence at Quinn's side startled him. Tai appeared, slapping into Quinn's left hand the jeweled sword that had fallen.

Standing over the kneeling Ghinamid, Quinn kicked him in the chest. The lord yanked to face this new assault as the birds lifted from him a moment, flapping to adjust their positions. One of Ghinamid's eyes was a ragged hole. In a surgical thrust, Quinn drove his sword into the eye. Ghinamid fell backward, toppling heavily.

Numb, Quinn stared at the Sleeping Lord's body.

The thought came: *I killed him with my left hand.*

Drones still rustled over Ghinamid body. He hoped they wouldn't turn on him, a new prey. But the birds swarmed over the body, determined that Ghinamid would remain in a permanent sleep.

CHAPTER THIRTY-NINE

PETER DEFANTI WALKED TOWARD THE VAULT BUILDING, pushing down hard on the panic that threatened to overtake him. The camp was in an uproar; people had waited about twenty minutes for the promised meetings in the dorms, but neither John nor Booth had showed up. Now a group of six people had decided to go into the crossover vault and were heading that way when Peter caught up with them.

Peter nodded at them, team leaders for logistics, engineering, nanochem, astrobiology, and physics. "Anybody have any goddamn idea what's going on?"

MSap engineer Shaun Coe looked at him like *he* should know. That he didn't filled Peter with foreboding. Something had gone awry. Something to do with Lamar Gelde. Lamar said there were meetings arranged, but it seemed there weren't. The sapient engineers were furious that they hadn't been brought in on problems immediately. The more Peter thought about it, the more he wondered if, when he and Lamar had talked for a moment outside the vault a half hour ago, he'd actually been trying to get away. If he didn't want to go across, no one would greatly care, but if he was hiding things, decamping with the thought of turning them in, that was—well, that was a disaster.

Now they'd go down to the control room and find out what the hell was going on.

As Peter, Shaun, and the rest of the group descended the stairs to the transition room, they were assaulted with a pungent odor too organic for the cleansed and metallic corridors. Peter thought it might be blood.

Shaun flipped his handheld light on and looked at the wall. An unmistakable red smear stained the wall. In the silence, everyone understood that their investigation had just turned deadly serious.

"Anybody armed?" whispered one of the engineers.

Logistics chief Jennifer Wren, who had gone a few steps ahead, pointed to something around the corner where the corridor zagged to give access to the control room. Joining her, Peter saw the weapons locker lying open.

Mike Jacobsky from nanochem took a handgun, bristling with sensing wires, and powered it up, while several of the others did the same. Mike aimed the weapon at the door. He fixed DeFanti with a look. "You want to knock?"

Peter shouted for John to open up.

When the door opened, an unarmed John Hastings faced four guns pointed in his direction.

"Oh, Christ," he moaned. "Not again."

With the truth of the last few hours finally out, Booth sat alone on the hard metal floor, indescribably weary. He'd chosen the engine vault as a place to wait, the place he'd be most likely to find peace to think.

Peter and his gaggle had come down to the control room and taken it over, demanding answers, and none too gently. So it all came out, all the surreal and ruinous events of the past hour and a half. After they'd finished debriefing him, Peter had called a general meeting back at the mess hall. They disregarded Booth for now, his bad judgment and mishandling of things temporarily set aside in favor of greater matters.

Blanketed by the engine's incessant bass drumming, Booth looked around him.

The woman from the Entire was gone, of course. The wires that had bound her wrists lay in a tangle on the floor where she'd been trussed up. Lamar had freed her. No doubt she'd lend a bit of credibility when he went to the police, in where?—the Tri Cities? Peter DeFanti had sent a security team after Lamar, but Lamar would have been using his dashCom the moment he left the compound, and might be meeting with the police on a road between here and Richland right now.

He stared up at the renaissance engine. It was a marvel of quantum tech married with vision. Somewhere across the branes was a universe cooling toward death. That universe, known on faith alone as the Entire, was doomed. Even the masters of such technology as Titus Quinn had described couldn't save it, not without fuel, a colossal source of it. The renaissance engine could have solved the issue, for a small price. *Let us come over. For God's sake, let the human race start over again.*

The great engine looked like a beast in a bathrobe, its bulk made broader yet by the coolant foam cocooning it. The powerful drumming in the vault comforted Booth. The machine was here, faithfully purring in its standby status. All that remained was to send over a few good men and women and to let the engine fulfill its purpose. That was delayed, but not thwarted. Who would believe Lamar, anyway? It could take hours or even days for anyone to muster an intervention. If it was just a few police cars from the Tri Cities, Shaun and Peter planned to keep them at bay for a time. But as soon as shooting started, the local gendarmes would get serious reinforcements, and renaissance would be over for good.

The general meeting would go on for a while yet. Maybe they'd decide he'd blown their mission and have to be tied up next to the engine, to feel the first impact of detonation. Or worse, they'd decide to deactivate. Dismantle.

It was during these moments, sitting alone in the dark of a September night in the old reactor cocoon, that Booth Waller decided to go it alone. The engine wouldn't go to waste. The dream was still vivid in him. It wouldn't crash because of a fretful old man and the gutless wonders assembled in this compound.

It could not be a coincidence that the woman of the Entire had arrived during the crucial time of their migration. Titus Quinn must have learned their exact timing, probably from Helice, under duress. Then he'd sent the woman as the first sortie, to confuse and confound them. That being the case, it was likely a lie that those crossing over were being murdered by the Tarig. Helice Maki might not be dead, and was perhaps even now working on their behalf to stop Quinn's maneuvers.

Therefore, it might all be salvaged. It *would* be salvaged, he decided.

Some people had already gone over to the Entire. Surely some of them were alive. Perhaps all of them. It wouldn't take two thousand individuals to form a gene pool. They'd always known that a few good people could engender a viable population. Genetic manipulation could take care of errors. It filled him with a surge of sweet relief to know that he had recourse. Renaissance had recourse.

He stood up, relief flooding the dark alleys of his body where, moments before, there had been despair. Oh, to feel hope again, that sharp love of the future! Looking around him, he stretched out his arms, letting his heart pound to the same cycle as the engine.

If Peter's meeting called for a stand-down, Booth would cut Peter and the rest of them out of the chain of command. He would light the fuse for the transform.

When he went over, the Tarig would thank him for it. It was their only hope.

Bullets sprayed across the hardened exoshell of Stefan Polich's personal Nova Class Mercedes. If Stefan had needed final proof of Lamar's incredible story, this was it. His men held their fire, waiting for their chance to land a hit. Crouching next to him were Caitlin and the woman whose name, she said, was Anzi. He was acutely aware of her strange and flagrant presence, but there was no time to think about her now.

When the cars had swooped down on them, Stefan's people were waiting. They'd pulled their cars into a barricade and took positions behind them, training twelve pathetic close-range handguns on their assailants. From the vehicles facing off across a few dusty yards of road, considerably more fire power. Their attackers had pulled up just out of range, having scanned the sweeps on Stefan's guns, taking their measure. They'd also called for him to surrender, but that couldn't happen. Caitlin made sure all of his guards knew they'd have an extravagant bonus if they stayed in the fight.

One of his men had turned careless, taking a shot in the chest. They couldn't even retrieve his body from the spot where he lay in the ditch. Stefan's hands were trembling, waiting to use his pistol, wondering if he had the courage to put his head up over the hood of the car and just fucking shoot. But they were out of range anyway, so he didn't have to test his bravery yet.

Next to him, Caitlin was showing Anzi how to use a gun. The two women were calm and grim, wasting no words. Somehow in the last hour Caitlin had accepted the woman as legitimate. Titus Quinn hadn't exactly sent her. She'd been in another dimension—the nature of which she could only haltingly describe—and had returned to see Titus fighting the Tarig who were killing those crossing over. Crossing over. Helice Maki had been working on her own transition platform, the slimy bitch. Her plan was evil almost beyond belief, unless one considered how often their miserable species had acted on paranoid and horrific ambitions. He needed to know more, but they'd barely had time to get the basic story as their pursuers came at them.

Stefan had called everyone he could think of. But people were in bed, and getting through to them had yielded nothing so far. He knew people in DC—but you didn't call them at 1:00 in the morning and get them to a phone easily, even if you were Stefan Polich of Minerva Corporation.

Caitlin crawled over to him, behind the command car, the one that they'd already deformed into its crashform, hard and fireproof. "Any luck?" she asked, voice low.

"No. I've got two generals and a joint chiefs staffer calling me back. If they do. I got through to a private security firm, one that can muster air and ground support. They're looking over a contract." He gazed at her in the spillover light from surrounding headlights. "I'm sorry, Caitlin. I should have . . . I didn't believe you. Maybe I didn't want to believe you."

Not bothering to answer him, she glanced over at Lamar, leaning against the former wheel of Stefan's car. "I say we give him a gun."

"You're shitting me."

"Give him one. They're going to come after us. They know we're sending out calls." She tilted her head in the direction of the enemy cars, now beginning to ratchet up the assault.

Booth waited outside the vault building, grateful that the darkness prevented him from contemplating too closely all that would be sacrificed in the coming minutes. But it was all going to die anyway. The brightest star in the sky had already died for the Tarig. Sirius, star of legends. The masses, of course, didn't worry about Sirius. If it had been worth worrying about, the newsTides would have told them.

A cluster of flashlights streamed out of the mess hall three hundred yards away.

He had a few moments to try and guess their decision. Plunge forward or fall apart. Do the job, or squander it all.

DeFanti led the way. When they got closer, the small crowd held back a few yards and let Minerva's big man convey the news.

The answer came clean and brief: "We're powering down, Booth. For now." DeFanti glanced in back of him. "The vote was to power down until we figure out what Helice is facing, or if she failed."

"A close vote?"

"No. Overwhelming. We haven't decided what comes next, except to take the engine off line." He waited for Booth to react, but got no foothold. "The Tarig may be killing us. We'll wait for another signal from Helice. If it doesn't come in three days, we'll dismantle things." He added, "If we even get that chance after Lamar is done spilling the story."

Booth nodded. "Where's John Hastings, then?"

"John?"

"I want to ask him something. It's important."

DeFanti called out for John, and from the forward edge of the group— possibly the group that had come to handle taking the engine off line—the mSap engineer came forward.

Booth regarded him, heart pounding. "You agree with this decision?"

John paused, snaking a look at DeFanti. "No, no I . . . don't. We're ruined here." He shot a look at DeFanti. "You know it, Peter. Lamar will sic the police on us. I voted go."

Bless his geekish heart, bigger than most, Booth had to admit. "Let's do it then." He jerked his head at the door. "Step inside, John."

DeFanti raised a hand to forestall him. "I said we're done, Booth."

Booth rounded on him. "What the fuck do you care if a couple more people go over?"

"The group . . ."

"Yeah, well let the group give themselves up, then. Fine. If I want to go, if John does, what do you care?" He eyed John pointedly. "Get inside, now." John shuffled forward, but DeFanti grabbed his arm.

"We're shutting—"

Booth stopped his protest with a right hook to the jaw. As DeFanti staggered back, Booth rushed for the door, John at his side. Booth yanked the metal door open enough for the two of them to slide through, even as John was stuttering, "They'll come after us . . ."

Booth slammed the door closed and locked it, using the crude slide bar left over from the Eisenhower Administration. "No, they won't."

He leaned against the cold metal door as people beat on the other side of it. "John," he said, locking gazes with the man on whom everything now depended. "We're going over. Go armed if you want. I'm taking a gun. Up to you." He shook his head. "He shouldn't have tried to stop us. What difference does it make to them?"

John had no answer to that. He let himself be pulled along to the dressing rooms.

"We'll do this right. No contaminants."

They donned their white jumpsuits, with John moving more slowly all the time, perhaps reconsidering. The engine thrummed louder than ever before, like a stampede of cavalry.

"Look," Booth said. "If you don't want to go, all right. But at least send me." They zipped up their suits. "But we've come this far; you should go with me. Up to you."

"All right, I'm going."

They slipped into the corridor and down the steps. Booth kept a mental patter going to keep up his spirits, his purpose: *Renaissance still works. It will work. We're going over.* He'd rather die on the other side than go to prison for the rest of his life.

Outside the control room, Booth stopped at the weapons cache. "I'm taking one. You?"

John shook his head.

Perfect. "Okay, then, let's go." Entering the control room, Booth said, "How's it work then, how is there time for the last person to go over?"

John's Adam's apple bounced as he tried to find his voice. "I set a sequence for a three-minute interval, then it's automatic. A three-minute pause now for the first, and three minutes between."

"Good. Are you ready?"

"No, I . . . how can I be ready?" John tried again to swallow, failed. "It's too fast."

"You want to spend the rest of your life in prison with a nice hairy felon for a roommate?" At John's look, Booth said, "Do it, then."

John gave a short nod. He touched the screen. As the sequence loaded, console lights flashed, and Booth hoped they were the right ones.

Booth said, "Either you go first, or me; which do you want?"

"You go."

At that, Booth drew his gun, activating it. "Wrong answer. You're going first. And you'll set the engine to go."

John's face fell into panic. "The engine?" He looked helplessly at the door, though he must have known he'd be shot dead if he tried for it.

"We don't need two thousand people, John. There are dozens of people over there. We can engineer our way to a new beginning. The Tarig will help us, because we're going to save them. Turn on the engine."

John stood unmoving, stunned or terrified, or both.

"You've got a couple of choices. I can kill you, or you can turn the engine on and go over first. I'll be the last to leave."

"You're going to kill me anyway!"

"No, you've got that wrong. I need you on the other side. I need every single person who has the guts to go. I hope that's you. Is it?"

John looked at the gun. He'd seen close-up what it could do. "Yes." He punched in a code. After a beat, a shuddering rumble vibrated through the vault. By Christ, it was the engine lighting up. It was renaissance. Without it, the masses would follow. They weren't welcome.

"Go, then," Booth said.

John bobbed his head at the control board. "I'm going to voice the code. It'll be good for two crossings."

John's voice came out thready but clear: "From the dark to the bright." Then he fled from the room. In a few seconds he was through the door to the

transition chamber. He stood at the top of the stairs, counting off two minutes, fifty-five seconds.

In the control room, Booth was counting, too. John moved down the
stairs, holding his breath at the last minute, ridiculously holding his nose.

Then Booth was in the hallway, feeling the roar of the engine shake his
bones. He opened the door and strode to the side of the pool, counting out
the three-minute wait.

CHAPTER FORTY

Storm wall, hold up the bright,
Storm wall, dark as Rose night,
Storm wall, where none can pass,
Storm wall, always to last.

—a child's verse

QUINN STOOD OVER THE BODY OF THE FALLEN LORD. He didn't know how long he stared as the birds settled into a resting swarm, still claiming their prey. He noticed Tai approaching with a flask of water. Quinn drank. He thought of the Tarig watching from their vantage points. What would they do next? Were they solitaires, hoping for his victory, or loyal old guard, ready to complete the destruction of Titus Quinn, the one they'd started on the hill of manses?

As the adrenaline levels fell off, he looked around him, finding that, near the Magisterium, a great crowd of functionaries swelled, staying well back, on the margins of the plaza.

He turned to Tai. No sword would help against those numbers, but he gave the jeweled sword into his keeping.

"Anzi," he said to Tai. "Where is she?"

"Master Quinn"—he looked at Quinn with something uncomfortably like worship—"she went to the Rose. So she said." Tai told him what had happened in the moments after Quinn had said goodbye to her and entered the plaza.

Heart sinking, he scanned the plaza in the direction Tai pointed. It was the place where the renaissance people had come through. Had Anzi believed you could cross both ways? Oh, Anzi, Anzi. Why didn't you ask me . . . why did you rush into the place that could kill you? Did you think you could stop them?

It was true she had disappeared. She had gone into some transition place, but unless Demat had made it possible to traverse both ways, she could have rushed to her death. And *had* Demat already arranged the doorway to take Quinn home? If so, he could just follow Anzi now. He took a step or two forward.

It was a plain section of the plaza; it wasn't even clear exactly where the doomed people had come through or where Anzi had stepped through. Perhaps that spot had a geometric relation to certain features of the plaza. He might have taken careful note of the place if anyone new emerged, but it had been some time since Ghinamid had murdered the last one.

"Tai, where is the door? Where did Anzi leave the plaza?"

"Master Quinn . . . I think . . . somewhere over there"—he waved his hand uncertainly—"I was watching you, not her."

He drank the last of the flask of water. Tai took it from his hands, acting as his servant, his second. Every joint and corner of his body hurt; his right arm raged in pain and, exhausted, his mind felt sluggish. He could cross over now. *If* Demat had arranged passage. If.

"Master Quinn? Will the Tarig kill us now?"

"They might. I don't know, Tai. We wait."

Quinn made a slow circuit of the bodies, looking at who had been part of the monstrous regime that Helice Maki came to the Entire to install. Some of the bodies were unrecognizable as human. He had been prepared to join them a few moments ago. Instead, he and a flock of birds had killed the Sleeping Lord.

Should he follow Anzi, trying to guess at the exact point she went through? The Tarig still observed him from their high, safe perches. Did they fear him, or were they waiting for direction from the next group of Five? Because the Five were dead, he thought, all except the lord of Ahnenhoon. Others would fill in, and the cycle would perpetuate. The decision of whether to use the crossover point hovered around him, rich with possibility. Everything depended on knowing whether Demat had enabled passage to the Rose—or if Anzi had taken a gamble and perhaps lost.

He found himself looking through the bodies for Lamar Gelde. When Quinn had first agreed to return to the Entire, Lamar had said, *Remember that*

I'm an old man. He'd wanted paradise, the demented old fool. He'd wanted the same thing that everyone wanted in the deepest centers of their being: to live, and live longer than the natural order permitted. Whereas, once you accepted the real order—that you would die like those gone before—you could live your life with the sweet intention to make it matter.

He stood over the body of a woman. She had black hair. Not Anzi, he noted with guilty relief. Cradled in the curl of her chest and stomach lay a very small dead child. He turned away, his heart shrinking, wrung dry.

Joining Tai once again, he waited for the Tarig to stir. He had no idea what came next.

As the waiting stretched on, Tai at last laid the sword on the ground. Then he drew something from his pocket. "I don't want this, Master Quinn. It's a thing of evil." He made a gesture that Quinn should take it, a small cylinder with a dull coating.

Quinn took it, bemused.

Tai went on, "Hel Ese called it a finder. She told me to locate the place where I could put a cell of destruction on the tower." He glanced at Ghinamid's Tower. Quinn remembered that Demat had told him a small explosion had been set off there.

It looked like a folded controller. He pushed the ends of it, and it opened. On its surface, a touch pad. Tai's intake of breath showed his surprise.

"Did she say its purpose?"

"Yes, to find the tower."

Quinn's thoughts circled, trying to find a landing. "But it's for something else as well," he murmured. "The inside is for something else."

"She said for me to keep it; she might want it back."

He felt as though Tai had punched him in the chest. *She might want it back.* In his left hand, the hand where, from this time forward, he would hold important items, he held a possibly very interesting item. *She might want it back.* When she came to the Ascendancy, Helice wouldn't have wanted anything on her person. The Tarig would have taken it. But Tai, her erstwhile accomplice, might safely keep it.

Quinn closed the controller, and it rolled up into a small cylinder again. "Tell me how it worked."

"I held it and walked through the plaza. When the machine grew warm, I knew it was the right place to put the . . . what she called the cell."

Tai looked up, staring across the plaza. Tarig were moving in mass down from the palatine hill onto the plaza.

Quinn unfolded the device again. It lay in his palm.

Tai picked up his sword as the Tarig advanced.

"Put it down, Tai." Swords were useless now. He looked up at the bright, letting its light warm his face for a moment. The gods are good after all, he thought. "Tai," he said, letting a smile come to his face, "you've just saved us from a bad end." It was so much more than that, but there was no time to explain. Tarig streamed off the hill of manses, and a lord was separating from the pack and coming forward.

Tai looked confused. "I? Saved? But . . ."

Quinn stopped him midsentence. Tarig were streaming onto the plaza, hundreds of them, in their shimmering skirts and vests. They stopped some fifty yards away. The lord who would speak for them came closer. He bore an air of easy authority, and something else; maybe curiosity.

Quinn held up the controller. "Stay back." The lord stopped.

Holding the device in his hand where the lord could see it, he went on. "I hold sway over the door to your home, my lord. Just as Helice did."

"Perhaps," the lord answered. "You seem to have sway over the flying drones and our stricken lord." He gestured around him.

"You're finished here, my lord. I'm desperate, and I won't argue. Don't give me cause to worry."

The lord regarded him and the device in his hand. "We are Lord Inweer."

That gave Quinn pause. It was Lord Inweer's brightship, then, that had come over the plaza as he'd fought Ghinamid. Inweer from Ahnenhoon. "We can parlay, then."

"We wish to," the Tarig said, deep and slow.

"I'm not in a very good frame of mind. You killed my wife. You threatened to kill the Rose. I could take revenge now. Maybe I will. If I destroy the door, does it strand you here?" During this speech, Tai had begun trembling hard. "Steady," Quinn murmured.

Inweer hadn't moved. "Perhaps we do not care."

"I think you care. I think you're afraid if I kill the connection to the Heart, you'll lose your nice solitaire lives. Maybe the destruction will take the Entire with it." He wondered for a brief flash how Helice could have risked that. But she had been willing to risk everything and All.

"That is surely a reason for talking, Titus Quinn." He gestured with a hand. "May I approach?"

"Not too close."

Inweer came within ten feet, regarding Quinn with as much scrutiny as Quinn, in his turn, focused on the lord.

"You and the woman Hel Ese worked together, ah?"

"No. But I have her controller."

"You need not have fought Lord Ghinamid, had you that power."

Quinn brought Tai forward from the position he'd taken just behind Quinn's shoulder. "This young man didn't know what Helice had given him. He kept it for her. The controller came to me too late to help with Ghinamid." The edges of the plaza were teeming with every sentient who lived in the city, above and below the plaza. The center of the stage was Quinn's upraised hand holding the device that could destroy the transit point.

"So, Lord Inweer, here's how we begin: I can activate the mSap from a distance." He hadn't those commands just yet, but the lord couldn't know that.

Inweer watched him, utterly still. "We detected the controller from our manses above. We thought you had it in on your person. But it was this other sentient who had it." Inweer turned his gaze on Tai, a darker gaze, and one that made the young man shrink back. "If we thought you bore only a sword, we would not have watched your fight uncaring." His gaze came back to Quinn. "We are ready, Titus Quinn. Speak to us. Let us parlay."

He had Inweer's attention. His body began to feel light, as though he'd been carrying something immeasurably heavy and had just set it down.

"Bring me a chair. If I fall down, I'm likely to activate the thing by mistake. I'd hate to see that happen, but I'm tired after my dance with your king." It was a rude statement, but he didn't care. A little offense was in order. Maybe quite a bit, eventually. He took a profoundly deep breath to clear his head. He was bluffing. Best to remember that.

"And send them away." Quinn waved at the crowd of Tarig. "One of you is enough, *ah?*"

He turned to Tai. "Stay by me. Are you up to this?"

"Yes, Master Quinn. I am up to it."

Meanwhile Inweer toed his boot into the plaza, tracing a circle. Up from the hot surface of the ground came a bud, then a round bench. The lord stepped back from it, giving Quinn space to come forward.

Quinn moved to the newly formed bench and sat, with Tai moving with him, taking a position just in back of him. Quinn clutched to the controller like he'd hung on to the handholds he'd used to climb down the face of the Magisterium.

The lord extruded another bench and sat across from him. It was a calming move, bringing the Tarig down to Quinn's level.

"You will shut down the machine at Ahnenhoon. It's over, that part of fueling the Entire is over."

"Yes."

It was too simple, but it was still the right answer. "Do it now. Take a brightship down there and kill it."

Inweer's attention crooked to one side, where a group of legates was approaching. Cixi, with an entourage.

Her timing couldn't be worse. "Keep her well back. She can wait."

With a wave of his hand, Inweer stopped her progress. Without missing a beat, he said, "We do not need a brightship, nor to go to Ahnenhoon to cease its functioning."

To Quinn's relief, Cixi and her minions retreated to the perimeter. Doubtless the old dragon still had a few power moves up her silken sleeve.

"Do it however you do it. Now, Lord Inweer. You understand it's all I care about at this moment. It's all you should care about."

"One understands. The Rose is your home. The Heart is ours. We preserve them both, ah?" He pointed a closed fist at the Tower of Ghinamid, until the sound of a profound, low chime flooded down, stinging Quinn's ears. The lords on the edge of the plaza turned to look in that direction, as did Cixi and her minions waiting on the other edge. The waves of sound fled outward into the air, into the world. The birds that had been rustling over Lord Ghinamid's body rose into the air, speckling the plaza with their exodus.

Inweer nodded. "It is done."

Just like that? Shadows came and went as the drones collected into a pattern above, then knifed away to the palatine hill, to their hidden roosts.

He didn't know whether Inweer had just done something with a flick of his hand that Quinn himself had spent all his energy over hundreds of days trying to accomplish. He had no choice but to assume for now that Inweer had shut down Ahnenhoon.

Off to the side, a sudden movement. A man appeared, one of the white-robed travelers. So, they were still coming.

Quinn said to Inweer, "Tie him up. Bind everyone who comes through."

The lord regarded him with what, again, Quinn took for curiosity. "Your own people?"

"Bind his hands and watch him, Lord Inweer. There will be others."

Inweer ordered it done, speaking so low Quinn wondered how the other Tarig could hear him. One of them came forward, and as the terrified man backed up, staring wildly at the bodies, the Tarig grabbed him and forced him to his knees.

Quinn didn't recognize him. There was no time for him at the moment. "The engine. It's shut down?"

Seated across from him, Inweer placed his hands on his knees. "As it should have been, long ago. We brought this calamity to ourselves with Ahnenhoon. Johanna instructed us so. For as much as one listens to women."

"She is dead?"

"She took her last glimpse of the Entire in my arms."

"I should put an end to this place right now," Quinn murmured.

"Talk instead. Fewer will die that way."

Quinn's fingers rested on the touch pad. The lavender gloaming of Deep Ebb had begun to give way to Between Ebb. A morning, of sorts.

He regarded Lord Inweer, wondering if, even with Quinn's threats, the lord might be playing an elaborate charade, or whether it was well and truly over. He looked down at the controller. With time he would figure out how to access its systems. For now, unfortunately, he was bluffing.

But one thing was true: At this moment, seated on a bench in the plaza of the gods, he controlled the Ascendancy.

CHAPTER FORTY-ONE

In the lead car, Lamar was wedged into the backseat between two over-sized goons. They held their guns casually between their knees, as though they had no fear of shooting their nuts off. Lamar was armed too, a little measure of undeserved grace from Caitlin. He was to lead them into the best position, coming around off-road to the back side of the dorms. They had eleven guns left, if you included the woman from the other side, who'd never fired one until a half hour ago. But it wasn't those guns on which the future of the planet depended.

It depended on the guns in the air.

A thrilling *whuf whuf whuf* overhead blanketed the night with urgent power. Bright swaths cut the desert into ribbons as six copters threw down dramatic cones of light. The game was on. Goddamn, but Lamar was almost happy. No, he *was* happy. If he'd had a chance to take a piss before they piled in the cars to follow the air strike, his happiness would be complete. It was a sad commentary on the state of national defense that the army wasn't here. No, not so much as the CIA or even the damn Border Patrol. Stefan Polich might be an almighty mega dog of industry, but he couldn't rouse the armed forces at midnight to take seriously a threat with an epicenter in Eastern Washington.

No, it had been Minerva's chief competitor, EoSap, that had come through with the air power and a few big guns. EoSap, Minerva's arch competitor, very interested in the Entire, having run spies since the first right-turning neutrinos got snagged at the Ceres space platform. So that had been Rob Quinn who'd been coming back from EoSap when Lamar insanely blew him up on the freeway. Spilling her story, Caitlin had turned to her husband and they'd split their efforts: Caitlin to Stefan at Minerva, and Rob—with all the authority of being Titus Quinn's brother—had gone to EoSap. Even as Polich was calling them from the desert, they were mobilizing to have a look-see. A looky-look with headlights, military trained security, and nice big weapons.

So EoSap, combined with Minerva's five cars, was going to stop the fuckers. Of which Lamar had been one, to be sure. But making amends, now. Mighty amends.

Lamar pointed out the window. "Over here." The driver veered around to put them behind the dorms. In the distance, he saw flashes of fiery action, maybe hugging around the engine vault. Last ditch stand there? By the reaction from outbursts of guns here and there, renaissance was not standing down, or at least some weren't. Lamar wondered how many really cared to take an armed stance. Christ, they were PhDs and planners, not trained fighters.

The car bearing Stefan and Caitlin pulled up parallel to the dorms. Everyone piled out, staying low to the ground, using the cars for barricades. Lamar leaned back to catch Caitlin in his sight, thinking he'd come to her side. But she caught his eye. A slow shake of the head told him he didn't have permission to apologize; to say, I'm sorry I killed your husband. Not yet.

Two of the EoSap copters settled down further off, too valuable to put in harm's way. But the real death-dealing was riding inside the things—EoSap's security, looking from here like they had more gravitas as soldiers than Stefan's bouncers.

He listened, wincing, to the sporadic fight. Someone took a hit; a terrible one. He couldn't know what was going on anywhere, much less over at the engine vault. But people were dying, or would die—for what he now saw as a revolting, pious, and murderous ideology. That had to stop. And Lamar was perhaps the only one who *could* stop it.

At the backside of the dorm, a shadow passed behind the window. Certain that someone was inside, Lamar cried out, "It's me, Lamar!" They were listening. They couldn't help but listen. "We need to let it go, it's too late now. Save yourselves, can you do that?"

At the other end of the car, kneeling by the hood, Stefan's bodyguards watched him in contempt and shook their heads.

Then came the response from inside the building: "Don't come in, we're armed."

Who was that? He didn't know everyone. But he thought it might be Eamon McConnell. "Just give it up!" he shouted. "The army's coming, folks. Give it up, you know? Before more people die."

Lamar waited and watched. No gun smashing the window, pointing at the enemy. Maybe they were talking it over. Eamon was a quiet guy, their best doctor. He wouldn't be looking to fight.

"Eamon!" He decided to shout the name. More shadows at the window. "I'm coming over to talk."

He stood up. The security guy next to him snarled, "Shit, head down."

But Lamar was the only one who could talk to them. And he *would* talk to them, if they'd let him, or damn the whole thing, and let come what may.

As he began walking away from the shelter of the car, Stefan's man lunged at his legs. Evading him, Lamar staggered away from the car, throwing his gun down, raising his hands. "Just talk," he shouted. "That's all."

Silence from the dorm.

Lamar took a step forward.

A shot took him in the forearm. Another, the chest. The violent shock stole his breath, lit up his brain in internal fire. He was lying on his back, staring up. Shouts over there, in the desert; gunfire somewhere. *Stars over him. Why so small?*

Pain flashed in his chest, but it didn't matter. The body was remote from him; he was wandering, lost, a short distance away. Not where he had thought he might be at this time and place. Not in the Entire. Not even in the Rose. The world was so small; it was in the fist of his mind. Then the fist opened, and there was nothing there.

Weapon fire split the air once more. Something burned over by the big building. The explosive sounds of hand weapons traced the paths of fighting. But whether there were two fronts or seven, it was hard to tell.

Standing back in the wall of cars, Anzi watched another air machine fly in, like a dirigible but very loud. She saw a flash of light by the blockish building that dominated the plain. In the explosion, she thought that the machines of war had found their focus. A gun rested in her hand. Press thumb into the slot. . . . But she didn't want to use this thing that she didn't know how to properly employ.

The woman who was the wife of Titus Quinn's brother touched her forearm. Anzi turned to her.

"The battle's slowing," the woman with the difficult name said. Anzi smiled at her. She was a favorite person of Titus's. She and her young children.

"I hoping so."

The woman whispered, speaking slowly so that Anzi could understand, "Tell me how Titus is. You said he was fighting? Does he have help?"

"No help against the lords. I not see him win." She looked at the wife of Titus's brother. "Shall I give him message? Tell him you are good, and small childs also? He so loves small childs of his brother."

They ducked low at a renewed burst.

When Caitlin didn't answer, Anzi said, "Lamar the uncle, he dying?"

"Yes. You can tell Titus that. But Lamar was with Helice Maki. He did bad things."

"Oh. Uncle with Hel Ese." That was sad news. She collected her news, wondering if she would ever deliver it.

"Anzi." In a pause in the fighting, the wife of Titus's brother hesitated. "How do you know Titus Quinn?"

"We . . . I help him in the All . . . then separating, since throwing chain away. You know chain, he bringing in to help Rose?"

Caitlin did not know, so Anzi said what she could of the chain and what had been done and not done. She didn't know how to express in English the finer points with which Titus measured his actions and responsibilities.

"You seem close to him, Anzi."

"Yes."

Anzi hesitated to say more, because they hadn't yet spoken of Johanna and how the first wife was dead. Had Titus reported that on his last sojourn home? Anzi wasn't sure. That was a time when he had heard, erroneously, that Johanna had died of grief.

The wife of Titus's brother said, "You love him."

"Yes." And then, because she was still waiting, Anzi said, "And Johanna dying, and Titus hearing. Titus and I . . . word for together?"

The wife of Titus's brother said very softly, "Lovers?"

Anzi thought she knew that word. It meant love and sex. How to answer that? Finally she said, "We marrying, when could at last."

The woman crouching next to her took on a strange expression, perhaps longing?

Anzi said, "I wanting go home for him."

The woman reached out and held her hand. "Yes. Yes, of course you do."

At a count of thirty-eight seconds, Booth heard the first assault.

He stood at the edge of the transition pool, staring back at the door. There was no lock on it. Counting: thirty-eight, thirty-seven. Just a few seconds more. John was already gone over. Booth next.

The noise overhead was horrendous, a series of concussive jolts. They were taking out the main door—twenty-seven, twenty-six—but they didn't know they had to be in a hurry, they'd take their time—twenty-three . . .

The door slammed open. Instead of a force of men, it was only Peter DeFanti, not even armed. Booth yanked up his weapon. But he'd wired it down for the crossing, and before his thumb hit the indent, DeFanti was on him, jerking him away from the lip of the pool, pounding a fist into his face.

Reeling away, Booth struck him in the temple with the gun. DeFanti went to his knees, head bowed. As Booth swept back for a kick, DeFanti launched himself at Booth's knees. Booth teetered, losing his footing on the side of the pool, grabbing DeFanti's shirt as he fell, and they both went over, hitting the viscous fluid, splattering matrix, hitting so hard, Booth lost the air from his lungs.

Transition coming, let it be now, but it was eleven, ten, nine . . .

Entangled with DeFanti as they both struggled in the matrix, Booth gulped a throatful of fluid, oh God, gagging, drowning. Booth's gun floated in the matrix, hitting him in the elbow as he thrashed. He floundered, air, please, a breath of air. DeFanti was flailing, trying to get to the stair. A glimpse of a leg going up the stairs, and Booth grabbed him by the ankle, pulling him out of sheer hatred, boiling outrage that . . .

Transition.

There were two people together, where one had been programmed.

The crossing went awry.

The constituent pieces—not even molecules, but fundamental particles—floated into the void. The multiverse would recycle them, as it did all useful things.

The waters in the pool calmed. Above, the engine paused. Then it clicked over into ignition mode.

It was a mighty surge. The gravity wave spread out, beginning the quantum transition that would have dissolved all matter. But it had no cohort in the Entire. Missing the connection as it had been programmed, the engine ceased its throbbing and fell silent.

The security forces that EoSap had hired spread everywhere through the vault, into the corridors, dressing rooms, control room, transition room. They found one body stuffed into the end hallway behind the control room. Someone who'd been shot in the face. Those who thought they'd seen Peter DeFanti rush ahead into the vault must have been wrong, because he was nowhere to be found.

Night deepened in the desert. Those who were going to die, did. The rest gave themselves up, coming out of the dorms and the dining hall, and even straggling in from the scrub. They were herded into corrals. Stefan and others conferred, made their calls.

The police were standing some thousand yards away, having instructions from a Special Forces unit of Fort Lewis to stand off until an incident commander arrived.

The compound was eerily quiet. People kept looking at the reactor vault as though it was a time bomb. But the hulking steel cocoon was silent as the stars. No one knew why the engine in the vault had gone off line. Perhaps the assault shook its quantum base or the coolants failed. For an awful moment, Caitlin wondered if she had mistakenly set all this in motion in her paranoia. But the renaissance people were already admitting things, though the stories were varied and bizarre. Some lied, some cast blame elsewhere, but there could be no denying the machine that occupied the place of the old nuclear reactor.

Some moments before, Caitlin had taken Stefan to one side and made her last request of him. In return for his help, she promised that she would speak strongly for him with Titus. And since Stefan still hoped that Titus could pull strings in the Entire—lucrative ones for the company—Stefan Polich did not turn her down.

Leaving him to accomplish his delicate task, she left his side and walked over to the reactor building. It was off-limits, but the group was disorganized enough not to notice when she went inside, past the ruins of the outer door.

Here, in the anteroom of the old nuclear reactor, a cold, stale air tinged with smoke was giving way to a desert breeze. It was growing cool outside, as the remnants of the warm day escaped into the clear sky. It felt good on her weary eyes. Caitlin touched the drapes of the dressing rooms as she passed them, thinking of people undressing for the gas chambers of Auschwitz.

She had little curiosity about the transition stage, below. People had gone over, one at a time, stepping on what she thought of as a scale, where you weighed in, taking the measure of your load of sin and bullshit. She had little pity for those who, Anzi had said, were cut down on the other side.

Keeping to the upper level, she savored the quiet time, walking the old perimeter corridor between the outer steel and the old reactor building wall. Her thoughts turned to Rob, Rob who had been a hero at the last. The man who saved the world, bringing EoSap for the good of the world and a handsome profit. She would have to learn what arguments he'd used. And all this time, she'd thought it would be Titus who made the winning save in whatever game had been afoot. But it wasn't any longer clear what she had thought Titus would do, or wouldn't do, except that he wouldn't have her. But it didn't matter anymore.

Anzi's declaration, far from breaking her heart, had freed her. That lightening of the burden of desire, resulting from a few words from the beautiful woman with the white hair, greatly surprised her. Things seldom proceeded as you expected. Thank God.

She walked slowly through the old nuclear reactor and listened to her footfalls against the metal floor grids until she was ready to go outside again.

CHAPTER FORTY-TWO

It is always a day.
The bright is never dark,
The Nigh flows ever on.
There will be time,
Under the sky,
In the forever land.
Only wait for me.

—a love song

BY THE TIME ZHIYA REACHED THE PLAZA, Quinn had turned command over to his lieutenant, Li Yun Tai. The young man sat on a seat that had been raised between Ghinamid's Tower and the nearest bridge. At his side lay a jeweled sword. In his hand he held the device that controlled the Heart. Zhiya couldn't see all this quite yet as she hurried toward the middle of the plaza; the knot of legates by the pillar had told her. But where was Quinn?

She sucked in a hot breath from the glare of Prime of Day on the stones and gamboled toward the cluster of people at the center of things. Walking at her side were the three stalwart Chalin fighters she'd been permitted by her escort, a steward of the Great Within. But what was permitted and not permitted anymore remained the most interesting question in the history of the Entire.

With no Tarig in view, she felt acutely aware of the functionaries of the Magisterium milling on the edges, murmuring and certainly plotting.

As she came closer, she saw Quinn, oddly, sitting at Li Yun Tai's feet. The reason for this soon became clear. He was asleep.

Quinn sat on the ground, his head thrown back against Li Yun Tai's knee, gone to dreams. She had to admit he looked nothing like the conqueror the steward had described, the one who killed the Sleeping Lord—*killed him*—and who had his foot on the collective Tarig neck.

The young lieutenant acknowledged her with a nod. He so thoroughly gripped the device he'd been given that his hand looked like a claw. He watched the crowd from the Magisterium with the apparent intention of blowing up the kingdom if anyone approached. Zhiya believed that, in his exhaustion, he might actually do it. The device was said to control the Tarig doorway home, but everyone believed that if the man of the Rose were to use it, the Ascendancy could not survive the tumult.

Two Ysli guards provided by the Tarig stood a few paces away. There was no sign of the reported bloodbath.

After a brief exchange with Li Yun Tai, Zhiya knelt beside Quinn, noting that he wore fresh clothes: a heavy quilted vest, a plain brown tunic and pants, and a soldier's boots. His wounds, reportedly to arms and legs, were hidden, but a slash on his face into his hairline had begun knitting up. The Tarig had beaten and tortured him, but that had been several days ago, before the Sleeping Lord woke up, enraged by the permanent opening of a door between the All and the Rose. The steward had told Zhiya that Quinn's right arm was nearly useless.

She put a hand on his good shoulder and whispered, "Quinn, it's Zhiya." He didn't stir. "Quinn."

Still nothing. Zhiya investigated a covered litter a few paces off. Li Yun Tai had said that Quinn had sent for it and that Lord Inweer had granted him this, and much, much more. Inside, a pile of old clothes, a chamber pot, a few water flasks. So this litter and the bench outside comprised Titus Quinn's command site. A strange billet, but the day was strange.

Returning to Tai's side she had him relate all that had happened. He told how Hel Ese had cozened him into helping her and how he had pushed her from the edge of the city. Zhiya had never seen the four-minute ride and would have liked to have been there. He related how Master Quinn, as he called him, had climbed down the *outside* of the Ascendancy to confront Hel Ese and all with a right arm still healing from the gash of a Tarig claw. He told how, once Lord Ghinamid had perished, Quinn had asked for the removal of the bodies. Also, that the swarm of legates be forbidden access to the plaza and that a litter should be sent as a washstall. That Lord Inweer had agreed to these simple things. And then the large thing: the removal of Ahnenhoon.

At Quinn's request, two Ysli guards, formerly clerks of the Magisterium, had been ordered into the plaza by Lord Inweer. Although Quinn felt confident enough to sleep, he still feared Cixi and her servants. They were to stay on the margins, and did. Li Yun Tai was not clear where the Tarig had gone, but not even one was in sight either on the plaza or on what Zhiya could discern of the hill of manses.

This young man had remarkable self-possession. As a mort, he likely had had little to do with the bright city, its Tarig kings or magisterial proceedings. Perhaps this accounted for his steadiness and clarity, she thought. He had no concept of what was really transpiring. But she took him for a devoted attendant since Quinn trusted him with the device.

Li Yun Tai wore clothes rather fancier than Zhiya thought necessary: dark green and orange silks and a sublegate's padded jacket with an excellent embroidery of a spinner. Well, he advances quickly, Zhiya thought. Can preconsul be far behind?

After hearing Tai's account, Zhiya crouched once again in front of Quinn. "My dear," she murmured. "Wake up. Zhiya is here."

He stirred, leaning into Tai's knee. Stymied, she looked up at Tai, who was no help at all.

"You have water?" Zhiya asked him.

Tai glanced at a flask by the bench. Zhiya opened the stopper and poured the contents over Quinn's head.

He came to life, sputtering.

"I tried being nice, but you wouldn't wake up." Quinn looked at her uncomprehending. She knelt next to him. "You are the lord of the Ascendancy, dear boy. It simply won't do to sit on the ground."

He pulled himself up, taking a seat on the bench vacated by his lieutenant. His right arm appeared to have some movement, at least below the elbow.

Li Yun Tai sent one of the Ysli guards for a basket of food. The other kept watch at the site where the young mort said the sacrificial humans had appeared in the plaza.

Zhiya gave Quinn the flask of water, and he drank. While he slaked his thirst, she asked, "Ghinamid died with your sword through his eye?"

Quinn mustered a scrape of voice. "Makes a good story. But the drones pecked him to death."

"Where have the Tarig gone, my dear?"

"Resting. Or whatever they do when they aren't pretending to be alive."

"And Anzi?"

"Gone. The Rose. I'll stay here until she comes back." He looked behind him, perhaps remembering the earlier scenes in this plaza. "Lady Demat was Chiron, returned. We might have guessed that. I set a bargain with her, and what I hope is that she braced open the door for me to cross over, and when Anzi went through she got there safe."

Zhiya blinked. Chiron was helping him?

"She set a condition. That I return to her."

Oh, there was a story here. "And would you have?"

He looked at Zhiya, clearheaded, it seemed, at last. "I don't know. It was my word I gave her. Are those things still important?"

"No. Not when you rule the Entire."

His attention was back on the exact spot, apparently un-demarcated, where the Roselings came through. "Anzi took my place. Going over. To stop them."

Zhiya sighed. None of this made much sense, but this was no time for sorting the details. Except for one—hardly a detail: "But Lord Inweer stopped things on this side? He shut down the engine?"

"Yes. So he said." He looked to the place where he had last seen Anzi. "One man came over from the Rose and survived. I talked to him. He said that they were on the verge of setting off the engine in the Rose. But it won't mean anything, because Inweer shut Ahnenhoon down first." He glanced at her. "It was a close thing, Zhiya. It could all have gone wrong."

"And didn't."

"Didn't. But there's still a problem."

Grinning gods, of course there were problems. The Tarig were still in their mansions, and the Magisterium was ready to revolt.

He waved the little device. "I don't know how the damn thing works."

By the Woeful God, he was *faking* it. She moaned.

A stir of people near the doors to the lift drew her attention. Another group had arrived at the nearest pillar station. Among them stood a woman with dark hair, wearing vivid yellow silks.

"My daughter," Quinn breathed.

Zhiya had only seen Sen Ni once before, but she was hard to miss. A red figure in a navitar's robes stood next to her.

"I said I would give her the Ascendancy."

Zhiya had to close her eyes to steady herself. By the Miserable God, the *Ascendancy?*

Quinn was about to make the biggest mistake of his short stay in the Entire. Fortunately, his daughter had been instructed to wait at the edge of the plaza, and did. Since Quinn was sitting, Zhiya didn't need to lean in far to whisper in his ear. "She'd make a bad queen. The one in red is her navitar counselor, Geng De. As a child, he fell in the Nigh and came up evil."

"Evil? I doubt that. Don't you?"

"Put it this way, then: Mother said this navitar has broken the code of the Nigh. He has gone beyond seeing the possibilities to changing them. That's why mother said that he *weaves*. Navitars swear never to weave—not that they could—but it's talked about, and they swear never to try. This one has already done so."

"Weave what?"

"The future." She fixed him with a look. "Evil isn't the wrong word."

"Your mother is sometimes confused."

"My spies say he sees Sen Ni every day. My advice is to wait a few arcs before you embrace her."

Quinn was looking the man in red over carefully. "What does your mother think the navitar wants?"

"Control, dominion. The usual villainy."

"If he weaves the future, why didn't he weave me out of it? He's no friend to me."

Was she supposed to argue every point? Yes, she supposed she was. He was half dead from his wounds and in shock from too much bright on his head. "He may well have bent the future. Anzi is gone. You're bluffing with the little machine. Who knows? But one thing I'm sure of: he made Sydney the Mistress of Rim Sway. Not only did the Tarig give her that as a ruse, they changed their minds and gave it to her in truth. If I were a fiend, I'd have had her head off."

He hadn't taken his eyes off Sen Ni's delegation. "She's waiting for me, Zhiya."

"First you'll have something to fortify yourself, then we'll ask her to come forward." She looked around her. "Can't a great leader get a dumpling around here?"

Li Yun Tai was taking command of a stacked basket of food, brought on the run by one of the guards. But when he brought it forward, Quinn shook his head. Either he was impatient to see his daughter, or impatient to be done with it.

Quinn looked at Zhiya, murmuring, "Do I look a fool? Sitting here on a bench with a jewel-studded sword?"

"You look as you should. But you'd look better with an ebb's rest." Zhiya mightily wished Quinn would postpone this interview, but since he would not, she reluctantly sent one of her Chalin guards to summon the girl.

Sen Ni came forward. Her yellow tunic and pants bore a brocade down the sides, and her hair was pulled high, set with tasseled combs. Zhiya thought she looked young, but not weak. She walked like one who had ridden beasts and walked home when thrown off. Her eyes, Zhiya noted as Sen Ni drew closer, were dark as a Tarig's. She'd forgotten about that troubling feature.

Quinn made to rise, but Zhiya put a hand on his shoulder and pushed hard. "You sit, or I'll kick you in your bad arm." He obeyed.

Despite instructions, the bad navitar had followed Sen Ni. The Ysli guards looked to Quinn for direction, but he waved them back. The murmur of the crowds on the perimeter ceased, as every pair of eyes in the Ascendancy watched the small group in the middle of the plaza.

"You are master of the bright city," Sen Ni said without preamble.

"Sen Ni," he said, using the name she preferred. "Who is this with you?"

"Geng De, a navitar and a friend."

"Ask him to give us privacy."

She turned to Geng De. The navitar murmured, but Zhiya heard him say, "In this strand, I am with you."

Sen Ni did not dismiss him, and it cooled Zhiya's heart to hear him talk of *strands*. He meant strands of reality. Oh, her mother was right.

Quinn regarded Sen Ni for a long moment. "I can't trust him. He's against me."

"You mistake him."

"He suggested that my Tarig captors kill me when I turned myself in at your door."

Sen Ni frowned, turning again to Geng De.

"I made a suggestion," the navitar said, his voice as high as a boy's. "That is true. But it is too late to kill him now." The young navitar looked at Quinn with an even, placid face that galled Zhiya more than a sneer.

Sen Ni bit her lip. "He's my ally, and has been since I walked into Rim City. I've lost every advisor. Even you have a mort and godder." She snapped her eyes to take in Tai and Zhiya. Zhiya held her gaze, refusing to be intimidated by this girl of legend.

Quinn responded, "You have Mo Ti."

"No, I don't."

Zhiya watched this down-spiraling conversation, fearing that Sen Ni would win by virtue of the ties she had on Quinn's heart. The time had passed when Geng De might have left without loss of face for Sen Ni. Now he was staying, and Zhiya would have liked to dispel his satisfied look.

Quinn's daughter turned the conversation. "I've come because of our bargain. Helice is dead. I helped you as much as I could. Didn't I?"

"Yes." Quinn sat still as stone.

The silence turned Sen Ni's face dark. "I was to have the Ascendancy. You were to give me the Tarig. *On a platter*, did you say?" She nodded. "You don't want all this. Leave it to those who've worked for it."

"I never wanted the Ascendancy," Quinn said. "But I mean to keep the Rose safe. Would you do that?"

Zhiya knew that Sen Ni couldn't answer this truthfully. The Entire's life depended on the death of the Rose. If not with the engine at Ahnenhoon, then with another. Sen Ni would not let her world vanish.

Daughter and father gazed at each other. Finally the daughter said, "The engine at Ahnenhoon has gone silent. Isn't that what you wanted? And we had a bargain. You gave your word."

Again, Quinn was silent. Zhiya had just advised him that vows didn't matter when you ruled. She hoped he'd take it to heart.

Sen Ni glanced at the palatine hill. "Lord Inweer came, I was told. What did he offer you?"

"The engine gone. What else could he?"

She shook her head in obvious contempt. "You are becoming one of them again."

He barely restrained a wince. "I love you with all my heart, but I can't let you have power that you'd turn against the Earth."

"You believe I would—or even could—hurt something a universe away?"

"I think your navitar might." Perhaps only Zhiya saw him trembling. "Dismiss him, Sen Ni. Do this thing for me. Let me advise you. Bring me to your side."

"To my side?" She almost laughed. "Was that our bargain? I don't remember that part." She paused, regarding her father. "I'm no longer a child. I choose my own counselors, people who've proven true to me. To survive, everyone needs someone strong at their side. I've had Riod, I've had Mo Ti. Now I have Geng De. You will need to trust us."

Quinn shook his head. "He fell in the Nigh, Sen Ni. He came up broken. A broken man can't rule or advise the one who rules."

They gazed at each other, locked in a dreadful silence.

Finally Sen Ni whispered, "Say it." She looked up at the bright. "Say your answer."

Zhiya couldn't move or breathe.

But it was as though Sen Ni's looking away gave Quinn the courage to speak: "No. My answer must be no."

Sen Ni settled her gaze back on her father. When she spoke, her voice fell into a harsh whisper.

"Prince of the Ascendancy again, then."

She shook her head. "My navitar says that won't last long." Then, turning away, and accompanied by Geng De, she walked back toward the plaza's edge.

As she did so, a small figure ran out from the crowd of functionaries. She was very short and dressed in elaborate brocade, gleaming under the bright. Her shoes came off as she ran. It was Cixi. The Ysli guards ran forward to restrain her, but Quinn called out to them. "Let her greet Cixi. A minute only."

Sen Ni fell to her knees before the high prefect, and the two of them fiercely embraced. It was a spectacle that held those assembled at the edges of the plaza transfixed. Flinging decorum aside, Cixi clung to Sen Ni, rocking her, patting her head. It was as though they were mother and daughter, Zhiya marveled. Another story. All to be told in its time.

When Zhiya looked at Quinn again, she saw tears streaming down his face.

When the reunion had gone on long enough, the Ysli guards took Cixi by the arms and pulled her back. The red navitar, in turn, pulled Sen Ni away toward the waiting lift.

Zhiya stood by Quinn's side, seeing Sen Ni enter the lift and then watching as Cixi, shaking off her the guards and her legates, walked with great dignity back to the Magisterium.

Titus Quinn sat in front of his pavilion. Sentients had been streaming in for several hours, paying their respects, boldly or slyly asking for preference or favors; some—those who weren't too terrified to do so in full view of the palatine hill—bent the knee in front of Quinn and Zhiya. The king and the dwarf, as she liked to say.

Set in the middle of the plaza, the large tent, supported on poles, served as Quinn's quarters. He had thought of places easier to defend—such as Cixi's audience chamber in the Magisterium—but, in the end, he chose something open and away from spy tunnels.

He had spent many hours seated on this bench, and he sat more easily now that Helice's mSap had been found. Zhiya's attendants found it in Rim City hidden beneath a trash heap.

The God's Needle was seldom visited in Rim City, a place that favored the Religion of the Red Throne. Thus neglected, even by its alcoholic godder attendant, the mSap had been safe on the Miserable God's altar beneath a small mountain of trinkets, handmade crafts, and food offerings. Zhiya removed the machine to a warehouse she owned under another name, it being too precious to risk bringing to the Ascendancy.

Nevertheless, the machine sapient was operating splendidly, according to John Hastings. He was the only one from the Rose who'd survived the crossing, having arrived following Ghinamid's death. It was also John Hastings who had traced the mSap using the controller and who had optimized the communication between the controller and the mSap. Now Quinn had immediate access to the mSap's dedicated function: to shatter the door to the Heart.

Once John and Quinn had spoken, it had taken only a few minutes for them to come to an understanding. John Hastings would either pledge an oath of support to Quinn or be thrown off the edge of the city. Zhiya had suggested the bargain, and Quinn had agreed. He was surrounded by enemies and needed none in his own midst.

John had also told him the sweet news that Anzi was alive, and had, by God, slowed the renaissance people down, made them doubt themselves. She was alive, but a universe away. He let himself bask in the relief of her safety, pushing away worries of what came next for them.

Quinn heard with grim silence how Lamar had been a part of it all, but had redeemed himself at the last. It was a long story of how renaissance had come apart at the end; how Booth Waller had broken at the last, forcing John to program the great engine. It made Quinn trust John the more that he admitted to that. As to forgiving him—Quinn set all such considerations aside for the sake of having a quantum engineer in the Entire. Whether the man was rehabilitated or merely terrified of falling did not greatly matter at the moment.

Anzi had survived, and had done what Quinn had meant to do, but in point of fact, probably never could have accomplished. He was contaminated with the past, and Anzi was fresh to the game and had played her part well, for an act she must have made up on the spot. He thought if she returned, he would give her the Magisterium. She was the most capable of anyone who had helped him.

But first they would by God have a wedding night.

The pavilion he'd set up in the plaza faced the place where she would return. No one had come through since John Hastings, however. Somehow, Lamar must have brought things at Hanford to a halt, but whether aided by the marines or the police, neither Quinn nor John could know. Eventually, he'd learn the outcome. Because he'd go home. But it couldn't be soon. Thus he was left to worry that the passage between worlds might decay enough to jeopardize the needed lock on the respective passage of time.

Zhiya had marshaled a force of fifty guards from her force of trusted godders, spies, and thieves, who had been arriving by threes and fours for the last hours. Inweer wanted no army in the Ascendancy, and Quinn respected that wish for now. His hold on the Tarig was tenuous, even if he no longer needed to bluff.

The dilemma was that he didn't know what he wanted or should want.

It seemed that, to secure the Rose, he had to control the Entire. The Tarig might be hamstrung, but there were other parties in the dispute. The Magisterium. The population of the land. Sen Ni.

He thought on these things as he sat outside on his bench, Zhiya and Tai nearby.

Tai stood behind him, having taken on the role of seneschal, valet, and bodyguard. Wearing the jeweled sword that Quinn scarcely thought he knew how to wield, Tai had become a tireless organizer as well as Quinn's personal assistant. Now and then Tai would come up with an English word, such as "food," "sleep," and "important visitor," looking inordinately proud if he got it right.

Quinn surveyed the plaza. No Tarig appeared on the visible avenues of the hill, much less near his pavilion. Lord Inweer said he would retire for a time, perhaps conferring with the other solitaires. The Tarig were still a problem in many respects. He tried to think through what accommodation could be made with Inweer, if any. Perhaps the Tarig should all go home; but could the Entire remain intact without them?

Zhiya sat on the ground beside him, refusing to share the bench. She was his sole advisor and second in command. Under her direction, emissaries had been sent to the Magisterium to assure every sentient that their place was not automatically in jeopardy. Even Cixi was allowed to remain for now, provided that she either brought the steward Cho from his prison or provided proof of his death. The death scroll came soon thereafter, to Quinn's great regret. Cho had provided him the redstone containing Johanna's warning of the purpose of Ahnenhoon. Quinn asked for a poet to create a grave saying, and one went into seclusion to produce it.

A line was forming for sentients who'd had the courage to make the trip to this uncertain city. Many did and wanted to come forward to greet Titus Quinn; among them were acquaintances, merchants, functionaries, and the curious.

Here, standing before him was a man who claimed to have served him a nicely charred meat skewer four hundred days ago during the great godder expedition to the Nigh. Quinn thanked him and took down his name, receiving his promise of cooperation. He had no idea if he'd ever met him before.

Next in line was a Gond on his litter who said he was on his way home and would convey Quinn's greetings to the nests of the forest. Quinn sent greetings. Tai had them written with a flourish on an activated scroll by a legate seated nearby.

The day continued in this manner, until toward Last of Day came one he knew. The Hirrin, Dolwa-Pan, who had long ago given him a ride in her sky bulb.

She made a leg, in a Hirrin bow, and eyed him coldly. "So you repay hospitality," she said without greeting.

"Was there hospitality? Did I sleep through it?"

"I gave you hospitality, oh yes? To the very reach of the minoral, and now you harass the gracious lords. I am disappointed also, that you deceived me, Titus Quinn."

"That I regret. You did help me with transport and never knew I was a fugitive. You haven't suffered for it, I hope?"

"No. But you won't see further favors from me. I am a princess among Hirrin, and I shall have little good to say of you."

Hirrin were used to speaking their minds, and this was a welcome respite from the fawning that had gone before. "I'd like to have your forgiveness, Dolwa-Pan, but I'm a slayer of Tarig, so that's hopeless, I suppose."

"Slayer. So it's true." She flicked a glance at the Tower of Ghinamid.

Quinn said, "Since we're speaking truth, I have to admit that Lady Demat set the birds against him, and he toppled from a surplus of them."

Dolwa-Pan sniffed. "I'd have my heart chime back."

"And so you would if it was in my keeping. I'm afraid my wife has it." At her look of surprise, he said, "You'll be the first to learn, Dolwa-Pan, what her name is. If interested."

She took an almost involuntary step closer. "Oh, perhaps."

"Her name is Ji Anzi. Of Shulen Wielding. She went on a dangerous mission to the Rose, and I'm waiting for her to return. You may remember the woman I traveled with. If she still has the keepsake I gave to her, you will have it back."

Dolwa-Pan puffed a little air through her lips. "That is a tender thing, to wait for one's love to come home."

"It's a hard thing."

"Oh, it is. You wait here for her, you say?"

"Yes, until she comes."

Again, the puff of air that was the Hirrin sigh. "Please keep the heart chime, Excellency." She bowed again and nodded at him as she left.

At last Quinn went inside the pavilion to rest. There were a dozen items waiting for his approval, those things that Tai and Zhiya decided they couldn't dispatch on their own. A meeting with Lord Inweer at Early Day tomorrow. They would continue to parry and thrust and learn what each wanted and what each must have.

Then there were the scrolls sent by Cixi. Up to a dozen, now.

"Read them," he told Zhiya.

Zhiya turned to Tai. "Read them, Tai, and tell us what you think." She shrugged at Quinn. "One must use people's talents or exhaust oneself."

"So that's the way, even here." Quinn went to his private section of the pavilion, as Tai eagerly sat at a makeshift desk and activated the first scroll.

Following Quinn into his private quarters, Zhiya murmured, "Does he have to wear a sword indoors?"

"Yes." Quinn would not have parted Tai from the jeweled sword for love nor money. The young man had earned his embellishments and then some.

When Quinn came out of the washstall, Zhiya said, "It would be a lot easier on the functionaries around here if you'd decide on a title." She grinned. "You know the one I prefer."

Yes, *king*. "Let them flounder."

"You don't make it easy on people. You keep changing your name and your face. Give them a handle on you."

But then he'd have to decide what he was. In Sidney's voice, *Prince of the Ascendancy* came uncomfortably to mind. He changed the subject.

"Any word of Su Bei?"

She shook her head. "We watch Rim City. Nothing."

The old man had never come to the city. With his minoral collapsed, Quinn feared he'd died in the calamity.

A rustle at the flap of his quarters. Tai stepped in. "Master Quinn." Nothing Quinn had said could persuade Tai to call him anything else.

"Master Quinn, others are gathered outside. Among them are two named Yulin and Mistress Suzong, who are certain you will see them quickly."

A smile came to Quinn. He felt it poke into his face, still stiff from the cuts he'd taken. "By God, Yulin and Suzong."

Zhiya led the way from his quarters and out onto the plaza.

The old bear stood some paces from the bench, looking thinner than before, but with a strange joy on his face. At Yulin's side was Suzong, who, glimpsing Quinn, made as deep a curtsy as was possible for a woman of one hundred thousand days. She also looked mightily pleased. It touched him.

But when they stepped aside, he saw the real reason for their joy. Someone else stood with them.

It was Anzi.

She stood by her quasi-uncle and aunt, supported on one arm by Suzong, because she had just come through . . . come over . . . come home.

Quinn rushed forward, taking her into his one good arm. He held her so hard that Yulin roared with laughter, and Suzong shushed him, and even Anzi laughed. Finally pulling back, he looked at her magical presence.

"We aren't dead," he said with true wonder.

"I thought I was. I thought you were."

They sat on the bench as everyone gave them room in a wide circle. He held her face between his hands, struggling to keep his right arm raised. He couldn't speak.

"Titus," she whispered, "the lord did not kill you."

"Birds . . ." he said, not thinking clearly. Her hair was matted around her face as though she'd come out of a swamp; her face, pale and strained from her ordeal. But still, she was beautiful. He felt that if he could just look at her for a few hours more, he would never ask the Miserable God for anything again.

For the next hour he kept her on his left, where his good hand could reach for hers, and he could, even while talking with Yulin and Suzong, assure himself that she was still there. She would not take any rest, and the truth was, he couldn't bear for her to sleep just yet.

At last, stories exchanged, Suzong knelt in front of Quinn.

"You have our fealty, Titus Quinn. This time, we will hold steady." She eyed Yulin, who tried and failed to look both noble and contrite.

Quinn turned to Tai. "Have the scribe write that down."

Happy to be in charge of such a high task, Tai rushed off to supervise a particularly beautiful document, complete with a seal he had spent some hours devising: one with a stylized Rose that long ago he'd admired on a bolt of silk in his father's shop.

ABOUT THE AUTHOR

K AY KENYON, nominated for the Philip K. Dick and the John W. Campbell awards, began her writing career in Duluth, Minnesota, as a copywriter for radio and TV. She kept up her interest in writing through careers in marketing and urban planning, and published her first novel, *The Seeds of Time*, in 1997. She is the author of eight science fiction/fiction works, including *Bright of the Sky* and *A World Too Near*. Recent short stories appeared in *Fast Forward 2* and the *Solaris Book of New Science Fiction: Volume 2*. Her work has been translated into French, Russian, Spanish, and Czech. When not writing, she encourages newcomers to the field through workshops, a writing e-newsletter, and a conference in eastern Washington State, Write on the River, which she chairs. She lives in Wenatchee, Washington, with her husband, Thomas Overcast.

Visit Kay Kenyon online at www.kaykenyon.com.